*Conv*

*Yours'*

For better,
for worse,
for convenience...

or for love?

# Conveniently Yours

**IN NEED OF A WIFE**
by
**Emma Darcy**

**DANGEROUS ALLIANCE**
by
**Helen Bianchin**

**NO WAY TO BEGIN**
by
**Michelle Reid**

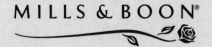

MILLS & BOON®

*MILLS & BOON and MILLS & BOON with the Rose Device are registered trademarks of the publisher.*
Harlequin Mills & Boon Limited,
*Eton House, 18-24 Paradise Road, Richmond, Surrey, TW9 1SR*

CONVENIENTLY YOURS
© by Harlequin Enterprises II B.V., 1999

*In Need of a Wife, Dangerous Alliance and No Way to Begin were first published in Great Britain by Mills & Boon Limited.*
as separate single volumes.

*In Need of a Wife* © Emma Darcy 1994
*Dangerous Alliance* © Helen Bianchin 1994
*No Way to Begin* © Michelle Reid 1991

ISBN 0 263 81534 X

05-9902

*Printed and bound in Great Britain
by Caledonian Book Manufacturing Ltd, Glasgow*

Initially a French/English teacher, **Emma Darcy** changed careers to computer programming before marriage and motherhood settled her into a community life. Creative urges were channelled into oil-painting, pottery, designing and overseeing the construction and decorating of two homes, all in the midst of keeping up with three lively sons and the very social life of her businessman husband, Frank. Very much a people person and always interested in relationships, she finds the world of romance fiction a happy one and the challenge of creating her own cast of characters very addictive. She enjoys travelling and her experiences often find their way into her books.

Emma Darcy lives on a country property in New South Wales, Australia. She has been successfully writing for Mills & Boon® since 1983, and has written more than sixty novels, which have been published worldwide.

# *IN NEED OF A WIFE*
## by
### Emma Darcy

# CHAPTER ONE

HE WAS a complete stranger. He had brought his three-year-old son to the same harbourside park Sasha had brought her nine-month-old daughter. In half an hour of desultory conversation across a sandpit where their children played together, all she had learned about him was his name, Nathan Parnell. He was also the sexiest man Sasha had ever met.

He made a pair of jeans and T-shirt look like indecent exposure. The casual but open affection with which he touched his son conjured up visions of the tactile pleasure he would give a woman. It brought goose-bumps to Sasha's skin.

And those riveting blue eyes. When she spoke they focused on her with concentrated interest as though she were the most important person in the world. Sasha found it difficult to tear her gaze away from him. Even when she forced her attention back to Bonnie, who was being entertained by his little boy, she was intensely aware of the man lounging on the grass on the other side of the sandpit.

'What I need...' he spoke in a musing tone, not so much to her as to the world at large, yet the deep baritone of his voice made her ears tingle with anticipation to hear what his needs were '...is a wife.'

Sasha's head jerked up, her dark eyes wide with shock. She quickly flicked the fall of her long black hair over her shoulder to cover up her reaction to the startling statement. She had been secretly envying Nathan Parnell's wife, and berating herself for having wasted so many years on Tyler Cullum while all the best men were taken. The whimsically appealing smile Nathan Parnell directed at her set her pulse racing.

'Tell me honestly,' he invited. 'Would you consider the position?'

Warning bells rang in Sasha's mind. Strangers who made odd propositions in a park were definitely to be avoided, no matter how sexy they were.

Her gaze quickly swept their vicinity. Most of the people who had been nearby earlier seemed to have wandered off. There was an old man sitting at one of the benches, reading the Saturday newspaper, a young couple under the trees closer to the water, two middle-aged women apparently watching the leisure craft sailing by on the harbour, all of them a fair distance from the sandpit and all of them strangers.

She probably looked like part of a family group, Mum and Dad and their two kids, and people in the city tended to steer clear of others' troubles. This was time to get out.

'I'd better be going,' she said, trying not to look too hasty as she began gathering the plastic blocks Bonnie had thrown around.

'You haven't answered the question,' Nathan Parnell reminded her, not exhibiting any discomfiture whatsoever. 'I need a wife, and to satisfy my curiosity I'd like to know whether you'd consider the position.'

'Definitely not.'

'Is there something wrong with me?' he asked.

With his attributes, he could probably have the choice of any woman in Sydney. He probably knew it, too. Sasha cast him a quelling look. 'I thought you were already married.'

'I was. Past tense.'

It gave her pause for thought. Maybe he was a widower in desperate need for someone to mother his little boy. Although why he'd pick on her, after the barest acquaintance, left a lot of questions up in the air. Was he impressed by her manner with Bonnie? Was that the only yardstick he had for a wife? Or did he find her attractive enough to fancy her in his bed, as well?

Curiosity prompted her to say, 'I don't want to raise a matter that might be painful to you, but what happened to your first wife?'

'She's gone. Hopefully to hell and perdition.'

It was certainly no salute to the woman he had married. Which gave Sasha every reason to be circumspect with this man. 'I'm sorry things didn't work out better for you,' she said, resuming her block-gathering. To keep him talking until she could make her getaway, she asked, 'How did she die?'

'She didn't. More's the pity,' he said with an edge of bitterness. 'Though the marriage wasn't a dead loss. I got Matt. Thank God he takes after me.'

'Then you're divorced,' Sasha deduced, wanting the situation spelled out.

'No other way out of the problem.'

Sasha knew how messy such problems were. She didn't have to divorce Tyler Cullum because they weren't married in the first place, but effecting a separation was just as traumatic as any divorce. She wondered how any mother could leave her child behind, as Nathan Parnell's wife apparently had. Then, with a spurt of her own bitterness, she supposed there were women, as well as men, who didn't want their lives loaded down with children.

Nathan Parnell took her silence for complicity and resumed his proposition. 'Consider the advantages. We could go back to the old way of doing things. Set up a marriage contract...'

'What makes you think I'm free to marry?' Sasha demanded, thinking he was assuming one hell of a lot in talking to her like this.

'No wedding-ring.'

'Many people think marriage isn't valid any more,' she argued, although it was Tyler's opinion, not hers.

The blue eyes blazed incredulity. 'You're still living with a guy who didn't bother to marry you when you had his child?'

'It does happen these days,' she flared at him, painfully aware of the mistakes she had made.

'Why isn't he with you?'

'Because...' It was none of his business, but somehow his eyes pinned her to a reply. 'Because I left him,' she finished defiantly. 'He wasn't good to me, and he wasn't good to Bonnie.'

'There you are. Same problem I had,' he said with satisfaction. 'We'd both be better served if we worked out a sensible contract. Set out what we're prepared to give to the marriage, and what we can expect from each other.'

'You're talking about a marriage of convenience.'

'Absolutely.'

'What about love?'

'Definitely out. It causes havoc and creates chaos. Turns sensible people into raving lunatics. The Greeks had it right. They called it Eros. The eighteen months of madness before passion cools and reality sets in.'

'Well, you might not think it's worth having, but I do,' Sasha said emphatically.

She grabbed her holdall and stuffed Bonnie's play blocks into it. Her dreams might have been tarnished by her experience with Tyler, but she was not about to give them up and become as cynical as Nathan Parnell.

'What did love do for you?' came the sardonic challenge. 'How long did it take you to find out your lover was a dead loss when it came to commitment and responsibility?'

She faced him with grim determination. 'It wasn't love. Not real, deep-down love. And I'm not going to settle for anything less next time around. If there is a next time. I'd rather manage on my own than compromise myself again.'

'How will you know this *real, deep-down love?*' he asked sceptically.

'I'll know.'

She wasn't at all sure of that but she stood up in disdain of any more of his arguments, then bent to lift Bonnie over her arm and brush the sand from her legs.

She was conscious of Nathan Parnell swinging himself into a sitting position but he didn't rise to his feet.

'It's pie-in-the-sky,' he stated mockingly.

'You can hardly say your attitude is normal,' she retorted.

'Normality is a fantasy. People aspire to it because they're so frightened of being themselves.'

'Well, now I'm free to be myself,' Sasha tossed at him.

'If you married me, you'd be even more free to be yourself.'

'Free?' She cocked a scornful eyebrow at him. 'Wouldn't I have to share your bed?'

'Minimally. Marriage isn't legal without consummation. Would once in a lifetime be asking too much of you?'

'Once! What kind of marriage is that?'

His eyes danced over her from head to toe, openly admiring the shining fall of her long black hair, the curves of her figure which were faithfully outlined by her T-shirt and jeans, the shapeliness of her long legs.

'Perhaps I could manage more if you really wanted me to,' he suggested, flashing her a smile that had the kick of a mule. His eyes held a definite glint of earthy wickedness as he added, 'You have lovely skin. Smooth and creamy. Must be like satin to touch.'

Sasha could feel the cream burning into fire-engine red as she remembered wanting to know how it would feel to be touched by him. Her gaze dropped to his hands, lightly resting on his knees, and she had a moment of lustful speculation that was totally unlike her.

Fortunately, Bonnie recalled her to her senses by squirming and crowing her eagerness to be returned to her playmate. Sasha hoisted her daughter up against her shoulder, holding her more securely, defensively.

'This is getting beyond the pale,' she said, her eyes flashing contempt for his concept of a convenient marriage. 'Where do you get such ideas from?'

He shrugged. 'They popped into my head.'

'So you ask the first woman you meet, or happen to be with, to be your...' Words failed her.

He grinned, totally unabashed. 'There is a certain zest to it, springing into the unknown. It could be a glorious adventure for both of us.'

'Or a trip to hell and perdition,' she reminded him with waspish intent, hoping he felt the sting in the tail. 'Don't forget that,' she added for good measure.

'Doesn't apply. No love involved.'

'Which is where I opt out. Thanks for the offer but it has no appeal to me.'

She leaned down to pick up her bag, telling herself she was crazy to have listened to him for so long, crazier still to feel tempted into listening some more. Sex-appeal was a trap. It faded fast once one got down to the nitty-gritty of making a relationship work. Tyler had conclusively proved to her that a relationship without love had no hope of bringing any real or lasting happiness.

'Can't I play with the baby any more?'

'I don't think the baby's mother wants to stay, Matt, and we have to respect other people's wishes.'

It was a gentle answer. Sasha saw an arm reach out and gather the little boy into a comforting closeness with his father, a loving touch that put an ache of yearning in Sasha's stomach. If Tyler had been like that with Bonnie... But he hadn't, and any last hope of him ever changing had died the night she saw him shaking their child as though she were nothing but a rag doll.

As she straightened, the bag firmly clutched in her hand, Sasha tried her best to project proud independence in turning away from the disturbing influence of Nathan Parnell's presence. But her heart caught at the mournful look in his small son's eyes.

She was well acquainted with the loneliness of being an only child. But Matt did have the love of his father. And Bonnie had her love. The last thing children needed was to be caught in the warfare of a relationship that wasn't based on love.

Reassured that she had done the right thing in leaving Tyler, and was doing the right thing in leaving Nathan Parnell, Sasha stiffened her spine and bestowed a warm smile on the little boy.

'Thank you for playing with Bonnie.'

'Can we play again another time?' he asked.

'I'm afraid not.' She saw the disappointment in his eyes. 'I'm sorry,' she added, then turned quickly and walked away, wondering how different their lives might have become if she could have given another answer.

In her abstraction she did not see the figure striding across the park on an intercepting course.

'Sasha!' he called.

She heard the strident anger in the voice. It arrested her mid-step. She turned towards the source, knowing already what she was about to see, knowing she was about to be involved in another confrontation, this one much more serious than the minor skirmish she had just played out with Nathan Parnell.

She knew the owner of the voice.

It belonged to Tyler Cullum.

# CHAPTER TWO

SASHA watched Tyler approach. She had once thought him sexy, but now she saw him as nothing more than a slick sophisticate, consumed with self-interest. He was more smoothly handsome than Nathan Parnell, conscious of the latest fashions, stylishly lean, and affecting a temperamental moodiness that he considered artistic.

Why she suddenly thought of Nathan Parnell as warm and honest and earthy, she didn't know. Contrast, she supposed. Nathan Parnell was a bigger man, his strongly boned face marked with expressive character lines, his dark hair an unruly toss of waves that looked finger-combed, if combed at all. There was nothing artificial about him. He was comfortable with who and what he was and not frightened to lay that out to anyone else.

Sasha told herself she had nothing to be frightened of, either. She didn't have to please or appease Tyler any more. She was free to be herself and go her own way.

But all her fine resolutions didn't stop her stomach from twisting into a knot of apprehension as Tyler came to a halt in front of her. She stared defiantly into

stormy grey eyes, deciding she had a definite preference for vivid blue.

'You could have told your parents which park you
were going to,' Tyler sniped. 'This is the third one I've
had to look through.'

'I don't understand what you're doing here, Tyler,'
she said truthfully. 'You were glad to see us leave a
week ago.'

He made a visible effort to control his irritation.
'Well, I was wrong, Sasha. Now that I've had time to
think about it...'

'I've had time to think about it, too. I wasn't wrong,
Tyler. For me, it's finished.'

'You're being unreasonable, Sasha. Just because
I'm not as patient as you are with Bonnie...'

Her expressive dark eyes flashed contempt at his
hypocritical excuse. It forced Tyler to a concession.

'All right. I'm sorry for blowing up, but she *was*
driving me nuts.'

'She won't any more. If you'll excuse us...'

Before she could move, Tyler stepped forward and
snatched her carrier bag out of her hold. 'You're not
going anywhere until we've talked this out.'

Sasha fought to remain calm, disdaining any attempt to retrieve the bag. 'Talking won't make any
difference to my decision, Tyler.'

She saw the struggle on his face. He found it difficult to accept that she could actually walk away from
him without a backward glance. 'Listen to me, Sasha,'
he demanded, mollifying the demand with a cajoling
tone. 'I miss you. I even miss the baby. The apartment feels empty without you.'

The glib persuasion didn't have the substance to reach past other memories. Sasha eyed him with bleak weariness. 'What you're missing, Tyler, is a convenience you've got used to. Find another woman to look after your needs. The one you tumbled in your studio might oblige.'

It riled him. 'I told you that was a one-off thing.'

'You're free to do whatever you like with whomever you like, Tyler. But not with me and Bonnie.'

His temper flared. 'I came to say I was sorry. What more do you want?'

'Nothing. There's nothing I want from you, except for you to go away and leave us alone.' She held out her hand for the bag. 'Please?'

He ignored the appeal. 'Where do you think you're going to live? You're being totally selfish squatting on your family. They don't have room for you.'

'I intend to find a place of my own.'

'Sure! That will be real easy with a baby in tow and no steady income. You're not thinking straight, Sasha. It's time you stopped sulking and came to your senses.'

'There's no point in this, Tyler. Please give me the bag and let us go.'

'You're being stupidly stubborn. Come back home with me and . . .'

She started walking away without the bag, sick of the argument, sick of everything to do with Tyler, wanting to put him behind her once and for all.

He caught up with her and wrenched one of her arms away from Bonnie, his hand closing around it with biting strength and jerking her around to face him. 'Don't turn your back on me! I came to talk to you.'

'It's no use!' Sasha cried, shocked at being forcibly held and struggling to free herself. Bonnie started screaming at the jolting.

'You're upsetting the kid,' he accused.

'Let me go and she'll be fine. We'll both be fine.'

'You're coming home with me.'

Pulling her after him, denying her any choice, he set off across the park, heading back to where he must have parked his car.

'Stop it, Tyler!' Sasha tried digging her heels in but that caused her to stumble when his relentless forward progress dragged her along with him. 'I don't want to go with you,' she protested.

He didn't so much as slow his pace. 'You're coming whether you like it or not.'

'This won't get you anywhere,' she fiercely promised him, pulling and straining against his iron-tight grip. She was hopelessly incapacitated by the need to hold on to Bonnie who was now screaming at the top of her lungs. Sasha was reduced to pleading. 'Let me go, Tyler. You're hurting me.'

'If you stop being a stubborn mule, you won't get hurt.'

'Let the lady go.'

The command startled both of them. In harnessing all her strength to resist Tyler's caveman tactics, Sasha had forgotten about witnesses. Tyler turned to glare at the man who had suddenly thrust himself into an intervening role. Sasha stared at her self-appointed rescuer in dazed disbelief.

Nathan Parnell had shed his sexy air of relaxed indolence. He looked very big, very strong, and very determined.

'Butt out, mister,' Tyler snapped at him. 'This is none of your business.'

Sasha felt a hot surge of humiliation. Being manhandled in public, and having her helplessness witnessed by Nathan Parnell and his son, was degrading. She should have handled this confrontation with Tyler more tactfully, although how she could have stopped him from turning it into an ugly spectacle she didn't know.

'Let her go or I'll...*break*...your arm.'

The words were loaded with menace. Her uninvited champion stepped forward, obviously prepared to execute the threat.

The shock of it brought Sasha's miserable train of thought to an abrupt halt. Why did men have to be so...so primitive? There was going to be a major physical confrontation unless she did something to stop it. And it wasn't necessary.

'It's all right,' she cried. When all was said and done, she *was* capable of standing up for herself. Tyler didn't mean to do her any physical harm, she was sure of that.

Nathan Parnell didn't back off but he stopped. 'It certainly will be,' he said, 'when the gentleman releases you and returns your bag.'

To Sasha's knowledge, Tyler had never been faced with the threat of physical violence before. With imminent danger temporarily averted, shock gave way to bristling bravado. 'Who the hell do you think you are?' he demanded.

'Parnell. Police officer. Off duty.'

The economy of words reinforced the command of the man and the identification made his stance even more intimidating. It gave Tyler pause for thought. He finally decided discretion was the better part of valour and released Sasha's arm.

Sasha reacted rather than acted. Her self-protective instinct made her step back out of Tyler's reach. Her maternal instinct urged her to soothe Bonnie's alarm. She was too shaken by what had happened to initiate any further resolution to this dreadful scene.

The erstwhile stranger from the sandpit stood his ground, eyeing Tyler as though he were a prime suspect in a murder case.

'You don't understand, Officer,' Tyler blustered. 'This is nothing but a domestic argument.'

'Want to come down to the station and have a friendly chat about it?'

Tyler didn't care for that challenge, either. 'This is ridiculous. Cops everywhere. Isn't there any freedom left in this country?'

'Yes, sir, there is. Freedom for women and children as well as men. Now, if you don't mind, hand over the lady's bag.'

'She has her hands full with the baby. *Our* baby,' Tyler argued.

Nathan Parnell turned to Sasha who was still trying to calm Bonnie. He addressed her quietly, politely, giving no indication that they had met and talked before.

'Would you like me to carry the bag for you, ma'am? I'll give you safe escort to wherever you want to go.'

Sasha felt confused. The authority he had brought to the situation was helping to end it, but she didn't want to get involved with the law. She didn't want to get any further involved with Nathan Parnell, either. He was just as bad as Tyler in wanting a *convenience*, and his he-man display didn't impress her any more than Tyler's did.

'You go with him, Sasha, and you'll never see me again,' Tyler vowed, fuming at having been put in the wrong.

It made up her mind for her. She didn't *want* to see Tyler again. 'Thank you, Officer. I would be grateful for your help.'

He turned back to Tyler and held out his hand. 'The bag please, sir.'

Tyler tossed it at Nathan Parnell's feet, glaring intense hostility at Sasha for her part in his humiliation. 'Don't think you can come crawling back to me. This is it, Sasha. I gave you your chance.'

She made no reply. Nathan Parnell scooped up the bag, stepped between her and Tyler, and took a gentle hold on her elbow to steer her in the direction he wanted her to go. 'If you'll come this way, ma'am ...'

Sasha hesitated, unsure what she would be getting herself into by going with him. Leaping into the unknown was not her idea of a 'glorious adventure'. Then she remembered his son and realised he must have left the little boy somewhere. Matt should be getting his father's attention.

She moved decisively, submitting to Nathan Parnell's escort, embarrassed by the trouble she hadn't been able to avoid, but relieved to put Tyler behind her. She wondered if it made her a coward, taking the easy way out, but what possible good could it do to continue a post-mortem argument with Tyler? The decision was made. There was no going back.

Matt was, in fact, sitting on the grass a little distance away, gravely watching their approach. Sasha wished he hadn't seen that ugly tussle. It must have disturbed him as much as it had disturbed Bonnie. It rocked children's sense of security when adults fought together.

'Get the rest of your things out of my apartment tomorrow or I'll throw them out,' Tyler shouted after her. 'Your parents will really love having to house all that. They won't have room to move.'

Sasha shuddered, hating the vindictiveness, hating the fact that four years of commitment had come down to this horrible parting.

'Just keep walking. Don't look back,' Nathan Parnell murmured.

She would never have guessed he was a police officer, although he certainly fitted the part, now that she knew. His height, his strong physique, the aura of being in command, unruffled by anything.

'I don't want to make any charge against Tyler,' she said, casting an anxious glance at him.

The compelling blue eyes gently probed hers. 'You don't think he'll trouble you any more?'

Sasha tore her gaze away, fighting a turbulent range of feelings related to his closeness and the caring way he'd looked at her. She was not a little girl in need of his protection, and she was *not* going to succumb to his proposition of a loveless marriage for the sake of having him at her side. He was not a comfort to her at all. He was disruptive and disturbing and the sooner she got away from him, the better.

'I'm quite sure Tyler has wiped his hands of me,' she said stiffly.

She hoped so, anyway. She felt that Tyler had too much ego to leave himself open to another rejection. From now on he would only think bad things about her and consider himself well rid of a relationship that had demanded too much of him anyway. She wondered what explanation he would give to their mutual acquaintances, then decided she didn't care.

None of them had been close friends. Although Joshua, Tyler's business partner, had always been kind. And perceptive. Joshua McDougal had been the only constant associate throughout her four years with Tyler. Social convenience had dictated the pattern of their life. If people weren't *fun,* they were quickly discarded.

Once she had thought Tyler's merry-go-round of people was the answer to all of her dreams. No more loneliness. Lots of people, happy to know her, happy to have her in their company. But it hadn't been real. Not deep-down real. And when it had come to the solid realities of life—responsibilities, commitment, building a solid future together, simply being there when needed—Tyler was, to use Nathan Parnell's words, a dead loss.

She had made the right decision. But it did leave her with some weighty problems, as Tyler had so nastily reminded her.

Matt hopped up to join his father in escorting her and Bonnie from the park. 'I didn't know you were a police officer, Daddy,' he said enquiringly.

It gave Sasha a mental jolt. She had accepted Nathan Parnell's claim without question, but out of the mouths of children came innocent truth.

'When did you become a police officer?' Matt relentlessly pursued the question as children always do.

'When needs must, Matt,' came the quiet reply.

Sasha realised he had supplied what he considered the situation demanded. But who was he really?

The answer exploded through her mind. A man who needed a wife, that was who, and he'd just made the opportunity to proposition her again. Nothing like a white knight to the rescue to soften a woman's heart and mush up her brain. Well, not this woman, thank you very much, Sasha vowed. For the time being, she was through with men.

She stopped walking.

They all stopped walking.

Matt looked up at her. 'My daddy can do anything,' he stated proudly.

'I don't doubt it,' Sasha bit out. She turned to confront the man who considered *when needs must* a good enough reason for arranging matters as he saw fit. 'Do you have anything at all to do with the law, Mr Parnell?'

His craggy, handsome face relaxed into a slow, heart-melting smile. 'I don't mind if you call me Nathan.'

Sasha battled to remain firm in her resistance to any tactics he might employ to persuade her to his way of thinking. 'You didn't answer the question,' she said tersely.

The smile quirked into winsome appeal. The effect was so sexy, Sasha could feel certain nerves quivering in response. 'I practised as a barrister for a while,' he said in a voice that had undoubtedly swayed juries, especially if the jurors were all women.

Sasha refused to be swayed. 'Did you get thrown out for malpractice?' she demanded.

He looked affronted. 'Of course not. I'm a very law-abiding citizen. I like legality. That's the beauty of marriage. Or, at least it would be with a properly drawn-up contract.'

Sasha was not going to get sidetracked on to that issue. Just for once, she was going to pin this man to a proper answer. 'Do you or do you not practise as a barrister now?'

'I do not. I gave it up.'

'Why?'

He shrugged. 'The judges didn't agree with me all the time.'

That didn't come as a surprise. 'I don't agree with you, either,' Sasha asserted.

'Over what?' He looked innocent. 'Have I done something wrong?'

'Threatening bodily harm. I don't believe in violence, Nathan Parnell.'

'Neither do I. None eventuated, did it?'

'No.'

'I rest my case.'

He looked positively smug. It exasperated Sasha into saying, 'I bet you're not always right.'

'My daddy's never wrong,' Matt said, looking up at his father admiringly. 'He told me so.'

'Brainwashed,' Sasha muttered, but she couldn't stop a smile at the precocious little boy.

It was a mistake. Nathan Parnell read it as compliance with their company. 'So, which way is home?' he asked, gesturing for her to indicate direction. 'Matt and I will see you safely to your doorstep. If you like,' he added belatedly, but with a smile that could have buckled her knees if Sasha weren't made of sterner stuff.

It was time to effect the parting of the ways. Nathan Parnell was not the law and Sasha was not about to let him take the law into his own hands any more than he had. She had the distinct feeling that he could twist anything to his purpose, including her if she didn't take herself out of his orbit.

'Thank you, but there's no need.' She looked around. 'Tyler's already gone.'

'What did he mean about having trouble with your parents?'

'I'll have to find a place of my own.' She heaved a rueful sigh. 'It's not easy. Work's been hard to get, and I'm not exactly over-endowed with the world's riches.'

Bonnie had fallen asleep. Sasha shifted her into a more comfortable position against her shoulder then held out her hand. 'May I have my bag now?'

'Sure you don't want me to carry it? It's no trouble.'

She resisted temptation and shook her head. 'I don't have far to walk.'

He handed over the bag. The blue eyes played a last bit of havoc with her pulse-rate as he said, 'Well, good luck with your job-hunting, and I hope you find a decent place to live.'

She met his gaze steadily, resolutely. 'Good luck with finding a wife.'

That was it. She set off and didn't look back, determined to put everything that had happened today behind her. Somewhere, somehow, she would make a good life for herself and Bonnie, even if she never found a man who would love both of them.

'Hold on a moment!'

Nathan Parnell's voice trapped her into looking back. Then the sight of him jogging after her with Matt enjoying a piggy-back ride and happily shouting 'Giddy-up, Daddy,' trapped her into stopping and staring at them. They were both so... heart-tuggingly attractive.

She was still standing like a store dummy when Nathan pulled up beside her. 'Here,' he said, bending over to slip a piece of notepaper into her bag.

'What is it?'

'I just thought of a place where you might get friendly accommodation. I wrote down the woman's name and her phone number. You could try it if you want to. The rent's negotiable.'

'Thanks, but...'

'Don't spoil it.' He grinned. 'That's my two good deeds for the day.'

Then, leaving her with the image of twinkling blue eyes, he was off again, his son bobbing up and down excitedly as his father broke into an obliging canter.

He was, without a doubt, the sexiest man Sasha had ever met.

# CHAPTER THREE

SASHA was desperate. It was impossible to stay on with her parents. Their small two-bedroom apartment was uncomfortably overcrowded since she had been forced to retrieve all her possessions before Tyler threw them out. On top of that, a nine-month-old baby did not understand or make allowance for the daily rituals of a retired couple. The unavoidable disruption to the household routine was giving rise to tensions that made life difficult for everyone.

She and Bonnie had to get out.

Day after day Sasha searched for a suitable place but what was affordable was unthinkable: dingy basement bedsits, neighbourhoods where no young child would be safe, dank, sunless rooms that had an unhealthy smell about them. She would have coped if she had only had herself to consider. It was Bonnie's welfare that concerned her. Once again Sasha opened her handbag and took out the piece of paper Nathan Parnell had given her. She hadn't wanted to put herself in a position where she was beholden to him for anything. She had told herself it was better for her if she avoided any possible connection to him. But was it better for Bonnie?

Sasha glanced at her watch. It was almost three o'clock. This time last week she was sitting beside a sandpit in a park, discussing marriage with Nathan Parnell. His image came vividly to mind.

So what if she did run into him again? He hadn't harassed her. He had respected her wishes. And Sasha had promised her mother she would find accommodation as soon as possible. This piece of paper was a chance to nothing. *When needs must,* she thought grimly.

Sasha picked up the telephone and dialled the pencilled numbers with both apprehension and determination, then stared at the woman's name on the notepaper as she waited for the call to be answered.

Five minutes later she had an address in Mosman and an invitation from Marion Bennet to 'come right on over'. However, when Sasha arrived at the recommended 'friendly accommodation', she was thrown into uncertainty about her course of action.

She stared at the magnificent two-storeyed home, unable to believe she had written down the right address. This place had to be worth a fortune, set as it was on harbour frontage and in grounds that had to encompass a couple of acres. Sweeping lawns and long-established gardens gave it an awesome look of prime real estate.

It probably cost a fortune to maintain, as well, Sasha reasoned. Perhaps having tenants helped the owner keep it. In any event, if she had somehow misheard the house number in the street, the best thing to do was find out and ring Marion Bennet again.

With a steadily purposeful step, Sasha made her approach by way of the long gravel driveway. It swept around in a semicircle so visitors could be driven right to the portico that framed the entrance to the house. Sasha couldn't help feeling like an intruder as she walked up and pressed the doorbell.

To her startled surprise, she heard it play a few bars of 'Jingle Bells'. It reminded her that it was the last week in November and all the shops were full of Christmas cheer. She hoped she could make Bonnie's first Christmas a happy one.

One of the double doors opened. Sasha was faced with a woman of similar age to her mother, grey hair neatly groomed, her rather buxom figure comfortably dressed in a loose-fitting top and casual cotton trousers. Her hazel eyes were bright with interest as they swept over Sasha in quick appraisal.

Sasha had dressed professionally in a navy skirt and white blouse, stockings, low-heeled court shoes. Her long hair was wound into a smooth top-knot and she had applied a light make-up to give her face some colour. She hoped she looked like a sensible, responsible and trustworthy person.

'Mrs Bennet?' she asked on a slightly anxious note.

The woman gave her a friendly smile. 'That's me. And you must be Miss Redford.'

'Yes.' Sasha smiled in relief. She had the right address after all.

But it still didn't look right when Mrs Bennet stood back and waved her forward. The foyer extended in a wonderful pattern of mosaic tiles to a magnificent polished cedar staircase that curved up to the top floor.

'We could go up that way, but there's another staircase by the kitchen that you'll find handier,' Mrs Bennet explained, leading Sasha into a side passage. 'I'm afraid there's no private entrance to the nursery and nanny's quarters.'

Apparently that was the accommodation for rent. Feeling somewhat intimidated by her surroundings, Sasha simply nodded.

'I'll give you your bearings as we go,' Mrs Bennet continued. 'The formal rooms are on our right, the TV- and breakfast-rooms on our left.'

She opened doors as they passed them, giving Sasha a glimpse of luxurious living on a scale she had never met before. The ceilings had to be at least fourteen feet high, and the furniture was out of this world.

Between the breakfast-room and the kitchen was a lobby that served the second staircase. This was much less grand than the first, the treads not so wide, and there were three landings as it angled around the wall to the upper floor.

As she followed Mrs Bennet's steady climb, Sasha had the sinking feeling that, however negotiable the rent was, this setting virtually precluded its being within her means. She should bring the matter up now to save wasting her own and Mrs Bennet's time, but the temptation to see what was being offered was irresistable.

'This is the nursery.'

Sasha was ushered into a bright, airy room, predominantly lemon and white, and containing every possible facility a mother and baby might need: storage cupboards, shelves, a changing table, a cot, a comfortable rocking-chair.

The nanny's quarters were equally spacious and complete. The bed-sitting-room had all the facilities and comforts provided in a top motel: a double bed, writing desk, small lounge suite, table and chairs, television, telephone.

Sasha couldn't even dream that the asking rent for this marvellous place would be in her capacity to pay. She tried to find some fault so she could retreat from the situation without loss of dignity. It was difficult to find a fault, but she came up with one.

'I need a private telephone line,' she said.

Mrs Bennet nodded a ready acceptance. 'I'm sure that can be arranged.'

'I need it for my business,' Sasha said defensively.

'Do you sell things from home?' Mrs Bennet enquired.

'No. I find things.'

She saw the incomprehension in the older woman's eyes and explained further.

'I find whatever people want found. It started with research for family trees, finding long-lost relatives, beneficiaries for wills. But it branched into tracking down family heirlooms and other things. The provenance of paintings or other works of art. Finding the owner of some rarity that someone wants to buy. Mostly people don't know where to start or where to go for the information they want.'

'What an interesting occupation! Do you get many people wanting your services?'

'Not too many lately. But I do use the phone a lot when I'm working.'

'It must save you considerable legwork,' Mrs Bennet said appreciatively, then dismissed the issue, leading Sasha through another doorway. 'I'm afraid the kitchenette is more or less limited to serving a baby's needs than cooking meals, but of course you'll have free use of the kitchen downstairs.'

It looked more than fine to Sasha. It was sheer luxury after what she had seen this week. It provided a small refrigerator, kitchen sink, a microwave oven, ample storage cupboards, and a benchtop with several power points.

Then there was the en-suite bathroom. It contained a bath for the baby as well as a separate shower stall if she preferred that herself.

Satisfied that Sasha had seen all there was to see, Mrs Bennet led her back into the nursery and pointed out one of the windows. 'The swimming-pool is fenced for safety. You're welcome to use it as you please. And the grounds. As I said, you don't have a private entrance but we tend to live as a family here. No one will mind your coming or going through the house, front or back entrance.'

It was time to bite the bullet on the question of rent. The case was hopeless but Sasha had to know. 'Mrs Bennet, you've been wonderfully kind showing me around, and I'd love to live here, but I don't know if I can afford it. If you'd give me some idea . . .'

The older woman smiled. 'Well, that's up to you, my dear. These rooms are simply being wasted with no one in them. What would you like to pay?'

It put Sasha on the spot. She wished a definite figure had been stated. Much easier to say no than to have to reveal the truth of her situation. Her mind went through a feverish calculation, stretching her means to the uppermost limit of what she might be able to reasonably pay each week without running into trouble.

'I don't have much work at the present moment, but I do have a bit of money put aside,' she explained. 'I can afford...' It was so inadequate, it would barely cover the cost of a bedsitter in the poorest part of Sydney.

'Go on,' said Mrs Bennet helpfully, her eyes soft with sympathy.

It seemed insulting to offer so little. In a voice she hardly recognised as her own, Sasha spoke the fateful words. 'A hundred dollars a week.' She could feel the blood burning through her cheeks. She turned aside, not wanting to face the reply, feeling humiliated and defeated.

'I'm afraid that won't do, my dear. I'm afraid that won't do at all.'

Mrs Bennet had seemed such a nice person, but making her propose a figure that exposed how destitute she was...it was belittling and demeaning. 'I'm sorry to have wasted your time,' Sasha said tonelessly, and headed for the door.

'What you are offering is far, far, far too much.'

It made Sasha pause. Was she hallucinating? Was her hearing defective today? She could not conceal the surprise she felt, nor did she attempt to hide it or disguise it as she swung around in disbelief. 'I must have misheard. I thought you said I offered too much money.'

Mrs Bennet looked puzzled. 'Didn't Mr Parnell tell you?'

Completely confused about what was going on, Sasha repeated what she had been told. 'He said the rent was negotiable.'

'So it is, my dear, but under the terms of the will of the late Seagrave Dunworthy there is a *caveat* on the property that prevents any room, or any number of rooms, from being let or rented beyond a certain price. The rental that may be charged up to that maximum figure is negotiable, but if the owner were to accept any figure above that price, then the owner would be liable to litigation which could effectively cause a disinheritance and loss of ownership.'

Sasha's professional curiosity was piqued. In the course of her work she had read a lot of strange and eccentric wills, but none like this. 'Are you sure of your facts? I've never heard of such a thing.'

'That's what I've been told, and I have no reason to disbelieve it,' Mrs Bennet assured her.

Sasha hesitated fractionally, then plunged to the heart of the matter. 'Then how much is the maximum figure that can be charged for a room or a set of rooms?'

'Five guineas a week.'

Reading old documents had made Sasha familiar with this unit of currency. It predated the introduction of decimal currency in 1966, and its real vogue was in the nineteenth century, although it had still been used in auctioneering circles, and particularly the horse-racing industry, up to a couple of generations ago. She did the mental calculation of converting this old coinage into pounds and shillings, and then into dollars and cents.

'That works out at ten dollars and fifty cents.'

'That is correct.' Without the slightest loss of aplomb, Mrs Bennet explained the position so that Sasha could appreciate it properly. 'You can negotiate any figure you like for the rent, up to a maximum of ten dollars fifty.'

Sasha still couldn't make herself believe it. 'The will must be very old to have been written in such terms,' she said, driven to question the validity of what she was being told.

'I don't have any information on that,' Mrs Bennet replied, looking totally unconcerned by such a consideration.

'Surely with the effect of inflation ...'

'I've been led to believe there is no mention of the effects of inflation in the will of the late and highly esteemed Seagrave Dunworthy.'

'Oh!'

Sasha didn't know where to go from there. Faced with the unbelievable that was apparently irrefutable, her mind went into numb stasis.

Mrs Bennet eventually jolted her out of it. 'Really, my dear, you must make up your mind whether to take the rooms or not,' she said in a kindly but matter-of-fact voice. 'I do have other things to do.'

'Yes. Well, of course I'll take them. In the circumstances.'

However dubious the circumstances were, Sasha told herself she would be stupid to look a gift horse in the mouth. Particularly in *her* circumstances.

'In that case, I must tell you now that the terms of the agreement are very specific,' Mrs Bennet said with an air of serious warning. 'Firstly, any benefactor of the revered Seagrave Dunworthy must speak of him in the most laudable terms. Otherwise they may lose the benefits conferred on them by the will.'

'Oh, I'll certainly do that,' Sasha said with feeling. 'He must have been a wonderful man.'

'Highly esteemed,' Mrs Bennet agreed. 'And secondly, the rental conditions are very precise. The money must be paid each Friday morning, after nine o'clock, and before the grandfather clock in the entrance hall chimes the twelfth stroke of the twelfth hour at midday.'

The eccentricity of this instruction seemed to add a ring of substance to the rest of Seagrave Dunworthy's will. 'I can't pay in advance?' Sasha asked.

'Definitely not.'

'Ten dollars fifty,' Sasha repeated in dazed bemusement.

'For convenience, ten is better,' Mrs Bennet advised. 'Then we don't have to worry about change.'

'Ten,' Sasha agreed, wondering if she had fallen through the looking glass like Alice. 'I get all this for ten dollars.'

'Well, if you'd like to negotiate...'

'No, no. Ten dollars is fine. I'll pay it first thing on Friday morning.'

'After nine o'clock,' Mrs Bennet reminded her. 'Now let's go downstairs and I'll give you duplicate keys for the front and back doors. Then you can move in whenever you like.'

'It will be tomorrow.'

'That's fine, dear.'

Sasha was in such a daze that it wasn't until Mrs Bennet was escorting her to the front door that a niggle of curiosity slithered into her mind. 'Does Mr Parnell know about the terms of Seagrave Dunworthy's will?'

'Oh, yes, dear. Mr Parnell is a lawyer. He explained all the terms of the will to me.'

A man of many parts, Sasha thought. Retired barrister, white knight, boy scout, the sexiest man she had ever met, and what else?

'I don't know what we would have done without Mr Parnell,' Mrs Bennet continued. 'We ran into terrible trouble. My husband was robbed of his business, although we couldn't prove it in court. We lost everything: our livelihood, the roof over our heads, all the money we had saved. We had nowhere to turn until Mr Parnell suggested this place and got us settled here.'

'He did that for you, too?' Sasha mentally added Good Samaritan to the list.

'Such a kind man.' Mrs Bennet opened the front door and smiled at Sasha. It seemed to be a 'welcome to the family' kind of smile. 'My husband will help you carry your belongings in tomorrow if you need a hand, dear. I'm sure you'll be very happy here.'

'Thank you.'

It seemed ungrateful to linger, taking up more of Mrs Bennet's time, but the memory of all those grand rooms prompted one last question. 'Does anyone else live here besides you and Mr Bennet?'

'Why, of course, dear. I thought you knew. Mr Parnell lives here.'

# CHAPTER FOUR

BY EIGHT o'clock on Sunday night, Sasha had moved herself and Bonnie into the Mosman mansion. She was unpacked and as settled as she was ever likely to be in this household. She didn't know how long her occupancy was going to last, but she was going to make the most of it while she could.

Bonnie was fast asleep in the nursery. Sasha had the luxury of the nanny's quarters to herself. She took a long, hot shower, pampered herself by putting on her peacock blue satin robe, then brushed her hair as she made a critical assessment of herself in the vanity mirror.

She had never been called pretty. Tyler had said she was elegant. Fine bones, a long neck and the straight fall of black hair to below her shoulderblades had been her main attractions to him. She wondered what Nathan Parnell saw in her, apart from her skin. She did have fine skin, but she had always thought of it as pale, not creamy, and tonight there were signs of stress and fatigue under her eyes. The last few weeks had not been easy.

Sasha put down the hairbrush and strolled into the kitchenette. A cup of coffee, then she would see what was on TV. She switched on the percolator, feeling a deep sense of satisfaction in not having to consider anyone but herself.

She hadn't seen Nathan Parnell all day. Mrs Bennet had told her he and Matt had gone visiting; Sasha didn't ask with whom or where. She was determined not to show any interest in him. But Mrs Bennet had told her other items of interest.

She and her husband rented the servants' quarters on the other side of the main kitchen. Nathan Parnell employed them as his housekeeper and handyman. This very convenient arrangement gave rise to grave suspicions in Sasha's mind.

Nathan Parnell liked convenience. He also used the law to suit himself. Seagrave Dunworthy's highly eccentric will could very well be an invention of Nathan Parnell's fertile mind. It had brought him the Bennets, who obviously served him well, believing they were the recipients of remarkable good fortune. With the same good fortune extended to Sasha, he might be counting on getting himself a compliant wife.

If so, he could think again. Desperate situations required desperate solutions, but Sasha couldn't believe her situation would become so desperate she would consider marriage in any circumstances to Nathan Parnell.

The more Sasha pondered her position here, the more it seemed to her that it didn't matter whether Seagrave Dunworthy was an authentic person or not. All she had to do was believe in him implicitly and esteem him so highly that no one could ever fault her on that score. The terms of his will not only allowed her to live here cheaply, but also independently of Nathan Parnell's good will or humour. As long as she paid her rent within the required time on Fridays, Nathan Parnell could have nothing to complain about.

The percolator boiled.

There was a knock on the door.

'Come in,' she called, wondering what Mrs Bennet had forgotten to tell her this time.

Sasha poured coffee into her cup, heard the door open; then realised several moments passed without a word being spoken. Surprised into looking for the reason, Sasha lifted her head and was abruptly jolted out of her complacency. Marion Bennet was not her visitor at all. It was Nathan Parnell.

He stood by the opened door, apparently as transfixed by the sight of her as Sasha was by him. He was dressed in navy trousers and a white shirt, yet Sasha was instantly assailed by a sense of dangerous intimacy and a heart-choking awareness of dangerous virility.

Her mind registered shirt buttons left undone, a deep V of tanned chest with a sprinkle of dark curls, rolled-up shirt-sleeves, muscular forearms, the damp sheen of hair freshly washed, electric blue eyes that sent sizzling sensations pulsing to sensitive places.

She was suddenly, flamingly conscious of her nakedness under the silk of her robe. Her skin sprang alive with awareness. Her nipples tightened. She searched frantically for something to say, anything to disrupt the current of serious sexuality flowing between them.

'I thought it was Marion Bennet.'

He didn't seem to hear. She needed something less obvious, more earth-shaking. Nothing came to mind.

'How striking you look in that vibrant blue.' His deep baritone voice seemed to throb through her. His mouth slowly curved into a whimsical smile that was somehow loaded with sensuality. 'I don't suppose you're wearing it for me.'

'No.'

'What a waste.'

Sasha desperately gathered her wits, determined not to be drawn into anything she didn't want. 'I have to thank you for suggesting this accommodation,' she said, trying for a neighbourly attitude.

His smile broadened. 'Your gratitude would be better directed to Seagrave Dunworthy. I was merely the intermediary. A cup of coffee will be repayment enough.'

'I was getting ready for bed.'

'So was I.' The blue eyes twinkled wickedly. 'And I thought of you.'

'As an afterthought of the day's activities?'

Sasha laughed. It was the only way to break the tug of his attraction and hopefully lift the conversation to a lighter note.

'The day's activities concerned you. I went to see Hester Wingate.'

'Is that someone else who's left some kind of marvellous will from which I can benefit?'

'No, but she's working on it. And she wants your services.'

'In what capacity?'

'Marion told me your profession was finding things. Hester is eager to employ your expertise.'

'You got me a job?'

'To make sure you could pay the rent.'

And keep me here, Sasha reasoned. Nathan Parnell was irrepressible, and probably ten steps ahead of her. She had no doubt that behind the twinkling eyes was a determined will to have his own way. He was not shy of playing any trick to get it, either. What have I let myself in for? Sasha wondered, then tried again to assert some control over the situation.

'Don't you think it's rather improper to visit me in my bedroom? Is this what I'm to expect?'

He shrugged. 'You're free to evict me if you want. But then you wouldn't know about the job.'

He had an indisputable point there. She needed work. She also needed this accommodation. But she didn't need a husband who didn't love her and Bonnie.

'Does a cup of coffee cover that favour as well, or are you expecting more?' she asked in dry challenge.

'I like mine black and two sugars,' he said, and promptly shut the door.

'Sit at the table. I'll bring it over,' Sasha instructed, wary of allowing him to set a cosier scene. As it was, he hadn't really answered her question and she wanted some firm distance between them. Like a good solid slab of wood.

'Did Bonnie settle down OK?' he asked affably, lessening her tension by doing as he was told.

'Sound asleep,' she replied.

'So is Matt,' he said with satisfaction.

Which instantly put the thought of *bed* in Sasha's mind. She fought off the idea that Nathan was thinking their children were conveniently accounted for. He had gained admittance to her room, but it was more than ten steps to her bed and she was definitely not going to give him any encouragement whatsoever in that direction.

Having surreptitiously checked that her robe was securely wrapped around her, Sasha took both cups of coffee to the table and settled herself on the chair opposite his.

'Now tell me what this job is about,' she invited, intent on keeping strictly to business.

His mouth twitched. 'Muck-raking.'

'Then I'm sorry you've wasted your time on my account. I'm not into scandal or anything defamatory that would hurt other people.'

She placed her elbows on the table, picked up her cup, lifted it to her mouth and sipped, hoping he would take the hint that the reason for him being with her was now limited to coffee-drinking.

He grinned openly, undeterred by dismissals or hints. 'Hester Wingate is ninety-two years old. Or, at least, that's what she admits to. She's probably older. She's the last of her tribe. All her friends, brothers, sisters have passed away. There are a few old scores she never got to settle. But that doesn't deter Hester. She wants the information for the *other side*.'

'What other side?'

'The vast beyond. The next life. I'm not quite sure how Hester sees the *other side*—whether they're all going to be together in heaven, or hell, or somewhere entirely different. But whatever it is, Hester wants to be prepared for them who done her wrong in this life.'

Sasha couldn't help being amused. 'Well, that does rather change the situation,' she conceded. 'You mean she wants to muck-rake in the far past about people who are dead and gone.'

'Precisely. Every last skeleton in every last closet. Nothing to be overlooked.'

'Can she afford my services?'

'What do you charge?'

Sasha hesitated. She really needed a good substantial job. If the old lady was a pensioner, it was unlikely she could pay much, but anything was better than nothing in her present straitened circumstances, and often one job led to another.

'The accepted rate is twenty-five dollars an hour plus expenses, but most people can't afford too many hours at that rate,' she said with rueful honesty. 'Usually, because I can't get much done in an hour, I put in a couple of hours for every one I charge.'

'Well, that's one way to get rich,' he drily remarked.

It made Sasha feel defensive, which drove her to an aggressive reply. 'It takes a long time to dig up real substance.'

'I'm sure it does,' he agreed. His eyes twinkled with infectious good humour, completely defusing any offence given. 'Hester has a lot of old scores to settle. If you're any good at giving her what she wants, you may end up being fully employed for years.'

The prospect of full employment for a while sounded too good to be true. Sasha's suspicions were aroused. 'Precisely who is this Hester Wingate and what connection do you have with her?'

'I'll take you to meet her if you're interested in the job. I do her legal work.'

'Then the law is still your profession.'

He shook his head. 'I only do it for Hester because no one else would put up with her.'

'A favour, you might say,' Sasha prompted.

'Very much so.'

And a favour for a favour seemed very much down Nathan Parnell's alley. Sasha's suspicions moved up a notch. 'She sounds extremely eccentric.' And possibly primed for the part by her legal consultant.

Nathan rolled his eyes. 'Believe me, you'll earn your money. I've redrafted her will at least twenty times. She had another codicil for me today.'

Another will. Another fertile invention by Nathan Parnell? 'Nothing could be more eccentric than Seagrave Dunworthy's will,' Sasha posed, wanting to see if he reacted to the connection.

He gave her a crooked smile. 'Want to bet on that?'

Maybe it was all true. Sasha had to admit to being intrigued by the prospect of investigating the situation. Besides, a job was a job, and, if she was promptly paid for the work she did, what did it matter if Nathan Parnell was behind it? As with this accommodation, as long as she believed everything was genuine, there was nothing for her to worry about.

'Where does Hester Wingate live?' she asked, getting down to practicalities.

'Church Point. In actual fact, I am commanded to bring you to her in time for morning tea tomorrow.

You are to bring your baby with you.' His eyes made an eloquent appeal. 'It would save me a lot of trouble if you agree.'

'You don't mind being ordered around?'

He sighed. 'I find it easier to fit in with Hester than not to.'

Despite her suspicions, Sasha was amused. The idea of a little old lady getting the better of Nathan Parnell was so unlikely, she wanted to see it for herself. 'It's very kind of you,' she said.

'I take it you're agreeable to the plan?'

'It couldn't be more agreeable,' she assured him. 'And I'm very grateful to you for thinking of me.'

'It was no hardship.'

His eyes locked on to hers, telling her it was a pleasure, the kind of pleasure a man took in doing something for a woman who was of keen personal interest to him.

Sasha's stomach quivered. She forced her eyes down. Her cup was still in her hands. She drank the coffee as though it were a life-saving necessity.

He picked up his cup. He had long, lean fingers, neatly manicured nails. Was he the kind of lover who would take and give sensual pleasure, tracing exquisite patterns on her skin with those fingers? Sasha caught her breath at the sheer eroticism of her thoughts. She had to get Nathan Parnell out of here before something inappropriate occurred. She waited until he finished his coffee, then tried to bring their business together to a quick conclusion.

'What time should we leave in the morning?'

'Can you be ready by nine-thirty?'

'Yes.' She stood up and gave him a weary smile. 'But I do need a good night's sleep.'

'I'll leave you to it.'

To Sasha's intense relief he rose to his feet without any attempt to prolong this encounter. She led the way to the door, opened it, then steadied herself to bid him goodnight.

'Thanks for all your help, Nathan.'

He paused beside her, his vivid blue eyes capturing hers with concentrated purpose. He was too close, disturbingly close.

'Would passion suffice?' he asked.

She felt his hands on her waist and knew he meant to kiss her. Probably he wanted more. Without a wife...

Her heart clenched, hit turmoil, and shattered into chaos. She shouldn't let him...she shouldn't...but a kiss was just a kiss. She could stop it at that. A kiss didn't commit her to anything. There were many reasons for giving him this little pleasure. He'd done a lot for her. He wanted it. And he was the sexiest man she had ever met.

In mind-spinning fascination she watched his mouth coming towards hers. She hadn't kissed anyone but Tyler for over four years, and in recent times there had been little feeling left in that. Mostly desperation. Often resignation. But that was gone now, and she was free to please herself, free to accept a kiss from another man, and she wanted to know what it would be like.

His lips moved lightly over hers, tempting, tantalising, encouraging her to respond. No demand. No pressure. Nothing to be frightened of. Her hands slid up to his shoulders, allowing him the freedom to gather her closer. He didn't. It was a long, slow kiss, one of sensual invitation and exploration, caressing away Sasha's thoughts. She went with him, following every step, entranced with the journey of escalating sensation.

A sigh, mingled with regret and satisfaction, whispered from her lips when he ended the kiss. The pleasure of it still lingered in her mouth. She wanted to taste more, and very quickly.

'Stolen kisses are the sweetest,' he murmured against her ear.

She opened her eyes and stared dazedly at him, wondering if he had felt anything special. 'You call that passion?' she taunted, piqued that he was still in control of himself.

'No. I call *this* passion.'

She saw the flare of desire in his eyes. Then his mouth claimed hers again, and his arms enfolded her, and his hands moulded her body to his, and there was no holding back. No control. Not for either of them.

Precisely how their passionate immersion in each other came to an end was a hazy area in Sasha's mind afterwards. Had they both pulled back, not having expected to feel so much? A mutual inter-reaction? Or had Nathan sensed some hesitation on her part, and given her the benefit of any doubt in her mind?

She heard him say, 'Tomorrow,' in a deep husky voice. There was a gentle disengagement, his hands steadying her before slipping away. Then he was gone.

She headed for her bed, barely aware of what she was doing, automatically switching off lights. She stretched out luxuriously between the sheets, her body still tingling with the sensations Nathan had aroused. She ran her fingers lightly over her lips. They weren't swollen, but they still felt highly sensitive.

Nathan Parnell had certainly delivered passion. She could very easily have ended up in bed with him. He had been fully aroused, urgently aroused, and the hard pressure of his need against her stomach had been like some wild aphrodisiac, triggering a sense of elation through her mind and a pounding excitement through her body. She had lost all track of any common sense in the dizzying pleasure of feeling wanted by such a desirable man. She had wanted him, too.

In retrospect, she was glad they had stopped where they had. Plunging into physical intimacy would have given her an involvement that had gone far too far, far too fast. Passion was not love. And it wouldn't suffice to hold a marriage together, either. She would have to disabuse Nathan of that idea.

On the other hand, he was a very intriguing man, attractive on many levels, and Sasha didn't want to discourage him completely from pursuing a relationship with her. It might lead to much more than passion, given time to get to know each other properly. Thanks to him, they were ideally placed to do precisely that.

A pleasurable little bubble of anticipation danced around Sasha's mind. Seagrave Dunworthy was a marvellous man. Hester Wingate sounded as though she was an equally marvellous woman. Nathan Parnell might rearrange his ideas on what made a marvellous marriage. Who knew what tomorrow might bring?

# CHAPTER FIVE

SASHA woke the next morning to what seemed like a different world. She could hear Bonnie babbling her contentment with whatever was in her line of vision in the nursery. A new home, a new job, and a new life, Sasha thought, and with a zest for getting on with it she sprang out of bed and headed for the bathroom.

Today she was going to look as good as she could. She would wash and blow-dry her hair into shiny sleekness. She would wear her fashionable, lipstick pink coat-dress and black patent high heels. She would dress Bonnie in her best clothes. There was a lot to do before she met up with Nathan at nine-thirty.

Time flew by. She had Bonnie strapped securely into her carrycot ready to carry downstairs when Nathan appeared at the nursery door. Sasha had left it open to facilitate her exit.

'Need some assistance?'

'I was just coming,' she replied, quickly scanning his face to see how he felt about what had happened between them last night.

The look he gave her came from a man who knew what he liked and had no inhibitions about showing it. His eyes danced appreciatively over her face and the long gleaming tresses of her hair, then simmered reminiscently over the curves of her figure and the shapeliness of her stockinged legs. The pleasure and satisfaction in his smile spread a warm glow under Sasha's skin.

'I've never seen any woman look so superb in that colour,' he said with flattering directness.

'I'm glad you think so.'

Dressed in a silky three-piece blue-grey suit, with a blue and gold tie to set it off, Nathan Parnell looked a very distinguished man of considerable class, devastatingly handsome, and master of his world. But not master of hers, Sasha swiftly amended, not unless she could feel it was absolutely right.

'Red might be more stunning on you,' he said consideringly.

She laughed in self-conscious pleasure at his interest in her appearance. 'I do have a red satin evening dress but I didn't think it was appropriate for the occasion.'

'I shall make sure an occasion arises.'

Excitement welled up in Sasha. He really meant to pursue a relationship with her. Or was he thinking she would make a suitably ornamental wife, as well as a desirable woman in his bed?

'Where's Matt this morning?' she asked, remembering he didn't come unattached.

'At playschool. It gives him the chance to mix with other children.'

He stepped forward to bend over Bonnie in her carrycot, smiling down at Sasha's baby and letting her curl her little fingers around one of his. Bonnie blew a few bubbles to show her appreciation of his attention.

A good father, Sasha thought.

He picked up the carrycot and the accompanying holdall, lifting his heart-tugging smile to Sasha. 'Ready?'

'Yes, thank you.'

She followed him downstairs, resolving to find out more about him on their drive to Church Point. All she really had was a stack of impressions, some of them well-founded but hardly what one might call solid information.

A white BMW was parked at the front steps. She watched him place Bonnie's cot on the back seat and secure it properly. He saw Sasha settled into the front passenger seat, waiting until she had her safety belt fastened before closing the door. It made her extremely aware of his physical closeness, and when he joined her in the car she couldn't help giving him a cursory look, matching his body against her memory of how it had felt pressed against her last night.

His eyes suddenly caught hers. For a moment there was a simmering promise in them, as though he, too, was remembering what they had shared. Then he turned his attention to starting the car and getting it on the road. Sasha sat very still, her heart zipping up and down a scale like a hammer on a xylophone. Nathan Parnell intended it to happen between them. It was only a question of *when*.

It couldn't be today, Sasha thought, not with Bonnie present. A sense of shock rippled through her. Too far, too fast, her mind hammered in swift reaction.

She had never been a promiscuous person. Despite her discontent with Tyler, she had remained faithful to him, and never once fancied any other man. Casual sex did not appeal to her. She wanted more than temporary passion. She wanted the deep, forever kind of love.

'When you're not drawing up codicils for Hester Wingate's will, what do you do?' she asked, determined that their relationship progress how she wanted it to progress. If it was to progress at all.

He slanted her a twinkling smile. 'I play computer games.'

She sighed her exasperation. 'I mean, how do you exist?'

'Most people would say very comfortably. I guess it depends on what your ambitions and priorities are.'

'Are you saying you're retired from work?'

'No. But I am in a position to choose what I do.'

'Which is?'

'Do you like diamonds, Sasha?'

She couldn't see the relevance of this question but she automatically looked down at her left hand, thinking of the engagement ring she had once hoped for from Tyler. 'As much as most women, I guess,' she answered, striving for a careless note. Was he thinking he could buy her with a diamond ring?

'There's an exhibition in the city. The best of the coloured diamonds from the Argyle Mine in the Kimberleys. The pinks are my favourite.'

She glanced at him in surprise. 'You like pink diamonds?'

'Fabulous. Would you like to see them? I'll show you how I protect them. With a computer game.'

'I'd like that.'

She couldn't imagine what he had to do with diamonds, nor what he did to protect them, but she wasn't about to miss out on full enlightenment. With this kind of car, and the classy suit he was wearing, Nathan Parnell was not exactly on government welfare. Nor were there many people so wealthy that they could afford to wind down and work at their own convenience at such a young age.

'How old are you?' she asked.

'Thirty-four.'

'Are you anti-social?'

He gave her an amused look. 'Do I act and talk as though I'm anti-social?'

'No,' she conceded, and thought how paradoxical he was. Why hadn't he found a woman of his own class to marry? Why pick on her, a stranger he'd met by complete chance in a park? Perhaps she should simply adopt his attitude of 'wait and see', instead of asking questions. Besides, she rather liked the surprises he sprang on her. It made life very interesting.

She turned her mind to the fast approaching interview with Hester Wingate. She had never been to Church Point, but knew it was on the innermost edge of Pittwater, a playground for sailing boats and other water sports. It was protected from the sea by the long Palm Beach peninsula, and renowned for its wealthy and prestigious marinas and yacht club. It was an expensive area in which to live.

Because of Hester Wingate's age, Sasha expected her to live in an old-style home. She was staggered when Nathan turned his car into the driveway of what could only be called a modern and luxurious villa, a huge pink and white construction that had two levels of Mediterranean-style verandas overlooking the sparkling expanse of water. The grounds were a luxuriant mass of tropical ferns and palms, hibiscus and frangipani trees. A gardener was raking up dead leaves.

'She can definitely afford twenty-five dollars an hour,' Sasha said with satisfaction.

Nathan laughed. 'Try thirty or forty. She'll respect your expertise more.'

They alighted from the car. Bonnie was fast asleep. Nathan took the carrycot. Sasha collected the baby's bag. They started up a massive concrete staircase that curved up to the lower-level veranda.

Nathan caught Sasha's hand. 'For courage,' he said, his smile a promise of support.

'Is she so formidable?' Sasha asked, inwardly marvelling over how good an act of friendliness could feel. Friendship was more important than passion.

'Depends on her mood. But, yes, she can be difficult.'

Sasha hoped Hester Wingate was disposed to like her. She wanted this job. It could mean a lot to her.

They reached the veranda. A huge variety of exotic plants in exotic pots suggested the owner was a collector of the unusual. Nathan led Sasha to a white aluminium dining setting which was positioned to catch the breeze off the water and a steady stream of sunshine. He placed Bonnie's cot on the table.

'I'll give Hester a call.'

He was very familiar with this house, Sasha thought, watching him slide open a set of glass doors and stroll into a vast living-room. It made her wonder once more if the job with Hester Wingate was a genuine one, or a contrivance agreed upon between Nathan Parnell and an old and trusted friend who could afford any indulgence.

Sasha dropped the holdall on one of the chairs and waited. She took several deep breaths to calm herself. Voices alerted her to their approach. The image Sasha had conjured up in her mind of Hester Wingate was blasted to pieces by a completely different reality.

She was little. She was old. She used a walking stick. But that was definitely the only concession to her ninety-two years, and even the walking stick was an elegant ivory and silver fashion statement.

Her hair was like a finely spun candy-floss confection in a silvery mauve colour. She wore a flowing caftan that shimmered with pinks and blues and aqua. Her eyes were a fascinating light blue, twinkling with lively interest, radiating energy. She stopped in the doorway between the living-room and the veranda and gave Sasha a thorough once-over that might have been rude from anyone else, but quite clearly Hester Wingate assumed it her right to examine guests as she pleased.

'I see,' she said, nodding vigorously. 'So this is the girl who is creating all the fuss.'

Sasha felt she had been catalogued under the wrong identification. She looked to Nathan for guidance.

'Under the will of...' Nathan began blandly.

'Don't pay any attention to him,' Hester commanded. 'Young women are meant to create a fuss. To leave a trail of devastated men in their wake. It's the only thing young women can do effectively.'

But it wasn't true. Not in this case. Unless Nathan had made a fuss about giving her the job.

'Are you clever?' Hester fired the question point-blank.

Sasha was at a loss as to how to answer. Fortunately Hester Wingate didn't require a reply. She appeared to be adept at holding conversations where only she spoke.

'It's a matter of bloodlines,' she said, and stepped over to the table to examine Bonnie. 'Never buy a horse without examining its bloodlines.' She shot a piercing look at Sasha. 'Do you understand that?'

'I have no intention of either buying or selling a horse,' Sasha said weakly. 'I've come about a job.'

'Now there's a child anyone might be proud of,' Hester declared, giving Bonnie her nod of approval before turning the full blast of her attention back to Sasha. 'Is she healthy?'

'Yes.'

'Are you healthy?'

'Yes, I'm healthy, too.'

Her eyes skated down Sasha's body. 'I like to see a woman with good wide hips. Saves a lot of problems.'

Sasha burned. This was going too far. It made her feel she was being regarded as a brood mare about to be put to stud.

'I whinny when I'm given oats for breakfast,' she said, flashing a withering glare at Nathan Parnell for his part in subjecting her to this absurd farce.

'Spirited,' Hester remarked as though Sasha had scored another high mark. 'Let me see you smile.'

'Madam, I must protest...'

'I will not work with either unpleasant or eccentric people. They are the two types of people I cannot abide.'

Sasha couldn't help smiling at the whimsy of this speech. Hester Wingate appeared to be both.

'Good teeth,' Hester said with satisfaction. 'My dear, you have passed all the tests so far. You have the job.'

'Thank you.' Sasha had nothing else to say. She didn't know if she had just been approved of as a suitable wife for Nathan Parnell, or as a suitable person to be in Hester Wingate's employ.

'Do sit down and make yourself comfortable, dear.' It was another autocratic command. 'Nathan, set the baby down just inside the door so we'll hear her when she wakes. Jane will bring morning tea in a few minutes.'

Sasha eyed Nathan with dark suspicion. He must have told Hester Wingate about his intention to enter a marriage of convenience and that Sasha was his selected candidate for the position of his wife. This job was almost certainly bogus, a means of persuading her that supplying solutions to needs was better than a love match.

His response to her look was to spread his hands in a gesture of innocence, and roll his eyes to suggest Hester was beyond his control.

Sasha didn't believe that for a second, but there was no profit in walking out in high dudgeon. Better to bite her tongue and sit this out. She could decide later what she was going to do.

Hester took the chair at the head of the table. When they were all settled, she reached over and patted Sasha's hand. 'I hope you don't mind, my dear, but at my age I don't have time for social chit-chat. Get on with the job. That's what I say. I take it you agree.'

'Definitely,' Sasha agreed with mixed feelings.

'When we start I'll take you to the history room. I've collected all the family bibles. All have been tampered with.' Hester paused for effect. 'It's a sad day when it's no longer possible to believe in the dates entered in a bible.'

'What do you want me to do about it?' Sasha asked.

'Find out the truth. Dig up the dirt. Nail everybody that can be nailed.'

'Is that all you want?' With a list of names and dates, it was an easy matter to check them. There wouldn't be many hours involved.

The old lady eyed her warily. 'I hope you're not suffering from false confidence, my dear. You are dealing with some of the world's greatest scoundrels.'

Sasha found that easy to believe. They weren't all dead, either. One of them could very well be sitting opposite her. However, she adopted a professional air and spelled out *her* credentials for the job.

'I assure you, Mrs Wingate, it is quite straightforward. I've done this many times before. Civil registration was introduced into New South Wales in 1856. From that time onwards, there's been a legal and compulsory requirement for all births, deaths and marriages to be registered. Before that, there are baptismal and marriage and funeral entries in church registers. I can obtain these . . .'

'Is bigamy against the law?' Hester archly demanded.

'Yes.'

'That's what I thought.' She gave Sasha a knowing look. 'I wouldn't rely on every member of this family's observing the law all the time. Not when it comes to bigamy. And not in other matters either.'

Sasha flashed a simmering look at Nathan Parnell. He was certainly of a similar breed.

He gave her a wicked grin that confirmed he took an unholy joy in doing things *his* way. It also confirmed he was thoroughly enjoying this little contretemps between her and Hester Wingate.

'And this is only the beginning, my dear,' Hester went on. 'Many peculiar things happened in my family. I want answers to every question.'

Sasha wanted a few answers, too. 'I'll need to get as much of the background as you can give me, Mrs Wingate.'

The aforementioned Jane arrived with a traymobile loaded with refreshments. Either Hester Wingate had a good appetite or she expected Nathan and Sasha to eat plates of sandwiches, cakes, scones, and pastries.

'Now tell me, my dear,' Hester commanded, eyeing Sasha with challenging interest. 'How much do you charge for your services?'

Sasha was more than ready for that question. Since eccentricity was the order of the day, she was not to be outdone. 'Fifteen guineas an hour,' she said, rolling it out as though it was her standard fee and not to be blinked at. It translated to thirty-one dollars, fifty cents, which gave her a nice little bonus for heartburn.

'Oh, yes!' Hester cried in delight, turning a beaming smile to Nathan. 'She *is* clever!'

'There are two other conditions,' Sasha added. 'I'm only to be spoken of in the most commendable manner. And the money is to be paid on Fridays between the hours of nine a.m. and noon.'

If some devious game was being played, Sasha had decided she could play it with the best of them.

Hester Wingate leaned back in her chair, the enquiring blue eyes looking even more quizzical. 'How *very* clever of you! And perceptive.'

Uh-oh, Sasha thought. Had she gone too far? 'I hope I wasn't being impertinent,' she said in a swift attempt to mend fences. After all the job, bogus or not, did offer an easy and much needed income.

'Not at all,' Hester assured her. 'You've struck on the one person I want you to concentrate on most of all. Every bit of dirt you can find. He is the greatest rogue and villain that ever lived. He destroyed my life.

To get revenge on him when I meet him on the other side . . . my dear, I would pay you anything.'

'And that person is . . . ?' Sasha prompted.

Hester frowned. 'I thought you already knew.'

'I'm not sure,' Sasha replied with a sinking feeling. Was she reading this situation wrongly?

'Why, my dear, the man in question is your benefactor.'

Sasha looked towards Nathan Parnell, desperately hoping she misunderstood. Despite his highly individual personality, and very wrong ideas about marriage, she wanted Nathan Parnell to be a *good* man, not a villain.

'Seagrave Dunworthy,' Hester said with hatred in her voice. 'The man I want to malign and crush is Seagrave Dunworthy.'

Sasha was stunned, all her assumptions shattered in one blow. There could be no doubting the depth of feeling emanating from Hester Wingate. Seagrave Dunworthy had been a real person. His eccentric will must be real as well. Hester Wingate's dirt-digging venture was real. The prospect of full employment for a long time to come was real. She had been told the truth.

Her eyes flew to Nathan Parnell. He *was* a good man. He had rescued her from Tyler, directed her to accommodation that met all her needs and more, directed her to a job that would help set her on her feet financially. He was better than Santa Claus.

Except there were two catches to the gifts he bestowed. The kind of marriage he wanted was anathema to her. And Sasha was now faced with a first-class dilemma.

If she did the job Hester Wingate required, and dug up dirt on Seagrave Dunworthy, she risked losing her low-rent accommodation at Seagrave Dunworthy's house. It was impossible to sustain a pose of highly esteeming a man if she proved he was a rogue and a villain.

The answer came to her. Nathan would know a way around the problem. He had got her into this mess. Now he had to get her out of it. And Sasha would make sure he did.

She smiled at him.

He smiled back at her.

Sasha's heart did a weird little flip.

How could she feel this sense of togetherness with a man she barely knew, a man who had no belief in the lasting power of love?

# CHAPTER SIX

SASHA was shown the history room. Arrangements were made for her to examine all the contents the following day. Hester said Brooks, her chauffeur, would collect Sasha from Mosman and drive her home again. Nathan suggested that Hester acquire a photocopier. Hester told him to organise the purchase and delivery. She wasn't interested in mechanical things. That was what men were for.

How different it would be if it were a horse, Sasha thought, surprising herself with how readily she was accepting what would have been an alien world to her a week ago. But she couldn't allow herself to be swept too far from her own objectives. There were problems to be resolved, and the sooner she did it, the better.

She waited until they took their leave of Hester and were in the car again with Bonnie settled in the back seat. 'What did Seagrave Dunworthy do with his life?' she asked, wondering if Nathan Parnell was prepared to malign their benefactor.

'I never knew him personally. He died around the time of the First World War.'

Sasha had the feeling it was an evasive answer. 'Do you have a copy of his will?'

'No.'

'Well, I'll soon get one. And since this job was your brilliant idea, and you do have legal expertise with wills, you can tell me how I can satisfy Hester without breaking the "highly esteemed" clause.'

'Easy.' He grinned at her. 'Dig up the dirt Hester requires, then prove it's all wrong. A vicious attack by vicious people on a highly esteemed and worthy man.'

'Thank you. I knew you'd have an answer,' Sasha said drily, thinking Nathan had better be proved right on this important point.

He chuckled. 'You have quite a talent for answers yourself. You handle Hester very well.'

She was amused by his admiration for her stand on giving as good as she got. Although initially she had been completely thrown. 'There was a moment when I thought she might go so far as to check my muscle tone and sprinting ability.'

'Your muscle tone is great.' His voice throbbed with appreciation.

Sasha's amusement died. Had last night's embrace been a coldly calculated way of checking out her body? 'If you've been summing me up for *breeding* potential . . .'

He grinned at her look of outrage. 'Making babies wasn't on my mind when I had you in my arms.' The teasing twinkle melted into something much more direct. 'Making love was.'

A flood of heat suffused Sasha's body. She knew he was merely stating the truth, and she couldn't deny she had been tempted, but it was time to spell out her position. Unequivocally.

'That wasn't love. It was passion. And it will not suffice.'

'Pretty powerful stuff, all the same.' He raised his eyebrows at her. 'Are you saying you don't want to sample the experience again?'

She struggled between honesty and caution. His eyes wouldn't let her lie. 'No. But...'

'Encouraging.'

'...I want more than that,' she finished emphatically.

'You'll get it,' he said with relish.

'No. I meant it's not enough.'

'I can do better.'

'I'm not talking about sex, Nathan,' she cried in exasperation. 'I'm talking about...about sharing... and caring.'

'Good manners. That's what you're talking about. If you'd like to tell me what gives you the most pleasure...'

'Forget it.' So much for a sense of togetherness, Sasha berated herself. She and Nathan Parnell were on a totally different wavelength when it came to love. 'It's too soon after Tyler,' she argued. 'I hardly know you. I don't know that I want to know you. You could turn out to be as great a villain as Seagrave Dunworthy.'

Sasha gasped in horror at what she had said. She had just lost her accommodation for Bonnie and herself.

Nathan Parnell broke the strangling silence, his voice pitched low, but certainty behind every word, a seriousness she had never heard before, except for one occasion. 'When needs must,' he said. 'We all have to do things we'd rather not. What do you know, really know, about Seagrave Dunworthy, apart from titbits of gossip? Who knows anyone? I could have sworn I knew my ex-wife. I bet you thought you knew Tyler. We were both wrong.'

He was right about that, but Sasha couldn't bring herself to concede the point. She didn't want to open her mouth again after the awful blunder over her benefactor. She was intensely grateful to Nathan for excusing it.

She pondered the unpalatable truth of what he'd said. It was all too easy to be fooled by images, never really knowing what went on beneath the surface of a person. Maybe life was a lottery. Either good or bad luck ran with whom you drew as a partner.

On the other hand, she did have some freedom of choice in whom she selected and when she selected them. With Nathan Parnell, it was definitely too soon, and she would never accept *his* terms for marriage, no matter how attractive she found him.

She belatedly realised that Nathan had driven past the turn-off to the Mosman house. 'Where are you going?' she asked, her head swivelling around to check she was not mistaken.

'To the exhibition centre at Darling Harbour,' he answered matter-of-factly.

The diamonds!

Sasha relaxed. Her curiosity was piqued. It would surely reveal another facet of Nathan Parnell's extraordinary life.

It was a quick journey into the city. Nathan casually parked the car in a place reserved for VIPs at the exhibition centre. Sasha didn't say anything. Let him take the consequences when he was found out.

Bonnie had slept through the entire trip. The sound of the car doors being opened and closed woke her. Nathan elected to lift her out of the carrycot and carry her in his arms, insisting she was no burden at all. Bonnie made no protest at this arrangement, snuggling happily against his shoulder and cooing approval at Nathan.

Sasha was privately amazed at Bonnie's ready acceptance of him. Normally she cried if a stranger picked her up, especially a man. Even when Tyler had made an effort to appear fatherly, Bonnie had sensed his inner rejection of the role, exasperating Tyler with her non-co-operation in playing the adoring daughter.

Plainly it was different with Nathan. He looked perfectly comfortable with a baby perched in his arms. A big man but a tender one. A rock. A protector. Bonnie must sense that, Sasha decided. Maybe instincts were more trustworthy than any knowledge.

As they walked along together, she started wondering about Matt's mother. Didn't she miss him? Sasha couldn't understand a mother giving up her child unless forced to by painful circumstances, yet Nathan had implied that Matt's mother was like Tyler, hating the responsibilities of parenthood.

The hurt must have gone very deep when Nathan realised he'd made a mistake in his choice of wife. Clearly he did not want to subject himself to that kind of hurt again. But Sasha was sure it was a worse mistake to give up on love altogether. A marriage of convenience was not the answer.

On entering the main hall at the exhibition centre, Sasha very quickly realised diamonds were not the dominant feature on show. There were huge displays on all the mining ventures: models and maps and diagrams and videos of gold mining at Kalgoorlie; iron mining at Pilbura; copper mining at Mount Isa; silver-lead-zinc mining at Broken Hill; coal mining from the Newcastle region; opal mining at Cooper Pedy; and, of course, diamond mining in the Kimberleys, as well as many others.

School groups were being led around by teachers who were intent on broadening the education of their pupils. There were crowds of other people, as well, satisfying their interest in the natural resources of a country that was rich with minerals and precious stones.

'If you don't want a geology lesson, we'll go straight to the showroom,' Nathan said, refocusing Sasha's attention on why he had brought her here.

'Lead the way,' she replied, realising they didn't have unlimited time. Matt would have to be picked up from his playschool at some reasonable hour.

Two security guards stood on either side of the doorway into the showroom. Sasha was amazed there weren't more in evidence when she saw what was displayed with such little protection. There were signs saying no touching was allowed, and people were not to stray in any way beyond the roped off areas, but the nuggets and precious stones were not in locked glass cases. They were arrayed on velvet-covered stands, their full glory undiminished by any barriers to the naked eye.

The coloured diamonds were the centrepiece in the room. They *were* fabulous. Sasha had only seen white diamonds before. She was fascinated by the range and brilliance of the colours. They were worth a king's ransom. The most outstanding was a pink.

'Gorgeous, isn't it?' Nathan murmured.

'Magnificent,' she agreed.

'It really doesn't catch the light to best advantage on that velvet,' he suggested.

'The notice said no touching,' she warned, catching the drift of his intent.

'You're right,' he agreed. 'Let's take the diamond home and study it there.'

With a nonchalant air, he placed one leg across the roped off area. Nothing happened. Then, to Sasha's dazed disbelief, he reached out and palmed the diamond from its stand.

Her shocked eyes followed the movement.

Just as swiftly, the diamond was secreted inside Bonnie's pilchers, hidden in the folds of her nappy. Maintaining every appearance of total innocence, Nathan Parnell calmly stepped back into the visitors' area and turned to view the opals on the other side of the diamond display.

All hell broke loose.

Alarms soared up a scale of decibels. Klaxons whooped. Bonnie started wailing. The two security guards filled the doorway, ordering those in the showroom to stay precisely where they were. Excited yelling was accompanied by a stampede of running feet from the hall outside.

Sasha froze. Nathan Parnell was a jewel thief? He was using *her* baby as an accomplice in a diamond heist? Could he possibly think she would let him get away with it? Did he possibly think *he* could get away with it?

No wonder he had disagreements with judges about what constituted justice! He had handed her a lot of surprises but this was beyond the pale. No way would she involve herself with a thief!

The guards parted to allow more men into the room. The sirens stopped. The klaxons stopped. After all the noise the silence was startling. The first man pointed an accusing finger straight at Nathan. 'I've got you,' he said with absolute conviction. 'You put the diamond in the baby's nappy.'

Sasha felt a surge of relief. At least she didn't have to accuse him herself. But was she incriminated by being with him? Would anyone believe she wasn't an accessory in these circumstances?

'You made the baby cry,' Nathan admonished, making a great show of trying to soothe Bonnie.

Sasha was dumbfounded by his calm and cool demeanour. How could he remain so unaffected in the face of being caught red-handed?

An older man pushed forward. He glared long and hard at Nathan Parnell through his gold-rimmed spectacles, brushed a hand over his receding hairline, then with an air of dull resignation he said, 'All right, Mr Parnell. You've proved your point.'

'Did you get a good shot of me on video, Daniel?' Nathan drawled, tilting his chin this way and that in mock posturing. 'Did I show up well from every angle? Which profile gave the best result?'

Sasha shook her head in bewilderment. He sounded like a horribly vain movie star wanting his ego stroked.

Daniel's gloom appeared to deepen substantially. 'Mr Parnell, you photograph brilliantly from any angle. I really prefer not to choose a specific shot. But I ask you...I beg you...is it possible for you to visit the display and *not* set off the alarms, and *not* have your photograph taken?'

'Daniel, if I recollect perfectly...' his voice dripped with silky reasonableness '...harsh words were spoken...'

'Mr Parnell, no man regrets, genuinely regrets, as much as I do that I called you crazy.' Daniel's voice gathered a passionate momentum as he continued. 'No man can more sincerely believe that I made a great error of judgement when I said this protection system could not work. No man could have been more wrong when I said, if this system could work, you were the last person in the world capable of making it happen. No person could be more sincerely, genuinely regretful of past mistakes, and I beg you, I beseech you, I pray that you will take this admission as an act of contrition, a true humbling of self.'

Daniel took a deep breath. There was a pitiful crack in his voice as he confessed, 'You are making my life hell, Mr Parnell. Please...please...will you stop setting off the alarms?'

'The system works, Daniel,' came the stern reproof.

'It does indeed, Mr Parnell,' he agreed effusively.

'You're absolutely convinced of that, Daniel?'

'I shall laud this system, and your genius in making it work, to the four corners of the earth, Mr Parnell.'

Nathan sighed. 'Well, if you're prepared to guarantee it that far, I'll stop testing it.'

'Thank you, Mr Parnell. Thank you. Thank you.'

'You can now have your diamond back, Daniel,' he said, as though bestowing a great favour. He extracted it from Bonnie's nappy and started polishing it on his lapel.

'Kind of you, Mr Parnell. Very kind.'

'And I won't set the alarms off again. Or have my photos taken.'

'Mr Parnell, I'll mention you as a beneficiary in my will. Thank you.'

Nathan held out the diamond and Daniel gratefully accepted it. With great care and precision, he positioned it on its stand, then stepped away with the air of a man who'd had a great burden lifted from his shoulders.

'Computer games,' Sasha muttered, intensely relieved that it was a case of Nathan Parnell nailing someone rather than being nailed himself. He might be a rogue but he wasn't a villain.

Nathan grinned at her. 'I like practical results, even from games.'

'It works. It all works,' Daniel repeated with fervour, then made a hasty withdrawal.

'Seen enough?' Nathan asked Sasha.

'Yes, thank you.'

'Sorry about upsetting Bonnie. I didn't think of that.'

'You didn't think of my heart, either.'

'Maybe I did.' His eyes danced with unholy mischief. 'You don't have any hankering to lead an exciting life?'

'Not so I've noticed,' she replied drily.

'Don't worry about it. A little more exposure, a little more training, and you'll soon be doing things you never thought possible.'

'That is highly unlikely.'

'We'll see,' Nathan said blithely.

They made their exit from the exhibition centre, thankfully leaving behind the speculative interest of onlookers. Sasha breathed in the sweet air of freedom, released from the prospect of visiting Nathan Parnell in Long Bay Gaol. Whether it was sheer relief or Nathan's outrageous behaviour she didn't know, but she broke into laughter at the whole crazy incident as they walked towards the car park.

'What do you find so funny?' he asked.

He didn't look at all amused. Perhaps he thought she was laughing at his idea that more exposure to his way of living would immure her to anything happening.

'It just feels good to be alive,' she answered. He certainly put some new zest and zing into her life. In fact, she couldn't remember ever having had such a wildly eventful day. Maybe Nathan was right. Not only had she sustained a number of shocks, she seemed to be thriving on them.

She grinned at him. 'Next time you decide to walk into such a prestigious place and play a game with one of your toys, you could give me a hint that pandemonium is about to break out.'

'Hey, wait a bit,' he cautioned. 'That wasn't a game and it wasn't a toy.'

'Well, you found it amusing enough when you were doing it. I find it more amusing now.'

'That was very serious business,' he insisted.

'Getting your photo taken,' she mocked. 'Ringing all the bells. Driving that poor man to distraction.'

It didn't get the kind of response Sasha had grown used to from him. The eyes that bored into hers had no twinkle. His face suddenly looked older; grave, hard, bitten with a determination to survive any odds.

'If that *poor* man hadn't said what he did to me, I wouldn't have gone to the US to develop my system. If I hadn't gone to the US, I wouldn't have kept custody of Matt. If I hadn't been contracted to prove my system at the exhibition, I wouldn't have had to come back to Australia. Because I came back into the country, and got found out, I've got a custody case to fight...' for the first time he sounded and looked like a man under great stress and strain '...and the inevitable consequences.'

'Is there anything I can do to help?' The impulse to give whatever sympathetic comfort she could was instinctive.

Nathan Parnell looked at her, a fierce blaze of emotion making his eyes even more vividly blue. There was no surface amiability or pleasantness now. Sasha wondered if she could ever know the inner core of this man, if any one person could ever really understand another.

'I've run out of time,' he grated. 'I need a wife.'

# CHAPTER SEVEN

SASHA felt her heart being squeezed. The force of his emotion was frightening and hurtful in its striking power. Sasha had never experienced anything like it. The urge to take it upon herself to solve his problems was compelling.

It took all her concentrated willpower to resist it, to turn her head away, keep walking. She was acutely conscious of him walking beside her, carrying Bonnie, a man who loved his son as she loved her daughter.

She didn't need to ask why a wife was so necessary to him. He had said enough for her to put two and two together. It was clearly related to keeping custody of his child. She felt sorry for him, deeply sorry that he was faced with the possibility of being parted from Matt. His love for the little boy had tugged at Sasha's heart from the moment of meeting in the park.

Nathan Parnell touched her in a way no man, or any human, had ever touched her, but she couldn't be his wife. Not as a convenience. His need to be married had nothing to do with her, not as the person she was. Sexual attraction was no basis for marriage. Neither was compassion. Sasha wanted to be loved, to be the only woman her husband would ever want beside him because no other woman would ever mean as much.

Tears pricked at her eyes. It wasn't fair that she should feel so drawn to a man who only wanted to marry her to secure his son from his ex-wife. And what about Matt's mother? Nathan had taken their son out of the country to keep custody, possibly bypassing the law, taking it into his own hands to do what he considered right. Maybe the woman had been grieving for her child. Sasha had only heard Nathan's view of his first marriage. How could she judge what was right and wrong?

They reached the car. Sasha remembered what she had thought about Nathan parking in a place reserved for VIPs. She hadn't known he was entitled to do so. It reinforced how little she knew about his life, what drove him to be the man he was. In the same way, he knew next to nothing about her. The idea of a marriage between them was dangerous. She had to stop thinking about it.

It was worse when they got in the car. Sasha was even more aware of him and it wasn't simply physical awareness. She felt pain and purpose pulsing in the silence. She desperately searched her mind for a way to break away from it, to separate herself from his need.

'So, you're now in the security business,' she said. His job was the only diversion she could come up with.

'More or less,' he answered, his tone uninterested, his thoughts clearly focused elsewhere.

82     IN NEED OF A WIFE

'Would you mind explaining to me how your computer game works?' Sasha persisted.

There was little enthusiasm in his voice at first. Sasha suspected it was only good manners prompting his replies, but he gradually warmed to the subject under her skilful questioning.

She found out that touching the objects under protection did not set off the alarms. The public were deceived about this so they didn't put their fingerprints on things. The system worked on the principle of what Nathan called a violation of space.

Apparently this was very important to Nathan. He expounded on the theme on their way back to Mosman. The violation of space was measured or triggered—Sasha wasn't quite sure which—by comparing digitalised information from different sources—whatever that meant.

The whole concept sounded ingeniously clever. Any kind of normal movement close to the protected objects was discounted. It was the opposite of a video security system that sought to capture every piece of information, over ninety-nine per cent of which was wasted. This system excluded irrelevant information, only reacting to a very specific computation.

It was all a bit too technical for Sasha to fully comprehend but she listened intently because Nathan was clearly proud of his work, and from the sound of it he had every right to be.

They were close to home when Nathan turned the car off the main route. 'We're back earlier than I expected,' he said, 'so I'll pick Matt up and save Marion the trouble of doing it later on.'

They stopped at a pre-school kindergarten centre. Nathan was able to park right outside the gate. 'This can take up to ten minutes or so, Sasha,' he warned. 'Do you want to come with me?'

'I'll wait here if you don't mind.' She needed the relief from keeping up a friendly interest and trying to ignore what was none of her business.

He had no sooner left her than Bonnie awoke. The motion of a car always put her to sleep, but once it stopped there were invariably cries of protest. Sasha decided a little distraction was in order. The kindergarten playground was swarming with small children taking part in one activity or another. Sasha lifted Bonnie out of the car and strolled over to the wire fence, knowing her baby daughter would soon be fascinated by the novelty of watching other children at play.

'Bonnie!' An excited cry pealed across the playground. A group of boys broke apart as one of them raced towards the fence. 'Bonnie, it's me, Matt!'

It was, indeed, and Bonnie responded as though she remembered him, waving her arms and gurgling with pleasure.

'Did Daddy bring you?' he asked Sasha, his face wreathed in a happy smile, his blue eyes dancing with delight.

'Yes.' Sasha nodded to the building. 'He's gone inside to collect you.'

'I'm out here,' Matt said unnecessarily. He turned to his friends who had followed him over. 'See? I have got a baby to play with,' he said triumphantly. 'She's a little girl, and my Daddy said I could help look after her 'cause she's living in our house now.'

'Boys are more fun than girls,' one boy observed.

'I like girls,' Matt said very seriously.

Sasha couldn't help smiling.

One of the other boys eyed her up and down. 'Are you Matt's mother?'

'Course she is!' Matt insisted, wheeling on the doubter. 'I told you she was coming.'

Sasha, who had opened her mouth to deny it, promptly held her tongue. She remembered the taunting in her own childhood about the lack of a father. No one believed she had one because he was mostly away in the navy. She had always felt the odd person out. What harm was there in letting Matt win at least one round with his playmates?

She would have to correct him once they were alone together. She could not allow him to continue the fiction. But for the present, it didn't matter much at all. In fact, it was quite flattering to be accepted so readily. Perhaps it reflected the little boy's deep inner yearning for a mother.

'Are you going to live with Matt now?' another boy asked, checking out the facts.

'Yes,' Sasha answered. 'Bonnie and I have come to stay.'

Matt beamed his pleasure in her affirmation. 'I can show Bonnie lots of things,' he said, his eyes shining at the prospect of having a ready admirer at hand from now on.

'Matt! Your father's here,' a woman called, beckoning him into the school building.

Matt sped off like a frisky colt, running and leaping for joy that his world was set to rights, at least for one day. The other boys trailed away from the fence, and Sasha returned to the car.

A minute or two later, Nathan and Matt appeared, the little boy swinging on his father's hand, skipping along beside him, obviously cock-a-hoop about having a 'family'.

Matt was strapped into his car seat beside Bonnie. As Nathan drove them home, the little boy excitedly told Bonnie of his favourite toys and what they could do with them. Bonnie made approving noises.

'I'll drop you at the front door before I garage the car, Sasha,' Nathan said as he turned the BMW into the driveway. 'If you'd like to leave the carrycot and simply lift Bonnie out, I'll carry it up for you later.'

'Can I get out with Bonnie, Daddy?' Matt asked.

'We'd better go and see Marion first, Matt. If it's all right with Sasha, you can then visit Bonnie.'

Sasha turned to give the little boy a welcoming smile. 'Whenever you're ready, Matt.'

'It'll be real soon,' he replied eagerly.

The car stopped at the front steps and Sasha quickly assured Nathan she didn't need him to get out and help. She collected her holdall, picked up Bonnie, thanked Nathan for everything, and closed the car doors on father and son.

As she unlocked the front door and entered the house, Sasha wished she could enjoy a sense of homecoming. The events of the day had left her with very mixed feelings about how to handle living here with Nathan Parnell and his son. Last night it had

seemed relatively clear-cut. Even this morning she had
thought all the choices were hers to make. Which they
were. But they didn't feel quite so clear-cut any more.

Her arms full with carrying Bonnie and her bag,
Sasha pushed the front door closed with her shoulder, then noticed that the double doors from the
lounge to the foyer were wide open. Marion must be
doing some cleaning, Sasha thought, and looked in to
say hello to the housekeeper.

There was a woman in the room but it wasn't Marion Bennet. Nor could she be remotely connected to
cleaning. She had made herself comfortable in one of
the armchairs, a drink in one hand, a smouldering
cigarette in the other, and she had the look of being
perfectly at home, having been born and bred to a rich
and luxurious setting.

On catching sight of Sasha, she raised a finely
arched eyebrow that somehow projected both curiosity and condescension. 'Who have we here?' she asked
in a tone that simulated interest but had absolutely no
heart in it.

Sasha did not reply. Her mind was busy trying to
place the face which was elusively familiar to her. The
woman crushed her cigarette into an ashtray and stood
up. She wasn't beautiful. She was elegant. She was
class from head to toe.

Blonde hair was tucked into a smooth French pleat
but an artful fringe added a soft dash of femininity.
Her make-up made the most of an interesting and very
individual bone-structure. She was tall and exces-
sively slim. The tailored cream suit she wore was pin-
striped with navy. Pearls made the perfect accessory.

She strolled towards Sasha, one hand still nursing her drink, a smile playing on her rather thin lips, a superior smile, not one with any warmth in it.

'I'm Nathan Parnell's wife,' she said. 'Who are you?'

# CHAPTER EIGHT

BIGAMY leapt into Sasha's mind. The bottom fell out of her world. Nathan Parnell hit the lowest rung of the ladder, and was shelved in the darkest, deepest recess in the basement.

Yet . . . he had been good to her. And kind. She forced out the necessary words with the necessary aplomb. 'I thought *ex-wife* was the situation.'

The woman shrugged. 'Life is change. Change is life. Discords can be turned into melodies. Who can say?' Again the smile without warmth, an automatic mechanism that declared she was in control of herself and everything else.

But she *was* the ex-wife. Sasha was satisfied that Nathan Parnell had not lied. His position zoomed out of the basement cellar and returned to the top of the ladder. She might not want to marry Nathan Parnell herself, but she certainly didn't want any other woman getting him before she made up her mind. Whether it was his ex-wife or not simply didn't matter. Not to Sasha.

'Don't count on a melody,' she said, wanting to shake the woman's insufferable confidence.

'Oh?' The eyebrow lifted in supercilious amusement. 'You're in a position to judge, are you?'

'I live here.'

The woman's calculating grey eyes flicked to Bonnie, studied her for a moment, then dismissed the baby as of no account. She added a curl of condescension to her smile. 'Nathan always was a sucker for down-and-outs.'

It ripped the mat out from under Sasha's feet momentarily, but she came back fighting. 'That's to my advantage, don't you think?'

'Dream on.'

The derisive reply was cuttingly dismissive. Sasha struggled for a suitable riposte.

'Elizabeth!'

The whip-like command in the call of the name snapped the friction between the two women. They turned to look at its source. Nathan Parnell had entered the lounge by the door from the hall. He did not look at all pleased to see his visitor.

'Yes, darling. I've come back,' Elizabeth drawled in a sacharine sweet voice.

'What for?'

No warmth there. Good, Sasha thought. No move to greet his ex-wife in any welcoming way, either. He stood by the door, grim-faced, his eyes ablaze with bitter suspicion.

Elizabeth strolled away from Sasha, but not towards her ex-husband. She stopped in front of the fireplace, as though establishing her hold on a commanding position. The three of them now formed a triangle, all equally separated. Sasha began to realise how formidable this woman was.

'You need a wife, Nathan,' Elizabeth stated without preamble. 'I'm qualified for the job. More experience than any other woman. I'll even forgive you your indiscretion.' She glanced at Sasha as though she were a *mycobacterium leprae bacillus.*

Nathan said nothing. His gaze did not shift from his ex-wife. Sasha suddenly felt very much out of place, an interloper in highly private business.

'If you'll excuse me...'

'No.' Nathan's attention snapped to her, the blue eyes compelling in their intensity of feeling. 'Please stay. I want you to hear.'

'You're always so cautious and conservative, Nathan,' Elizabeth mocked.

'If you're sure,' Sasha said uncertainly.

'He wants you as a witness, you fool! Not that it will do him any good.'

The scorn stung. Sasha looked at Nathan's supremely superior ex-wife and felt a slow, deep anger start to burn. Tyler, in his worst moments, used to call her a fool. He implied all women were fools, driven by their hormones. Here was a woman calling her a fool, and Sasha wasn't about to take it, not from anyone.

'I'll bet she doesn't have any hormones,' she gritted between gnashing teeth.

'Too damned right,' Nathan agreed. 'Perceptive of you. No hormones.'

The woman viewed Sasha with icy contempt. 'Beware of slander. I have a law degree, the same as Nathan.'

Dismissing Sasha as too trivial for further consideration, she turned back to the target of her visit. 'We have a custodial case on our hands, Nathan. I came to give you a choice. You can remarry me and play the part of the adoring husband, which you do so well, for the next twelve years. In that time I will become the first female premier of this state and have two terms in office.'

Enlightenment burst through Sasha's mind. The vague familiarity of the face—Elizabeth Maddox— prominent campaigner on television in the last state election—the consummate speaker for *women's* interests.

'That satisfies my needs,' she continued, uncaring of the naked and grasping ambition she displayed. 'You get to keep Matt, Nathan. That will satisfy your needs.'

'If *needs must*.' It was the voice of hopelessness.

Sasha was appalled at the deal offered and Nathan's response to it. 'That is so unfair!' The words poured from her lips before she could bite her tongue. 'It's blackmail!'

The woman shrugged. It was of no consequence to her whether it was fair or not. Sasha's heart plummeted to the same basement dungeon where she had previously put Nathan Parnell. She looked at him in desperate appeal. Was there no way out of this poisonous woman's plot?

He misread her look. 'Elizabeth didn't become avaricious for power over people until after we married,' he said, as though wanting Sasha to understand there was some mitigation for his mistake in marrying the woman.

'It took me a while to realise my potential,' Elizabeth agreed. 'But I made it big. And I'm going to make it bigger. One day I'm going to be the first female prime minister of this country. My name will be enshrined in every history book.'

The gloating pride in her voice sent a wave of revulsion through Sasha. The self-aggrandisement was sickening enough, but then she had the gall to look at Nathan as though he were an object of pity.

'And what will you have done, Nathan? What will you achieve?' she mocked.

He made no reply, simply staring stonily at his ex-wife. And Sasha suddenly understood. There was no point in talking caring or kindness or generosity of heart to a heart of stone. Nor would Elizabeth give credit to any genius of mind that was not bent to amassing and cementing power.

'I'll expose you,' Sasha said, fiercely hating everything Elizabeth Maddox stood for. 'I'll repeat this conversation. As a witness. I'll sell it to the newspapers. I'll...'

Elizabeth laughed at her. 'You'd be digging yourself a hole you'd never climb out of, you poor, pathetic idiot. You couldn't pay off the damages I'd collect in a lifetime.'

'I could show up your rotten hypocrisy so you'd never get elected again,' Sasha flung back at her.

'No one would believe you by the time I finished ripping your character to shreds,' she retorted with chilling confidence. 'In the courtroom I can make black look white and white look black.'

She looked pointedly at Bonnie, then eyed Sasha with malicious intent. 'I think I'd portray you as a...tramp. A gold-digger. A sleazy gutter bitch who's trying to sell something more profitable than what's between her legs. I can do it, too, can't I, Nathan?'

'Yes,' he agreed heavily. 'You can do it, Elizabeth.'

She didn't bother acknowledging the affirmation. Her cold reptilian eyes kept projecting their lethal message straight at Sasha. 'That was the difference between us. Nathan was an idealist. He wanted truth and justice, no matter at what cost. I wanted success. I won. Nathan lost. That's true, isn't it, Nathan?'

'Yes,' he agreed even more heavily. 'You won. I lost.'

It answered all the questions Sasha had had about why Nathan was no longer a barrister. And why he took the law into his own hands to correct what he perceived as wrong.

Elizabeth bestowed her smarmy smile on him. 'That's the way it's always been between us. You recognise and accept that, don't you, Nathan?'

'I hope you never make yourself Minister for Justice,' he said, hating his defeat yet apparently powerless to evade it.

'Why would you lose the custody case?' Sasha pleaded to him. 'If the family law court has already found in your favour...'

'Please explain it to your moronic friend, Nathan.'

He took a deep breath. He looked directly into Sasha's eyes, yet his own were curiously blank. There was nothing to be read of what he was feeling. His voice was toneless as he stated the position.

'The reality was that Matt would have interfered with Elizabeth's working schedule. I interfered with it and she got rid of me. The responsibility of a child was a worse interference so she got rid of Matt. At the time, that image of Elizabeth and her ambition suited her requirements. My petition to the court for custody was not contested. It suited Elizabeth to let me have Matt then. But when it comes to court again, she will argue mental fatigue and harassment, undue pressure by a big powerful man on a defenceless woman. Allegations will be made of physical threats . . . is that right, Elizabeth?'

'It barely scrapes the surface of what will happen, Nathan,' came the taunting promise.

'Now that Elizabeth has her eye on high office, she has to project family values, loyalties, caring and concern for people.' A touch of acid crept into his voice at associating such things with a woman to whom they meant nothing. 'What was good for her ambition before is now a liability. Voters want to see personal warmth. Matt is to be her showpiece . . .'

'And you, darling,' Elizabeth drawled. 'Devoted husband and father. I want both Matt and you to give my new image solid credibility.'

His jaw tightened. It clearly took an effort to unclench his teeth and continue. 'It will be argued in court that I prevented Elizabeth from knowing her own son because I went to the US which prevented her exercising visiting rights.'

Sasha couldn't let that pass. 'But you went to the US because Daniel rejected your system and . . .'

'We're not talking about truth, Sasha,' Nathan cut in, a thread of passion breaking through the monotone. 'We're talking what will be argued.'

'You've learnt a lot in the last year or so, Nathan,' Elizabeth remarked, then enjoyed herself by driving a few more nails into the argument. 'Alienation of natural love and affection ... I'll have a field day in the Press. Women everywhere will naturally sympathise with my plight against this bullying man.'

It was a total travesty of justice and she relished it, Sasha thought, feeling both helpless and hopeless in the face of such consciousless and callous manipulation of others' lives.

Nathan didn't bother explaining any further. The situation was explicit enough. He was up against a ruthless woman who didn't care what damage she did as long as she won her own way.

Seeing that she was not about to draw more blood from Nathan, Elizabeth shrugged carelessly and said, 'Where is the child anyway? I suppose I should see him.'

If looks could kill, Nathan Parnell's look would have killed Elizabeth right there. She should have gone to hell and perdition, Sasha thought.

'If you want me to fall in with your scheme, Elizabeth, you damned well put on your best political act with Matt.'

'Mummy awaits,' she syruped back at him.

He glowered disgust at her and left the room.

Elizabeth finished her drink and set the glass on the mantelpiece. She turned to Sasha. 'I suppose you're paying some pittance rent under the will of Seagrave Dunworthy?'

Sasha disdained a reply. She wasn't going to feed this woman's malice.

Elizabeth sneered. 'What an old fool he was. Brain the size of a peanut. A walrus could have outperformed him in high intellectual capacity. And making such a clown of himself, at his age, with all that passion over such a contemptible girl, illegitimate child and all.'

Sasha held her tongue. She had no idea what Elizabeth was talking about and she wasn't about to show ignorance.

The other woman's gaze travelled around the room as though cataloguing its contents. 'Still, he did leave something of value and substance. Pity I'll never inherit, although, of course, under a tontine, anything is possible.'

A tontine! Sasha's mind did a swift whirl. Seagrave Dunworthy's will must be more eccentric than she'd thought. Under a tontine, the beneficiaries of an annuity shared in a trust, the shares increasing as each beneficiary died, until the whole went to the last survivor. Did this mean that Elizabeth Maddox was related to Seagrave Dunworthy? Or were Nathan and Matt?

The avaricious grey eyes returned to Sasha. 'Don't bet on staying here, rent or no rent. I'll make sure you'll very quickly lose any desire to remain under this roof.'

Nathan came back in, leading Matt by the hand. The little boy lagged a step behind, hesitant about what was expected of him. Nathan squatted down so that his eyes were on a level with his son's. He spoke softly but very seriously.

'Matt, I want you to meet someone very special to you. The most special person in the world. It's your Mummy, Matt.'

The little boy's gaze fixed on Elizabeth.

She gave her automatic smile. 'Hello, Matt.' It was the indulgent voice of a politician on an ingratiating mission, a concession to Nathan's demand. She held out her arms, inviting the child to run to her.

He did not. He sidled closer to his father and put his arms around Nathan's neck.

'Please, Matt,' Nathan gently begged. He tried to ease the stranglehold of Matt's arms, urging him into acceptance. 'Come with me and meet your...'

'She's my mother,' he whispered, flinging an arm out of Nathan's hold and pointing backwards at Sasha, but not looking at her. 'The same as Bonnie, Daddy.'

'No, Matt. You know we cannot tell a lie...'

'You said you were a police officer.'

Nathan winced. He was lost for words, for an adequate reply.

Sasha stepped in, trying to retrieve the situation. 'I'm your pretend mother, Matt. I love being your pretend mother, but Elizabeth is your real mother.'

'No, she's not,' Matt cried, and shook his head in adamant rejection.

Elizabeth's arms dropped to her sides. 'Let the boy go,' she said, and promptly cast aside any pretence of a maternal role. 'I merely wanted to see what he looks like. He takes after you, Nathan. Nothing of me there at all. What a pity. A fine-looking boy apart from that. He'll photograph well.'

Nathan struggled to his feet. 'Can't we try...?'

'No. It's years before he becomes a voter,' Elizabeth said, as coldly practical as ever. 'Then he may comprehend my real worth.'

Again Nathan's jaw tightened, but he swiftly unlocked it to attend to his son. 'Do you want to go back to Marion, Matt?'

The boy fled the room without a backward glance. Nathan heaved a sigh and closed the door before turning to face Elizabeth again, his face etched in stoic resignation.

'Now let's get down to business,' Elizabeth said crisply. 'Do you want to marry me and keep the child, Nathan? Or do you want to lose a battle on the front page of the newspapers, as well as in the courtroom? What's your choice?'

*When needs must,* Sasha thought. The situation was very clear to her now. If Nathan Parnell was married to another woman, and they had a good, stable, old-fashioned, permanent relationship, the child's welfare would best be served, in the eyes of the court, by leaving custody as it was, with the father who could offer his son a secure family life. Visiting rights would go to Elizabeth, but Sasha had seen enough. The visiting rights would never be exercised.

'Come, Nathan, the decision does not call for deep reflection,' Elizabeth snapped impatiently. 'Make up your mind.'

His lips compressed. Sasha could feel his hatred of the decision facing him, yet, knowing his love for his son, she was also intensely aware of the sense of inevitability hanging over it.

Elizabeth, scenting victory, could not resist one more shaft. 'And you can throw this presumptuous hussy out of here today,' she said with a contemptuous toss of her hand at Sasha. 'I wish to occupy your bed tonight. See if you are still as expert as you once were.'

Manhood... fatherhood... she was taking him for everything. And Sasha knew Nathan would sacrifice it all to safeguard his son. The distaste on his face at this very moment would be swallowed. Whatever he had to do, no matter how dreadful it would be, he would do it for love of Matt. A rock. A protector.

His lips parted to form one word.

Sasha got in first. She did not recognise her own voice. It issued forth like the disembodied utterance of a spirit from another world.

'Mr Parnell does not have a choice.'

For the first time Elizabeth looked discomposed. She had been hanging on Nathan's word, already tasting her malicious triumphant success, knowing how he had been going to answer.

'Rubbish!' she hurled at Sasha, furious at the interruption. 'Everyone has choices.'

'Not in this case,' Sasha said with quiet determination. 'As a man of honour, Mr Parnell is already committed to a different future. He has asked me to marry him. And my answer...'

She felt him look at her. She looked at him and felt a wild sense of exultation as she saw the light of salvation in his eyes, the incredible reality of a miracle that he'd been given no reason to expect or hope for.

On a bursting wave of adrenaline, Sasha walked towards him. 'My absolute and unequivocal answer...' her voice gathered an evangelical passion '...is yes. I will marry him. Yes. And I'll stand by his side, in court and out of it, and fight his fights with him, against anyone and anything.'

She stopped in front of him and the admiration in his eyes was all the intoxicant she needed to drive the heady recklessness further. She wheeled to face their mutual enemy. 'You may not realise it yet, Elizabeth, but you're a loser. And you've just lost everything.'

'Nathan...' There was fury and frustration in the demand.

Sasha felt his arm curl around her shoulders, supporting her stand. 'I have a wife, Elizabeth,' he said, his voice strong and vibrant. 'So get the hell out of here. Sasha and I have matters of importance to discuss.'

# CHAPTER NINE

SASHA had been so caught up with disposing of Nathan's ex-wife that she hadn't stopped to consider the consequences. They came to her hard and fast as Elizabeth Maddox made her final exit from Seagrave Dunworthy's home. At least, Sasha hoped it was the final exit.

She was beginning to realise what an incredibly reckless thing she'd done in committing herself to a marriage she didn't want. It could ruin her life. And Bonnie's. Nathan Parnell might be the sexiest man she had ever met, but however expert he was in bed, it wouldn't make up for a loveless relationship. On top of that, she would be trapped into staying with it by Matt, who wanted her to be his mother.

As the front door closed behind Elizabeth Maddox, the arm around Sasha's shoulders felt more like a prison bar than a source of comfort. 'I need to sit down, Nathan,' she said, but what she really needed was space and distance between them so she could start getting things in perspective.

Without a word he led her to one of the chesterfield lounges flanking the fireplace. She sank onto the soft down cushions and let Bonnie slide to her lap. The scene with Elizabeth had been harrowing and Sasha felt drained of initiative. Yet whatever she now said to Nathan Parnell was probably going to be the most important conversation of her life.

She groped for words and how to express them. She looked around the lounge, seeking inspiration. Such a beautiful room: chairs and sofas upholstered in silk brocades—peach, pale green, ivory and gold—their richness enhanced by a cream carpet that was both fine and thick. Elizabeth Maddox had fitted into this room. It was the appropriate gathering place for people of class to relax and enjoy each other's company. Nathan Parnell looked right in it, too.

Sasha didn't fit at all. Not only was her bright lipstick pink dress a jarring tone, she simply wasn't used to an elegant lifestyle. It made her acutely conscious that she knew nothing of Nathan's friends, or the society in which he moved.

She wished he would sit down, preferably in the chesterfield opposite her, but apparently he wasn't going to. As though wanting to exorcise Elizabeth's image from this room, he stood where she had stood, in front of the fireplace. His hands were linked behind his back. He appeared to be studying the subtle peach shades around the veining in the marble top of the table set between the two sofas.

Sasha tried to read his face. What thoughts were running through his mind? There was no sign of joy or relief. No glance of gratitude to Sasha. No flash of wicked blue from his eyes. His demeanour was gravely introspective.

'Perhaps,' she began nervously, 'I acted somewhat hastily.'

In an instant his eyes were locked on to hers. 'You were *magnificent.*'

It took Sasha's breath away. No one had ever thought her that wonderful before. She was sorely tempted to bask in the sweet intoxication of his admiration, but it was like the blissful afterglow of great sex. It wouldn't last.

'I shouldn't have let myself become involved,' she said, trying to get things on to a more practical level.

'Joan of Arc would have been proud of you.'

He was making it very, very difficult. 'There has to be another way out,' she said desperately.

'There is.'

Sasha looked at him incredulously. 'There is?'

The blue eyes bored into hers, intensely watchful. 'If you want it.'

'What do you mean, *if* I want it? You don't imagine I really want to marry you, do you?'

'It felt like a good idea to me.'

'That's because it's convenient,' she scoffed.

'You haven't felt a rather special feeling developing between us?'

Nathan Parnell had something up his sleeve. Probably an ace. Or a joker. Having seen him in action at the exhibition centre with the diamond, Sasha had little doubt it was a winning card. She could feel the confidence of the man and knew from hair-raising personal experience it would not be unfounded.

She had already entangled herself once. She was not going to do it again, not if there was a way out. She would treat Nathan Parnell with a great deal of circumspection, play her own cards very close to the chest, admit nothing. He was not going to get her more involved when she quite desperately needed to get herself uninvolved.

After her Joan of Arc triumph over Elizabeth, it was perfectly obvious that *feelings* could lead one badly astray. Sasha was not about to discuss such a dangerous and treacherous subject.

'I don't know what you mean,' she answered warily.

'Do you feel an animal magnetism between us?'

Sex, he meant, and that had to be trouble. 'Absolutely not,' she said primly.

'Do you feel a real need to be together for the sheer joy of being together?'

'I don't mind talking to you,' she conceded. That was relatively safe.

'A rapport that's beginning to be beautiful to share?'

She raised her eyebrows. 'When I don't know half the things I need to know about you?'

'Falling in love could have more to do with instinct than knowledge.'

'I've never heard anything more ridiculous in my life. How arrogant can you get, thinking I'm falling in love with you?'

He sighed and dropped his gaze, releasing Sasha from the disturbing directness that she had fended off with brick-wall effectiveness. She was congratulating herself on not letting down her guard when he shattered it with a sad personal reflection.

'Well, I guess the feeling is all on my side.'

Sasha's heart flipped around. Nathan Parnell, falling in love with her? That put a different complexion on things. Maybe she should stop giving blanket denials. If there was a real possibility... On the other hand, she had told him she wouldn't marry without love. This could be a ploy to win her over to the idea that a future together might be the answer to all her dreams, while its only real purpose was to solve his problems.

Would he be that low?

She scrutinised him as he studied the marble top again. He looked very sober and serious. If there weren't a determined jut to his chin, she might have said he looked depressed. After all, he had every reason to be depressed with the situation he faced with Elizabeth.

Sasha reconsidered. Maybe she should marry him. In name only, of course, just to get him over the hump of the legal situation. She wouldn't commit herself to a consummated marriage. There would have to be a way out. She could be a pretend wife and a pretend mother until the danger from Elizabeth was over. And then...

'Sasha...' He lifted pained eyes. A sharp touch of regret, a dull edge of resignation. 'There's been a grave misunderstanding. I don't quite know how to tell you this...'

Was it the truth? The unvarnished, unbent truth? Sasha had the impression of a great pit yawning open before her feet. Nathan was deadly serious and, whatever the misunderstanding was, it was going to affect her. Badly. She could feel it coming.

'Spell it out, Nathan,' she said, impatient to know the worst.

He hesitated. 'Let me get this absolutely clear. You really don't want to marry me?'

Sasha hesitated. Was she blocking off a door she really wanted left open? 'The circumstances are hardly propitious,' she said carefully, trying to keep all the options open.

'I can't help the circumstances, Sasha.'

'You did say there was another way,' she reminded him.

'You'd rather I take it?'

'That would certainly be best for me.' It gave her more time to explore what was happening between them, to make sure it was not a passing fancy.

'So what you said to Elizabeth was a ploy, a strategy, a tactic?'

'It was like you with Tyler in the park. Telling him you were a police officer to make him stop what he was doing to me.'

He nodded, closed his eyes briefly, then made a fair attempt at a grateful smile. 'I thank you, very sincerely, for standing up for me.'

'No one has the right to force their will on others. Elizabeth has no more right to do that than Tyler or anyone else.'

'I agree.' He nodded some more, took a deep breath, then added, 'And now that Elizabeth has been suitably diverted, I can get on with what really has to be done.'

Sasha frowned at him. 'What do you mean, Elizabeth was suitably diverted? I *saved* you from Elizabeth.'

'Yes, you did. I've never seen anything to equal it. Inspirational. I'll remember this day all my life.'

Sasha was somewhat mollified by the accolade but he hadn't answered her question. 'How will you beat her custody case if you don't marry me?'

'There is an alternative.'

'Yes?'

'When you were moving in yesterday, Matt and I went visiting. Marion told me you were short of work, so I interested Hester in your potential. But Matt and I did one other thing, as well.'

'What?'

'I signed a contract... establishing that... well, the long and short of it is that I've contracted another marriage arrangement.'

'You did *what?*' Sasha could scarcely believe her ears.

'She's a nice young Polish woman. Needs permanent residential status in this country. The problem was quite simple really. She wants...'

The wrath Sasha had felt against Elizabeth Maddox faded into insignificance. Two atoms collided. Nuclear fusion was about to take place.

'Nathan...' her voice shook with explosive energy '...do you realise that a few minutes ago I sacrificed myself, and Bonnie, and our future... we sacrificed ourselves for you? I went into battle for you, giving everything I had? I...'

'No one could more deeply appreciate...'

*'And you are already contracted to marry another woman?'*

'I had to do it.' He looked bewildered by her furious outburst. 'Time was running out. I told you so.'

Sasha hoisted Bonnie up to her shoulder again and rose to her feet. 'Precisely what did you have on your mind when you got me to come to this house, Nathan Parnell?'

'I didn't get you to come,' he protested. 'You needed a home...'

'You got me a job, as well.'

'So you'd have some income if you needed it.'

'And the very first night, after coming home from your Polish woman... Is she beautiful?'

'Well, yes, she is. I have to make the marriage look credible to Elizabeth, and...'

It was like waving a red rag at a bull. Sasha saw blood-red. 'So after coming home from your young, *beautiful* wife-to-be, you had the unspeakable duplicity to try your *passion* out on me.'

'That wasn't premeditated, Sasha. It happened.'

'Stolen kisses are the sweetest,' she jeered, then raged off around the room, firing words back at him like a hail of shotgun pellets. 'You were eyeing me over the moment you entered my room. If I hadn't put the table between us and kept you talking, you would have tried something more much sooner. As it was, we almost ended up in bed. If I hadn't made you control yourself...'

'Dammit, Sasha, I was the one who pulled back! I didn't want to take advantage of you. I know what it's like after a long relationship breaks up. The feelings of worthlessness...'

'I have never felt worthless in my life. Do you hear me? Never! And don't tell me you were thinking of pulling back this morning. You were openly planning to have an affair with me.'

'Of course I want an affair with you. Any man would. It's not necessary to *plan* these things. They happen. People do it all the time. I wanted to know if you felt what I did. And what's more...' a dangerous glitter leapt into his eyes '...I think you do, Sasha. You feel it every bit as strongly as I do. And that's why you're reacting like this.'

'If you think I'm going to share you with a beautiful...'

'Cut that out. You know why I'm going through with this marriage. It has nothing to do with love or loving. It's to collect a piece of paper....'

'What about the consummation?'

'I'll close my eyes and think of you.'

'How dare you! How dare you flaunt...?'

'I'm trying to mend fences.'

'Too late. The horse has bolted.'

'Let's see if it has.' He started walking towards her, his eyes sizzling with intent. 'Everything you said to Elizabeth was a ploy, was it?'

'Mostly,' Sasha snapped. She headed for the door. She was not going to do battle with animal magnetism.

'You were *magnificent*, Sasha.'

He was using that voice on her again. And those blue eyes of his were dynamite. 'I despise you,' she flung at him.

'I'm falling in love.'

It halted Sasha momentarily. 'Go try that line on the beautiful Polish woman you've contracted to marry.' She doggedly resumed her retreat towards the door.

'I don't know why you're taking this so badly.' He looked genuinely puzzled, and frustrated, and exasperated. 'I've only done what I quite openly discussed with you when we met in the park.'

'Good for you. Go right ahead. See if I care.'

His hands reached out in appeal. 'I want to placate you. How was I to know you'd come back into my life and give me some of my greatest moments?'

'That's what men always do. Justify themselves. No matter what,' she shot at him scathingly.

'It's not as if Urszula will be living with me.'

Sasha reached the door and opened it. She cast one last furious look at Nathan Parnell. 'By all means use the law as you wish to sort out your problems, Nathan Parnell. Please leave me out of them in your future planning. I won't be your witness ever again. I won't be your lover. Ever. I won't be a pretend mother for Matt, either, because that will end up breaking my heart. So you'd better straighten him out, too. Then get to work on yourself.'

'I'm sorry.' He looked bereft.

She slammed the door shut behind her. To Sasha's mind, it was the metaphoric slamming of a lot of doors on things she was never going to think about again.

Bigamy, she thought in towering outrage as she stamped up the stairs to the nanny's quarters. It was no better than bigamy.

# CHAPTER TEN

FOR the next few days Sasha saw very little of Nathan
Parnell. Occasionally they passed in the foyer or hall.
She bestowed a frosty, 'Good morning,' or 'Good afternoon,' on him, disdaining any answer to the provocative things he chose to say to her.

Matt did not visit the nursery. Marion Bennet offered to mind Bonnie whenever Sasha had to go into
the city to search through the archives for the facts
Hester wanted. Sasha usually came home to find Matt
playing with Bonnie in the Bennets' apartment, but
she let that pass without comment. It involved no
emotional attachment for herself and she was sympathetic to the little boy's loneliness.

Hester Wingate remained true to the autocratic behaviour of their first meeting, but Sasha found herself enjoying the old lady's highly individual view of
the world and its inhabitants.

Hester loved thoroughbred horses and bloodlines.
Breeding them had made her fortune, which accounted for her predisposition to judge things from
the stallion's point of view.

She was an amazingly colourful character, unique
in Sasha's experience, brutally direct in all her opin-
ions and beliefs and blithely dismissing anything she

considered not worthy of her attention. She was the perfect antidote to any brooding over Nathan Parnell's perfidy. That was reason enough for Sasha to like being with her, but the liking quickly became genuine for Hester herself.

Sasha's first action, on Hester's behalf, was to obtain a copy of Seagrave Dunworthy's will at the probate office. The clauses Marion had told her about were there, almost verbatim. There was a lot more besides. There was no beneficiary called Parnell; no beneficiary called Wingate; no beneficiary called Maddox, or any other name that Sasha recognised. The tontine existed, but the money was all diverted to a series of trusts.

Apart from the task of digging up dirt on Seagrave Dunworthy and Hester's other associates, Sasha had to check all the dates in the tampered bible. These related to the Dawson family with five sons and eight daughters. It took Sasha many hours to gather every birth, marriage and death certificate, but it didn't solve the problem.

Most of the children, at one time or another, had had a valid reason for altering their ages upwards. Four of the girls married before they reached the age of consent, and two of the boys enlisted in the army for World War One before they reached the minimum age. There was no obvious way of telling what was cause and what was effect. Did the boys enlist in the army knowing they were under age, or did they genuinely believe in the dates in the bible? It was very puzzling.

Sasha was so bent on evading Nathan Parnell that she almost missed paying her rent between nine a.m. and the twelfth stroke of noon on Friday. It was only when Hester paid her for her work that she remembered. Hester immediately ordered Brooks, her chauffeur, to drive Sasha home again.

It seemed the height of irony to be racing the clock in a Rolls-Royce for the sake of paying ten dollars, but Sasha was mightily relieved when she made it home with five minutes to spare. She bolted into the foyer and ran straight into Nathan. He had just emerged from the library which was directly across the foyer from the lounge.

'Please get out of my way!' she cried. 'I have to pay my rent.'

'I paid it for you.'

She pulled out of his steadying grasp and tried to catch her breath. She glared at him uncertainly. 'Why did you do that? Don't tell me you still want me living here.'

His eyes were piercingly blue, projecting the same concentrated interest in her that had held her captive in the park. 'I want you to stay.'

'It won't do you any good,' she warned, holding out the ten-dollar note she'd had ready to give to Marion Bennet. 'I don't want to owe you anything.'

'As you wish,' he said, taking the note and pocketing it.

'Do you pay rent?' she asked bluntly, discomfited by the thought he might somehow be the owner of the house.

'Of course.'

'How much?'

'The full five guineas. Ten dollars fifty.'

Sasha frowned. He couldn't be the owner, yet he obviously had a say in who came here. Without him, neither the Bennets nor she and Bonnie would have benefited from Seagrave Dunworthy's strange terms about the house. Nathan had to have some connection to the owner.

'What does Marion do with the money?' she asked.

'It goes into a trust account. But there is something which is far more important that I'd like to discuss with you. Do you know how many days it is to Christmas, Sasha?'

It was the first week of December. Sasha hastily calculated the time, thankful she now had the income from Hester enabling her to buy Bonnie some lovely gifts for her first Christmas. 'Twenty-two days,' she answered, which gave her plenty of time to shop.

Nathan looked triumphant, as though he had scored a major victory. Sasha recollected that this was the longest conversation they'd had since Monday. Not that it was any great deep and meaningful communication.

'This might be the season of goodwill to all men,' Sasha observed acidly, 'but I'm reserving my goodwill for women. And not all of them, either.'

'I'd like you to come to a pre-Christmas party with me, Sasha,' he said, an eloquent appeal in his eyes sliding straight through her defences and worming its way into her heart.

'Whatever for?' she demanded testily, resenting the ease with which he affected her.

'Because your friendship and support mean a lot to me.'

He sounded genuine. He looked genuine. Sasha couldn't ignore the fact he'd given her a lot of support when she was in desperate need of it. This home. Her job. 'Is it a special occasion?' she asked warily.

'It's not something I can pass up without giving offence. The judge has been like a father to me and——'

'What happened to your real father?' Sasha had become very curious about bloodlines.

'He fell off his horse in a polo game and broke his neck. I never really knew him.'

Horses again, Sasha thought.

'All my friends will be there, Sasha...'

She wouldn't mind seeing what his friends were like.

'...and they're aware of the custody case coming up. They know what Elizabeth is like. I'd rather not have to listen to sympathetic comments all night. If you'd come with me...'

His mention of the custody case and Elizabeth snapped Sasha out of her treacherous musing. 'Why don't you take the beautiful Polish woman you're going to marry?'

'Because I can't bear to be with her,' he said evenly.

Sasha was fascinated. 'Then you've made a poor choice of wife, haven't you?' she said silkily. 'When have you contracted to marry?'

'Next Wednesday.'

'Well, you've made your bed, Nathan. I don't think you have any option but to lie in it,' she said with some asperity.

'Sasha, I've tried to break that contract. I can't. I've never felt so desperate in my life. There's no way out.'

He certainly looked harassed, but Sasha was wary of accepting anything at face value. 'How have you tried?' She needed details.

'I lined up twenty different males who were prepared, with some inducements, to marry her in my place. Urszula is demanding specific performance from me. She won't be bought out of it and I can't find a substitute she'll accept.'

Urszula knew a good thing when she saw it, Sasha surmised, and was hanging on for more than Nathan had bargained for.

'The problem is I wrote the contract myself,' he continued. Sasha thought she heard a hint of desperation in his voice. 'It runs about five lines. It's in simple English. And there's no escape clause anywhere. I thought I was binding Urszula. Now it's me who's caught.'

'I told you in the park that what you proposed to do was not a well-thought-out arrangement. Love comes first. Then the marriage.'

'I fervently agree with you. I rather like your more direct approach. You're not selfish or grasping. Quite the contrary.'

Not exactly selfless, Sasha mentally corrected him. She didn't want to interrupt when he was speaking so well.

'There's so much I find admirable about you, Sasha. Others will admire you, too. We should get to know each other better. Having you at my side tomorrow night...it's a first step. It would commit you to nothing, Sasha, and I promise you'll have a good time. Let's have one night together.'

It was similar to granting one last favour to a condemned man. Nathan had certainly done her some favours. It ill behove her to refuse him this simple boon. Besides, it was a long time since she had let her hair down and had a good night out.

Nathan wasn't married yet. Perhaps . . .

'All right. Just this once,' she said with pointed emphasis. Sasha didn't want him to get any wrong ideas about what this party might lead to between them.

He gave her a sparkling smile that danced down Sasha's spine and hit her solidly in the solar plexus. 'I'll make the arrangements with Marion to mind the children.'

He was off before she could have second thoughts.

The second thoughts came anyway.

It was quite safe to go with him. Nothing would happen unless she wanted it to happen. But it was living dangerously.

# CHAPTER ELEVEN

SASHA knew she shouldn't wear the red satin evening dress. It was strapless. It was figure-hugging. It had a slit up the centre seam at the back of the skirt for ease of movement, but there wasn't a man alive who wouldn't see that slit as provocative.

Tyler had chosen the dress. His professional eye admired dramatic effect. With Sasha's pale skin, her thickly lashed dark eyes and long black hair, her above average height and her fair share of feminine curves, the red satin dress delivered dramatic effect. It could be said . . . with oomph.

It was almost certainly wrong to wear it to a judge's Christmas party. The women there would probably be in black or cream or white, all understated class but extremely elegant and expensive. Not that the red satin dress was cheap. It wasn't. But it wasn't subtle. It was, to put it succinctly, a traffic-stopper.

What did it matter, Sasha reasoned to herself, if she raised eyebrows or drew stares tonight? She didn't know the people who would be at the party. She would probably never meet them again. She could please herself without any regard to what others thought, taking a leaf out of Hester's book and not caring a fig.

She had the right to be colourful. She was free to do as she liked. No obligation to anyone. Committed to nothing. That was what Nathan had said. He had also said she would look stunning in red.

Sasha had to admit to a deep primitive urge to stun his socks off. It would teach him a lesson for getting tied up with his Polish woman and not waiting for her. As for thinking she would have an affair with him, he had been undeceived on that matter in no uncertain terms when she'd told him she wanted love and commitment.

Sasha took another look at herself in the mirror. She *was* playing with fire. She *was* living dangerously. The cautious, common-sense side of Sasha knew all along she shouldn't wear the red satin evening dress. The devil made her do it.

The arrangement was that she meet Nathan in the foyer at eight o'clock. She didn't go down the back stairs. She had left Bonnie with Marion an hour ago, bathed, fed, and ready for sleep. This was her one night with Nathan before he married, and Sasha saw every reason to get full value out of it right from the start. She heard the grandfather clock in the foyer strike the first of eight strokes as she reached the head of the grand staircase.

He was waiting for her.

The clock tolled again as she stared at him. The note seemed to reverberate through her heart.

He was dressed in a formal black dinner suit, black bow-tie, white dress shirt. Why men always looked their most handsome and distinguished in such clothes, Sasha didn't know. All thought processes halted. Nathan Parnell was *stunning*.

He glanced up and saw her. An involuntary look of sheer wonderment passed over his face. He turned towards her, slowly, as though he might be deprived of a life-promising mirage if he wasn't careful. A hand lifted, impulsively reaching out its invitation to come to him. His vivid blue eyes consumed her.

Sasha had the sensation of floating down the stairs. She was barely aware of her legs moving. She reached the foot of the staircase and Nathan was there to meet her, and she put her hand in his, and there was silence for several dream-like moments, silence except for the swirl of feelings that whispered dreams could come true.

'Stunning,' he said simply.

'Thank you.'

'You've already made it a night to remember.'

As gratifying as that statement was, it brought Sasha back to reality. 'You'll have plenty of nights to reflect on that,' she reminded him pertly.

'All the more reason to live for the moment,' he replied, not the least bit abashed as he took her arm and tucked it around his.

It was the gentlemanly way to escort her to the car, Sasha reasoned, so she let him get away with it. However, she was intensely aware of him matching his steps to hers, his closeness, their togetherness. She could even smell his aftershave lotion. Somehow it was sexy, too; spicy, enticing and very male.

Once in the car, Sasha decided talk was the only way to ward off the animal magnetism that was gathering force by the second. Silence definitely had the effect of feeding it.

'Tell me about the people I'm going to meet at the party,' she said brightly.

Nathan was slow to answer. Sasha surmised that it was taking him a few moments to concentrate his mind. 'Judges, lawyers, layabouts, the rich, the poor, the famous, the infamous. They'll all be there. A cross section of society.'

It was a very general reply. Sasha had meant him to be more specific with names and character sketches. 'I thought you didn't like judges,' she remarked.

'On a continuing downward spiral,' he replied with feeling. 'There's not one of them, not *one*, who would find in my favour to break the contract with Urszula Budna. They were unanimously unhelpful. I know, because I checked them all.'

'You can't do that! Trying to solicit favours from judges!'

'Desperation,' he agreed. 'Anyway, it didn't work. Not one of them could find a loophole anywhere.'

So the marriage was inevitable.

Depression closed around Sasha's heart. She felt sorry for Nathan, sorry for herself, sorry for the shutting off of what might have been possible between them. A sense of futility in the evening ahead of them stirred a surge of rebellion. None of this was her fault. She had to get on with her own life.

'I have no sympathy for the mess you've got yourself into, Nathan. Self-inflicted,' she tartly reminded him. 'And I'm not going to carry a long face around with me all night. I'm going to enjoy myself.'

'If the primary function of a young woman is to leave a trail of devastated male hearts in her wake, you should enjoy yourself. Immensely,' he said with a touch of heavy irony.

'Enjoy myself I will, but not at the expense of others.'

Apparently he had no comeback to that. Sasha could feel him looking at her, willing her to look at him, but she kept her gaze fixed on the traffic ahead.

'I think it's the love in your heart that puts the bloom in your cheeks, the light in your eyes. It irradiates your person, Sasha, giving you a beauty that——'

'Please stop this nonsense.'

'I don't mind admitting I'm falling in love with you. What's your problem?'

Urszula Budna, Sasha thought savagely, but she wasn't about to admit anything. In the circumstances, any admission would not lead anywhere good. 'This is the most useless conversation I've ever had. I'd rather talk about the weather.'

Nathan lapsed into silence, obviously declining to wax lyrical about the weather although it was the kind of night made for lovers. Sasha was acutely aware of that when they reached their destination and she stepped out of the car. A full moon was rising. It was a cloudless starry sky. The air was warm and balmy with the sensual pleasure of a feathering breeze off the harbour.

They hadn't travelled far. Sasha was not surprised to find that Nathan's paternal judge lived in what could only be called a stately home. Like Seagrave

Dunworthy's mansion, and Hester Wingate's luxurious Mediterranean-style villa, it stood on a large chunk of prime real estate which had been moulded by expert gardeners into a splendid setting. It was nothing more than another extraordinary part of Nathan Parnell's extraordinary life, Sasha thought flippantly, refusing to be impressed.

There was even a parking attendant to remove and take care of the BMW. That was indicative of what was to come. Sasha held her head high as Nathan escorted her inside. Nothing and no one was going to intimidate her tonight. She was as good as anyone else and a darned sight better than some.

Her confidence was given a boost by their host's reception. The venerable judge was well into his sixties but there was nothing jaded about his appreciation of Sasha. Having warmly welcomed her, he raised enquiring eyebrows at Nathan.

'I had an idea that might help.'

'Yes?' Nathan encouraged.

'Change your religion. Become a Mormon.'

Having delivered this opinion, the judge turned to greet other incoming guests.

Nathan looked quizzically at Sasha. 'That might solve the problem.'

'*If* you can find a woman who won't mind sharing a husband,' Sasha remarked sweetly, 'you're welcome to her.'

'I thought as much,' Nathan muttered darkly. 'You're not at all helpful.'

That was the limit of their private conversation. Nathan was hailed by friends and they were quickly drawn into a congenial group of people. Most of the introductions floated into Sasha's ears and out again. Too many names to remember. She was met with speculative interest, of one kind or another, from both men and women.

The men tended to envy Nathan, and the women envied her. It was good for Sasha's ego, yet it was an empty satisfaction. She didn't really *have* Nathan, and she didn't really *want* other men's interest.

Nevertheless, Sasha sparkled as she had never sparkled before. She drank French champagne. She nibbled gourmet delicacies from silver trays. Dinner-jacketed waiters circulated with endless supplies of tempting treats and Sasha in her red satin evening dress was definitely not a neglected guest.

She received charming care and attention, flirtatious care and attention, bold and purposeful care and attention. Nathan, however, seemed oblivious to all this. *His* care and attention was faultlessly courteous. Nothing more, nothing less.

Sasha found herself fuming with frustration. Nathan concentrated his interest on the conversations directed towards him. The women who drew that sexy focus of attention in those riveting blue eyes lapped it up and did their utmost to retain it. Men seemed to lobby for his approval. They all, men and women alike, basked in Nathan Parnell's personal charisma.

Sasha finally decided she had had enough. She bestowed her best brilliant smile on a notorious gambler who whisked her off to the ballroom and propositioned her as he demonstrated some blatantly suggestive dance steps. She didn't know whether to be flattered or outraged. In the end, she laughingly parried his wicked but good-humoured banter.

It reminded her of her resolution to enjoy herself. Emboldened by the gambler's success at removing Sasha from Nathan's side, other men asked her to dance with them. No objection came from Nathan and Sasha danced her feet off, gaily accepting invitation after invitation. She bubbled with vivacity. Every time her partners returned her to Nathan she glowed with the pleasure they had given her. Nathan smiled indulgently. He did not ask her to dance with him. He appeared to be having a perfectly fine time without her at his side.

Having got this heartburning message, Sasha danced on without bothering to return to his side. She didn't need *him,* either. There were plenty of men flocking around her, panting for her attention and lapping up every responsive flash in *her* eyes. There were men ready to get her another glass of champagne, men ready to please her palate with whatever food she might fancy, men hanging on every delightfully bubbly word that spilled from her red satin lips.

It was highly irritating to Sasha that such an idyllic situation should become extremely tiresome. But it did. She took the only possible relief that pride allowed her. She retreated to the ladies' powder-room and did some quiet seething while she ostensibly repaired her make-up.

Nathan Parnell was no more falling in love with her than the man in the moon. He hadn't even bothered to try taking her out to the romantic patio beyond the ballroom to show her the moon.

Matt was definitely wrong about his daddy's being able to do anything. Nathan Parnell had either resigned himself to defeat, or didn't care enough to compete for her undivided attention. Sasha was disappointed in him. Deeply disappointed.

Since her 'good time' had worn thin, and Nathan obviously didn't require her, Sasha saw no point in staying at the party any longer. She hoped Nathan would have the good manners to take her home upon request. If not, she would order a taxi. She was about to sally forth from the powder-room with this purpose in mind when she was confronted by the last woman in the world she wanted to see.

Elizabeth Maddox.

Nathan's ex-wife effectively blocked Sasha's exit with a stance that exuded haughty scorn. Sasha returned a bored look that hid quite a few explosive little questions—like whether Nathan had known Elizabeth was going to be here, and had he planned on using Sasha's presence to camouflage his real marriage plans from his litigious ex-wife?

'You don't look Polish,' Elizabeth opened up with gimlet-eyed suspicion.

'You don't look like a piranha,' Sasha retorted.

'So, Urzsula Budna thinks she has teeth, does she?' Elizabeth gave Sasha's dress a contemptuous once-over before lifting pitying eyes. 'Well, from tonight's performance, my dear, they're certainly not sunk into Nathan. That's why you've been playing up to every other man.'

This was clearly a case of mistaken identity and Sasha was tempted to blow Nathan's strategy wide open. He hadn't done the decent thing by her. He hadn't even done the indecent thing. He had been totally, callously and recklessly indifferent.

'You really want him and you can't get him,' Elizabeth sneered.

That goaded Sasha to resume battle stations. 'Sounds as if you're stating your own position,' she drawled, flicking her eyes over the sleek silvery gown her antagonist wore. 'A dead fish seems a more apt description than a piranha.'

Elizabeth resumed her haughty air. 'I had Nathan precisely where I wanted him. You do not.'

Sasha couldn't let that pass. 'I like a man to simmer before bringing him to the boil. It's called living dangerously. But very exciting.'

Another woman entered the powder-room. Elizabeth had to step aside and Sasha seized the opportunity to leave. She headed straight for where she had last seen Nathan. He was engaged in some lively debate with a raven-haired beauty and a bunch of lawyers.

Sasha hooked her arm around Nathan's, flashed her teeth at his companions, then brought their discussion to a dead halt.

'Please excuse us, ladies and gentlemen. Nathan needs to dance with me. His legs might get broken if he doesn't do it right now.'

'She Who Must Be Obeyed,' Nathan intoned, but without resistance.

They all laughed.

Nathan swept Sasha away towards the ballroom, stroking her arm as though she was a ruffled cat that required soothing. She didn't purr. As far as she was concerned, fur was about to fly.

'To what do I owe the honour?' he asked, a silky satisfaction in his voice.

'Don't get tickets on yourself,' Sasha warned. 'You're a sneaky rotten scoundrel who'll say anything that'll give you an advantage.'

He gave her a hurt look. 'When have I not spoken the truth to you, Sasha?'

'Falling in love with me,' she scoffed at him, 'was a villainous lie.'

'Undeniable fact.' He swung her into his arms as they reached the dance floor. 'Feel my heart. It's almost bursting with the excitement of holding you close to me.'

She declined the invitation, her eyes flashing dark scorn. 'Why didn't you ask me to dance with you?'

'I was respecting your wishes regarding freedom of action.'

'What wishes?'

'Not to be with me. To enjoy yourself with others,' he answered blandly.

'I didn't say that.'

The blue eyes lit with hope and devilish desire. 'You mean I misunderstood? You wanted to enjoy yourself with me? I could have danced all night with you? You wouldn't have refused if I asked?'

The arm around her waist pressed her closer. He executed a turn that frotted their thighs together in a highly intimate manner. A dangerous current of warmth raced through Sasha.

'The only reason I'm dancing with you now is to show your ex-wife I can have you any time I want,' she gritted.

'You can,' he assured her with fervour. 'I can't sleep at night for thinking of how it would be between us. I want you so much...'

Sasha stamped on his foot to concentrate his mind on the real burning issue. 'She's here! And you knew she was going to be here, didn't you?'

'Who?'

'Elizabeth!'

'Do you know how tantalising it is when your breasts heave like that? Irresistible. I feel...'

'Your ex-wife is watching us,' Sasha almost yelled at him in frustration.

'Put your arms around my neck. Let's give her some dirty dancing. I can do it with you. Elizabeth won't be left in any doubt about how deeply you stir me.'

She glowered at him as she followed his suggestion. 'Not too dirty. I don't want you getting pleasure out of your trickery, Nathan Parnell.'

'I promise that whatever happens, I won't be pleased. I also swear to you I didn't know Elizabeth would be here,' he said solemnly, his eyes burning into hers. 'I do know she wasn't invited. She must be with another guest.'

Sasha cogitated on that statement for several moments. Nathan made it very difficult for her to concentrate. Full body contact, and the way he was making the most of it, was extremely distracting. His expertise in dancing not only left nothing to be desired, it flowed and pulsed with a sexuality that was stimulating a lot of other desires.

Surely he would have been doing this before if he'd known Elizabeth was here. Being a stand-offish escort didn't fit the scenario of trying to keep the wool pulled over his ex-wife's eyes. Sasha had to concede it was more probable that she had leapt to a false conclusion. Nathan Parnell was not guilty as she had charged him.

'Elizabeth thinks I'm your Polish woman,' she said. 'She knows about Urszula Budna.'

'Marriage application forms. She'd do a check to make sure we're really getting married.'

'But I'm not Urszula Budna.'

He gave her a heart-melting smile. 'I know. Thank you, Sasha.'

She struggled against melting. 'What for?'

'Thumbing your nose at Elizabeth. Sticking by me again in spite of your reservations.'

'I can't abide people like her,' she defended.

'You have great principles. An admirable mind. A generous heart. A beautiful body.'

He was screwing them all up with what he was doing in this dance, Sasha thought, torn between the need to keep fighting him and the need to give in to the pleasure of simply feeling him and the feelings he stirred in her.

Elizabeth was watching, she told herself, and that was justification enough to act with a certain amount of uninhibited élan. She wriggled a little closer. Nathan's hands slid to her hips, swaying her into a seductive rhythm that was definitely dirty. It aroused more than a simmer of excitement.

'Stop it,' she hissed.

He bent his head, his warm breath tingling her ear as he whispered. 'I want to, but I can't. Do you know how erotic you feel in this dress?'

She had known all along that she shouldn't have worn it.

'It's so sensual,' he murmured huskily. 'So hot, so vivid, so *you*.'

'Dance me out to the patio.'

'Great idea!'

'It's cooler out there,' Sasha suggested, acutely aware of her own heated response to the hardness pressing into her stomach.

'Let's leave. I don't want to be with anyone else but you.'

'Nathan...' Her voice quivered and died. She was suddenly breathless, confused by the strength of her own desire to have him to herself. Before she could make up her mind whether to stay in the safety of numbers or go with him, he whirled her down to the end of the ballroom, his legs imprisoning hers in a rhythm that was too intensely exciting to break.

He scythed through the crowd with purposeful haste, scooping Sasha along with him, stopping for no one, only pausing at the front door to ask someone to order his car to be brought immediately. Then they were outside, and in the intoxication of the moment Nathan swept Sasha up in his arms and carried her down the steps to the driveway. There he let her slide to her feet, moulding the pliant softness of her body to his rampant virility as he kissed her with a devouring passion that Sasha was powerless to resist.

She didn't hear the car pull up beside them. She didn't hear its doors being opened. Her heart thundered in her ears, her head swam with dizzying sensations, her body revelled in the wild pulse of desire that beat from him to her in throbbing waves. She had never known anything like it.

Nathan lifted her into the passenger seat. He fastened the seatbelt for her. His lips roved over hers, reluctant to break the thrall of sensuality. She heard his sharp intake of breath as he pulled back. Her door was shut. She watched in a daze as he strode quickly to the driver's side. Then he was beside her, revving the engine, accelerating them on their way, and his hand took possession of hers, fingers interlacing, gripping, wanting so much more.

A voice in the back of Sasha's mind told her she'd better think about this and think fast.

But she didn't want to think.

This was a time for doing.

# CHAPTER TWELVE

IT WAS going up the stairs that dispelled Sasha's pleasurable haze of anticipation for what would happen next. If Nathan had carried her, she might still have clung to feeling swept away from any thought of tomorrow. The mechanical act of placing one foot after another beat home the knowledge that each step took her closer to Nathan's bedroom, and there was no commitment to anything other than satisfying the need burning through both of them.

He was still gripping her hand.

As they reached the top of the stairs she halted, turning to him with wary, accusing eyes. 'It's the dress, isn't it? I shouldn't have worn it.'

He touched her cheek with tenderness. 'It's not the dress. It's the woman inside it.'

'But...'

'We'll soon get rid of the dress. Then you can see for yourself.'

He headed for the nanny's quarters, drawing her after him, making any protest about proceeding with him untenable. He was leading her to *her* door.

'You're going to marry another woman,' she said, but even to her own ears her voice failed to carry much conviction.

'I'm not married yet.'

'How can you possibly get *out* of the contract?'

He looked sternly into her eyes. 'Suicide is always a good last alternative.'

It was no alternative as far as Sasha was concerned. Nathan was so vital, so... attractive in every way. The thought of him dead put a queasy hollowness in her stomach. She wanted him, wanted him for herself, and the prospect of never having him suddenly made a wasteland of her future life.

He opened the door to her bed-sitting-room.

She hesitated. Was she ready to commit herself to an uncertain fate with him? 'Maybe we should...'

The blaze of desire in his eyes seared the thought from her mind. 'Now,' he said with a deep throb of passion. 'This is the moment we've both been waiting for. The moment of truth.'

Sasha knew there was something wrong with that statement, although there was something right in it, too. Before she could identify the flaws in the argument that would clarify what she should or shouldn't do, Nathan manoeuvred her into the danger area and she was in his arms with the door shut behind them.

He kissed her.

It fuzzed up her mind very badly. She had the sensation of her legs moving backwards, being pushed along by piston-like thighs, but there was a lot of other sensational things happening so she wasn't absolutely sure about that until she toppled on to the bed and found herself underneath the man who was still kissing her, trailing a hot, hungry mouth down her throat, cutting off her breath, making her feel giddy with his ardour.

'I drank too much champagne. Otherwise I wouldn't be letting you do this,' she gasped out, trying to explain the strong urge to unrestrained wantonness that was pumping through her body.

'More champagne,' he breathed in her ear. 'That's what we need. More champagne.'

He started to move away from her. She pulled him back because she didn't think she could handle any more champagne, not when she should be trying to think of other things. Nathan misunderstood. His mouth ravished hers with increasing intensity, kissing her again and again, excitement escalating into a writhing desire that was frustratingly restricted by their clothes.

Nathan suddenly raised himself, straddling her as he tore his arms out of his jacket and hurled it on to the floor. A sobering splash of reality gave Sasha the strength to make one last effort against committing herself to the unknown.

'Let's not be too hasty about this, Nathan,' she pleaded, uncertain whether the point of no return had already been passed in making up her mind as to what she should, or should not do.

'You're right.' His eyes had a feverish glitter. 'I don't want to be tempted into taking you prematurely. We should have the pleasure of slowly undressing each other, being naked together.'

'That's not what I meant.'

'It's what I meant. I'll do the tricky bits first.'

He pushed his cufflinks free and tossed them in the same direction as the jacket. Then he started on his bow-tie. The pressure of his loins had her pinned to the bed. The heat of his body, the controlled strength of his thighs, the promise of seeing him as all raw male, made a heady intoxicant for Sasha. She didn't really want to move, but there was a niggle in the back of her mind that wouldn't go away.

'I won't have you *taking* me,' she said more strongly.

'Wrong label. Politically incorrect. Forgive the expression.' He flashed her a wicked grin. 'I want you to take me, too. All of me.'

That conjured up tantalising images. Her stomach contracted excitedly, warningly, as he discarded the bow-tie and proceeded to undo the studs of his dress-shirt.

'What do you think you're doing?' she croaked.

'Taking my clothes off. Better to get them out of the way. Frustrating otherwise.'

'You can do that in your own bedroom,' Sasha said shrilly. The glimpse of bare skin from the gape in the fabric made naked fact of fantasy, and what if he didn't feel the same about her as she did about him? What if...?

Again came the grin that undermined any train of reason. 'No novelty in that. Done it many times before. If you'd like to help me...'

'No!' She swallowed hard. 'I think we should talk sensibly about this, Nathan.'

He raised a quizzical eyebrow. 'When it's your turn I won't use any hands to undress you. Just my mouth, teeth, lips and tongue. What do you think of that?'

Her mind boggled. Could he do it? 'But this doesn't solve anything,' she wailed somewhat desperately as he shed his shirt and threw it on to the ever-growing pile.

'My word it does, Sasha. It solves a lot of things,' he replied fervently.

He had a torso that would make any woman go cross-eyed. Sasha was no exception. It was not often one saw a splendid arrangement of muscle, skin and bone. Her impression in the park was absolutely correct. A perfectly proportioned lover.

It's not human to resist, she argued to herself, and Nathan was right. It would solve a lot of things. Like knowing instead of wondering. Tentatively she reached out, stroking her fingers over the flesh from the waist up. He flinched and she could see the muscle spasm under her touch. It made her feel... powerful. Nathan had his little sensitivities, as well. She could touch him and... On a wave of wild exhilaration she put the tips of her stroking fingers into her mouth and sucked them.

'You taste good.'

He laughed joyously as he raised himself on to his knees. His hands unfastened the waistband of his trousers. The zipper followed. 'Now you can do it all the way over me.'

Her eyes widened at the bulge in his underpants. He looked so...*big*. Her mind fluttered to Tyler. She had never been intimate with any other man. She couldn't

remember feeling so . . . mesmerised . . . by the sight of
Tyler. Nathan was different. Nathan was enticingly
different, excitingly different, magnificently different. And he certainly wanted her as much as, if not
more than, she wanted him.

Her hands moved to draw his trousers down, to see,
to know, to touch. He leaned over her and ran his
tongue over the swell of her breasts above the bodice
line of her dress. ''You taste good, too,'' he murmured. Then his teeth closed over the edge of satin and
tugged.

Good heavens! she thought, he's really going to do
it. Undress me without using his hands.

'There's a zip at the back.'

'I'll get to it.'

'You'll need help. You can't do this by yourself.'
The strapless bodice was boned to mould around her
breasts and it was impossible to tug it down without
undoing the zipper first.

'Trust me. I can do it,' he growled, having moved
the satin enough to dip his tongue into her cleavage,
making her impatient to feel the hot, tingling caress on
her nipples. What would he make her feel when he
reached them?

'You undressed yourself with the tricky bits,' she
argued.

'True.'

'It'll be better if I undress myself.'

He sighed. 'If you must.'

'Stand up for a moment.'

He moved swiftly, unpinning her. He was off the
bed, ridding himself of the last of his clothes before

Sasha found enough presence of mind to sit up. What she saw made her breath catch in her throat, made her temples pulse with a roaring of blood. Her mind glazed with the wonder of taking all of him. An experience, she thought, a once-in-a-lifetime experience no woman in her right mind would pass up. Even if it was wrong.

She swung herself off the bed, turning away from him so she wouldn't be caught staring. He was tearing off his shoes and socks. Her legs felt quivery. Her hands were tremulous. She fumbled over the hook and eye. She finally managed to get it apart, grabbed the head of the zipper and scorched it down her back.

As the red satin slid off her body to pool at her feet, Sasha heard Nathan's sharp intake of breath, knew they were definitely beyond the point of no return now, and didn't care. A wild exultation filled her mind as she stepped away from the dress and turned to face what was to come.

For this one night I'll do anything I want, anything I like, she thought, casting off all the inhibiting shadows that might encroach on the blissful sense of freedom. She had wanted Nathan Parnell almost from the first moment they met, and the wanting had increased with everything he'd done for her, everything he was. If she never had him again, she would have him tonight.

He stared at her, his eyes feasting on what she had bared for him. 'Perfect breasts,' he groaned, stepping closer to cup them in his hands. The warmth of his palms and the caress of his fingers felt perfect to Sasha.

She ran her hands up his arms, over his shoulders, revelling in the naked strength that was bared to her. He felt like polished wood, hard and satiny smooth, but he was warmly, wonderfully alive. His hands suddenly slid around her back, pulling her into an urgent embrace, flattening the soft pliant fullness of her breasts against his chest, flooding her body with the throbbing heat of his. His fingers raked her pantihose down, clearing the curve of her bottom so he could fill his hands with its roundness and press her into an even more intimate awareness of his arousal.

'You're too excited!' she exclaimed.

'Disagree.'

He had no time for words. He bent to roll the sheer nylon down her thighs and his mouth closed over one of her breasts, and he used his lips, tongue, teeth, with such exquisite eroticism that Sasha thought she would die from the pleasure of it. She grasped his head and forced it to her other breast, wanting to feel it there, too. She lifted her leg so he didn't have to move away to complete the removal of the stocking. He took her shoe with it. The other leg. The other breast.

Please. More. Yes, yes, yes. She didn't know if she said the words or whether they simply pulsed through her. Free of the other stocking and shoe, his hand sliding between her thighs. Yes, there, too, yes, yes, and he did it with caring softness, sweet blissful caresses along the sensitive folds, soothing and exciting, more and more exciting, an arc of vibrating excitement from her breasts to the rhythmic plunging of his fingers, but fingers weren't enough. She wanted . . .

'Nathan...' Her hands clawed at his back, tugged at his head, frantic with urgency.

He responded with a surge of strength, lifting her, sliding the hard power of his virility to the centre of her need. She coiled her legs around his waist, leaned back, and moaned with ecstatic relief as she felt the massive force of him enter her, filling her, pushing past the convulsive spasms of muscles that closed and expanded around him, reaching further, further, stretching for...

'Let go, Sasha. Let go.'

Her mind was in chaos, unknowing what he meant. Her legs were locked around him. She couldn't let him go... except her arms. She let them slide limply from his neck and he caught her securely as she fell back, supporting her bottom and waist. And he began rotating like a ballet dancer in a spin. She stretched out her arms, her hair floating as he turned and turned... a carousel of throbbing intimacy, the connection deeply inside, undulating, all of him, all of her.

There was a sharp tingling through her skin as the blood drained into her torso, her face, her head. It was dizzying, intoxicating. The room was going around and around with the beat of his thrusting maleness, a pump of pleasure deep within her, strong and constant as she floated around it, melted around it, shattered into a million exploding pieces around it.

Then he caught her to him and laid her back on the bed, stacking pillows under her so she didn't need his support, and his hands were free to stroke her in harmony with the stroking within. An erotic feather-touch under her hipbones as he slid forward, a light

palm pressure on her stomach as he deepened the
thrust, the uplifting capture of her breasts as he drove
to the end, then all the way back again with the mind-
blowing anticipation of the next slow plunge, and the
next.

It was beautiful, enthralling, hypnotic in its repeti-
tive pattern, yet the desire to touch him stirred Sasha
to lift her heavy arms, reach out, capture his face. It
broke his concentration. His eyes met hers and they
stared at each other in dazed wonderment. She pulled
his head down and kissed him with all the love and
yearning for oneness with the mate of her heart and
mind and soul. The uninhibited outpouring of her
passion shattered his control. She felt his body start to
tremble.

He tore his mouth away. 'Sasha . . .' It was a hoarse
breath of need. 'Sasha . . .' An acknowledgement of
what she did to him.

She found the strength to rock with him as he fren-
ziedly sought the fulfilment of release. It came with a
great shuddering cry from him, and again it was
'Sasha...' like a bursting dam of feeling that could not
be contained any more.

She did not know if it was a moment of truth. She
wrapped her arms around him and held him close. She
didn't speak. Her feelings went beyond words. But her
heart beat its own refrain . . . Nathan . . . Nathan . . .

# CHAPTER THIRTEEN

A LOUD rap on her door stirred Sasha from deep sleep. She found herself half sprawled over Nathan whose eyes were closed, but, as she started to move, his arm instinctively curled more firmly around her.

'Sasha, are you awake?'

Marion Bennet's raised voice was a clear call to attention. The thought of Bonnie jerked Sasha up with a guilty start. How late was it?

'Whass wrong?' Nathan slurred sleepily.

'Hush!' She clamped a hand over his mouth, her heart galloping at the thought of Marion walking in on them.

'Sasha?' Another louder knock.

Sasha managed a reply. 'Yes. Hold on a moment. I'm coming.'

Nathan heaved himself up on one elbow as she hurtled out of bed and ran to the wardrobe. He watched with a smile as she quickly wrapped herself in the turquoise silk robe. She frowned a warning at him, and he kept a discreet silence as she went to the door.

Mindful of the chaos of clothes on the floor, not to mention the man in her bed, Sasha squeezed around the door, carefully blocking any view past her as she addressed Nathan's housekeeper.

'Sorry I slept late, Mrs Bennet. I'll come and get Bonnie now.'

'She's fine, dear. Harry and Matt are playing with her out in the back garden. It's your visitors. I wasn't sure what to do about them. So I'm checking with you first.'

'Visitors?' Sasha hadn't expected anyone to call on her, except perhaps her parents, and they would telephone first. 'Who are they?'

'A Mr Cullum and a Mr McDougal.'

Tyler and Joshua! What did they want? 'I'd better get dressed.'

'Will I ask them in?'

'No!' Her emphatic refusal startled Marion. Sasha quickly tempered her voice. 'I'll go and talk to them, Mrs Bennet. Did you leave them waiting on the portico?'

Marion nodded. 'It wasn't polite but I had orders not to let anyone harass you.'

Sasha didn't have to ask where the orders came from. He was in her bed. 'I'll get dressed and go down to them straight away.'

'Take your time and don't worry about Bonnie. When you're ready is soon enough,' Marion assured her.

Sasha whirled back into her room as the housekeeper headed for the back staircase. She shut the door, took a deep breath, then met Nathan's acute blue gaze.

'Who's McDougal?' he asked.

'Tyler's partner. They share a photographic studio.'

'What do they want?'

She shrugged to express her lack of knowledge.

'Is this trouble, Sasha?'

'I doubt it. Not with Joshua along.'

'I'll come with you.'

'No. *I'll* handle this. *You* clean up the evidence.'

She waved at the wild array of clothing on the floor. He grinned, the memory of last night's wild abandonment sparkling in his eyes. Her heart jiggled as though he had it on a yo-yo. Regretfully, it wasn't last night any more. It was tomorrow.

'I've got to get moving, Nathan.'

She hurried back to the wardrobe, grabbed some fresh clothes, and raced off to the bathroom. By the time she emerged, washed, hair brushed, clothed in jeans and T-shirt, Nathan was gone and the floor was swept clean of any reminder of their intimacy. She found the red satin evening dress hanging up. She didn't pause to wonder where he'd put the other telltale items.

As she hurried downstairs to meet the man who had shredded the trust she had given him, Sasha had to wonder if she had committed the ultimate foolishness in succumbing to her feelings for Nathan Parnell. Whatever the outcome of their union, it was done now. At least her relationship with Tyler was well and truly resolved. She had no regrets about leaving him and had no desire or intention of ever going back to him.

If he had brought Joshua along to act as his advocate in a reconciliation, she had to make it absolutely clear there would be no future for them, except for

Tyler's rights as Bonnie's father. Despite this resolution, Sasha opened the front door with some trepidation. Tyler was a man of many moods, most of them volatile. Initially his uninhibited responses had been a source of attraction. Somewhere along the line they had become self-indulgently excessive.

They weren't on the portico. They were both at the foot of the steps, leaning against a huge king-of-the-road four-wheel-drive Range Rover, complete with bull bars and insect screens. It was not the kind of vehicle Sasha would have readily associated with Tyler, but apparently he or Joshua had the use of it this morning.

Tyler was stern but Joshua had a smile for her, giving his characteristic gesture of peace and goodwill. The tension inside Sasha eased slightly. Joshua's long, loose-limbed body seemed permanently relaxed. Unruffled by anything, he presented the absolute contrast to Tyler's air of restless energy.

'Quite a step up, Sasha,' Tyler drawled derisively, casting a glance over the impressive façade of the house.

'How did you find me, Tyler?'

'Your parents gave me the address so I could write to you.' He gave a harsh bark of laughter. 'What's it like, living in a mansion?'

'The same as anywhere else. It's the people who count.'

'And I don't count any more.'

'Not in my life, Tyler. I'm not blaming you. We didn't fit together in the end.'

Tyler chewed that over in his mind. Then his face lightened and he jerked his head sideways. 'What do you think of *her*?'

Puzzled, Sasha looked about, trying to locate the female in question. No one in sight.

Tyler didn't notice. He slapped his hand down on the bull bar. 'When you walked out on me, I had to find a replacement. Josh and I pooled our resources and we bought this. We've named it *Mary Bryant*. How does that strike you?'

Replaced by a car, Sasha thought numbly. She couldn't trust herself to any words. She raised her arms slightly, opened the palms of her hands and heaved her shoulders. Let him make what he could of that expression of his inadequacy.

Tyler didn't notice that, either. 'We're off to the interior,' he declared with an air of triumph. 'Take the greatest photos ever taken. Coffee-table stuff. We won't be back for years. We might never come back.' He grinned at his partner. 'Will we ever come back, Josh?'

'Never,' Joshua agreed amiably.

Sasha had the strong sensation that this was all meant to be very vengeful and threatening from Tyler, but somehow it struck her as a great idea.

'I'm glad you're doing what you really want to do,' she said in a conciliatory tone. She did not want to part bad friends with Tyler. There might come a time when Bonnie wanted to know her father and Tyler did have an attractive side. It was responsibility that weighed him down.

'I do care for you and Bonnie,' he jerked out.

'I know that, Tyler,' she replied sadly, thinking of the wasted years. 'But you need your freedom.'

'You understand.'

'Yes, Tyler, I understand.'

She looked at Joshua with knowing eyes. His reflected the same knowledge. They both knew it was easier for Tyler to travel lightly without the burden of a wife and child. She looked back at Tyler and managed a generous smile.

'I hope this venture leads to all you ever wanted.'

'Yes... well... I have to admit it's a relief you've taken it like this, Sasha,' he acknowledged. 'We weren't getting on so well, but it made me feel inadequate for wanting to duck out on you and Bonnie.'

Sasha understood that, too. It was a question of pride and self-image. Tyler didn't like to feel badly about himself. No doubt it had driven him to the abortive attempt at reconciliation in the park, despite his desire to be free of any encumbrances.

'It's OK,' she assured him. 'It wasn't working for either of us. It's better we go our separate ways.'

'I'll pay you maintenance for Bonnie, Sasha. Josh convinced me I should. What we figured...'

Tyler's voice trailed into silence. Both he and Joshua stared past her and she felt Nathan's presence like a force-field, generating potent elements that changed the *status quo*. The surprise on Tyler's face tightened into pugnacity.

'You! What the hell are you doing here?' Tyler demanded, his eyes furiously accusing Sasha of putting him in the wrong again.

'I live here,' Nathan answered blandly, and, much to' Sasha's consternation, put his arm around her shoulders, laying claim to her, flooding her body with a hot awareness of his. Then to compound the possessive action, he asked, 'Can I help, darling?'

Tyler gave Nathan a scathing look. 'You're the cop who broke up my talk to Sasha in the park. If this is your home you must be the most corrupt cop in the whole damned police force. You've got to be worse than Shags Bordello, worse than...' He was lost for words.

Joshua eyed Sasha with some concern. 'If you've got yourself involved in something...'

'I left the police force after I won Lotto,' Nathan interrupted, explaining away the unexplainable.

'Some people have all the luck,' Tyler muttered bitterly. 'I've never won Lotto.'

'Precisely,' Nathan agreed.

Tyler turned truculently to Joshua. 'She's found a new lover. One that can supply her with more than I ever could. That's what's to blame.'

'Is that right, Sasha?' Joshua asked, not as ready as Tyler to leap to conclusions.

'Yes, it is,' Nathan confirmed before she could begin to defend herself against the accusation of being a heartless gold-digger. Her mouth opened and snapped shut in stupefied shock as Nathan rattled on.

'Absolutely correct. Expressed very succinctly. Sasha is much better off living with me. So is Bonnie. Took to me straight away. I always wanted a ready-made family.'

Tyler looked as if he was about to burst a blood vessel. 'I was trying to do the honourable thing,' he seethed. 'Now I've changed my mind. You're not getting one damned thing from me, Sasha. No maintenance. Nothing for the kid, either.'

'Hold hard there, Tyler,' Joshua said lazily. 'We haven't heard Sasha's side of this.'

'Not one cent! Let him look after her and his ready-made family. All my work. He's getting what he wants. All my hard work wasted.' With a dismissive wave of his hand, Tyler headed for the driver's side of the *Mary Bryant*.

Sasha recognised the futility of saying anything. Even if it was possible, it was too late to correct the impression Nathan had so deliberately and effectively imparted.

Tyler hurled himself into the driver's seat. Joshua threw up his hands and hurried to the passenger's side. Tyler was starting the engine when a white Porsche zipped into the driveway, passed the Range Rover, ducked in front of it, braked fiercely, and came to a gravel spitting halt.

Out whirled Elizabeth Maddox.

The expression on her face promised that revenge was sweet. She didn't so much as flick a look at the rumbling Range Rover. Her sleet grey eyes glittered at Sasha and Nathan as she strode between the two vehicles.

'I told you not to come here again, Elizabeth.' Nathan had steel in his voice.

It didn't stop her. She started mounting the steps, her arm sweeping up to point an accusing finger at

Sasha. 'She is not Urszula Budna, and don't think you're going to get away with fraud. Urszula Budna has come to see me. She is now my client.'

Nathan pretended to have a heart attack. Sasha didn't see anything humorous in that at all.

'I'll blow this case wide open,' Elizabeth crowed. She sneered at Sasha then intensified the sneer for Nathan. 'This mistress thing on the side. You're going to lose the custody case, as well. You are a walking disaster, Nathan. I'll strip you so bare, there won't even be any bones left for the carrion to peck out.'

Nathan's eyes narrowed. 'I think you're in for a spot of bother yourself, Elizabeth.'

'Don't be ridiculous. Nothing is going to hurt me. I even bought a new car to show my contempt for your behaviour. In fact...'

While Elizabeth was rebutting Nathan's opinion, Sasha watched in fascination as Tyler exited his vehicle and slowly ascended the steps behind Elizabeth. He tapped her on the shoulder, interrupting the spate of words flowing from Elizabeth's lips.

'You sprayed my car with gravel. You hit *Mary Bryant*.'

Elizabeth barely noticed the hiatus. 'Don't interrupt me while I'm speaking.'

'You got out of the wrong tree this morning,' Tyler said more menacingly.

'Please go away.'

'Aren't you going to apologise? Say you're sorry?'

'Will you please go away?'

'OK.'

Tyler walked back to the vehicle that was designed for hard work and hard living. Sasha breathed her relief. Then she saw what he was going to do as he reversed his new pride and joy, braked, and revved the powerful engine. She closed her eyes.

'Don't close your eyes while I'm talking to you,' Elizabeth fumed.

Sasha opened her eyes. The huge Range Rover charged forward. There was the sound of crashing metal as it rammed the back of the white Porsche. The rear end of the little car crumpled. The Porsche slewed to one side. Tyler reversed. He was going to ram it again in the side. Dazed, they all looked on helplessly as the bull bars bit into the driver's door, crunching it inwards, then trundled the whole car forward as though it were a smashed toy being bulldozed off to the scrapheap.

'That's my car!' Elizabeth screamed.

It was ear-piercing.

She forgot Nathan and Sasha, plunged down the steps, ran furiously to stop the metal carnage along the driveway, yelling unspeakable violence at the perpetrator. Not even the Pope could have found such words, even in prayer.

The Range Rover halted. Tyler reversed again.

'Stop it, stop it, stop it!' Elizabeth screeched.

It was already too late for that.

Tyler paused to lean his elbow on the window ledge of the driver's door and look down upon the perpetrator of the initial offence. 'Say you're sorry for hitting *Mary Bryant*.'

'Yes. No. I don't know.' It sounded as though Elizabeth had burst more than a blood vessel. She was having a cerebral haemorrhage.

Tyler put his foot on the accelerator.

'Yes. I'm sorry,' Elizabeth screamed. 'For God's sake! Don't do it again.'

The acceleration dropped to a throaty rumble. Tyler leaned out again, this time to give dictation. 'Say after me. "I'm sorry I hurt *Mary Bryant*."'

Elizabeth forced the words out. 'I'm...sorry... I...hurt...*Mary Bryant*.'

'If you'd said that earlier, it would have saved you a great deal of trouble. Let this be a lesson to you.'

Nathan and Sasha automatically strolled down to the driveway to survey the damage now that the worst appeared to be over. Elizabeth looked as though she was barely containing herself from flying at Tyler tooth and nail.

'And one more thing,' he said with a mocking leer. 'You didn't unman me one bit when you behaved like a bitch in heat between the sheets. I got the better of you there, too.'

Sasha closed her eyes. Had Elizabeth Maddox been another of Tyler's infidelities when he was taking photos for magazine articles on celebrities?

'You're nothing but an animal,' Elizabeth snarled.

'It takes one animal to recognise another.'

'Pig!'

'Sow!'

'Do I take it there's been some intimacy between you two?' Nathan slid in sweetly.

'One of your women on the side, Tyler?' Sasha asked.

Neither answered.

Tyler drove off, looking like an Olympic champion who had just received his gold medal.

'What happens to me?' Elizabeth wailed.

'I'll get Marion to call a taxi for you,' Nathan said dismissively.

'I can do that for myself,' Elizabeth snapped. 'I have a mobile phone.'

'Fine. We'll leave you to it.'

'Aren't you going to ask me in?'

'I think not,' Nathan said, completely unruffled.

He hooked Sasha's arm around his. They turned in unison and walked back up the steps. The last Sasha saw of Elizabeth was her isolated figure, surveying her wrecked Porsche and wringing her hands. She looked as if she could break into tears of frustration.

'We make a great couple, don't we?' Nathan said with ringing satisfaction as he closed the front door behind them.

'Do you still have to marry Urszula Budna?' Sasha asked, uncertain of where they stood after the latest development with Elizabeth, and the revelation of her affair with Tyler.

Nathan sighed. 'The contract survives, regardless of what Elizabeth did or did not do with Tyler.'

'So the situation remains the same.'

'No. We've got rid of Tyler for good now.'

Sasha frowned. 'Why did you interfere? He was going anyway. What you got rid of, Nathan, was any financial support for Bonnie.'

There was not one flicker of guilt in his eyes. 'If Bonnie is in need of anything, I'll fix it. Until such time as she can support herself.'

He was certainly an expert at fixing things, Sasha thought with heavy irony. He had been doing it for her ever since they'd met. If only they'd met sooner. Or after all the complications in his life had been sorted out. Why did she have to get involved with men who wouldn't or couldn't commit themselves to a straight line relationship?

'That's my commitment to you, Sasha,' Nathan said quietly, as though he had read her mind. 'I'll put it in writing if you like. Either way, I will look after you and Bonnie.'

The bittersweet assurance lifted some of the depression in her heart, but it didn't remove the one reality that dimmed any pleasure in thinking of a future together. 'In a few days, Urszula Budna will have more rights than she has now,' Sasha stated flatly.

'She has nothing to do with us, Sasha.' Nathan drew her into his arms, stirring memories of last night's soul-deep intimacy.

Sasha pressed her hands against his chest in protest at his power to swamp her with feeling. She lifted deeply vulnerable eyes to his. 'But you have to sleep with her to make the marriage safe against legal threat.'

'Nothing on this earth could make me do that after what we shared last night.'

'You really mean that?'

He smiled, a slow sensual smile that lit his eyes with a wicked sparkle. 'Let me show you,' he said, and pulled her into the library with him.

'Nathan, we can't——'

'We can.'

'The children——'

'Are being well looked after.'

'We mustn't——'

'Be long. OK. Time trial. Starting from now.'

He leaned her against the door and unfastened her jeans as he kissed her. Before Sasha knew what she was doing, her hands were active on his trousers. Desire was terribly consuming. Once it took hold, it took over. Time trials made it all the more exciting.

# CHAPTER FOURTEEN

'ENOUGH of these mournful sighs,' Hester remonstrated impatiently. She slapped the latest report on Sasha's findings face-down on the table and eyed Sasha sternly. 'What's the problem?'

'I'm sorry...' Useless to deny her distraction of mind. She couldn't stop thinking that today was Monday, and in two days' time Nathan was to marry Urszula Budna.

Hester waved dismissively. 'Nothing to be sorry about. What's Nathan done?'

There was no evading the acute perception in Hester Wingate's piercing eyes. 'It's not his fault,' Sasha answered glumly.

'Of course it's his fault,' Hester corrected with asperity. 'Men are always at fault. Nathan is a man. *Ergo,* he is at fault.'

'There's this Polish woman...' Sasha started off circumspectly.

'There always is. Men have two brains. The one in the unmentionable area causes all the trouble.'

A burning rush of blood scorched Sasha's cheeks.

Hester put her own inimitable interpretation on that. 'Seduced you as well, did he? Swept you away with passion?'

'Not exactly. Only a little,' Sasha demurred, too honest to pretend she hadn't been a willing participant in their mutual desire.

'At least you're better than Elizabeth Maddox. That woman is mad. Megalomania.' Hester leaned over and patted Sasha's hand. 'Don't you worry. It will all turn out for the best.'

'It can't,' Sasha said hopelessly. 'He's contracted a marriage with someone else and he can't get out of it. He wrote the contract himself and it's watertight. You see . . .'

Sasha explained about Elizabeth's machinations to get both Nathan and Matt back to bolster her image for political purposes.

Hester rose from her chair. Her diminutive form shook with deep emotion. 'Blood will tell. He'll find a way. Rotten to the core like his great-grandfather, but essentially a good man. One of the finest. Blood will tell. He'll find a way.'

Hester could have been speaking Egyptian for all Sasha understood. 'Are you speaking of Nathan?'

'He even looks likes his great-grandfather. Got the devil in him. Always had. But I thought he had enough of *me* in him to correct for that.'

Nathan had never fitted into any family tree Hester had given her. There was one item Sasha could latch on to. 'Who was Nathan's great-grandfather?'

Hester looked sharply at her. 'Haven't you found that out yet?'

'No.' It wasn't in her brief from Hester.

'Not much good at digging up the dirt, are you?'

Sasha bridled at the premature criticism. 'That's not quite true,' she defended. 'I haven't found out all the ramifications yet, and I wasn't going to mention it until I'd worked my way through them, but . . .'

Sasha hesitated, mindful of the security that the nanny's quarters provided her and Bonnie. She was on dangerous ground with this, but her professional expertise had been called into question.

'Go on,' Hester urged.

'It's about Seagrave Dunworthy,' Sasha said slowly.

'Is it, now?' The interest kindled in Hester's eyes took a mega-leap at that name.

Sasha decided that her independent occupation of that part of the Mosman house no longer mattered. She burnt her bridges behind her. 'Seagrave Dunworthy attempted to enter a marriage that would have involved him in bigamy.'

Hester sat down, a look of triumph spreading across her face. 'Is that so?' she encouraged.

'Yes,' Sasha said firmly. 'I have proof of the existence of the first wife and she was alive at the time the second marriage was to take place.'

'Absolute proof?' Hester queried.

'Absolute,' Sasha assured her. 'Certificates double-checked. The second marriage was to take place at St. Mary's Cathedral, Bishop Clancy officiating. It was the social wedding of the year. The bride turned up. The groom turned up. So did the brother of the first wife, uninvited and unannounced.'

'I don't need the details of that part,' Hester said sharply.

'Of course, once the existence of the first wife was made known, the wedding could not go ahead.'

'Get on with the good dirt,' Hester encouraged. 'This part is boring.'

'The name of the bride was suppressed in the newspaper. It turned out she had lied about her age and didn't have parental consent. There were also implications that she was pregnant at the time.'

'I'm interested in Dunworthy,' Hester snapped. 'Not in some flighty female.'

'He died soon after. Within two years. The death certificate states the cause as a fall from a horse. Some say he invited death, others that it was by his own hand.'

'Nonsense!' Hester scoffed. 'He was simply careless.'

'A few close friends said it was from an excess of passion.'

'Aggravated remorse, more likely.'

'His first wife was institutionalised in Zurich for deep psychological problems.' The diagnosis on the medical report was schizophrenia, but Sasha knew that was the popular label for any mental disorder in those days.

'In a word, she was mad,' Hester declared.

'Yes. After her death...'

'When was that?'

'A month before he died.'

Hester frowned. 'You've got uncontestable proof of the date of her death?'

'Yes. And once he was free of his legal obligations to his first wife, Seagrave Dunworthy made his extraordinary will. It was signed one week before his fatal fall from a horse.'

Hester sat for a while in brooding silence. She finally gave Sasha a beetling look. 'He was a callous, unfeeling man.'

Sasha shrugged, not prepared to agree or disagree with that judgement.

'Is that all you've dug up on him?' Hester demanded.

'I haven't had time to work through all the trusts and find out what they mean. But I did find one thing. I think it's something important.'

She had Hester's keen attention.

'Among the papers I examined there were archival files from Brumby, Blackridge and Bagwell. They were Seagrave Dunworthy's solicitors. In the correspondence, reference was made to a Mary Ester Dawson...'

Sasha paused, looking for a reaction from Hester. It was one of the names in the Dawson family bible where the dates had been changed. Hester stared at her unblinkingly, giving nothing away, waiting for her to go on.

'The letter is dated a few days before he died. I think the letter was meant to be passed on, but no one realised its significance until it was too late. It wasn't passed on and he received no reply to it. After he died...well, there was no point to it any more. Until I found it.'

'You have it here?' Hester demanded gruffly.

'Yes.'

'What does it say?'

'It's too deeply personal for anyone but Mary Ester Dawson,' Sasha said quietly.

A flash of pain sharpened Hester's eyes. 'You know that's me.'

'I guessed.'

'Show it to me.'

Sasha lifted the photocopy out of her briefcase. The old lady's hand shook as she took the letter written over seventy years ago. She read it slowly, devouring every word, going back to the beginning, trying to comprehend.

Sasha felt intrusive. She got up and strolled along the veranda, pausing to look down at the lush tropical garden below. The frangipani trees were in full bloom. They were called love flowers, pink yellow, cream, so richly scented, growing everywhere. It made the place look exotic and warm and tended and cared for. Yet for over seventy years Hester Wingate had believed her life had been ruined by Seagrave Dunworthy. But for a careless oversight in a solicitor's office . . .

She heard Hester cough and turned around. There was a different look about her, a lifeless look. Her skin was like old parchment, her mouth withered, her eyes colourless.

'I misjudged him, didn't I?' she said bleakly.

'Yes.'

'Too late.'

'Not too late to tell the truth about him,' Sasha suggested, walking back to be with her.

A fleeting smile softened Hester's lips. 'He is Nathan's great-grandfather. He was my lover. He was the father of my child. And there was never another man to match him.'

'The items in the will, the rent for example ...'

'It was to compel me to live in *his* house. It would never be economical to rent it out, and it couldn't be sold. It didn't work with me, of course. I've never put a foot inside that house. Ever.'

'Always to be spoken well of? Because of the gossip and calumnies and detractors?' Sasha prompted.

'He tried to make amends,' Hester acknowledged, 'but it was too late. I had him thrown out of the house. Took all his horses from him first, though. When I married George Wingate it wasn't much of a love match, but we did breed some of the finest thoroughbreds in the country.'

'It was Seagrave Dunworthy's love of horseflesh that made him put the rent in guineas.'

'We had so much in common. The day he died ... that was the day I married George. When I heard about it, I told myself I was glad. Savagely glad. It made me free of him. But I wasn't free of him ...'

'He loved you,' Sasha said gently. 'Deeply and passionately. He tried to do the honourable thing and marry you. There's a ring of desperation in that letter he sent to the solicitor. He might have been breaking the law, but it wasn't to hurt anyone. It was to set matters right. *When needs must ...*'

A solitary tear formed in Hester's eye and it trickled a lonely path down her aged cheek. 'He never made me cry. Never.' Then, brokenly, '*When needs must ...*'

Sasha curved her arm around Hester's frail shoulders. 'He loved you. There is no dirt.'

'I need to be alone. How is it that...'

'Yes?'

'...it took that old fool seventy years to make me cry?'

'I guess grief takes many forms,' Sasha said, aware that her bitter grief over the wasted years with Tyler had made her question the wisdom of her instinctive responses to Nathan. But not any more.

Life was too short to put off what she knew she wanted because of a set of irrevocable circumstances. Nathan might not fall off a horse tomorrow, but who was to say how long they would have together? It was stupid to brood over Nathan's paper marriage to a woman who had no rights to anything but a piece of paper in return. Sasha resolved not to let that stand in the way of what she and Nathan could have together.

She gave his great-grandmother an impulsive hug, then withdrew to pack away her papers and leave the old lady alone with her memories. She had walked to the end of the veranda when Hester called out. She paused and looked back. Hester was on her feet and hurrying after her.

'I didn't say thank you, Sasha.'

'It's just my job.'

'Thank you.'

Curiosity made Sasha ask, 'Would you mind telling me one last thing?'

'What is it?'

'The dates in the bible. I still don't know how and why they were altered. Was it because your younger brothers wanted to enlist in the army?'

'Good heavens, no! It was my sister, Isobel. I was with her while she did it.'

'So you could marry Seagrave?'

'My parents thought the age difference was too great.'

''But why did you pretend to me that you didn't know?'

'My dear, how else could I convince you I needed someone to work for me? If I hadn't found a job for you, Nathan would have made my life unbearable.' She gave Sasha a wise look. 'Take my word for it. When Nathan wants something he always finds a way.'

Sasha smiled. 'Thank you, Hester.'

On her way home, Sasha pondered the revelations that had answered so many questions in her mind. Nathan, being in the direct line of inheritance from Hester, would eventually become the owner of Seagrave Dunworthy's house. That was why he had the right to select who could rent rooms. That was why Elizabeth had considered she had a chance of inheriting, if Nathan had married her again.

What she found inconsistent with everything else Nathan had done was leaving it to chance whether she would come to his house and take up the offer of rooms. If she hadn't done that, and she might not have, they would have missed each other, because he had no way of finding her again. Yet, once she had come, he had gone out of his way to get her a job, as though it was important to him to keep her with him, even though he had already contracted a marriage with Urszula Budna. Somehow it didn't quite gell to Sasha.

Not that it mattered now. The past was the past. Holding faith with the future she and Nathan would share together was the important thing. When she arrived home and collected Bonnie from Marion's care, she told Marion that Matt was welcome to come up to the nursery after he got home from his playschool. She could not let the little boy feel unwanted any longer.

An hour later, Matt came pelting up the back stairs. He burst into the nursery, his face alight with pride and pleasure as he held up a big sheet of paper for Sasha and Bonnie to see.

'We did finger-painting today. This is my picture.'

Sasha regarded the stick figures with the expected interest. 'I like the colours you used, Matt.'

'Yes. I did you in pink, Bonnie.'

She obligingly gurgled her approval from the play-pen.

'This is Daddy in blue,' Matt went on. 'Harry's in green for the garden. I made Marion orange 'cause she gives me orange juice every morning. I'm brown. That's getting dirty from playing.'

He seemed reluctant to identify the last stick person. 'And the one in red?' Sasha prompted.

Matt gave her a shy but hopeful look. 'That's my pretend mother.'

'Well, she looks very nice and warm,' Sasha said with a smile. 'Would you like me to pin the picture up on the wall? Then we can look at it whenever we want to.'

Matt eagerly agreed and Sasha invited him to choose the best position for it. He watched her press the thumbtacks in. Then they both stood back to admire the result.

'The teacher said to paint our family,' Matt informed her.

'You did a fine job, Matt.'

It was Nathan's voice behind them.

'Daddy!' Matt ran to his father and Nathan swung him up for a hug. 'I can play up here now, Daddy.'

Nathan's eyes met Sasha's with an oddly tense and urgent look. 'Well, how about you play with Bonnie while I talk to her mummy, Matt?' he said, his voice warmly encouraging for his son.

There was instant agreement. With both children in the playpen, happily gathering and scattering plastic blocks, Nathan quickly drew Sasha into the adjoining kitchenette. He slid his hands around her waist, drawing her close, but his mind was not on kissing her. His eyes searched hers with an intensity that set her heart aflutter.

'There may be a way out of the contract. It's extreme. It's radical. And it involves you, Sasha.'

## CHAPTER FIFTEEN

HESTER was right, Sasha thought, her mind leaping with elation. When Nathan really wanted something, he found a way. Matt was right. His daddy *could* do anything.

Sasha flung her arms around his neck, her eyes sparkling with a great burst of happiness. 'You're the most wonderful man I've ever met!' As well as the sexiest. She went up on her toes to kiss him.

Nathan hesitated a moment, a brief conflict in his eyes. Desire won. His mouth took hers with passionate intensity. His arms pulled her into a fiercely possessive embrace. Arousal was so swift, Sasha broke away in alarm as she remembered the children.

'Matt and Bonnie...'

'I love you, Sasha.'

Her heart swelled anew. 'I love you, too.'

He looked deeply and seriously into her eyes. 'I need your help.'

'What do you want me to do?'

'Give me Tyler's address.'

Sasha was thunderstruck. 'What's Tyler got to do with you and me and Urszula Budna?'

'He's the linchpin to my present difficulties. Anyone who can bed Elizabeth and not feel unmanned has extraordinary powers, including tenacity of purpose. Tyler is the man I need for a desperate task. In military terms he'd be called "the forlorn hope". Not much chance of survival.'

'Radical' and 'extreme' suddenly took on a terrible meaning. Sasha shook her head vehemently. 'Not murder, Nathan. I've thought of that, too, but only figuratively, not literally. No, no, no, no, no! Not murder. And I don't believe Tyler would be capable of it anyway. He's irresponsible, occasionally violent, but definitely not a murderer.'

Nathan looked at her in amazement. 'You actually thought of murdering Urszula Budna?'

'Not really. It flashed through my mind. But I only wanted her to go away.' She felt defensive.

'You thought I'd contemplate murder?' There was a certain amount of awe in his voice.

'Not until this moment, no.'

'Perish the thought. You're never to think such a thing again.'

'I won't.' She hadn't really thought of it at all. She thought Nathan had. To distract his attention, she swivelled around to get a notebook and pen from the top kitchen drawer. 'I'll write down Tyler's address for you.'

Having done that, she tore off the page and handed it to Nathan, who quickly pocketed it then produced some papers of his own.

'I need you to sign these,' he said, spreading them on the kitchen bench.

'What are they?'

'Sasha...' He grasped her arms and turned her around to him. His riveting blue eyes bored into her heart again. 'Will you marry me?'

She took a deep breath to clear the sudden obstruction in her throat. 'I'd consider it if you weren't married to someone else.'

'I love you.'

'I won't commit bigamy.'

'I love you passionately.'

'We don't *need* to marry. But if there's a way...'

'There's a way.'

'I don't want you to mess up my life.'

'Mine's already messed up.'

'That's your fault.'

'Kiss me.'

'The children...'

'...won't see a thing.' He eased her back against the kitchen sink.

'You know what this leads to,' Sasha protested, aware of the thrill of excitement already quivering down her thighs.

'Only a kiss.'

'One.'

'As long as it lasts to the end of time.'

'No.'

'If you sign the papers I'll go and see Tyler.'

She grabbed up the pen again. 'This is only to get rid of you.'

'Here's the line.'

*'This is an application to marry under special licence!'*

'Covering all eventualities.'

She eyed him in alarm. *When needs must . . .* the words echoed through her mind. Was he the reincarnation of his great-grandfather? 'I haven't said yes yet.'

'This is not a contract. It's an application that can always be nullified.'

'Are you sure?'

'Certain.'

'I'll write that on it. This application can be nullified at any time.'

'Fine. It's always best to be cautious.'

Sasha was. Particularly over this point. Nathan had a definite tendency to take the law into his own hands.

'Thank you, my love.' He whipped the papers away the moment she'd finished writing, stole a quick kiss on her lips, then was off. 'I'll be back as soon as I've got Tyler lined up.'

'For what?' Sasha called after him.

'Best you don't know.'

He was gone.

Sasha couldn't follow him. The children needed her supervision. So she stewed over the plan, whatever it might be, for a considerable amount of time. Then she gave up on it. Nathan Parnell was a law unto himself. She might as well get used to living dangerously. He had certainly spoiled her for any other man.

Afternoon passed into evening. Dinner was eaten. The children were put to bed. Sasha went to bed herself after hours of impatience, waiting for Nathan to return.

She was woken by a nibble on her ear. 'Sasha, we're going to marry.' The words whispered through her mind. For a moment she wondered if she was dreaming. Then an arm curled around her waist and she rolled onto her back to check out the reality of the man lying in the bed beside her. Her lover. Her husband-to-be if he spoke the truth.

'I haven't set the date for a wedding,' she said, feeling she should be annoyed with Nathan for keeping her in the dark.

'I have.' He dropped a kiss on her nose.

Sasha sighed. What was the point in being petty? She loved him. She wanted him. And he was offering her the ultimate commitment to their relationship. 'What's your plan, Nathan?' she asked.

His lips grazed seductively over hers. 'It's a tight schedule.'

'How tight?'

'We get married an hour before I'm due to marry Urszula Budna.'

Sasha jack-knifed in shock, their heads bumping painfully as she knocked Nathan aside. She was too agitated to care. 'You're going to commit bigamy with her?' she squawked.

'No.' He pressed her down onto the pillow again and stroked her hair soothingly. 'If I'm already married to you, obviously I can't specifically perform the terms of the contract with her. It'd be against the law. A married man can't marry someone else.'

'That's true,' Sasha agreed on a wave of deep relief. 'But Urszula isn't going to be happy. And she's got Elizabeth as her lawyer.'

'That's where Tyler comes in.'

'How?'

'Firstly, he and Joshua McDougal will be witnesses at our wedding. Apart from showing Urszula our certificate of marriage, they can also swear to her that the deed has been done.'

Incredulity flooded Sasha's mind. 'You got Tyler to agree to that?'

'Yes. Then he'll marry Urszula in my place, giving her the right to stay in Australia and take out citizenship. Which was all she wanted from our contract before she got other ideas.'

'Tyler? Marry Urszula?' Sasha knew for a fact Tyler didn't believe in marriage.

'He doesn't have to live with her. He doesn't have to stay married to her. It's only a convenient legality,' Nathan explained patiently. 'He understands that.'

'How on earth did you persuade him into it?'

'I promised to save him from going to gaol. He needs legal representation for what he did to Elizabeth's car. I'm going to defend him. No one else could bring the same feelings of sympathy, understanding and compassion to the case that I will. Already I'm working on my peroration to the jury. I'll get him off.'

Sasha stared at him in dazed bewilderment. 'But that case won't come up before Wednesday. And Tyler thinks marriage is a gaol.'

'Not this one. No responsibility involved. It could be a perfect match. A marriage made in heaven. And it's another poke in the eye for Elizabeth. Tyler rather relishes that.'

'Ego. One-upmanship,' Sasha murmured. It fitted Tyler's character.

'Apart from which, what I'm going to pay him for marrying Urszula...' Nathan grinned. 'In Tyler's terms, it's the equivalent of winning Lotto.'

'A million dollars!'

'Nothing like it. But enough for Tyler to think he's got lucky for the first time in his life.'

Nathan started kissing her. His hands moved to do distracting things to her body. Sasha wanted to respond, but there was a clamour in her mind that insisted he was making a bigger mess out of the mess they already had. She lifted his head up, gulped in a quick breath and spilled out the worrying concerns he had raised.

'Can you afford it, Nathan?'

'For you, yes.'

'After we've paid for all this, are we going to be impoverished for the rest of our lives?'

Nathan told her what he was worth.

'Good heavens!' she gasped. 'Money like that can cause a lot of problems.'

'Sasha, darling, can we please face that problem when we come to it? The first thing is to get married. Let's concentrate only on that.'

She gradually relaxed. It was really rather marvellous thinking of how very much Nathan wanted them to be together and stay together. It added a special glow to their lovemaking, a deeper appreciation of his love and need for her. She smiled to herself as she remembered Nathan scorning love, saying it caused havoc and created chaos. He certainly thought it worth having now. Not pie-in-the-sky at all.

It was the real deep-down love this time. Sasha
could feel it in her soul. Perhaps the passion would not
stay as white-hot as it was now, but it was not a madness that would cool after eighteen months. It was
bonded in with mutual values, mutual beliefs, mutual
feelings, mutual instincts. Sasha knew the caring and
sharing and the continual building of both would always be ongoing for her and Nathan, the ready support of each other, the wanting that couldn't even
begin to envisage wanting anyone else.

He was her man.

She was his woman.

As they lay languorously together, feeling the sweet
bliss of utter contentment in the fulfilment of every
desire, Sasha's thoughts drifted over all Nathan's radical arrangements. She hoped nothing would go wrong
between now and Wednesday.

'Where are we being married?' she asked.

'Central Register Office. It's near St Mary's Cathedral.'

Sasha thought of Hester and her aborted marriage
to Seagrave Dunworthy. A church wedding didn't
guarantee anything. Neither did all the flowers and
finery that went with it. That wasn't the important
part at all. Not to Sasha. The Central Register Office
was fine by her.

'I must tell my parents,' she said, more as a reminder to herself than as a remark to Nathan.

'No!' he yelled like a scalded cat. The next instant
he had her flat on her back and was leaning over her
in urgent command. 'You mustn't tell anyone. Not a
soul. Not even Marion. It was bad enough that I had

to go to your parents concerning the details of the marriage application.'

'How did you know where they live?'

'Umm ... I suppose I looked it up in the telephone directory.'

Sasha knew that was wrong. Her parents had an unlisted number. She wondered what Nathan was being evasive about, then shrugged off the thought. It was irrelevant.

'Why mustn't anyone be told? Surely family can know. It's not as if ...'

'Sasha, people talk. Can't help themselves. Then other people talk to other people, and word gets around. Imagine this scenario. You're standing there as the bride. I'm standing beside you as the groom. And the question is posed ... is there any impediment to stop this man and woman from marrying?'

Her mind instantly flew to Hester and Seagrave.

'The last thing we need,' Nathan said vehemently, 'is Urszula Budna's brother turning up and waving a legal contract that I'm in breach of. Can you even begin to comprehend what a disaster that would be, and how the past repeats itself?'

# CHAPTER SIXTEEN

THE past did not repeat itself.

At ten o'clock on Wednesday morning, Sasha and Nathan were married in the Central Register Office. It did not have the grandeur of St Mary's Cathedral. A bishop did not officiate. But no one turned up to stop the marriage.

Owing to the secrecy that was maintained, Sasha was unable to wear a wedding-dress. However, she had spent part of Tuesday doing Christmas shopping. The present she bought for herself was a very expensive white silk suit. Sasha found it very easy to convince herself that her wedding-day was better than any Christmas Day she could ever have. It was perfectly reasonable, therefore, to open and wear her Christmas gift to herself on this more appropriate occasion.

Nathan, of course, looked as handsome as ever. In keeping with decorum, he wore a conservative but very smart grey suit.

The ceremony was brief. Efficient but effective, Sasha thought. Nevertheless, it had an unexpected and dazzling highlight. Nathan not only slid a wedding-ring on to the third finger of her left hand. He accompanied it with another ring featuring a fabulous pink Argyle diamond. It choked Sasha up for several moments. She looked at Nathan with swimming eyes. He assisted her in regaining her composure by kissing her until a surge of heat dried the tears.

Tyler and Joshua performed their role as witnesses with perfect aplomb, making it look as though it was an everyday event in their lives. They expressed congratulations, shook Nathan's hand warmly, kissed Sasha on both cheeks, and generally conducted themselves as though they were thoroughly delighted with the successful completion of phase one of *the plan*. They strolled outside to await the arrival of the next bride. At precisely eleven o'clock, a white Mercedes with government plates on it pulled up at the curb.

Out stepped a man who frowned at Sasha.

'The brother,' Nathan murmured.

He was followed by a woman who was quite strikingly beautiful and voluptuously curved.

'Urszula,' Nathan murmured.

Sasha reflected that she could have felt savagely jealous if Nathan's rings weren't on her finger.

There was a sharp intake of breath from Tyler.

Sasha cynically suspected he wouldn't mind consummating his paper marriage.

Then out of the car stepped Elizabeth Maddox.

'The lawyer,' Nathan murmured.

Elizabeth drew herself up to her full height for the purpose of looking down her nose at the waiting group.

'Your choice of witnesses, Nathan,' she invited, as if preparing for a duel with pistols. She ignored Sasha.

With a wave of his hand Nathan indicated Tyler and Joshua.

'What poor taste you have!' Elizabeth observed coldly.

'I think introductions are in order,' Nathan replied. 'This is my wife, Sasha Parnell. Beside me is my replacement bridegroom for Urszula. You have met before. His name is Tyler Cullum.'

Hell broke loose.

Elizabeth's strident responses indicated that not only were the dogs of war unleashed, but also the four horsemen of the Apocalypse. What was being called down upon their heads was about to make Armageddon look like a children's play yard.

Urszula's brother broke into violent argument and agitation. He saw a life of ease and luxury evaporating before his eyes.

Elizabeth went into legal argument as to why the marriage was void. Nathan urged Sasha to come home and consummate immediately. Elizabeth's blood-pressure soared to a new medical record before she conceded bitter defeat to a *fait accompli,* and turned her attention to punitive damages.

Urszula gave emotional outcries of piteous horror at the situation.

At this critical moment, Tyler stepped forward and into the ring. Urszula surreptitiously cast a glance over him as she held a hand to her bleeding heart.

'Pain and agony!' Elizabeth ranted in triumph. 'You'll pay for pain and agony. You'll pay for loss of reputation to my client. You'll pay for abrogation of her rights, arrogation of powers you don't possess, and derogation to Tyler Cullum . . .'

Tyler smiled at Urszula. It was a full blast double whammy smile of explosive impact. Many a lady had felt the full blast of Tyler's smile. Few recovered.

Urszula was no exception. The legal argument going on around her was falling on barren ground. Urszula was a realist. She half smiled back at Tyler.

Tyler had many attractions. At his charming best, most women would look and keep looking. Urszula kept looking. Sasha observed a certain animal magnetism flowing between Tyler and Urszula. Sasha understood that. She wondered if Urszula would like a trip to the great interior of Australia.

Tyler seized the moment.

He stepped forward and took Urszula's hands in his. 'You're the woman I've been waiting for all my life,' he said with winning fervour. 'I can make you happier than you've ever been before. I've got the money and I've got the time. I'll take photos of you that will be featured in every magazine in the country. You'll be famous.'

'I will?' Urszula's eyes filled with stars. 'Yes,' she said. 'Yes, I'd like that.'

'Don't listen to him,' Elizabeth snapped.

'I'll give you everything,' Tyler promised. 'Everything a woman can want. In return I require one thing.'

'Not children. I don't want children,' Urszula said anxiously.

'I have all I need,' Tyler assured her hastily.

'Then what do you want?'

'Fire your lawyer.'

Urszula turned a glazed look to Elizabeth. 'You're fired.'

Tyler curled Urszula's arm around his and swept his bride-to-be into the register office. Joshua belatedly followed, looking perfectly relaxed about all that had transpired.

'No, Urszula, no!' her brother yelled, running after her.

'Go and marry Elizabeth,' Urszula hurled back at him. 'I've got what I want.'

Elizabeth screamed a tirade of abuse after Tyler's retreating back. What she would do to him in court would be nothing compared to what she would do if she ever had him at her mercy.

'Time for us to leave,' Nathan said to Sasha. 'Now we can start planning a proper wedding and a proper honeymoon and a proper everything.'

'Don't they need a second witness in there?' Sasha didn't want any hitches in phase two of *the plan*.

'Let the brother come to his senses. I'm sure he will. Otherwise they'll have to use a clerk.'

The door of Elizabeth's Mercedes slammed shut. The car surged forward, away from the kerb, and Nathan stood looking after it for quite some moments.

'What are you thinking, darling?' Sasha asked, drawing his attention back to her.

'Elizabeth is a most erratic driver,' he said cheerfully, taking her hand. 'Let's go home. For ourselves. And for the children.'

WHEN NATHAN explained what their marriage meant to his son, Matt's eyes glowed with satisfaction in his own inner belief. 'I knew she was my mother. She's not my pretend mother any more. She's real.'

Nathan clearly had no inclination to correct him, yet fact was fact, and he could hardly ignore Elizabeth's natural claim on their son. Matt did have to understand in case Elizabeth still persisted in wanting custody.

'Matt, the other lady who came last week . . .'

'You were wrong about her, Daddy,' the little boy said with unshakeable conviction.

'Why am I wrong, Matt?'

' 'Cause it wasn't in her eyes.'

From the mouths of babes came the simplest of truths, Sasha thought. Elizabeth was his biological mother, but that had no meaning whatsoever to Matt. Maybe he was right.

He turned to Sasha, his eyes clear with the knowledge that was so clear to him. 'I felt it inside when you looked at me. Like at the park when you said you were sorry you had to go. And at playschool when I told the other kids.'

Her empathy for his loneliness.

'I felt it too, Matt,' she said softly. She crouched down to draw him closer to her, their eyes sharing the same knowledge. 'What your daddy was trying to tell you . . . the other lady is your birth mother. But I'm your real mother in here.' She pressed one hand to her heart and the other over Matt's heart. 'I always will be.'

They shared a secret smile of perfect understanding.

Then Matt turned his smile up to his father, 'See, Daddy?'

'Yes, I see, Matt.' The look he turned to Sasha was all she wanted to see. The deep forever love that would see them through their lives.

SASHA TOLD Nathan the proper wedding and proper honeymoon could wait until some time in the New Year. What she wanted most of all was a family Christmas.

The next day a huge van arrived in the driveway. It took four men to carry a large fir tree in a huge pot into the lounge. Only a room with a fourteen-foot ceiling could have accommodated such a tree.

They spent hours decorating it. When the happy task was finally completed, and Nathan switched on the string of coloured lights he'd draped around the branches, Bonnie thought it so wonderful, she took her first tottering steps.

On Christmas Day, Sasha's parents came to share in the festivities. The roast turkey had just been set on the dining-table when the doorbell rang. Sasha and Marion had their hands full bringing in all the accompanying dishes to serve with the turkey, so Nathan went to answer the call.

There was a murmur of voices. Sasha idly wondered who it could be. She didn't have to wait long to find out. Brooks entered the room, his arms laden with presents. Jane followed, carrying a big plate containing a massive plum pudding surrounded by bon-bons for the children. Behind them came a voice that Sasha recognised all too well.

Hester Wingate.

She entered the room, complaining bitterly as Nathan ushered her in before him. 'I broke my word. I swore I'd never enter this house that Seagrave built for me.' She found Sasha's eye and looked sternly at her. 'But I can hardly go to meet him on the other side without knowing he had done a proper job of it, can I?'

Sasha hastened to her side, uttering reassurances. 'Of course, you had to come and see for yourself. We'll set three more places at the table for you and Jane and Brooks, and have Christmas dinner together. Afterwards I'll show you through all the rooms.'

'I'd like that,' Hester agreed, 'but I still think I did better taking all his horses.'

'I'm sure that's right,' Sasha said, inwardly rejoicing that Hester had finally found peace and goodwill to all men. Especially with Seagrave Dunworthy.

LATER THAT NIGHT, when their visitors went home and the children were tucked up in bed asleep, Sasha and Nathan relaxed together on one of the chesterfields in the lounge. The lights were out except for those on the tree, and they reminisced over the day in a mood of blissful contentment.

'Life is full of chance,' Sasha mused. 'If we hadn't met in the park, if Tyler hadn't turned up, if I hadn't been desperate for a place to live, you would never have found me, Nathan.'

'Sasha, my darling, after we met in the park, nothing was left to chance. It was only a matter of time.'

'How could you be so sure I would come here?'

'I wasn't.'

'What would have happened if I hadn't turned up?'

'I would have come to you.'

She turned on him in exasperation. 'You didn't know where I lived. Or where I might have moved to.'

He grinned. 'Yes, I did.'

She suddenly recollected that he had found her parents' address, and not through the telephone directory. 'How?' she demanded.

His grin grew wider. 'Computer games.'

She heaved an impatient sigh. 'Stop teasing.'

'When I slipped the address of this house into your bag, I also slipped in a tiny technological device.'

'You bugged me?'

'No, darling. That's against the law,' he said sanctimoniously. 'I was simply tracking your bag. Wherever it went.'

'What if I'd left it in a bus? Or had it stolen?'

'The first stop gave me your parents' address. I figured they'd always know where you were.'

'Promise that you'll never do such a thing again.'

'I promise.'

'Why did you do it?'

'Because, my love, I was in need of a wife.'

**Helen Bianchin** was born in New Zealand and travelled to Australia before marrying her Italian-born husband. After three years they moved, returned to New Zealand with their daughter, had two sons then re-settled in Australia.

Encouraged by friends to recount anecdotes of her years as a tobacco sharefarmer's wife living in an Italian community, Helen began setting words on paper and her first novel was published by Mills & Boon® in 1975. Since then, Helen has written more than thirty romances which have been distributed all over the world. An animal lover, she says her terrier and Persian cat regard her study as much theirs as hers.

# DANGEROUS ALLIANCE

by

## HELEN BIANCHIN

# CHAPTER ONE

THERE was a soft thud as the Boeing's wheels hit the tarmac, followed by a shrill scream of brakes as the powerful jet decelerated down the runway.

The flight had been smooth and uneventful, and merely one in a series of many which Leanne had taken between the Gold Coast and Melbourne during the past five years.

With one exception. This time Paige wouldn't be waiting to meet her, and there would be no joyous reunion and exchanged laughter as mother and daughter attempted to catch up with each other's news.

An ache began behind her eyes, and she blinked quickly in an effort to dispel the threat of tears as she gazed sightlessly out of the window.

It wasn't fair that her beautiful mother should fall prey to a rare form of cancer, or that its stealthy invasion had proven to be so extensive that the medical professionals could only issue a grim prognosis. Within twenty-four hours of receiving the news, Leanne had arranged her flight and assigned a senior assistant to manage her beauty therapy clinic.

The engines wound down to a muted whine as the large jet wheeled off the runway, then cruised slowly towards its allotted bay.

Customary procedure completed, Leanne joined the queue of passengers vacating the aircraft, unaware of the appreciative glances cast in her direction. Vivid blue trousers and matching top in uncrushable silk accented her slim curves and were a perfect foil for her shoulder-length ash-blonde hair.

Within minutes she emerged into the arrival lounge, and she moved with ease towards the luggage carousel, her eyes skimming the conveyor belt for a familiar bag.

'Leanne.'

The sound of that faintly accented drawl tore the breath from her throat, and her heartbeat stilled imperceptibly, then kicked in at an accelerated rate. It took only seconds to compose her features before she turned slowly to face the man standing within touching distance.

His tall, broad frame was sheathed in impeccable suiting, and strong, sculptured facial features, piercing grey eyes and dark well-groomed hair completed an arresting composite that few women could successfully ignore.

As head of the vast Kostakidas empire, he emanated a dramatic sense of power that was coveted by his contemporaries and viewed with supreme caution by those who chose to oppose him.

Dangerous, compelling, and intensely ruthless. Lethal, she added silently as she summoned a smile in greeting.

'Dimitri.'

Five years ago she would have flung herself into his arms, accepted the teasingly affectionate brush of his lips against her cheek, and laughingly indulged in a harmless game of flirtatious pretence.

Now she stood quietly, her eyes clear and unwavering, their blue depths masking pain. 'I thought you'd still be in Perth.'

One eyebrow rose slightly, and his expression assumed an edge of cynicism in silent reproof. 'Like you, I rearranged my business affairs and caught the first available flight east.'

Her features were a carefully composed mask that hid a host of emotions. 'It wasn't necessary for you to meet me.'

He didn't say anything. He had no need. She was Paige's daughter and his late father's silver-haired angel. As such, he would accord her every consideration, and refuse to concede her desire for independence.

Leanne felt her body quiver slightly, and she forced herself to maintain rigid control. 'Have you seen Paige? How is she?'

His eyes held hers for a few timeless seconds, then his features softened. 'An hour ago,' he revealed. 'She is as comfortable as it is possible for her to be.'

Paige had earned Dimitri's affection ten years ago when she'd married his widowed father, and her warmth and generous nature had turned Yanis's house into a home, softened the hard edges of a cynical, world-weary man whose sole focus in life appeared to be escalating his empire to monumental proportions while grooming his only son to follow in his footsteps. The ensuing five years had resulted in an abundance of love and harmony, until tragedy had struck with a boating accident that robbed them of husband, father and stepfather, and placed Dimitri at the helm of the vast Kostakidas corporation.

'Which bag is yours?'

Dimitri had been educated in a number of countries, and his faint accent was an indistinguishable inflexion that lent itself easily to a fluency in several languages; Leanne shivered faintly as she attempted to maintain a mental distance from an intrusive memory.

'The tan,' she acknowledged, indicating its position on the carousel, and she watched as he extricated it with ease.

'Shall we go?'

It was crazy to feel so incredibly vulnerable, she chastised herself silently as she walked at his side to the sleek, top-of-the-range maroon-coloured Jaguar parked at the kerbside immediately adjacent to the entrance.

Within minutes Dimitri urged the powerful vehicle into the flow of traffic exiting the terminal, and Leanne directed her attention to the scene beyond the windscreen, feeling strangely loath to indulge in idle conversation.

The car's air-conditioning provided relief from the midsummer heat, and the sun's glare was diffused by tinted windows through which the sky appeared as a clear azure, with only a whisper of soft cloud evident on the horizon.

Nothing appeared to have changed, Leanne mused as the Jaguar picked up speed on the freeway. Weathered brick homes dulled by pollution and age-lined suburban streets, and narrow steel tracks embedded into main arterial roads provided a linking tracery for electric trams as they whirred noisily to and from the city.

She drew a deep breath, then released it slowly. Melbourne was a large, bustling metropolis of multinationals with a culture that was wide and varied. It was the place where she was born, where she'd grown up and attended shool.

There was an intrinsic desire to turn back the clock. Except that that was impossible, for you could never recapture the past, she reflected sadly.

Now she'd stay for as long as Paige needed her, and afterwards she'd return to the Gold Coast where, thanks to Yanis's generosity, she owned her own apartment and a successful beauty therapy clinic, ensuring not only financial independence, but a safety net that would enable her to sever the one remaining link to the Kostakidas family.

'No attempt at polite conversation, Leanne?'

His voice held musing humour, and she cast him a pensive glance.

'Your success in the business arena is well-chronicled in the financial reviews.' She kept her eyes steady, and she even managed a faint smile. 'Likewise, your social activities are reported in the tabloid Press.' She paused, then allowed her gaze to rove carefully over his superb frame. 'You're obviously in good health...' She trailed off, and effected a slight shrug. 'I'm sure we can spare each other a rundown of our respective love lives.'

For a brief milli-second his eyes resembled dark ice, then soft, husky laughter emerged from his throat, and unless she was mistaken there was a degree of brooding respect evident in the glance he spared her.

'You've grown up,' he drawled lazily, and pain momentarily clouded her eyes.

'At twenty-five, one would hope so,' she responded sweetly.

'I promised Paige I'd take you straight to the hospital,' Dimitri said minutes later as he eased the car off the freeway.

A chill fear clutched her heart, and she searched his chiselled features for a hint of reassurance, and found none. It was two months since she'd seen her mother, and she agonised that she hadn't detected even a glimmer of concern in Paige's voice, a slight hesitancy—anything that might have betrayed a glimpse of anxiety relevant to a worrying health problem.

How could such a thing happen? she raged silently. Paige ate all the right foods, exercised and played tennis, never smoked, and drank minimally. *Why*?

Ten minutes later the Jaguar swung through open wrought-iron gates and traversed a wide, pebbled driveway to park at the rear of one of Melbourne's most exclusive private hospitals.

As they passed through Reception the nurse spared Dimitri a smile tinged with a degree of wistful envy, whereas the sister in charge had no such qualms.

'Mrs Kostakidas is resting quite comfortably.' Her eyes held liquid warmth and a silent invitation, should the man at Leanne's side choose to give the merest indication of interest.

Leanne watched with detached resignation, and wondered whether her exalted stepbrother would choose to make another conquest. In his late thirties, he was an intensely sensual man whose power, wealth and sheer physicality drew women like bees to a honeypot. Yet he had a select coterie of women friends with whom he chose to dine and indulge in social proclivities. Inevitably, there were some he surely bedded, but not, she suspected, indiscriminately. A newsprint photo taken at a recent glitzy function came vividly to mind; it had named his female companion as Shanna Delahunty, only daughter of Reginald Delahunty, the insurance magnate.

'Paige's suite is to the right.'

The quietly spoken words served as a timely warning, for they gave Leanne the few essential seconds necessary to seek control before she walked into the luxurious suite.

Despite having been given the grim medical facts, Leanne found it impossible to relate the gaunt, pale-featured woman lying propped against a nest of pillows with her mother.

It wasn't easy to smile, and it took a tremendous strength of will to keep the tears at bay as she crossed to the bed and carefully embraced the slight figure. Paige's bones appeared fragile, and her skin felt like fine tissue paper. It was if the essence of her mother had gone, and Leanne wanted to scream out against the unkind hand of fate.

'Hello, darling.' The words were softly spoken, the smile truly beautiful, as if the flickering flame deep within had gained a small measure of renewed life. A hand lifted, and faintly trembling fingers brushed the length of Leanne's cheek. 'I'm so glad you're here.'

The desire to weep was almost irrepressible, and Leanne gave a slight start as Dimitri curved an arm round her shoulders. His silent strength acted as a protective cloak, and she stood perfectly still, her features carefully schooled as Paige feasted her eyes lovingly on her daughter's diminutive frame before shifting to the man at her side.

'Thank you.' The words were a soft whisper, and Dimitri's eyes were dark, liquid with affection, yet when they slid towards Leanne they became vaguely smoky in silent warning, and she stiffened fractionally as his fingers shifted and began a subtle massage of the fine bones at the edge of her shoulder.

'We'll leave you to rest,' he said as he leant forward to brush Paige's cheek with his lips. 'Leanne will call in after lunch, and we'll both visit this evening.'

'Yes.'

Paige's voice was barely audible, and Leanne managed to contain her tears until they were in the corridor, then they spilled over and began trickling in twin rivulets down each cheek.

The corridor seemed longer than she remembered, and by the time she slid into the passenger seat she was an emotional wreck.

'Why didn't I know she was ill?' Leanne demanded with a mixture of impotent rage and deep anguish, then, as a thought occurred to her, she turned towards the man who had just slid in behind the wheel. 'Why didn't *you* tell me?'

'Simply because I didn't know,' Dimitri assured her hardly. 'Paige and I maintain weekly telephone contact, and I dine at the house every few weeks.'

In between business trips that took him from one Australian state capital to another, and numerous countries around the world, his base was a spacious penthouse suite atop a stylish apartment block barely two kilometres distant from his late father's Toorak mansion.

'Paige showed no signs of illness? Nothing?' Leanne queried with disbelief.

'I last saw her five weeks ago, and, although pale, she assured me she was recuperating well from a virulent flu virus.' His eyes were dark, his expression reflective. 'I left the next day for a series of meetings in the States, then Paris, Rome, followed by a stop-over in Perth. A fax from Paige's medical adviser was waiting for me at the hotel,' he relayed bleakly. 'I rang you as soon as I had all the facts.'

'She must have suspected something, surely?' Leanne agonised huskily.

'The medical professionals informed me she's been aware of the severity of her condition for several months. It was her express wish to keep it private until such time as she required hospitalisation.'

Her throat felt painfully constricted, and she was barely managing to keep the tears at bay. Dammit, where was the slim pack of tissues she always carried? Moisture spilled over and ran down her cheeks, and her fingers shook as she brushed the tears away.

She heard his unintelligible oath, then a soft white square was pushed into her hand and he pulled her into the protective curve of his shoulder.

Her initial instinct was to move away, but she lacked sufficient strength to break free. Tears streamed silently down her cheeks and dampened his shirt, and she was vaguely aware of his fingers slipping beneath the weight of her hair to trace a soothing pattern across a collection of fragile bones.

She had no idea how long she remained there before she regained a measure of control. Only minutes, surely, she agonised despairingly

'I'm sorry,' she proffered in a slightly muffled voice as she attempted to pull free.

'For what, Leanne?' he drawled in cynical query. 'Dropping your guard long enough to accept my compassion?'

'I didn't——'

'Want to display any emotion in my presence?'

'No,' she retaliated bleakly, unwilling to show so much as a chink in her armour. She sat still and stared sightlessly out of the window, remembering all too vividly the numerous occasions when she'd deliberately sought his attention. Attention he'd affectionately fielded without hurting her vulnerable feelings, until the fateful night of her twenty-first birthday.

Leanne closed her eyes in an attempt to shut out a memory that was hauntingly clear in every detail.

Paige had provided a wonderful party with many invited friends, and Leanne had been so happy. No guest had been more important to her than Dimitri, and the secret wish she'd nursed that at last he would recognise her as a woman. Flushed with a dangerous sense of exhilaration, she'd flirted a little with every male friend, and enjoyed one glass too many of vintage champagne. At the end of the

evening, when everyone had left and Paige had retired upstairs to bed, she'd reactivated the stereo
system, selected a tape and teasingly begged Dimitri
to share a dance.

Emboldened, she'd pressed her body a little too
close to his and lifted her arms to clasp them around
his nape. The top of her head had barely reached
his chin, and she'd arched her neck, offered him a
bewitching smile and teased that he had yet to
bestow a birthday kiss.

It had begun as a teasing salutation, and had
rapidly transgressed to something so infinitely
sensual that she had simply discarded any inhibitions and given herself up to an exotic alchemy
without any clear thought as to where it might lead.

She'd had no idea of the passage of time until
she had been forcibly put at arm's length, and his
harsh words had sent her running upstairs to her
bedroom to weep until almost dawn.

The next day he'd flown to Sydney, and during
the ensuing weeks she had convinced Paige of the
necessity to exert a new-found independence away
from home, electing, despite Paige's protests, to
choose Queensland's Gold Coast as her base.

Paige had become a frequent visitor, and Leanne
had carefully arranged her weekends and holidays
in Melbourne to coincide with Dimitri's absence,
although it had been impossible to avoid him completely. If he was on the Coast, he made a point of
phoning and insisting on taking her out to dinner,
or to a show, or both... in the guise of dutiful,
stepbrotherly affection. His invitations had become
a challenge she coolly accepted, for she refused to

give him the satisfaction of knowing he still possessed the ability to ruffle her composure.

'Paige is a rare jewel who succeeded in capturing my father's heart, affording me unconditional affection without attempting to usurp Yanis's loyalty to his son.' Dimitri's voice intruded, and she turned her head to look at him. '*You*,' he added with quiet emphasis, 'were an added bonus.'

Latent anger rose to the surface and threatened to erupt in speech. 'You...' Words momentarily failed her. 'Bastard,' she finally flung in whispered anguish. It was the wrong appellation, and, worse, an unforgivable insult. But at that precise moment she didn't care.

The silence in the car was deafening, and she could sense his palpable anger. For a second she closed her eyes against the harshness of his features, then slowly opened them again.

Dimitri activated the ignition, then reversed out of the parking bay, and the crunch of tyres sounded abnormally loud as he eased the car towards the designated exit.

The exclusive suburb of Toorak hosted numerous homes belonging to the rich and famous, and the elegant residence that Yanis had built was no exception, she decided as Dimitri brought the Jaguar to a halt before a set of impressive wrought-iron gates, then activated the remote-control modem to open them.

The car swept down a wide, palm-lined driveway and drew to a halt beneath the *porte cochère* of a magnificent Mediterranean-style mansion whose white-rendered exterior and terracotta-tiled roof conjured up images of the hillside vineyard estates of the Côte d'Azur.

A grandly proportioned home, it contained over a hundred square feet of luxury living on two levels, with five bedrooms and six bathrooms in the main house, a guest cabana which included a lounge and bar, a free-form swimming-pool and a full-size tennis court.

Scrupulously maintained, its gracious formal rooms had been used to entertain Yanis's business associates, and family friends. A generous man, he'd lent his name to a few worthy charities, and a small fortune in much needed funds had been raised through a variety of functions held here over the years.

Leanne slid from the car, then followed Dimitri through double leadlight doors to the formal entrance hall—a stately marble-tiled room with a crystal chandelier and sweeping mahogany staircase.

Although it had been her home for the past ten years, Leanne never failed to experience a feeling of awe at the sheer magnificence of displayed wealth.

Cream marble-tiled floors graced the ground floor, and there was an abundance of expensive Chinese silk rugs woven in designs employing mushroom, pink, pale blue and green against a cream background. Expensive tapestries graced the pale cream silk-covered walls, and vied for supremacy with original works of art. Yanis had indulged Paige her love of Louis XVI furnishings, and much of the furniture had been imported from France and Italy.

Now a chill slowly traversed the length of Leanne's spine, and she had consciously to still the sudden shiver that threatened to shake her slender frame with the knowledge that, although Yanis had bequeathed this beautiful mansion to Paige for her exclusive use during her lifetime, upon her death it would inevitably revert to his son.

Which meant that within weeks Leanne would no longer be able to regard it as her home, for afterwards she knew she wouldn't be able to bear seeing Dimitri here with the woman he would inevitably choose to take as his wife.

It shouldn't be too difficult to reduce contact gradually to an occasional telephone call, a few brief, friendly written missives, followed by a card at Christmas.

'Leanne, it is so good to see you.'

A heavily accented voice broke into her reverie, and she turned at once to exchange a warm greeting with Eleni Takis—cook and housekeeper who, together with her husband George, took care of the house and grounds.

'Eleni.' There was evidence of barely contained tears, and a wealth of genuine affection.

'George will take up your luggage,' Eleni declared as she stood back. 'And lunch will be ready in thirty minutes.'

'You shouldn't have gone to any trouble,' Leanne protested, knowing she'd have difficulty in consuming more than a few mouthfuls of anything.

'Nonsense,' Eleni admonished, and her appraisal of Leanne's slender frame became faintly critical. 'You have lost weight. In one so small, that is not good.'

'If I ate even a half of what you served me, I'd
go back to the Coast half a stone heavier and one
dress size larger.'

Eleni looked slightly perplexed. 'But this time you
stay. Yes?'

'Any messages, Eleni?' Dimitri drawled, and
Leanne intercepted an unspoken warning in his
tone.

'Your secretary rang. She is sending you faxes.'

Leanne shot him a quick, enquiring glance as
Eleni departed, and met his dark, discerning gaze.

'Paige requested I take up temporary residence,
as she didn't want you to be in the house on your
own.'

Her stomach churned at the thought of having
to live, even for a short time, in such close proximity to a man with whom she felt the antithesis of
comfortable.

She drew a deep breath, then exhaled it slowly
as she sought to keep her voice light. 'I fail to see
why, when I've lived alone for the past five years.
Besides, Eleni and George live above the garages.'

His eyes narrowed fractionally. 'Go upstairs and
unpack. We'll talk over lunch.'

About *what*, for heaven's sake?

Her bedroom was spacious, airy, and had a
splendid view of the pool and gardens. The muted
colour scheme was restful, the furniture the epit-
ome of elegance with its imported silk upholstery,
and the adjoining *en-suite* bathroom was a feminine
delight in the palest pink travertine marble with
crystal and gold fittings.

Without further thought, she discarded her
clothes and stepped into the shower cubicle,

emerging minutes later to select elegant trousers and a top in pale sage-green cotton, then, dressed, she tended to her hair and make-up.

It was almost one when she entered the kitchen, and Eleni cast her a warm smile.

'You are just in time. Everything is ready, except for the bread.'

'I'll take it through,' Leanne offered promptly as she crossed to the oven. 'Anything else?'

'Just the lamb. The salads are on the table.'

It looked like a feast fit for a king, and far more than two people could possibly eat. There was chilled wine resting in a silver bucket, two exquisite crystal flutes, silver cutlery and the finest bone china.

Eleni took extreme pride in the house, preparing food and presenting a fine table. Paige was a gracious employer who attested that material possessions were useless if they reposed in cupboards and cabinets merely for visual display.

Dimitri entered the room within minutes, smiled indulgently at Eleni's fussing, then took a seat opposite Leanne as the older woman retreated to the kitchen.

'Wine?'

'No—thank you,' Leanne refused with the utmost politeness.

'The keys to Paige's Mercedes are in the top drawer of the cabinet in the foyer,' he informed her as he filled his glass.

'Thank you.'

His eyes narrowed slightly. 'You're hardly a guest, Leanne. The car, or anything else you need, is at your disposal.'

She was about to utter thanks for the third time, then opted against it, choosing instead to attempt to do justice to the excellent Greek salad Eleni had prepared.

Perhaps if she concentrated on food, this crazy ambivalence would disappear. It was quite mad, but she felt as if she was teetering on the edge of a precipice, and nothing could shake her acute feeling of apprehension.

Overwrought, overtired and consumed with anxiety—all of which was quite logical in light of her mother's state of health, she qualified as she speared a segment of feta cheese and attacked an olive.

The delicately roasted lamb fared little better, and she forked a few mouthfuls then pushed the remaining meat and accompanying vegetables round her plate before discarding it completely.

'Not hungry?'

'Eleni will disapprove,' she offered ruefully.

Dimitri pushed his napkin on to the table and leaned back in his chair. 'Relax, Leanne.' His eyes were dark, enigmatic, yet there was a tinge of mockery evident.

'What topic would you suggest we politely pursue? The state of the nation, the weather? Your latest property acquisition?'

'Paige,' he insisted quietly. 'Her wishes, and what we intend to do about them.'

Dear lord, he didn't pull any punches—just aimed straight for the jugular. 'There isn't a thing I wouldn't do to please her,' she assured him without hesitation.

'Without exception?'

She didn't need to think. 'Of course.'

Dimitri regarded her in silence for several long seconds, his gaze infinitely speculative beneath faintly hooded lids. 'Even assuming the pretence of a romantic alliance with me?'

# CHAPTER TWO

FOR an instant Leanne was robbed of the power of speech, then the colour drained from her face, leaving it pale.

'I don't find that suggestion very amusing,' she said at last.

Dimitri's eyes never left hers, their dark depths faintly brooding, and she had the instinctive feeling that he had already weighed all the angles and was intent on playing a manipulative game.

'I'm perfectly serious.'

The breath seemed suddenly locked in her throat, and she swallowed compulsively in the need to regain her voice. '*Why*?'

'Paige is concerned for your future,' he offered, noting the faint wariness which was apparent.

Logic vied with rationale, then mingled with a degree of angry resentment. 'I've lived an independent life for more than four years. My future is secure, and afterwards...' She trailed to a halt, then forced herself to continue. 'I'll simply return to the Coast.'

'Where you'll become an easy prey for fortune hunters,' Dimitri accorded indolently.

'Don't be ridiculous,' she denied at once. 'This house, everything, will revert to you.'

'The house, yes. However, there are annuities you will inherit from a number of Kostakidas-affiliated corporations. There's also an apartment in Athens, a home in Switzerland, and a villa in France. Jewellery, stocks, shares. Gifts Yanis bestowed on Paige during his lifetime. All of which will become yours.' He paused slightly, watching her expressive features carefully as the effect of his words sank in. 'Added together, their worth totals several million.'

It was almost impossible to comprehend, for, although she'd known her late stepfather's personal wealth had been measured in millions, she'd had no idea of its extent. It wasn't something she or Paige had ever discussed.

'Yanis gifted me the Gold Coast apartment, and the beauty clinic,' she said at once, perturbed beyond rational thought. 'I don't want or need anything else.'

'Those weren't my father's wishes. Nor,' he added quietly, 'are they mine.'

'I'll contest Paige's will in your favour,' she declared vehemently.

'Impossible. That eventuality has already been foreseen and legally negated.'

'It can all accumulate and be held in trust.'

His smile held a tinge of cynicism. 'Idealistic, Leanne, but scarcely practical.' He regarded her carefully. 'Paige and Yanis nurtured the hope that we might eventually become romantically attached, and it would give Paige peace of mind to believe that their fondest wish has eventuated. As it is, she's consumed with anxiety over the men who will beat a path to your door, professing undying love in order to enjoy a free meal-ticket for life.'

Her eyes widened, their blue depths darkening measurably as she wrestled with a desire to please her mother and the fear that she'd never emerge from such subterfuge unscathed.

'I'm no longer fifteen, and I do possess a degree of common sense. I don't think I need a protector.' Not you, she added silently. Dear lord, never you.

'We're discussing Paige,' he reminded her, with velvet softness.

'I don't want to deceive her,' she offered slowly.

'Yet you love her very much,' he pursued, and she shivered inwardly. 'Enough to enter into a pretence that will make her happy, and ensure her peace of mind?'

'What do you want, Dimitri? My unequivocal agreement to enact a lie?'

His eyes hardened fractionally, and his mouth curved to form a wry smile. 'Will it prove so difficult given the limited time-span?'

She closed her eyes, then slowly opened them. 'You know how to twist the knife, don't you?' she countered with a trace of bitterness.

His gaze didn't falter as he reached for his glass. 'Will you have some fruit, or would you prefer coffee?'

How could he sit there and switch so calmly from something of such personal magnitude to a mundane selection over lunch? Even as she contemplated the silent query, the answer followed. Dimitri was an astute businessman, well-versed in the cut and thrust utilised by power-brokers all over the world. He clinched deals worth millions, dealt with hardliners in the financial arena, and undoubtedly annihilated lesser minions on a day-to-day basis. Against such a formidable force, what chance did she have?

'Chilled water,' Leanne indicated, viewing him with circumspection as he took the carafe and re-filled her glass.

'Tell me about the beauty clinic,' he encouraged with apparent interest, and she suffered his appraisal with unblinking solemnity, all too aware of what he saw, for it was an image she knew in detail.

Pale, fine-textured skin, a delicate bone-structure, a wide, generous mouth framing even white teeth, a nondescript nose, wide-spaced deep blue eyes, and shoulder-length natural ash-blonde hair.

'It's successful,' she dismissed with a negligible shrug. 'Women like to look good, and most are prepared to spend money in the name of beauty.'

'Merely for self-gratification?'

'Of course. And pleasing a man.' She could recall instantly the features of several socialites who devoted much of their morning hours on a regular basis to one beauty treatment or another. Aromatherapy, a facial, brow- and lash-tinting, massage, waxing, manicure and pedicure, to mention a few. When that failed to revive the passage of nature satisfactorily, they resorted to the skill of cosmetic surgery. Chasing elusive beauty and maintaining it was an expensive pastime, and Leanne was a skilled beautician, dedicated to her craft.

Dimitri reached forward and extracted a peach from the fruit bowl which he proceeded to peel and stone before offering her a segment. 'No?'

The need to be free of his disturbing presence was overwhelming, and she excused herself from the table.

'I'll be caught up in the city for most of the afternoon,' he revealed as she got to her feet. 'Be ready at six. We'll visit Paige, then go on somewhere for dinner.'

Leanne was unable to resist the query. 'Won't Shanna object?'

His gaze was remarkably level. 'Shanna has nothing to do with my taking you to dinner.'

'You could always drop me home, then meet her later.'

'This conversation is going nowhere, Leanne,' Dimitri drawled hatefully.

'In that case, I'll give Eleni a hand clearing the table, unpack, then visit Paige,' she returned with the utmost politeness, and his husky laughter made her want to lash out in anger. Except that such an action would invoke his temper, and she'd already insulted him. To do so again on the same day would be the height of folly.

It was almost two-thirty when Leanne entered her mother's suite and her heart contracted as Paige complimented gently, 'Darling, you look so well.'

What could she say in return? It was difficult, much more difficult than she'd envisaged, and she simply pulled a chair close to the bed and sat holding Paige's hand.

'Dimitri is very fond of you,' Paige offered huskily. Perhaps medication had eased her pain, for she didn't seem to be under quite so much strain. 'Anything you need, he'll advise and guide you. He's given me his word.'

Leanne wanted to cry, and her vision began to shimmer with the onset of tears. Oh, dear God, she agonised, *help* me.

'Yanis loved you so much, almost as much as I do. He adored having you as his daughter.'

'He was a wonderful man.'

'Yes,' Paige agreed simply. 'As is his son.'

*No.* The single negation was a silent scream which seemed to reverberate inside her brain. Don't do this to me. She longed to say that Dimitri had been the embodiment of her fantasy hero, as seen through the eyes of a teenage child. Her problem was in discovering he had feet of clay.

'Everything I have will be yours. Property, jewellery,' Paige continued after a long pause. 'It amounts to a very sizeable inheritance, darling.'

Leanne felt her chest tighten with emotional pain, and her throat began to constrict as she attempted to gain some control over her turbulent emotions. 'I don't think I want to talk about it. It hurts too much,' she whispered.

'But I'm not afraid. Really,' Paige assured her gently, her eyes a soft blue without any hint of fear. 'My beloved Yanis will be there. And I don't want you to be sad.' Her eyes misted, and her lips curved into a soft, tremulous smile. 'If I could have one wish, it would be to see you happily settled with a man who will love and care for you. Marriage,' she continued quietly, and her fingers stroked Leanne's hand with an absent, abstracted movement. 'And children.'

Grandchildren you'll never have the pleasure of seeing, Leanne said silently. It wasn't fair. Paige would have made a wonderful grandmother.

Leanne was aware that any moment now she'd burst into tears. 'I am happy,' she said quickly. Too quickly. Paige's illness and level of medication hadn't diminished her perceptiveness in any way.

'Are you, darling?'

Unable to find any adequate words that wouldn't sound defensive, Leanne offered a shaky smile and launched into an amusing anecdote about something that had happened at the clinic. Then she left Paige to rest for an hour, and returned briefly with some of her mother's favourite roses as well as some fresh fruit in the hope of tempting her appetite.

It was almost five when she arrived home, and after alerting Eleni that she was back she moved swiftly upstairs, shed her clothes, donned a swimsuit and then made her way down to the pool.

Perhaps if she set herself a rigorous number of lengths she would be able to dispel the haunting image of her mother's pale features and the infinite sadness beneath her gentle smile.

It didn't work; nor did attempting to focus her thoughts elsewhere. Consequently she was feeling infinitely fragile when she descended the stairs a few minutes before six.

Dimitri was in the lounge, a tall glass of chilled water in one hand, and his dark eyes speared hers as she entered the room.

'A cool drink?' He indicated a crystal water-pitcher liberally filled with ice-cubes and decorated with sliced lemon and sprigs of mint.

'Please.'

He took a glass and filled it, then handed it to her, his expression musingly speculative as she carefully avoided touching his fingers.

He looked what he was: a well-educated man, well-versed in the analysis of humankind and aware of the limits of his control. It was a mantle he wore with uncontrived ease, and she felt a thousand light-years removed from his particular brand of sophistication. Which was crazy, especially as she'd been privy to an elevated lifestyle during the past ten years, and could converse knowledgeably on a variety of subjects.

It was Dimitri himself who unsettled her, for his degree of sensuality was a heady, potent entity she constantly fought against, aware that if she were ever to lose her inner battle the results would be totally cataclysmic.

He subjected her to an thorough appraisal, then let his gaze rest thoughtfully on the contoured pink fullness of her mouth.

'When you've finished, we'll leave.'

In the car he slotted a cassette into the stereo system and concentrated on negotiating the early evening traffic. Leanne conjured up a number of conversational subjects to pursue, only to discard each one, and she sat quietly as the sleek, powerful vehicle ate up the distance.

Paige had already eaten, and she brightened as Leanne preceded Dimitri into the room.

'You look lovely, darling,' Paige complimented her gently. 'That shade of blue does wonderful things for your eyes.' Her gaze shifted to the man at her daughter's side. 'Don't you think so?'

'Stunning,' Dimnitri agreed as he crossed to the bed and brushed his lips against Paige's temple. 'How are you feeling?'

There was such a depth of affectionate concern in his voice that Leanne's body quivered slightly, and she was conscious that her voice sounded a little too bright as she greeted her mother, then sank into a chair which Dimitri had pulled close to the bed.

He merely stood close behind her. Much too close. She was conscious of him with every muscle in her body, every nerve-end, and it was all she could do not to visibly jump when his hand came to rest on her shoulder.

Paige noticed the implied intimacy, and smiled. 'Where are you going for dinner?'

He named a restaurant that was not only ruinously expensive, but well-known for its fine cuisine.

Paige's eyes took on a luminous sheen. 'Is it a celebration of some kind?'

'Not quite,' Dimitri drawled, and Leanne felt his fingers tighten slightly over the fine bones at the edge of her collarbone. 'I'm hopeful that the combination of an excellent vintage wine and superb food will persuade Leanne to accept my proposal.'

The air became trapped in her lungs, impeding her breathing, and she could have sworn that the beat of her heart stopped before it went racing into overdrive. Words froze in her throat as he curved his free hand round the sensitive arch of her nape.

You bastard, she longed to cry out at him. An angry denial rushed to her lips, then died as she caught sight of her mother's expression.

Joy, pure joyous relief intermingled with a happiness so vivid it lit her features and turned them into something so incredibly beautiful that it brought any verbal negation that Leanne might have uttered to a halt.

As Dimitri had known it would. Just as he knew she wouldn't have the heart to do anything other than go to her mother's outstretched arms and accept the loving embrace, share her tears, then watch with a sense of stunned disbelief as Dimitri extracted a slim pouch and slid a large, pear-shaped diamond on to the appropriate finger of her left hand.

'You didn't breathe a word this afternoon,' Paige said huskily.

'Quite simply because I had no idea of Dimitri's intention,' Leanne responded with a calm she was far from feeling. The ring felt heavy, and she barely resisted the temptation to tear it from her finger.

'Yanis would have been so happy. As I am.' Her mother's words were faintly breathy, emotion-filled, and somehow Leanne managed a suitable response.

Presenting the façade of a newly engaged fiancée took all her acting ability, and it was a minor miracle that she managed to emerge almost forty minutes later from Paige's suite without having resorted to histrionics.

Leanne was silent all the way to the car, and she didn't utter a word as he reversed out of the car park and eased the vehicle on to the main thoroughfare, then her tightly controlled anger erupted in a heated flow of words designed to blister his hateful hide.

'How *dare* you?'

'Pre-empt your decision? It was a foregone conclusion, knowing the depth of your love for Paige.'

'That doesn't give you the right——'

'I care for Paige very much. Enough to give her pleasure for what limited time she has left. Surely

we can put aside our own differences long enough
to perpetuate an illusion?'

'That isn't the point!'

'What is the point, Leanne? Your resentment,
your anger? Surely the focus should be Paige
herself?'

She was too incensed to accede to his dictum,
and she flung furiously, 'I don't want to have dinner
with you.'

'I've made a reservation, and we both need to
eat. Why not share a meal together?'

'Because I'm so mad, I'll probably pick up the
soup plate and tip the contents over your head!'

'I shall consider myself forewarned.'

'Or the salad,' she muttered direly as he pulled
into a car park adjacent to one of Toorak's well-
known restaurants.

The ring was an alien manacle, and she slid it
off, ready to hand it to him the instant he cut the
ignition.

'Leave it on,' Dimitri ordered as she thrust it at
him.

'*Why*?'

'It stays on, Leanne.'

'Don't be ridiculous. It's far too valuable, and
too——' She had been going to say beautiful, because the stone in its setting was exquisite.
'Everyone will notice.'

'Precisely,' he conceded with dry cynicism, and
her eyes widened in shocked disbelief.

'You mean to go public with this?'

'Paige has a phone beside her bed,' he enlightened her. 'Her weakened state doesn't prevent
her from making calls.' He viewed Leanne's

dawning horror with musing cynicism. 'It will take only one friend to spread the news and within a matter of days it will have circulated among the social set.'

'You really mean to go through with this pretence *openly*?'

'Of course. It has to be seen to succeed.'

'Define *succeed*, Dimitri,' she insisted, aware that the whole thing was rapidly getting out of hand. Like a snowball accumulating in size as it gained momentum and assumed the very real threat of becoming an avalanche.

'A formal announcement in the Press tomorrow.'

'You mean you've actually gone that far?' Her voice rose. 'You damned egotistical, proprietorial *bastard*!'

'Watch your unwary tongue,' he warned silkily.

'Forgive me,' Leanne flung with unaccustomed sarcasm. 'I wasn't aware I shouldn't put up any resistance to a scheme I'm not happy with—*or*,' she added vengefully, 'dare to upbraid you for taking charge without my sanction.'

'Come and eat.'

'I don't want to eat, and I especially don't want to eat with you.'

'Nevertheless, you will.'

'I refuse to sit at the same table and *pretend*. The food would choke me.'

'Aren't you being overly dramatic?'

'Don't patronise me, Dimitri,' she said darkly.

'You used to be such an obedient child,' he relayed musingly.

'What would you know?' she flung. 'You were rarely there.'

'Did you want me to be?'

That was too close to the bone for comfort, and her eyes were startlingly clear in the subdued overhead lighting. 'You were thirteen years my senior, more sophisticated, and a thousand light-years ahead of me. Besides, a teenage stepsister would have cramped your style.'

'Yet there were occasions when I partnered you to several functions Paige and Yanis chose to attend,' he alluded with deceptive mildness.

She remembered them well, each one etched permanently in her brain. Now she felt resentful that he'd adroitly defused the immediate situation by orchestrating a subtle shift from her heated anger.

'This restaurant is one of your favourite haunts,' she reminded him stoically, then added the rider, 'What if Shanna is there?'

'We're all civilised adults,' Dimitri returned smoothly.

'This—this *farce*,' she said in a tight voice, 'is solely for Paige's benefit. If you dare to act out the part of adoring fiancé anywhere else but at the hospital——'

'Difficult to confine our actions, when it will be news in a variety of papers tomorrow,' he drawled.

'I'll never forgive you,' she vowed with renewed vehemence.

'Our first public appearance *à deux* is inevitable,' he told her drily. 'Besides, what excuse will you give Paige for a change in plan? That we couldn't wait to be alone together?'

She barely restrained herself from hitting out at him, and angry resolve prompted her to reach for the door-catch. 'Do you always use such devious tactics in a bid to achieve your objective?'

She didn't wait to hear his answer, and slid out from the passenger seat, choosing to walk on ahead of him. A fruitless exercise, for she'd scarcely taken half a dozen steps before he reached her side.

The restaurant was one she'd frequented occasionally with Paige, and its elegant décor projected an ambience that was frequently sought by the city's upper social echelons. Which was probably why Dimitri had selected it, she decided darkly as the *maître d'* proffered an effusive greeting before leading them to a prominent table reserved, Leanne instantly surmised, for the chosen, favoured few.

Dimitri ordered champagne, Dom Pérignon, and at Leanne's faintly raised eyebrow he merely smiled and asked the wine steward to fill her glass.

The lighting was subdued and attuned to intimate dining, but she felt as if she and Dimitri were the room's central focus. The diamond on her finger flashed with a fiery brilliance from myriad facets, and she pushed her hand out of sight on her lap, supremely conscious of its significance.

The restaurant catered for leisurely dining, and she selected the soup *de jour*, followed it with a prawn starter, refused a main course, passed on dessert and opted against the cheeseboard. The serving of each course seemed to take an age, and by the time coffee was brought to the table she was seething with impatience to leave.

To attempt to maintain a polite façade almost killed her, yet inherent good manners wouldn't permit a public display of anger.

And he knew, damn him, for he kept up a *divertissement* that was masterly, with an ease she could only admire but inwardly seethe at as he tempted her to try a morsel from his fork and refilled her flute with champagne.

The coffee was strong and aromatic, and she sipped it abstractedly, wishing only for the evening to conclude. She was tired, emotionally exhausted, and suffering the onset of a headache.

A predominate waft—*wave*, Leanne corrected wryly—of exotic perfume assailed her nostrils, and was immediately followed by the tinkling sound of a feminine voice.

'Dimitri, what *are* you doing here? I understood you weren't due back from Perth until next week.'

'Shanna.' Dimitri's greeting was warm, but not effusive.

Courtesy ensured an acknowledgement of his companion. 'Leanne.' The brunette proffered a brilliant smile. 'How are you? Are you down on holiday from the Coast?'

'Not exactly,' Leanne managed in polite response.

'Is this a family tête-à-tête? Or may I join you?'

'Leanne and I were just about to leave,' Dimitri imparted smoothly.

'Surely you could stay,' Shanna suggested persuasively. 'There's a group of us, just friends—we'd love you to join us.'

'Thank you—but not tonight.'

The *maître d'* hovered discreetly as Dimitri signed the credit slip, then moved unobtrusively out of sight.

Shanna's eyes moved to the empty champagne bottle. 'Celebrating a recent success, darling?'

'You could say that,' he responded, shooting Leanne a musing smile. 'Personal, not business.'

'You've aroused my curiosity. Is it confidential?'

'I've persuaded Leanne to marry me.'

Shanna's smile slipped for the space of a second, and Leanne could only commend her superb control, for, although the brunette's features portrayed surprised pleasure, her eyes held a darkness that contained bitter disappointment.

'You must tell me how you managed to convince Dimitri to make a commitment,' she said to Leanne.

A degree of humour was the only way, and Leanne tempered her reply with a musing smile. 'He simply slid a ring on my finger.'

Dimitri stood and held out his hand to Leanne. 'You'll excuse us, Shanna?'

Leanne had no recourse but to follow his lead, and she felt a certain sympathy for the attractive model. Rejection hurt like hell. Hadn't she suffered at Dimitri's hands more than four years ago? As she would again, a tiny voice taunted. How long after Paige's passing would he retract the engagement—a few days, a week?

'You've burned your bridges,' Leanne said as the Jaguar picked up a cruising speed, and she incurred Dimitri's dark glance.

'There were no bridges to burn,' he replied with deliberate mockery.

'She was your——' She couldn't say it.

'Lover?' he prompted.

'Yes!'

'We visited the opera on a few occasions, took in the theatre, and attended several parties and functions.'

'I don't care what you did together.'

'No?'

'You could have bedded a hundred women, for all I care.'

'I'm very particular as to who shares my bed.'

She was unable to resist the taunt, 'I'm not the one you should be attempting to reassure.'

He didn't answer, and there was something heady about having the last word. It lifted her spirits, and prompted an appraisal of her surroundings.

A dark indigo sky with a sprinkling of stars was at variance with the light summer shower that was as sudden as it was fleeting, necessitating only a few swishing turns of the wiper blades. Bright neon street-lights provided intermittent illumination, and cast long, deepening shadows from numerous trees standing guard on both sides of the suburban road.

There was the slight but distinctive sound of tyre-treads traversing wet bitumen, then the car slowed and paused as Dimitri activated the remote-control module that electronically opened the gates.

Within minutes another button released the garage doors, and the Jaguar slid to a halt between Paige's Mercedes and a luxurious four-wheel drive.

Once inside, Leanne made her way towards the stairs.

'Will you join me in a nightcap?'

'No,' she declared evenly. 'I'm going to bed. I'm tired and I have a headache.'

'I'm disappointed,' he said with studied indolence. 'I imagined the instant we reached the house you'd fly at me in a rage.'

'I want to,' Leanne assured him tightly. 'Badly. Unfortunately I don't possess the energy to launch an attack.'

A slight smile curved his mouth, and there was a gleam apparent in his dark gaze. 'In that case, I'll see you at breakfast.'

The words she wanted to hurl at him remained unsaid, and she ascended the stairs to her room where she undressed and removed her make-up before slipping between the cool, freshly laundered sheets.

She should have fallen asleep the instant her head touched the pillow. Instead, her mind was filled with a host of images, not the least being Paige herself, and the inimicable man who had temporarily taken charge of her life.

She had little comprehension of how long she lay staring at the darkened ceiling as the painful throbbing in her head deepened until she began to feel physically ill. Her body broke out in a sweat, then began to cool, and she knew any attempt at sleep without some form of medication would be useless.

Slipping out of bed, she crossed to the *en-suite* bathroom and rummaged through the bathroom cabinet for some pain-killers, only to curse softly on discovering that there were none.

She lifted a hand and pressed it wearily against her temple. Maybe there was something in the cabinet in Paige's suite. If not, she'd have to venture downstairs.

It took only a few minutes to discover that there was nothing stronger available than paracetamol, and she closed her eyes momentarily, then opened them again in restrained exasperation. Maybe if she took two now it would take the edge off the pain sufficiently so that she could sleep.

There was a tumbler on the marble-topped vanity unit, and she half filled it with water only to have it slip through her fingers and crash down into the marbled basin.

'Dear God,' she whispered shakily at the explosive sound of shattering glass. It was enough to wake the dead. The last thing she needed was to have to face Dimitri at this hour of the night.

Yet he appeared in the doorway within seconds, his features dark and forbidding.

She could visualise the scene through his eyes. A slight figure attired in a long cotton nightshirt, dishevelled hair, and pale features overshadowed by large eyes darkened with pain.

'I'm sorry the noise woke you.' Her eyes felt heavy and impossibly bruised. She lifted a hand, then let it fall helplessly down to her side. 'I'll pick up the glass.'

'Leave it,' Dimitri instructed brusquely. 'Eleni can attend to it in the morning.' His eyes swept to the foil strip of tablets, then to her pale features. 'Headache worse?'

'Yes.' She winced painfully, closing her eyes against his forceful image and the degree of sexual magnetism he exuded. The white towelling robe he'd hastily donned merely enhanced his height and breadth, and she was in no fit state to arm a mental defence against him. 'I'll just take these, then go back to bed.'

Without a word he leaned forward, extracted another tumbler, half filled it with water, then placed it in her hand.

When she'd swallowed the tablets, she replaced the tumbler, then made to move past him only to give a gasp of surprise as he leaned forward and lifted her into his arms.

'Put me down.' The protest was adamant, for the shift in gravity had caused her nightshirt to ride dangerously up her thighs, and she was acutely conscious of a loss of modesty.

His strength was palpable, and this close she could smell the faint muskiness of his skin mingling with a trace of aftershave. She had only to turn her head fractionally for her lips to come in contact with the edge of his neck.

'I can walk. There's nothing wrong with my legs.' Even a severe headache couldn't diminish the heightened degree of sensual awareness she felt at being held so close against him. 'Put me down!'

'Why so nervous?' Dimitri queried lazily as he gained the hallway and headed towards her suite.

'You're enjoying this, aren't you?' Leanne accused, choosing to emphasise her point by balling a fist and aiming it at his shoulder. A totally ineffectual gesture that reminded her of a butterfly senselessly batting its wings against a tiger.

'You possess an over-active imagination.'

He sounded amused, darn him, and she aimed a more forceful punch. 'Put me down, damn you!'

They reached her room, and he crossed to the bed and settled her carefully between the covers. 'I'll fetch the tablets in case you need them through the night.' Leanne closed her eyes against the sight of him, and prayed she might be asleep by the time he returned.

A hopeless appeal, for she was acutely aware of the moment he re-entered the room.

Her eyes flew open at the touch of his fingers as they brushed idly down her cheek.

'Sleep well,' he bade with teasing amusement, then he turned and left the room before she was able to summon a stinging response.

# CHAPTER THREE

LEANNE woke feeling refreshed and without any lingering trace of a headache. Quickly tossing aside the sheet, she crossed to the large expanse of panelled glass and drew back the drapes.

It was a beautiful day, the sun bright, the sky clear of any clouds. Without pausing for thought she caught up a swimsuit and made for the *en suite*, emerging five minutes later to pull on shorts and a T-shirt before making her way down to the kitchen.

'Morning, Eleni.' She greeted the older woman who was busily occupied scouring a skillet at the sink.

An affectionate smile creased Eleni's features as she dried her hands and turned to give Leanne her undivided attention. 'Ah, how is the headache this morning?'

'Gone, thank goodness,' Leanne said with relief, and, crossing to the large refrigerator, she extracted fresh orange juice and filled a glass, then sipped from it with undisguised appreciation.

'Dimitri has already left for the city.'

Thank heavens for small mercies, Leanne said silently. Facing Dimitri at the start of her day would have been too much.

'He intends calling into the hospital this morning,' Eleni continued, relaying the message she'd been requested to convey. 'And he'll be home at six, so you can both go and visit Paige together.'

Her dark eyes filled with expressive warmth. 'The news you are to marry gives me much joy.'

It was on the tip of Leanne's tongue to take Eleni into her confidence and reveal that the engagement was a sham conceived entirely for Paige's benefit. Except that something held her back, and she accepted the housekeeper's affectionate hug with equal warmth.

'Thanks, Eleni.' It was difficult to look suitably starry-eyed, but she managed a credible smile.

'What can I get you for breakfast? Eggs? French toast?'

Eleni adored making a fuss, and Leanne's smile widened as she wrinkled her nose in silent negation. 'We play this game every time I come home,' she responded musingly. 'A banana, toast and coffee will be fine, and I'll get it after I've had a swim.'

It was almost ten when she slid behind the wheel of the Mercedes and drove to the hospital. Frequent short visits would prove less tiring for Paige, and Leanne divided up the day accordingly.

If anything, her mother seemed a little brighter, and, although pale, her features no longer looked quite so drawn.

'Darling, let me have a look at your ring,' Paige requested within minutes of Leanne's entering the suite, and Leanne dutifully extended her hand. 'It's simply beautiful, and a perfect fit.'

She managed a suitable rejoinder, and endeavoured to display a degree of fascinated pleasure in the diamond's multi-faceted brilliance.

Paige's eyes assumed a faint, dreamy expression. 'I saw the announcement in this morning's papers.'

Leanne hadn't thought to look. She'd spent ages
in the pool, enjoyed a late breakfast, then rushed
upstairs to shower and change.

'A small, private ceremony held at home next
week,' her mother relayed wistfully. 'In the gardens.
Isn't that wonderful?'

'Yes, wonderful.' What else could she do but
agree?

'Have you decided what you'll choose to wear?'

'Not yet.' There was a rack of gowns in her
wardrobe, any one of which would be eminently
suitable for an informal engagement party.

'Dimitri has already conferred with my doctor,
and, with a nurse in attendance, there's no reason
why I can't be at the house for a few hours. A
wedding-gown is so special,' Paige enthused gently.
'You'll look stunning in white.'

Wedding. Who said anything about a *wedding*?
The feeling of panic momentarily robbed the breath
from Leanne's body. 'Paige——'

'I wish I was able to go shopping with you,' her
mother continued wistfully. 'There's that lovely
boutique in Toorak, and you must ring Vivienne.
She'll put everything aside and give you her undivided attention.'

A sense of disbelief washed over Leanne's body,
and she felt stunned ... but not for long. A slow-
burning anger ignited and began to flare, coursing
through her veins until she was consumed with it.

'Paige,' Leanne began, making every effort to
maintain control. 'Dimitri and I——'

'Have known each other for years. Ten in all.'
Beautiful blue eyes glowed with the immensity of
Paige's pleasure. 'This wedding will be so special.

I've longed for the day you get married, and I'm overjoyed that you're bringing the date forward for my benefit.' She lifted a hand and covered Leanne's fingers. 'I'm going to have Vivienne bring in some gowns so I can make a suitable selection for myself as mother of the bride.'

*Dear God.* What had begun as a harmless conspiracy was now raging out of control. The question was, *why?*

She had to remain calm. No matter how angry she felt, she couldn't allow Paige to suspect that things were not as they seemed.

'Has Dimitri been in to see you this morning?' she queried gently, and her mother gave a slight nod.

'Early, darling. On his way into the office.'

Dimitri was incapable of being manipulated, not even by the circumstances of Paige's illness. Which meant he had to be a willing participant.

It killed her to smile, but she managed a credible facsimile. 'I shall take him to task for breaking the news.' The chiding amusement in her voice masked the threat of intent. She planned to *slay* him. She also had to get out of Paige's suite before her animosity became visible.

'I'll leave you to rest for a while,' she said in a light voice. 'I have to ring Vivienne, and begin some serious shopping. I'll be back after lunch.' Leaning forward, she touched her lips against her mother's cheek, then swallowed quickly against the lump that rose in her throat as she glimpsed the faint misting of tears which was evident.

The moment she left the suite a cold, hard anger rose from within her, and by the time she reached

the car she was so maddened it was a minor miracle
that she reached the city without incident.

The Kostakidas corporation had offices on a high
floor in an ultra-modern steel and glass tower that
held the ultimate in executive furnishings.

It was years since Leanne had visited its revered
portals, and she moved with calculated calm towards Reception, unnerved by the stylishly attired
young woman whose hair, make-up and clothes
would have done credit to a model straight out of
*Vogue* magazine.

'Dimitri Kostakidas,' Leanne stated with quiet
authority.

'Mr Kostakidas is in conference,' the receptionist
relayed with polite regret. 'Do you have an
appointment?'

Leanne's expression was equally polite. 'Perhaps
you could inform Dimitri's secretary that his fiancée
is waiting to see him?' She even took the faint sting
from her words by proffering a slight smile. 'I'm
sure he won't object to the interruption.'

The girl's professionalism was superb. 'Of
course,' she acceded at once, and, picking up the
receiver from its console, she relayed the information, listened attentively, then replaced the receiver. 'Annita will be out in a minute to escort you
to Mr Kostakidas's private lounge.'

Almost immediately an immaculately attired
woman emerged into the foyer, her classical features expressing just the right degree of friendliness.

'Miss Foorde? How nice to meet you. May I offer
my congratulations?' Her smile appeared genuine,
and Leanne managed an appropriate response. 'If
you'd care to come with me?'

Dimitri's private lounge was sumptuous, with deep-seated armchairs in buttoned soft black leather, and strategically placed occasional tables. A double set of cabinets lined one wall and floor-to-ceiling glass provided a spectacular view of the city.

'Dimitri won't be long,' Annita informed her. 'Can I get you a drink? Coffee? Something cool? A light wine, perhaps?'

She'd like to pour boiling oil over his head, but that was purely wishful thinking! 'Iced water would be lovely.' At least it might cool her down, and she thanked her as the woman handed her a glass filled with ice-cubes and chilled water before taking her leave.

Five minutes passed, followed by another five, and Leanne began to ponder darkly whether Dimitri was genuinely unable to extricate himself or merely providing time for the dissipation of her anger.

Fat chance, she derided silently, unable to prevent the faint tensing of her body as the door opened and the object of her rage entered the room.

In a formal dark business suit he looked formidable. Invincible, indomitable, and infinitely dangerous to any unwary adversary.

'Leanne.' Dimitri's voice was deceptively bland. 'This is an unexpected pleasure.'

Her eyes flew to his, and their depths were alive with the fiery sparkle of restrained anger. An emotion which was so consuming, it obliterated any respect for caution.

'You know very well why I'm here,' she returned heatedly.

His dark, faintly amused gaze merely added ammunition, and she got to her feet, ready to launch into further battle.

'Shall we do lunch?' His voice was a calm drawl finely edged with humour, and her eyes resembled intense blue sapphires as they flashed wrathful fire.

'How can you stand there and calmly suggest *lunch*?' she flung with subdued anger.

One eyebrow rose slightly. 'Paige can surely be forgiven for displaying a degree of sentimentality. In the normal course of events a wedding follows the announcement of an engagement.'

'Precisely. Except the engagement isn't real, and there'll never be a wedding!' Leanne drew herself up to her full height and still felt diminished, for even though she was in four-inch heels he towered head and shoulders above her. 'You could easily have put a brake on her enthusiasm, offered a simple explanation without hurting her feelings. Why didn't you?'

Dimitri crossed to stand within touching distance, and his close proximity sent a shiver of acute sensation scudding down the length of her spine.

'Were you able to disenchant her?' he queried with dangerous silkiness.

'Don't insult my intelligence,' she flung with soft vehemence. She took a deep, calming breath, then launched into scathing attack. 'No one, not even Paige, could manoeuvre you into any situation you found intolerable.'

His faint smile held a wry cynicism that was reflected in the darkness of his eyes. 'Is the idea of marriage to me so unacceptable?'

The weight of his words penetrated her brain, and she looked at him aghast. 'What are you trying to say?' she whispered.

'We've known each other for years, we share a mutual affection, and have no false illusions that the other is marrying solely for the acquisition of sizeable individual assets.'

Her eyes widened in shocked disbelief. 'That's crazy,' she uttered huskily.

'Is it?' Dimitri probed cynically, his gaze startlingly direct. 'There isn't an eligible woman of my acquaintance who wouldn't run far and fast if my fortune suffered a drastic reversal.' His lips formed a twisted smile. 'An honest arrangement is infinitely preferable.'

Take a deep breath, an inner voice urged, and try to retain hold of your sanity. 'I don't believe this.' Desperation clouded her vision, a desperation so real it almost tore the breath from her throat. 'What about what I want from life?'

He lifted a hand and caught hold of her chin, tilting it so that she had to look at him. 'Happiness, the security of a man you can trust at your side. Aren't those important qualities?'

Standing so close to him made her conscious of an elevated nervous tension, together with an electric awareness that was terrifying, and she held his gaze with difficulty. 'What about *love*?'

He was silent for several long seconds, then he ventured silkily, 'How do you define love, Leanne?'

As the most finite emotion between two people so acutely physically and mentally attuned to each other that it surpasses all else, she thought.

'I know what I want it to be,' she responded quietly, and his mouth curved to form a faintly wry smile.

'Idealism versus reality?'

'I haven't yet acquired your level of cynicism.'

'I would be disappointed if you had.'

She felt her stomach execute a few painful somersaults at the implications of such a marriage. Did she possess the courage to go through with it? *Dared* she?

'It would be positively *indecent* to arrange a wedding one week after the engagement announcement,' she ventured slowly. 'What would people think, for God's sake?'

'Either that you were holding out for marriage before allowing me into your bed,' he proffered lazily, 'or we'd been careless with contraception and you were carrying our child.'

She was powerless to prevent the faint tinge of pink that rose to her cheeks, and she only just prevented herself from throwing her glass at him.

'Do you doubt my ability to pleasure you in bed?'

Delicate colour sufused her cheeks, and she almost died at the degree of indolent humour evident in the gleaming eyes so close to her own.

Every single instinct screamed for her to wrench out of his grasp, to insist *now* that she fully intended to denounce any plans for marriage and acquaint Paige with the truth.

Yet she was held captive by the degree of sexual chemistry that was apparent between them, the intrusive weaving of a sensual magic so intense that it was all she could do to resist the instinct to sway towards him and invite his kiss.

Inner resolve was responsible for the gathering of courage needed to adopt a suitable response, and she forced her mouth into a musing smile and allowed a gleam of humour to lighten her eyes.

'I'm sure you possess the requisite finesse . . .' she said with teasing mockery, allowing words to slip from her tongue without conscious thought. 'If not, I can enlighten you as to my . . .' she paused imperceptibly ' . . . preferences.' She deliberately raised one eyebrow and cast a seemingly careless glance round the room. 'I'm sure you could guarantee total privacy, but there's always the risk of interruption.' It took all her courage to continue, and she managed to inject a degree of teasing indulgence into her tone. 'Annita might be shocked if she caught her exalted boss and his fiancée immersed in the enjoyment of sex. Or worse.' She attempted a bewitching smile that held the temptation of Eve. 'I much prefer the bedroom, don't you?'

Dear God, what was she thinking of? It must be a form of divine madness to proffer such provocation, especially when she had absolutely no intention of following through.

'Privacy and comfort are a definite advantage,' Dimitri concurred with dangerous indolence, and she focused her attention on a point just behind his left ear.

Maybe if he thought she'd had several sexual encounters he wouldn't be so keen to go through with the wedding. A prospective husband could understand a long-lasting relationship, even more than one, given reasonable circumstances. But somehow she doubted that Dimitri would easily forgive promiscuity. Perhaps if she alluded to an active sex life, he'd be only too willing to agree to an annulment...

'I'll take you to lunch.'

Leanne's eyes flew to his, and she glimpsed the dark unfathomableness in his faintly hooded gaze.

'No,' she refused with a quick smile. The thought of sitting opposite him in a restaurant attempting to sip wine and fork food into her mouth would be more than she could bear. 'I promised Paige I'd be back at the hospital this afternoon, and I managed to get a hair appointment at five.' The latter was a fabrication, but she'd make a series of phone calls until she found a salon that would take her at that time. 'It will be easier for me to meet you at the hospital just after six.' All she wanted to do was get away from him, and she relaxed visibly as he turned towards the door.

'In that case, I'll walk you out to the lift.'

'I'm sure I can find my way.' Even to her own ears her voice sounded stiff, and she suffered his light clasp on her elbow and tried not to show her impatience as they passed through Reception.

Much to her relief, a lift arrived within seconds of pressing the call button, and she moved swiftly into the cubicle, infinitely glad when the doors closed and the lift began its electronic descent to the basement car park.

With the movements of an automaton she slid in behind the wheel and drove to Toorak where she successfully charmed Paige's hairdresser into giving her a late afternoon appointment. It was almost one, and she moved quickly towards the exclusive boutique Paige favoured. Even a few sample swatches would suffice, and perhaps a bridal

magazine or two—anything to appease her mother's
interest and divert her attention for an hour.
Fortunately Vivienne had already been alerted, and
there were numerous designs assembled from which
to choose.

Paige had set her heart on Leanne wearing a full-
length dreamy creation in silk and lace with a tiered
veil, and a bouquet of cream orchids. The fact that
Vivienne was in full agreement was a bonus, her
expertise proving invaluable as she suggested, advised, and enthusiastically planned turning what
Leanne had envisaged as a very small, intimate
wedding into the social event of the year.

'Attending *numbers*,' the vendeuse dismissed,
'mean nothing. The Kostakidas name is sufficient
to ensure that photos will appear in several newspapers and at least one of the country's leading
magazines. Dimitri will doubtless forgo any camera
crew in favour of a personal photographer, releasing one, maybe two photographs.' A bright,
lacquered nail jabbed the open page of a glossy
bridal magazine with fervour. 'So, everything will
co-ordinate perfectly. We understand each other,
*oui*?'

It was after three when Leanne entered the hospital, and she and Paige were chatting happily when
Dimitri entered the suite some ten minutes later.

Leanne's pulse leapt at the sight of him, and for
one brief second her eyes locked with his, only to
skate to a point somewhere in the vicinity of his
left shoulder.

The following thirty minutes became the longest
half-hour in her life as she conversed with ease,
although afterwards she had little recollection of a

word she'd uttered. Once, she chanced a glance in his direction and glimpsed a tinge of humour apparent in those dark, gleaming depths, and thereafter she studiously avoided meeting his gaze.

After half an hour Paige began to visibly tire, and Dimitri got to his feet in one fluid movement, indicating that they would leave her to rest.

Minutes later they cleared Reception and walked out to the car park where his Jaguar was parked next to Paige's Mercedes.

'Are you going straight home?'

His drawled query provided the impetus for her to be contrary, and she summoned a seemingly regretful smile as she slid her key into the lock.

'No. I still have a few things to do before the shops close.' She opened the door and slid in behind the wheel, dismayed to see how he stood indolently at ease between the open door, one arm propped against the roof as he leaned down towards her.

'Eleni has prepared a celebratory dinner.' The thought of dining at home *à deux* caused a pang of dismay, and she cast him a speaking glance as she activated the ignition and fired the engine, feeling infinitely relieved as he straightened and closed the door.

She reversed with ease, and as she drove off she saw him get into his car, aware as she paused to enter the flow of traffic that the Jaguar was right behind her.

Dammit, where could she go for two hours? What she wanted to do was go home, change into a swimsuit and lounge round the pool with a long, cool drink. And something to eat. Which reminded her that she hadn't eaten a thing since breakfast.

The city didn't hold any appeal, so she simply headed towards Toorak, found a parking space, then popped in briefly to see Vivienne. Afterwards, she collected a few magazines and wandered into a trendy café where she ordered a salad sandwich, iced water and a cappuccino.

She needed time to relax, and it was easy to sit quietly and leaf leisurely through the magazine pages for half an hour. The wisdom of lingering any longer on her own didn't seem prudent when it became obvious that her solitary presence had been noted and speculated upon by two young men who seemed intent to test their macho appeal at any second.

There was an exquisite lingerie boutique within walking distance, and she browsed there contentedly, choosing to purchase a cream silk nightshirt and a few essentials before enduring an unnecessary shampoo and fractional trim—opting to have the length caught into an elaborate knot atop her head, rather than flowing freely about her shoulders.

At least the style was cool, and she emerged from the salon at six, aware with every kilometre she travelled that it was bringing her closer to the hospital—and Dimitri.

The Jaguar was conspicuous by its absence in the hospital car park, and Leanne breathed a faint sigh of relief as she locked the Mercedes.

Reception was quiet, and she made her way swiftly down the corridor to Paige's suite, only to come to an abrupt halt at the sight of Dimitri sitting at ease on the edge of her mother's bed.

He stood as she entered, and his smile held musing warmth, although his eyes were dark and unfathomable. 'I had George drop me,' he enlightened her evenly as Leanne quickly masked her surprise.

She moved forward to greet her mother, then she sank into the chair Dimitri pulled forward. He, much to her chagrin, chose to stand behind her, and she was consciously aware of the faint, elusive tones of his aftershave mingling with the clean smell of his clothing.

Every now and again she felt his hands settle briefly on her shoulders, and each time her heartbeat raced into overdrive. The ensuing hour became a parody as she attempted to inject her voice with enthusiasm and display the expected interest in arrangements for her impending marriage.

'Mid-afternoon, one week from today,' Dimitri revealed. 'I've arranged the celebrant, caterers, flowers, and invitations for a handful of guests.'

Dear God, it was like riding a roller-coaster that wouldn't stop.

'A weekend at one of the inner-city hotels will have to suffice in lieu of a honeymoon,' he continued with regret.

They both knew it was merely an excuse based on the acute precariousness of Paige's health, but Paige pretended otherwise.

'You must go to Greece,' she enthused, her eyes misty with remembered pleasure. 'The islands are so beautiful. Santorini. Rhodes.'

'We will,' Dimitri assured her gently. 'I promise.' He leaned forward and brushed his lips against her temple. 'You're tired. We'll leave you to rest, hmm?'

Leanne followed his actions, then walked at his side to the car, handed him the keys, and slid into the passenger seat.

The distance between hospital and home had never seemed so short, and with each passing kilometre she found it impossible not to feel as if a trap was steadily closing around her vulnerable neck.

The Mercedes slowed before the impressive set of gates, then traversed the drive and slid to a halt inside the garage.

'A drink before dinner?'

Leanne registered the drawled query as they entered the house, and she paused in silent contemplation. She'd barely eaten anything at breakfast and only a sandwich since... Wisdom cautioned that alcohol in any form on an empty stomach was the height of folly. However, a small measure might give her the necessary courage to sit through a few courses of Eleni's gourmet offerings.

'Yes.' Decisiveness had to be an advantage, she considered as she preceded him into the lounge. 'A light white wine.'

Minutes later she sipped the cool, fresh chardonnay with appreciation, enjoying the faint warmth stealing invasively through her veins as it soothed a degree of elevated nervous tension.

'Is there anything you'd like to discuss?' she ventured lightly, and bore his slow, raking appraisal with equanimity for several minutes before fixing her attention in the vicinity of his right shoulder.

'Are you suggesting we indulge in the art of polite conversation?'

The drawled query held an element of humour, and she effected a slight shrug. 'Why not?'

'I gather anything is applicable,' he responded in vaguely cynical tones, the edge of his mouth lifting in quizzical speculation, 'as long as it doesn't touch on the wedding.'

Her stomach lurched, and decided not to settle too comfortably. Or maybe it was the effects of the wine.

'Or my ability to provide you with sexual pleasure,' he elaborated hatefully. 'As a matter of interest, how do you intend to measure my——?' he paused deliberately, then added with dangerous softness, 'Performance.'

Sheer bravado was responsible for her taking time to reply. That, and the need to shock. 'I've tried it, and found the experience to be vastly overrated.'

She had, once. With someone of whom she'd become very fond. And it had been a disaster. Simply because when the moment had arrived she'd panicked and called a halt before anything happened. Exit one very angry young man whose blistered riposte had rung in her ears for weeks. However, she had no intention of enlightening Dimitri of that fact.

'Indeed?' His voice sounded like velvet being shaved by the finest tensile steel blade. 'Perhaps I'll be able to change your opinion.'

Leanne pretended to accord him due consideration, her gaze dark and speculatively thoughtful. 'Perhaps,' she allowed with a faint shrug, aware that she was playing a dangerous game, and an extremely foolish one. 'Although you don't really turn me on.' She had to be mad, *insane*. Indulging in verbal foreplay with a man of Dimitri's calibre held all the potential dangers of an amateur juggling nitro-glycerine.

'Shall we go in to dinner?' Was that her voice? She sounded so calm, when inside she was quaking from an excess of nervous tension.

'Eleni has prepared your favourite moussaka,' he told her smoothly. 'She'll be upset if it begins to spoil.'

It took only one glance at the elegantly appointed table for Leanne to realise that the kindly housekeeper had utilised the finest damask, set out the best china, silver and crystal, and offset it all with elegant candles and flowers. A bottle of Cristal champagne rested to one side in a silver ice-bucket, and a single red rose lay diagonally beside each plate.

To one side lay a number of covered serving dishes, and Leanne was touched at the effort Eleni had employed to make this a special meal. It also made her feel like a traitor, for she knew Eleni's heart would be crushed should the truth of her alliance with Dimitri ever be revealed.

'Only a small portion,' she cautioned as Dimitri took her plate and prepared to serve the food.

As well as moussaka, there were parcels of minced lamb spiced with herbs and wrapped in vine leaves, delicious home-baked bread and thin slivers of veal dipped in egg and breadcrumbs and fried on a high heat that ensured a crisp coating on the tender meat. Delicate Greek pastries vied with a selection of grapes and cheeses to follow.

The food was delicious, Leanne knew, for Eleni possessed an enviable culinary flair. However, after the initial few mouthfuls she merely reassembled the contents of her plate, refused anything from the main selection, and just nibbled at a pastry before choosing a few grapes.

'Your appetite seems to have diminished to a point where it's almost non-existent,' Dimitri commented, and she effected a dismissive shrug.

'I didn't have lunch until late.'

'More champagne?'

Dared she? Somehow she didn't think so. 'No, thanks.'

They had maintained a discourse throughout the meal...polite *divertissements* that covered the state of the nation, the Kostakidas empire and the travels of its illustrious director. Sydney, Rome, Athens, Zurich, Lucerne and London within seven months was an impressive record.

Dimitri sat with ease, yet there was an inherent quality apparent, a primal essence that was wholly primitive. Intermingled with a devastating sexual alchemy, it proved a fearsome combination from which any sensible female would run and hide.

As the minutes ticked slowly by she began to feel stifled, supremely conscious of every pulsebeat, every single breath she took.

'I'll take everything through to the kitchen and put away the food.' It was the least she could do, and besides, Eleni would have retired to the flat she shared with George above the triple garage at the rear of the grounds. 'Then I'll make coffee.'

'I need to make an international phone call and send a few faxes,' he declared, unperturbed as he rose to his feet. 'Perhaps you wouldn't mind bringing my coffee into the study?'

She managed a negligent, monosyllabic reply, then systematically began placing everything on to the trolley before wheeling it through to the kitchen where she transferred food into the refrigerator before loading the dishwasher.

Ten minutes later the coffee was ready, and she poured some into a cup, filled a Thermos flask, then put both, together with cream and sugar, on to a tray before taking it to the study. It was a pleasant chore that she'd delighted in performing for Yanis on numerous occasions in the past, and the small table adjacent to the study door still remained, allowing her to set down the tray as she knocked before opening the door.

Dimitri was leaning against the side of the large rosewood desk, the telephone receiver held in one hand as he conducted a conversation in Greek to someone on the other end of the line.

Leanne's eyes flew to his tall, muscular frame, registering that he'd discarded his jacket, removed his tie, and loosened the top few buttons of his shirt.

With a hand thrust into his trouser pocket he exuded an aura of power that she found vaguely frightening, and she felt her stomach lurch, then contract with apprehension as she met his faintly hooded gaze.

She had no wish to eavesdrop on his conversation, despite being unable to comprehend so much as a word, and she moved silently to the desk, deposited the tray, then turned to leave, only to come to a halt as he caught hold of her wrist, successfully preventing her flight.

She looked at him in startled surprise, then opened her mouth to voice a silent protest, closing it again as he concluded his conversation and replaced the receiver.

His eyes were darkly inscrutable, and he cast the tray a quick glance, then raised an eyebrow in silent query at the single cup. 'You're not joining me?'

'No. It's too strong for my taste.' She made a controlled effort to keep her voice calm. 'Besides, I don't want to disturb you.'

All she wanted to do was run upstairs to her room, and she pondered the wisdom of inventing a headache—anything as a logical reason for escape.

'That's an interesting phrase,' he drawled as he stood up. He lifted a hand to her throat, then slid his fingers to cup her nape, impelling her forward.

She lifted both hands to his chest in an instinctive movement to prevent further contact, although the gesture proved fruitless as he curved an arm down her spine and pulled her close against him.

He was going to kiss her. She could see the gleam of intent mirrored in the depths of his eyes as his head lowered to hers.

She wanted to cry out, but no words emerged as his mouth closed over hers and began caressing with erotic slowness, his tongue a provocative instrument as it slid over her lips, then dipped into the moist cavern to tease and tantalise at will, demanding a response she found difficult not to give.

It was like being cast adrift in an unknown sea, and she felt terribly afraid, for there was a very real danger that she'd never make it to shore.

He wasn't playing fair, for his touch had undergone a subtle change as he created havoc with her senses and tipped her over the edge beyond rational control.

At her soft intake of breath his mouth hardened, taking possession with such innate mastery, she felt as if he was plundering her very soul.

All her senses were acutely attuned to this one man, and she felt achingly alive, her response generous and unbidden as he transported her to a place she had hitherto only visited in a host of wayward dreams.

A subtle shift in his hold as he pulled her close into the cradle of his hips made her shockingly aware of his swollen arousal, and she began to struggle, frightened of his strength and her own vulnerability.

Attempting leverage against his chest, she wrenched her mouth away from his . . . succeeding, she realised shakily, only because he chose to allow her to.

Dear lord in heaven, what had her foolish parrying invited? She wanted to turn and run, yet her limbs seemed frozen into immobility, and her eyes were wide and unblinking, their dark blue depths dilated to their fullest extent as she met his narrowed gaze.

His hands slid down her arms and curved against her ribcage, his thumbs brushing against the sides of her breasts, witnessing her instant reaction to his touch, the sweet burgeoning and sudden tightness of each vulnerable peak as he conducted an agonisingly slow, exploratory sweep that seemed to reach deep inside her, activating her sensual core until it flared and radiated through every nerve cell, every fibre, until she felt on fire.

It was damning, damnable, and there was nothing she could do to hide her response. Her mouth trembled, and she stood perfectly still as he lifted a hand and brushed his fingers across her softly bruised lips.

'I think we can dispense with any doubt that I fail to turn you on,' Dimitri taunted gently. His hand slid to her hair as he tucked a stray tendril back behind one ear. 'Go to bed.' He caught hold of her chin between thumb and forefinger, tilting it so that she had to look at him. 'And sleep—if you can,' he added softly.

She needed no second invitation, and only innate pride prevented her fleeing from the room and the inimical man who occupied it.

Instead, she forced herself to turn and walk slowly to the door, then closed it quietly behind her before making her way upstairs to her suite where she undressed, put away her clothes, removed her make-up, then slipped on a cotton nightshirt and slid in to bed to stare sightlessly at the darkened ceiling until sleep finally provided a blissful oblivion.

# CHAPTER FOUR

THE days leading up to the wedding passed in a blur of activity as Leanne slotted fittings and shopping in between visits to Paige in hospital. Then there was the essential liaising with Eleni and the caterers, the numerous phone calls. Not to mention the necessity of taking a hurried flight to the Gold Coast in order to ensure that the manager to whom she'd entrusted the beauty clinic was prepared to continue on a more permanent basis, to arrange for the leasing of her apartment, the storage of her treasured belongings, and, lastly, to collect more of her clothes.

When she got back to Melbourne Dimitri, whether by circumstance or design, appeared equally busy, for he left the house before Leanne emerged downstairs for breakfast, and returned in time to visit Paige. Two evenings out of the ensuing four he claimed a prior dinner engagement with business associates, and returned long after Leanne had retired for the night.

She tried to tell herself that she couldn't care less, that she didn't want his attention—or his extended affection.

Yet deep inside she knew she lied. With each passing day she became more acutely sensitive to his every glance and move. And he knew, damn him. He was a master at any game he chose to play. While she was a mere novice in several. The knowledge was evident in the faint gleam of his eye, the slightly twisted smile, and it irked her unbearably.

Friday dawned bright and clear, and Leanne became swept along on a swift-moving tide that saw the arrival of numerous people, each engaged for a specific task.

By noon the marquee, which had been erected the day before, was filled with its complement of tables, each of which had been set with linen, cutlery and crystal, and decorated with orchids. The caterers arrived and took care of the food beneath Eleni's eagle-eyed supervision.

At one o'clock Leanne escaped upstairs to shower and change, while Dimitri drove to the hospital to collect Paige and an accompanying nurse.

Vivienne arrived at two—ostensibly to help Paige dress, and to assist Leanne with her gown and veil. Forty-five minutes later the photographer descended, closely followed by the celebrant.

Paige looked incredibly frail, yet there was an inherent strength apparent, almost as if she'd marshalled all her reserves together in order to make it through the next few hours.

It was perhaps as well that there was no time in which to think. If there had been, Leanne was sure she'd never have had the courage to go through with it.

Instead, she found herself walking at Dimitri's side towards the flower-festooned gazebo at the edge of the gardens, aware of Paige seated in a wheelchair, and the celebrant's voice intoning a meaningful but brief ceremony legalising an alliance between Leanne Paige Foorde and Dimitri Yanis Kostakidas.

Wedding-rings were exchanged, and the groom kissed the bride.

There were more photographs, then champagne was served to the select collection of guests, followed by hors-d'oeuvres and more champagne.

The food was served at five-thirty, an epicurean delight featuring several European dishes to tempt the most discerning palate.

There were forty guests in all, and the only reason Leanne knew the number was because she asked Eleni. Most were people she knew, a few very well, others were business associates of Yanis and Dimitri, together with a handful of Paige's dearest friends.

At eight o'clock the guests, by prior arrangement, began to disperse, and when they had all gone Leanne slipped indoors to change out of her wedding-gown.

George had already stowed her bag, together with Dimitri's, in the boot of the Jaguar, and it was almost nine when Dimitri drew the car to a halt outside the hospital's main entrance.

Paige looked tired, her skin almost ashen and alarmingly translucent. But her eyes were alive, as bright and deep a blue as those of her daughter.

'We'll stay and see you settled,' Leanne declared gently, but Paige shook her head.

'No. I insist. Besides, I'm very tired.' Her smile was quite beautiful. 'Come and see me tomorrow. In the afternoon.' There was even a tinge of humour apparent in her voice. 'Not before.'

Leanne looked on helplessly as Dimitri lifted Paige from the car and placed her into the wheelchair, and there was only time for the briefest of affectionate hugs before a team of nurses converged and wheeled Paige out of sight.

She wanted to go home, to her own room, and forget the day's madness and all it entailed. Except that that wasn't possible.

For the past hour she'd felt akin to a dove held in the claws of a marauding hawk, heart fluttering almost out of control while she waited for the moment when he would strike and slash her delicate flesh to ribbons.

Leanne turned and walked back to the car, slipping into the passenger seat as Dimitri slid in behind the wheel.

'Would you like to go on to a nightclub?'

Images flickered through her mind of a dimly lit room, hazy with the pall of cigarette smoke and loud with the sound of music. There was always the chance that they might encounter Shanna if he chose one of the exclusive clubs he was known to favour on occasion, and somehow the thought of having to enact the part of an enraptured bride was more than she could bear. But the alternative of being alone with him in a hotel suite wasn't exactltly preferable, either.

Leanne shook her head in silent negation, then added a quiet refusal.

'Or somewhere for coffee?'

More than anything she wanted to slip out of her dress, remove her make-up, curl into a comfortable bed and go to sleep.

'No, thank you,' she declined with the utmost politeness. Leaning her head back against the cushioned head-rest, she simply closed her eyes as he fired the engine and sent the car purring smoothly out on to the street.

Ten minutes later the vehicle drew into the entrance of a stylish hotel, the concierge emerged to greet them and their bags were extracted while Dimitri took care of the registration.

Their suite was on a floor high above the city, large, luxurious, with appointments that put it in a class all of its own.

The porter deposited their bags, then retreated soundlessly after providing the usual spiel regarding the hotel's amenities.

The almost silent click of the door seemed unnecessarily loud, and Leanne cast a cursory glance round the room before allowing her attention to focus briefly on the kingsize bed.

Dear God, the days when a bride swooned with fear on her wedding night belonged in the Dark Ages. Yet the circumstances were far from typical; so, too, was the man she'd pledged to love and honour.

'There's champagne in the bar-fridge,' Dimitri drawled as he slid open his bag and began transferring clothes into the wardrobe.

Champagne? 'Why not?' she replied with an ineffectual shrug. It might also dispense with some of her nervous tension.

He crossed to the bar, extracted and opened the champagne, then handed her a slim flute.

Dammit, this room, the *bed*, was stifling her. Not to mention the man who seemed to dominate it. Maybe refusing to visit a nightclub hadn't been such a good idea, after all.

'We should have gone back to the house,' Leanne
ventured, and incurred his faintly musing glance.

'Why destroy the illusion?'

'Paige——'

'The hospital have this number, and that of my
mobile.'

There was nothing she could do to prevent the
haunted look that crept into her eyes, and she took
several sips of champagne in a desperate bid to gain
some measure of control.

'I'll unpack,' she managed with outward calm,
and, placing the flute down on to a nearby table,
she crossed to her bag and began removing clothes,
placing them on hangers, in drawer space; then,
collecting toiletries and nightwear, she made for the
adjoining bathrom.

She felt as tense as a tightly coiled spring, and
without further thought she stripped off her clothes
and stepped into the shower stall.

Warm water cascaded over her shoulders and
down her back, and for several minutes she simply
stood there, taking solace from the therapeutic fall
of water, then she reached for the soap and worked
a good lather before rinsing off.

Towelled dry, her toilet complete, she gathered
up a nightshirt and slipped it on. The silk whispered over her curves, its hem coming to rest at
mid-thigh. It wasn't exactly the ultimate in feminine
appeal, she decided as she cast her reflected image
a quick glance. However, she was damned if she'd
don a filmy nightgown in deference to her role as
a blushing bride.

Her hair was still piled on top of her head, and
her fingers went automatically to the confining pins,

loosening and discarding them before dragging her fingers through its length.

A pale-faced *child* with solemn eyes much too large for her delicate face stared back at her. Dammit, she looked about seventeen!

Years of fantasising about Dimitri in the role of lover was one thing. The reality was infinitely different.

Dear God, she'd never be able to go through with it—never, she despaired. Her hands curled round the vanity-unit surround, and her knuckles showed white as she attempted to gather together sufficient courage to move from the room.

Without giving herself time to think, she turned and emerged into the bedroom, coming to an abrupt halt at the sight of the large bed, its covers turned back, and the softened light of a single bedlamp. One glance in Dimitri's direction was sufficient to determine that he'd shrugged off his jacket, removed his tie, freed all the buttons on his shirt and pulled it free from his trousers.

He looked up and saw her, his gaze darkly inscrutable as he took in her cream silk nightshirt with its demure neckline and short sleeves. Then he moved towards the bathroom. 'I won't be long.'

Leanne lifted her shoulders in a negligible shrug. 'Take your time.' Take all night. In fact, take forever! she added silently.

Seconds later she heard the sound of the shower running, and she moved around the suite with the restlessness of a cat walking on hot bricks.

For one crazy moment she considered changing into her clothes and racing downstairs to call a cab, although that would achieve precisely nothing,

except highlight her own insecurity and incur
Dimitri's amusement.

Within minutes the shower stopped, and she
closed her eyes tightly, then slowly opened them
again. Tell him the truth, an inner voice urged.
Sure, she argued silently. After all the provocative
innuendo, would he believe her lack of experience?

A movement caught her eye and she turned
slightly to see Dimitri enter the bedroom, his tall,
muscular frame saved from complete nudity by the
towel hitched carelessly at his waist.

He looked magnificent, broad shoulders, deeply
tanned skin stretched over superb musculature, a
deep, curling mat of dark hair covering his chest
and arrowing down to a firm waist, and strong
muscled thighs.

Leanne unconsciously caught her lower lip between her teeth, and tried to shrug off a feeling of
helplessness as a tide of warmth swept through her
body. Dammit, she'd seen him in less as he'd swum
lengths of the pool. Why should the sight of a towel
hitched round his hips cause such a stir?

Her heart stopped, then lurched into a runaway
beat that visibly hammered at every pulse-point,
and his eyes assumed a dark inscrutability as he
watched the play of fleeting emotions chase across
her expressive features.

Her stomach clenched with pain, knowing that
he probably didn't care whether she slept with him
or not. It angered her considerably that she would
lose whether she chose to stay or retreat, for there
was nothing to win.

Yet, as much as she wanted to turn and walk away, a perverse little imp inside her urged her to play the challenge to its bitter conclusion. For if she lay unresponsive in his arms the loss would not be entirely hers. A subtle form of revenge, but one that would be very sweet.

Her chin lifted, tilting at a proud angle as she held his gaze with unflinching regard. 'Shall we get this over with?' Did her voice sound as strangled to his ears as it did to her own?

One eyebrow rose in silent query. 'Wham, bam—thank you, ma'am?' he taunted silkily as he moved slowly towards her.

His raking scrutiny was daunting, and his eyes flared for an infinitesimal second, then became faintly hooded as he lifted both hands and framed her face.

His head lowered to hers, and his mouth savoured her soft, trembling lips before beginning a tantalising exploration of the delicate tissues within.

All her fine body hairs rose in self-defence against his deliberate eroticism, and she gave a silent groan of despair as liquid warmth began coursing through her veins.

She closed her eyes and willed her body not to respond, hating the way he was able to reach down to her soul and kindle desire with such infinite delicacy that it was all she could do not to lift her arms and wind them round his neck.

Warning flares activated her nerve-endings as his hands slid slowly down and slipped beneath the hem of her nightshirt to shape her buttocks, then slide over her hips to explore the soft concave of her waist, before trailing up to cup her breasts.

There was nothing she could do to prevent the slight aching fullness as each peak pulsated beneath his touch, or the involuntary catch of her breath as he eased the slither of silk from her body.

It took immeasurable courage to stand still while every instinct demanded an attempt at modesty, and her eyes assumed a haunting vulnerability as he gently brushed his fingers across each breast in turn before trailing down to the soft, curling hair at the apex of her thighs.

Without a word his head moved down to hers, and she gave a startled intake of breath as his mouth settled over the hollow at the edge of her neck and began teasing with such erotic sensitivity that she was powerless to still the degree of heightened emotion surging through her body.

It was like an encompassing heat that liquefied her bones and tore at the foundations of any inborn reserve, creating an ambivalence that was vaguely frightening.

She wanted to cry out as he curved an arm beneath her knees, and she felt incredibly helpless as he sank down on to the bed, his large frame seeming to loom much too close as he shifted towards her.

Slowly, with infinite ease, he lifted a hand and began tracing the soft contours of each breast, pausing to tease first one tender peak, then the other, before trailing low to probe with disturbing intimacy, his touch so electrifyingly provocative that it attacked the fragile tenure of her control.

Fire leapt through her body, and she arched away from him, gasping as she failed to escape his invasion, and her heart began to thud alarmingly as his lips settled in a vulnerable hollow at the base of her throat, teasing with sensual skill the rapidly beating pulse before grazing slowly down to the gentle swell of her breast to savour the soft tracery of veins.

Leanne cried out as he took the tightening peak into his mouth and began to suckle shamelessly, using the edge of his teeth to wreak an erotic havoc that trod a fine line between pleasure and pain.

His touch became a physical torment, and she was unaware of the soft, guttural sounds emerging from her throat as his mouth trailed slowly down to begin the most intimate exploration of all.

She lost the fragile hold on her sensual sanity and went up in flames, a willing supplicant to a driving hunger so intense that there was no room for shock, only a wild, pagan need that surpassed any restraint, and she reached for him, instinctively begging him to ease the throbbing ache deep within her.

Yet he was in no hurry to comply, and she moved restlessly beneath his touch as exquisite sensation spiralled through her body, consumed by such agonising sweetness that she began to sob in helpless despair.

Then he moved, his hard length a primitive invasion, and she gasped out loud as he began to withdraw, only to repeat the action several times, rendering such exquisite torture that she rose up and pressed her mouth against his shoulder, unaware of the tiny bites she rendered on his flesh until she tasted the salt of his blood.

With one slow movement he entered her, and she gave a faint whimper of distress as he stretched delicate tissues unaccustomed to accommodating such turgid rigidity.

Unbidden, her hands instinctively pushed against his shoulders in a desperate bid to be free of him.

'You sweet fool,' Dimitri growled in husky remonstrance. Taking extreme care not to move, he lowered his head and trailed his lips across her cheek, tracing a path to her mouth, his breath mingling with hers as she attempted to turn her face to one side.

'Don't,' she pleaded desperately, except that he wouldn't permit any such escape, and her muffled entreaty became lost as his mouth settled over hers, soothing, coaxing, so that she was unaware of the subtle movement of his body until it was too late. There was no pain, just the intense sensation of complete enclosure as she tightly encased him in warm, living silk.

He remained still for several timeless minutes, watching the softly fleeting emotions that chased across her expressive features as unused muscles flexed and contracted in an age-old rhythm that seemed almost beyond her control.

Leanne gasped as he began to move, his slow stroking so exciting that she clung to him as he urged her beyond mere pleasure to a state of sensual radiance so essentially pagan, it was all she could do not to cry out with the pleasure of sexual fulfilment.

Afterwards he brushed her mouth with his own in a light, tantalising caress that caused her lips to tremble in damnable reaction.

Slowly, with infinite care, he caught her close and rolled on to his back, carrying her with him so that she lay cradled against his chest. One hand captured her nape while the other trailed down to rest at the base of her spine.

She could feel the powerful beat of his heart so close to her own, and his skin smelt faintly musky. For some strange reason she wanted to edge out her tongue and taste it, and the desire to stretch like a contented feline was almost more than she could bear.

Leanne was conscious of every nerve-end, the faint ache of unused muscles, the slight tenderness of her breasts as they pressed against the mat of hair covering his chest, not to mention the highly sensitised tissues deep within her.

'You played a dangerous game, little cat,' Dimitri chided gently. 'A lover displays more finesse with an untutored innocent than he affords a partner well-versed in the art of lovemaking.' His fingers travelled slowly up her spine, then slid to frame her face, lifting it so that she had no option but to look at him.

The muted light lent his strong features various angles and planes, and his eyes were dark and slumberous. For the life of her she couldn't remove her gaze from his mouth. It fascinated her, the slightly fuller lower lip, the curved shaping that was infinitely sensual.

Remembering just how erotic his plunder had been of her body brought a slow suffusing of colour to her cheeks, and she lowered her lashes in an effort to hide the intensity of her emotions.

'Please let me go,' she said quietly, and she attempted to push herself away from him—without success, for his hold tightened measurably.

'You're uncomfortable?'

Not physically. However emotionally, mentally, she felt incredibly ill at ease. 'I must be heavy,' she protested hesitantly, and sensed his slow smile.

'You're a lightweight,' he drawled, then cautioned musingly, 'Continue moving like that, and I won't be answerable for the consequences.'

'You're still...' She trailed off, unable to find the right words, and she blushed as he finished huskily,

'In possession of you?'

She suddenly felt very young, and extremely inexperienced. '*Yes.*'

His soft chuckle was almost her undoing, but he shifted carefully, then curled her close to his side.

Her body ached, inside and out, and she made no protest as he slid from the bed. Seconds later she heard the sound of running water, and within minutes he returned and scooped her into his arms.

To feel so acutely shy seemed ridiculous, given the degree of intimacy they'd shared, yet there was an innate reserve that forbade any further loss of inhibitions as he placed her in the capacious spabath, then stepped in to sit beside her.

It was easy to close her eyes and let the bubbling water provide its soporific magic, and afterwards she stood silently quiescent as Dimitri towelled her dry before leading her back to bed.

'Dimitri——'

Anything further she might have uttered died in her throat as he tugged her down beside him, and on the edge of sleep the last thing she remembered was the possessive trail of his fingers across her skin, and the brush of his lips against her hair.

# CHAPTER FIVE

LEANNE woke slowly, aware in those few seconds before total consciousness that something was different. The morning sun normally beat against the closed drapes from another direction, and she never slept nude.

Then she remembered.

Cautiously she turned her head, and discovered that she was alone. The rumpled sheets and tossed pillows were vivid reminders of how she'd spent the night and with whom.

And, as if that weren't sufficient, her body ached with the subtle evidence of Dimitri's invasion. She was extremely aware of her breasts, and their faintly tingling peaks. Sensitive tissues deep within her were still sensitive from his shameless possession as she'd followed an inherent instinct as ageless as Eve.

Even the mere thought of her response was enough to make a mockery of her intention to remain like ice in his arms.

*Ice*? She'd resembled a flame, consuming, generous, and blazing fiercely with desire.

Leanne closed her eyes against a host of chaotic memories, then opened them again.

Her eyes travelled to the electric clock on the nearby pedestal, and she gave a soft groan of despair, for it was well after eight.

'Breakfast?'

She raised her head at the sound of that drawled query, and pushed a shaky hand through the length of her hair. After last night, she really didn't want to face him at all.

Dimitri crossed to the bed and stood regarding her tousled appearance with musing indulgence. 'Orange juice, cereal, toast, coffee?'

Attired in jeans and a casual knit shirt, he looked indecently healthy, exuding a raw masculinity that was arresting and far too disruptive to her peace of mind.

'Start without me,' she said in a slightly husky voice, and felt infinitely relieved as he turned and retraced his steps to the table.

The tantalising aroma of bacon and eggs teased her nostrils, intermingling with strong, hot coffee. It made her realise just how hungry she was, and without hesitation she carefully draped the sheet around her and slid from the bed.

Collecting fresh underwear, she selected a slim-fitting cotton dress, then she moved to the *en suite*, emerging almost ten minutes later ready to face the day.

'I've already phoned the hospital,' Dimitri revealed as she took a seat opposite him at the table. 'Paige spent a reasonably comfortable night.'

Leanne managed a polite response, and concentrated on drinking her orange juice, then she opened the single-serving packet of cereal and poured it into the bowl, added milk, and began eating.

She was acutely aware of every movement she made, every breath she took in an effort to portray normalcy. Her entire body felt as if it was a tautly stretched wire, her emotions almost beyond any measure of control. It wasn't a feeling she was comfortable with, any more than she was comfortable with the man who aroused them.

'What would you like to do this morning?'

Leanne carefully replaced her cup down on to its saucer, and endeavoured to meet his gaze.

'We don't necessarily have to be together, if you have anything of importance...' She trailed off, her voice portraying extreme politeness.

His eyes narrowed fractionally. 'Now, why would you imagine I'd arrange anything more important this weekend than spending time with you?' he queried with deceptive softness.

It was crazy to feel so acutely fragile. 'Dimitri——' She foundered, wanting to scream out that she found it impossible to come to terms with the degree of intimacy they'd shared, or her own libidinous reaction.

'Don't hide from me,' he warned quietly, and, reaching out, he caught hold of her chin and tilted it fractionally so that she had to look at him. 'Or attempt to pretend we're not physically in tune with each other.'

'Damn you,' she cursed shakily, hating him. 'I'm not ready for that sort of honesty.'

'Perhaps not,' he drawled. 'But I won't allow you the illusion of psychological deception.'

'I'm going for a walk,' Leanne said tightly. 'I need some fresh air.'

'Finish your coffee,' he bade her easily, relinquishing her chin. 'We'll drive down to Frankston, have an early lunch, then visit Paige.'

She was mad to retaliate, insane to consider flouting him, but she was damned if she'd accept his direction with lamb-like docility. 'What if I'd prefer to stay in the city?'

'Do you foresee dragging me into various boutiques as some form of subtle revenge?' Dimitri countered, then he added musingly, 'Be warned, I'll insist you personally model every prospective purchase to my satisfaction.' His faint smile held humour at her expressive reaction. 'Changed your mind?'

She wanted to hurl something at him, and it irked her terribly that he knew. 'Frankston sounds good,' she managed sweetly, and, standing up, she retreated into the *en suite* to apply minimum make-up, then she collected her shoulder-bag and moved to the door.

The Jaguar was parked out front, the motor running, with the uniformed concierge standing in attendance, when they emerged from the main entrance. Leanne slid into the passenger seat while Dimitri walked round to slide in behind the wheel.

It was a beautiful day, the sun glorious in a cloud-free sky. Ideal for a scenic drive along the Mornington Peninsula.

The large car manoeuvred its way through inner-city traffic, then gathered speed as Dimitri gained the Nepean Highway.

Frankston was remarkably picturesque, with magnificent homes along the old Mornington Road area and Mount Eliza, the latter being a classy, trendy little community Leanne had visited with Paige on a few previous occasions.

Dimitri parked close to the sea, and they walked along the sandy foreshore. The salty tang smelled fresh and clean, and there was a soft breeze, warm from the summer heat, that teased the soft tendrils of Leanne's hair. Soft, pale sand lent a contrast to the blue bay sparkling beneath the sun's rays, and she felt an easing of inner tension as she walked silently at Dimitri's side.

There was a sense of togetherness that hadn't been in evidence for a long time... almost five years, she realised silently. For some strange reason she wanted to reach out and tuck her hand in his, to have him draw her close against him and raise her face to receive his kiss. To smile, and laugh a little, to share some of her innermost thoughts and question his.

Yet she did none of those things, and wondered why. Perhaps it was fear of rejection, fear that he would misconstrue her actions and place some sexual connotation on her innocent need for friendly companionship.

'Lunch?'

She paused by his side, and spared his arresting features a solemn glance. Then she smiled, her eyes blue and clear. 'Yes.' The sea air had renewed her appetite, and she felt the need for a long, cool drink.

He chose a small café that wasn't filled with weekend tourists, and ordered cold chicken with a delicious side-salad, and fresh fruit.

It was after two when they left, and almost three when they drew to a halt in the hospital car park.

Paige was asleep when they entered her suite, and in repose her features looked very pale, with a translucence that caused Leanne concern as she crossed to the bed and lightly touched her mother's shoulder.

Paige roused, and her eyes widened, then sparkled with pleasure as she eased into a more comfortable position.

'Leanne, Dimitri,' she greeted softly. 'Is it afternoon already?' Her gaze settled on her daughter in searching appraisal, as if seeking something indefinable, and Leanne wanted to cry out that love didn't come swiftly in the night, and sexual enlightenment was something else entirely.

'It was a beautiful wedding,' Paige voiced with a soft smile, and her eyes shone with remembered pleasure as they moved from Dimitri to her daughter. 'You looked wonderful, darling.' She turned towards her son-in-law. 'Didn't she?'

Dimitri reached out and caught hold of Leanne's hand, lifting it to his lips as he brushed her knuckles lightly. His eyes never left hers, and for a moment she thought she might drown in those dark depths. 'Beautiful,' he agreed gently.

Leanne couldn't breathe, and long seconds later she tore her gaze away from his, only to meet the small gleam of satisfaction in her mother's eyes.

Dear God, in a minute she'd choke, or blush. Or both.

'Now, what have you planned for the rest of the day?' Paige asked, and Dimitri smiled.

'A lazy afternoon. We drove down to Frankston this morning.' He leant forward and brushed his lips against her temple. 'We'll call in and see you before we go out to dinner.'

Leanne was silent in the car, and in their suite she moved quickly into the adjoining bathroom to change into a black maillot, over which she pulled a cotton T-shirt, then she gathered up a towel and a tube of sunscreen cream before emerging into the bedroom.

'I'm going for a swim,' she revealed, and glimpsed his lazy amusement as he looked up from reading from the day's newspaper.

'A desire for exercise, or a need for solitude?'

'*Both*,' she answered succinctly.

'Don't stay in the sun too long,' he warned softly.

Without a word she crossed to the door, opened it, then allowed it to close quietly behind her before moving towards the lifts.

It was a very luxurious hotel, and the swimming-pool was situated on the roof. A huge tiled affair with sparkling water, an abundance of sun-loungers, umbrellas, a small bar, and waiters in attendance.

There were also several people, which rather spoiled her quest for solitude. Although, to be honest, her reason for escape had been motivated by a need to be free of Dimitri's disturbing presence. At least for a while, she qualified darkly.

Possessed of a light tan, she smoothed in cream, slid her sunglasses in place, then lay face down on a full-length sun-lounger. Thirty minutes, then she'd change position, she promised herself as she closed her eyes and gave herself up to the relaxing warmth of the sun.

She must have dozed, for she came sharply awake at the touch of a hand against her shoulder, and she turned to see Dimitri stretched out on an adjoining lounger.

Attired in black silk swimming-trunks he exuded dynamic masculinity, together with an inherent vitality that was infinitely dangerous to her peace of mind.

How long had he been there?

'You're turning pink,' he said indolently, and she turned over and lay on her back.

'I slathered on heaps of cream,' she defended, and she closed her eyes in the hope of ignoring his presence.

With little success. After five minutes she simply gave up trying and slid to her feet. Seconds later she executed a clean dive into the pool, and stroked several lengths before resting momentarily at the pool's edge, then she levered herself on to the ledge and caught up her towel, watching idly as Dimitri followed her actions.

He was a good swimmer, utilising strong, clean strokes in a natural rhythm that reminded Leanne of a sleek jungle beast. Then she shivered slightly, and blamed herself for possessing a fanciful imagination.

Towelled dry, she caught the length of her hair and wrung the excess water from it, then she wound the towel sarong-wise round her slender frame as Dimitri levered himself from the pool in one easy movement.

Minutes later they took the lift down to their suite.

'Can you be ready in an hour?'

Leanne spared him a quick glance. 'Of course. Do you want to take the shower first, or shall I?'

'We could take it together,' he suggested with cynical mockery, and her eyes assumed a brilliant blue.

'I don't think so,' she declared evenly, turning away from him, and his soft chuckle was nearly her undoing.

Leanne was ready at six, looking elegant in a black velvet evening dress with exquisite gold beading. Created by the acclaimed Australian designer, Daniel Lightfoot, it was strapless, its hemline resting fractionally above the knee, and came with a matching evening cape. Purchased after one of his recent showings on the Gold Coast, it moulded her slim curves and provided a startling contrast for her silver-blonde hair.

Dimitri was already waiting when she entered the lounge, and his eyes gleamed in silent appreciation, then dropped lazily to the full curve of her lips before slipping down to the gentle swell of her breasts.

A pale tinge of colour crept across her cheeks as sheer sensation unfurled deep within her and spread through her body like liquid fire. For one small second her expression betrayed a haunting vulnerability, then she tilted her head fractionally and summoned a faint smile.

'Shall we leave?'

Paige was tired, and appeared weaker in just the few hours since they'd seen her last. Leanne experienced a terrible sense of foreboding as they drove into the city. There were words she wanted to say, queries that required reassurance. But she kept silent, knowing there could be no reassurance.

She would have liked to go home. *Home*, not the hotel suite where they were booked into for another night. And she wanted to be alone with the infinite degree of sadness which filled her heart—for the wonderful woman who was not only her mother, but her friend. Most of all, she wanted to rage against fate for stealing away someone so good, so very kind, before her time.

The restaurant was exclusive, expensive, and offered excellent cuisine.

Leanne ordered soup *de jour*, followed by a seafood dish, and opted for fresh fruit instead of dessert.

Dimitri chose an excellent white wine, and she took a sip from her glass, then set it down. After last night she felt ill at ease in his company, and she launched into a discourse of inconsequential small-talk touching on a variety of subjects but focusing on none.

It was almost ten when he indicated that they should leave, and Leanne walked at his side to the car, choosing to sit in silence during the short drive to the hotel.

Inside their suite, he queried mildly, 'Coffee?'

Leanne didn't even hesitate. 'No. It keeps me awake, and I didn't——'

'Get much sleep last night?'

He sounded amused, damn him, and it rankled unbearably.

'You've consciously avoided eye contact with me for most of the evening,' Dimitri drawled. 'Why so shy?'

'Perhaps because I am!' Leanne retorted, then hated herself for taking the defensive.

'You found last night's experience...' He paused imperceptibly, then continued with musing cynicism, 'Overwhelming?'

Soft colour crept over her cheeks, and she clenched her hands in silent anger. 'I think you——' She faltered, then took a shallow breath and continued, 'Deliberately set out to shock me.'

One eyebrow rose slightly and his mouth edged to form a faintly mocking smile. 'Not to please you?'

That he'd succeeded was something she was unwilling to admit—even to herself.

Her eyes skittered away from his, all too aware of the latent gleam in those dark depths, the slight cynicism apparent there.

A shaft of pain speared through her body, and she met his gaze with difficulty. 'You have the unfair advantage of vast experience,' she said stiffly.

His eyes gleamed with latent mockery. 'A repeat of which you'd prefer to avoid—tonight.' His hand trailed to her nape, tilting her head so that the extent of her fragility was exposed.

'I really am tired.'

'Then go to bed,' he said gently.

'Alone?' Her eyes felt far too large, and she was unable to prevent the tip of her tongue from running over her lower lip in a purely nervous gesture.

'No,' he drawled, watching the fleeting tinge of colour shade her cheekbones.

Leanne was mesmerised by his dark, gleaming gaze, and haunted by the sensually curved mouth that descended slowly to capture hers in a light, erotic tasting—teasing, yet withholding the promise of passion.

Then he lifted his head, and she felt strangely bereft as he gently pushed her to arm's length.

For a moment she stood hesitantly, unsure, then without a word she turned and made for the bathroom where she discarded her clothes, removed her make-up, then slipped into a silk nightshirt.

When she emerged he was already in bed, and she slid quietly in between the sheets.

She lay still and closed her eyes, then gave a start when he reached out and snapped off the bedside light.

'Goodnight, Leanne.'

His faint amusement curled like a painless whip round her heart. Deceptively soft, yet infinitely possessive.

She was in no doubt that he'd instigated a deliberate play upon her emotions, and it hurt like hell that she'd allowed him to succeed.

Without a word she turned on to her side, only to give a startled gasp as firm hands clasped her waist and pulled her into the warm curve of his body.

His arm rested on her hip, and one hand settled possessively over her breast, shaping the softness with easy familiarity.

She felt his lips brush her hair, and settle briefly against her temple, and she closed her eyes.

'Don't,' she pleaded, certain that she'd never be able to remain immune. Unsure that she even wanted to.

With minimum effort he turned her towards him, and her hands instinctively moved to his shoulders when his mouth settled over her own in a gentle, teasing tasting that gradually assumed passionate intensity as he drank deeply from the moist, sweet cavern, taking as much as she was prepared to give.

It wasn't enough, Leanne decided hazily as she uttered a murmured protest when his mouth left hers and began a tortuously slow path to her breasts.

She was hardly aware of the gentle tug that dispensed with her nightshirt, and she gave a soft moan as he took possession of one tender peak.

An arrow of desire shot through her body, radiating until every pore, every sensitised nerve-end seemed to pulse with sensual life. It became all-encompassing, all-consuming, and negated any logical thought except the need for him to ease the ache deep within her.

She wasn't aware of the guttural pleas that escaped her lips, or the groan of despair as he trailed a tantalisingly slow path over her midriff, down the soft planes of her belly, to offer succour to the most intimate cavern of all.

Several long minutes later she gasped out loud as he began a merciless assault that almost tipped her over the edge, and she reached for him, her fingers heedlessly pulling his hair as she begged him to stop.

It was sheer torment, and she was almost demented when he lifted his head and began to explore one inner thigh, nipping the tender flesh when she dug her fingers into the hard sinew of his shoulders.

Then he moved, and she arched instinctively as he entered her, sliding slowly through the tight, silken tunnel that stretched sweetly to accommodate him.

This time there was no pain, only the erotic sensation of complete enclosure as she absorbed his throbbing length.

It felt so good, so *right*, and she was beyond caring as he encouraged her to match his movements, increasing the pace until they were in perfect unison.

The warm turbulence became a tumultuous rhythm that tossed her high, suffusing every nerve-end with electrifying passion as he led her towards a climactic orgasm so complete, it transcended every emotional plane and left her spent, consumed with such agonising sweetness that she didn't possess the will to move.

She was dreamily conscious of the drift of his fingers as they caressed the softness of her breasts, and the gentle touch of his lips against her own.

The last thing she remembered was the sheet settling across her shoulders, and the human warmth of arms enfolding her close as she fell asleep.

It was late morning when Leanne and Dimitri checked out of the hotel and drove back to the Toorak mansion.

Eleni had prepared a veritable feast for lunch, and, although Leanne attempted to do the food justice, her appetite was sadly lacking.

Perhaps it was a sense of premonition, for no sooner had they vacated the dining-room than Dimitri took a call from the hospital to say that Paige had taken a turn for the worse.

They arrived to discover that she'd been moved into the intensive-care unit and placed under heavy sedation.

There was nothing anyone could do, except be there as Paige slipped in and out of consciousness.

The vigil lasted another two long days and nights; a vigil they both shared in shifts until the early hours of Wednesday morning when Dimitri took Leanne home.

# CHAPTER SIX

THE days following Paige's funeral slipped by, each a little less painful than the last as Leanne lost herself in completing innumerable tasks, and when there was none left she helped Eleni in the kitchen, conducted an unnecessary spring-clean, then diverted her attention to the gardens. Her actions were automatic, determined, and clearly indicative of a need to ease the grieving process.

There were times when it was all too easy to bring Paige's laughing features to mind, to visualise her smile and hear her lilting voice.

The memories they'd shared had been so very special, the bond between them closer than most. It was something she would treasure for the rest of her life.

Introspection began to intrude like a dark invader, and it seemed inevitable that Dimitri should become the central pivot of her existence, and their marriage.

With Paige's passing, there was no longer any need for pretence. Despite any resolution Leanne made, she was powerless to stop the acute sensations Dimitri was able to arouse, and she began to hate herself for the way she responded to the slide of his hand over her smooth skin, the touch of his mouth on her own.

Yet there was an inherent need to lose herself in his lovemaking, to become so caught up with the

wild surge of emotions that she forgot everything
except the magic of the moment. Afterwards she
slept, only to wake and face the reality of each new
day.

One morning, barely half an hour after Dimitri
had left for the city, she simply collected her bag,
informed Eleni that she'd be back by late afternoon,
then entered the garage and slid in behind the wheel
of the Mercedes.

It was a beautiful day, with only a few drifts of
cloud in a pale blue sky. The sun was hot, and she
automatically activated the car's air-conditioning
unit.

With no idea of where she would go, she simply
headed the car south and drove, instinctively
choosing the Nepean Highway and the Mornington
Peninsula.

The traffic was heavy until she cleared the outer
suburbs, then it began to ease as she neared
Frankston.

There were any number of beaches *en route* to
Portsea at the furthest tip of the Peninsula, and
Leanne eased the car to a halt on a grassy verge at
the seaside town of Rosebud overlooking the expanse of Port Phillip Bay.

For what seemed an age she gazed out towards
the horizon where the sea merged with the sky, lost
in reflective thought.

Almost unaware of her actions, she slid from the
car and locked it, then set out along the sandy
foreshore.

A faint breeze tugged the hem of her skirt and
teased the length of her hair as she walked. In the
distance a few seagulls took to the air from their

forage for food, circling low out over the water before gliding back to dig their long, curved beaks into the wet sand.

Every now and again the silence was broken by a keening gull, and after a while Leanne turned and began retracing her steps, surprised just how far she had come.

Inevitably her thoughts turned to Dimitri and their marriage...an alliance conceived from loyalty for a woman they had both adored.

A dangerous alliance, Leanne conceded, aware of the depth of her own emotions. She had little doubt that Dimitri viewed the marriage as a highly successful merger, for it tied several loose ends neatly together. His father's bequest to Paige was now within his control. He had a wife for whom he held affectionate regard; someone he could rely on to act as his social hostess.

But was it enough? Could she bear it when mere affection was no longer sufficient, and he began to seek attention elsewhere? With someone like Shanna?

A sudden chill whipped through her body, and she hugged her arms close to her midriff. If he should turn away from her, she knew she'd wither and die.

She had wealth and property worth millions. The ability to have almost anything she desired, and to travel anywhere in the world. Yet what she wanted was beyond price.

The crazy part was that she already had his name; she occupied his house and his bed. The question was, could she occupy his heart? Dared she even try?

She was mad, insane to want it all. The sensible thing to do would be to confront him, offer him a release from the marriage, and return to her former life on the Gold Coast.

At least, if she instigated such a proposal, it would be less hurtful than going with the status quo and discovering somewhere down the track that he'd taken a mistress.

It was after eleven when she gained the grassy verge and walked the few remaining steps to her car. With deft movements she unlocked the door and slid in behind the wheel, then reversed out and urged the vehicle towards town. It was too early for lunch, but she felt the need for a cool drink.

After exploring the township of Rosebud, she drove to Portsea, where she ate her usual salad sandwich in a little café before heading home.

'Dimitri rang,' Eleni informed her as she entered the kitchen. 'I am to remind you of the dinner tonight.'

'*Damn*.' The curse whispered from her lips as she recalled the worthy charity to which Paige had lent her support, and the fundraising function scheduled for this evening. A prestigious event held in the banquet-room of a select inner-city hotel, it was guaranteed to be attended by a number of wealthy patrons.

She vaguely recalled Dimitri mentioning that they were to assemble in the hotel lounge at six for drinks. Which meant she had precisely two and a half hours to search her wardrobe for something suitable to wear, shower, and tend to her nails, make-up and hair before they had to leave.

She managed it with five minutes to spare, looking coolly sophisticated in a stunning electric-blue silk gown with matching beaded jacket. The colour highlighted the clear texture of her skin, and gave emphasis to her silver-blonde hair, which she'd deliberately styled into a swirling knot atop her head. Jewellery was confined to a diamond pendant, matching earstuds, and a slim gold bracelet at her wrist.

Dimitri looked devastating in a black dinner-suit, white silk shirt and black tie. He possessed an animal grace that reminded her of a jungle predator... sleek, powerful, and infinitely dangerous.

'Ready?'

His musing drawl made all her fine body hairs stand up in protective self-defence. 'To enter the fray?' she countered solemnly, and incurred his level gaze.

'You don't want to go?'

Leanne drew a deep breath and released it slowly. 'I'm not looking forward to the inevitable scrutiny we'll receive.'

His eyes narrowed slightly as they swept her pale features. 'I think you're being overly sensitive.'

She gave a negligible shrug. 'Perhaps.'

'Paige gave a lot of her time and effort to this particular organisation,' Dimitri reminded her quietly, his gaze direct and vaguely analytical. 'I'm sure she would have wanted us to represent her tonight.'

Leanne was unable to suppress the faint quickening of her pulse at his nearness. He had the strangest effect on her equilibrium, making her aware of a primitive alchemy, a dramatic pull of the senses that was devastating.

She managed to hold his level gaze, and proffered a slight smile. 'Yes, I guess so.'

The drive into the city took longer than anticipated due to the heavy flow of traffic, and the sheer number of cars attempting to park provided inevitable delays. Consequently it was after six when they entered the huge formal lounge adjacent to the banquet-room.

Leanne stood quietly at Dimitri's side, greeting numerous acquaintances who paused to offer a mixture of congratulations and condolences.

Several waiters and waitresses circled with trays bearing glasses of champagne, orange juice and mineral water, and Dimitri followed her selection of the latter.

'Darlings, how *are* you?'

Leanne turned her head slightly at the sound of a familiar voice, and she was unable to suppress a winsome smile at the sight of a plump matron whose flowing, multi-layered attire and large-brimmed hat had become her trademark. She was also a committee member and generous benefactor whose tireless efforts had helped raise hundreds of thousands of dollars over the years, Paige had assured Leanne several years ago on just such an occasion as this one.

'Alethea,' Leanne greeted her with genuine pleasure.

'*Thrilled* to hear of the wedding. Devastated about poor, darling Paige.' She looked almost tearful, then she brightened considerably. 'A good crowd tonight. With luck, the children's hospital

will acquire another mini-bus.' She reached out and
patted Leanne's arm. 'You're a sweet girl.'

With surprisingly lithe movements she turned and
moved through the groups of mingling guests.

It was an event which several people chose to
patronise in an effort to be seen, Leanne mused as
she allowed her gaze to wander idly, noting several
well-known personalities, a few of whom wore sufficient jewellery to provide an insurance nightmare.

At seven the doors to the banquet-room opened
and guests began to file in to take seats at their
allotted tables.

'Who are we seated with?' Leanne asked as
Dimitri took her elbow.

'Does it matter?'

Only the most insensitive planner would have
placed Shanna at their table, and Leanne breathed
a faint sigh of relief on her discovery that the tall
brunette was nowhere in sight.

But her relief turned to dismay when the stunning
model made a dramatic entrance halfway through
the first course. Attired in a strapless, backless
design in black velvet, she drew every eye in the
large room as she *glided*, for want of a better description, Leanne mused silently, towards her designated table, several metres away.

Far enough away to preclude any immediate
contact, Leanne observed with unaccustomed un-
charitableness, but close enough to be reasonably
accessible once the meal was concluded and the
tables were cleared.

Leanne finished her starter, then did justice to
the delicately stuffed breast of chicken with accompanying vegetables, and she declined dessert, re-

fused to be tempted by the cheeseboard, and opted for a slim flute of champagne as opposed to mineral water in the hope that it would soothe a growing sense of unease.

Entertainment for the evening was a thirty-minute fashion parade by both male and female models featuring garments by Australian designers, after which the catwalk was dismantled while coffee was served to enable those who chose to dance to take the floor.

It signalled an opportunity for friends to move from one table to another, and Leanne wondered just how long it would be before Shanna opted to grace them with her presence.

'Dimitri. *Leanne*'

The smile was bright, too bright, as the beautiful brunette slid into a vacant seat next to Dimitri, and Leanne matched it with a diluted version of her own, aware that her actions were the subject of veiled conjecture by several guests.

'Shanna,' she responded with friendly politeness, while inwardly damning the man at her side for the seemingly warm greeting he extended.

How did one cope in the presence of a husband's former mistress? Leanne agonised, hating the hard knot of pain in the region of her heart.

With considerable aplomb, innate good manners, and an excellent attempt at acting, an inner voice told her.

'Poor Leanne,' Shanna purred with feigned sympathy as she lifted a hand and let her fingers rest lightly against Dimitri's arm. 'You must be *lost* without Paige.'

Steady, Leanne counselled herself silently. Just go with the flow. 'As well as being my mother, she was my best friend,' she offered with quiet honesty, and glimpsed the faint glimmer of envy in the model's beautiful eyes.

'How—quaint,' Shanna ventured before shifting her attention to Dimitri. 'I'm throwing a party tomorrow night.' She paused, then gave a sultry smile. 'My apartment. Any time after eight.'

Leanne unconsciously held her breath as she waited for him to answer.

'I don't think we can make it,' Dimitri drawled. Only Leanne, and possibly Shanna, saw that his smile didn't quite reach his eyes. 'Perhaps another time?'

Shanna recovered quickly. 'Of course, darling.'

Her make-up was perfect, Leanne noted, from the gloss covering the soft fullness of her lips, to the skilful application of eyeshadow and liner, and she was unable to suppress the uncharitable thought as to how the model shaped up first thing in the morning.

Dangerous shift—she grimaced inwardly—for it inevitably led to how often Dimitri had woken in Shanna's bed, and was closely followed by contemplation of Shanna's obvious expertise in the art of sexually pleasuring a man. It had to be light-years ahead of her own.

Leanne dearly wanted to escape, except that such an action would be observed and assessed, only to be classed as immature. So she stayed, sitting seemingly relaxed, offering a polite dissertation when the occasion demanded ... which wasn't often, for

Shanna made it patently clear that Dimitri was the focus of her attention.

Eventually the tall model rose to her feet, gave Leanne a slight smile, pressed glossy-tipped scarlet nails to Dimitri's arm, then wafted off in a cloud of heavy perfume.

'Dance with me.'

Leanne forced herself to meet Dimitri's gaze, and her eyes were wide and unflinching as the dark, unfathomable depths conducted a steady appraisal of her features.

He took hold of her hand, threading his fingers through her own, and she felt them tighten as she attempted a surreptitious bid for freedom.

There really wasn't much she could do except comply, at least, not in public, and with a gracious smile she rose to her feet and allowed him to lead her on to the dance-floor.

She was a competent partner, possessed of a natural grace, and she moved into his arms with ease, feeling the customary surge of warmth on contact with his body.

He held her close, his hold lightly possessive, and she had the strangest feeling that if she attempted to break free he would refuse her release.

The temptation to rest her head into the curve of his shoulder was motivated by her own traitorous soul, not her mind or the pain in her heart which ensured that she danced with such utter correctness that her constricted muscles began to ache from the strain.

Dimitri didn't offer so much as a word, although once she could have sworn she felt the brush of his lips against her hair.

When the music changed, he led her back to their table, his hand firm against the small of her back.

'Would you like to leave?'

Leanne turned slightly and looked at him carefully. She didn't want to stay, but she wasn't sure she could bear to be alone with him. She knew for certain that she didn't want to share his bed . . . at least, not tonight.

'Do you have an early start in the morning?' The query was polite, and she tempered it with a smile that brought a faint narrowing to his eyes.

'No earlier than usual.'

'In that case, I'll leave it up to you.'

She saw a fleeting glittering gleam in his eyes, then it was gone. 'I think we've done our duty. It will take all of thirty minutes to reach the door.'

It took slightly longer as they paused at one table, then another, exchanging words with business and social acquaintances as they went.

The Kostakidas empire commanded immense respect, as did the man who held the directorial chair. His presence at any social soirée was a considered coup, and Leanne could only admire his effortless ease in fielding several invitations to up-coming events.

She was surprised to see that it was almost midnight as Dimitri eased the Jaguar from the underground car park, and she leaned back against the head-rest.

The traffic was minimal once they left the inner-city, and she was grateful for the soft music drifting from the car's stereo system, for it precluded the necessity to make conversation.

The streets in the exclusive suburb of Toorak were quiet, and in no time at all Dimitri brought the car to a halt inside the garage.

Once indoors, he moved towards the lounge. 'A drink?'

She hesitated, then gave a slight shrug in acquiescence. Why not? It might help her sleep. 'A light brandy, with ginger ale,' she requested as she followed him into the room.

With ease he removed his tie, then slipped free the top two buttons of his shirt. The action changed his appearance quite dramatically as he shed the outer trappings of sophisticated formality.

Minutes later he placed a crystal tumbler in her hand, and she sipped from it slowly, feeling the warmth steal through her body as the alcohol began to take effect.

He projected an aura of latent power, a distinctive mesh of dangerous masculinity and sensuality that was wholly sexual.

Unbidden, a warm ache began deep inside her, slowly spreading through every vein in her body. It was damnable, incomprehensible, she mused silently, hating him more at this precise moment than she'd ever hated anyone in her life.

'Tired?'

'That's a loaded question,' Leanne responded with enforced lightness. 'How am I expected to answer?'

His eyes narrowed faintly, then assumed an expression of indolent amusement. 'Why not with honesty?'

Her lips trembled slightly, and her eyes held a tinge of aching sadness. 'I don't want to sleep with you.'

He lifted a hand to her cheek, and she flinched away from the brush of his fingers as he trailed them along the edge of her jaw, then slowly traced the throbbing cord at her neck.

The breath seemed to catch in her throat, and her eyes clung to his, bright and intensely vulnerable.

'No?'

His gentle query proved her undoing, and she moved back a pace, her body stiffening as she fought to control her emotions.

'I won't be a substitute.' Her voice was quietly angry, and she was shaking inside, caught up in a complex web that threatened to engulf her fragile senses.

'For Shanna?' Dimitri pursued silkily, and she suppressed the sudden shiver that feathered the surface of her skin.

'I don't possess her——'

'Sexual proficiency?'

Her eyes began to ache, along with the rest of her body, and she resisted the temptation to offer a flippant reply. 'I can't think of a better term,' she agreed at last.

'There's a difference between a partner who performs the sexual act like a mechanical doll, preoccupied with the monetary rewards to be gained from the relationship,' he drawled, 'And a wonderfully warm woman who loses herself in the sharing of a mutual joy.'

Her eyes widened measurably at his implication. 'That's . . . deplorable,' she whispered.

'The truth,' Dimitri mocked with hateful cynicism.

Without another word she finished her drink, then, after placing the tumbler carefully down on a nearby table, she turned and walked from the room, uncaring whether he followed or not.

Upstairs she entered their suite and undressed, removed her make-up, released her hair, then she pulled on a nightshirt and made her way down the hallway to the room she'd occupied as her own.

The thought of sharing the same bed, just lying there waiting for him to slide in beside her, was impossible.

She told herself she didn't care about the consequences of her action as she folded back the counterpane and slid between the sheets.

For an age she lay staring sightlessly at the ceiling, feeling hopelessly torn by a host of complex emotions.

How could you hate someone you loved? she agonised. Jealousy was hell and damnation. She had married with no illusions, so what right did she have to be *jealous*?

Leanne was on the edge of sleep when she heard the faint click of the door opening, and her heart felt as if it jumped to her throat as Dimitri crossed over to the bed.

Without a word he reached forward, removed the covers, then lifted her into his arms.

'Leave me alone!'

'If you don't want to make love, that's your prerogative,' he drawled hatefully as he walked from the room. 'But we share the same bed.'

'Doesn't it matter that I might choose not to?' she cried, sorely tried by his inherent strength and indomitable will.

'Not in the least,' he declared as he trod the short distance to their suite.

'Damn you,' she cursed, struggling to be free of him and failing miserably. 'Damn you to *hell*.'

Without a word he lowered her on to the bed, then slid in to lie beside her, and she rolled on to her side away from him, curling into a protective ball, too tense to contemplate sleep.

She remained still for what seemed an age, almost afraid to move, aware of his recumbent form mere inches away.

More than anything she would have liked to turn and flail at him with angry fists, to verbally assault him for behaving like a dominant, tyrannical *brute*. Except that if she did it would have only one ending, and her victory would be no victory at all.

# CHAPTER SEVEN

LEANNE must have slept, for she woke to discover that the bed was empty. A quick glance at the bedside clock revealed that it was after eight, and with an audible groan she slid to her feet.

After a quick shower she donned cotton shorts and a top, then ran lightly down the stairs to the kitchen.

'Dimitri has already left for the city,' Eleni told her with a smile, and Leanne hid her relief as she retrieved orange juice from the refrigerator, then she crossed to the pantry for some cereal.

The day stretched ahead with very little perceived direction, and when she'd eaten she returned upstairs and changed into tailored white trousers and a matching blouse. Then she applied make-up, slid her feet into high-heeled white sandals, and caught up the keys to the Mercedes.

What she needed, she decided as she cleared the gates and began heading towards the cluster of shops and trendy boutiques at Toorak, was something constructive to do with her time.

Paige had been content to aid numerous worthwhile charities and serve on various committees. However, Leanne knew that that wasn't her scene, nor could she just stay at home doing nothing, or whiling away the hours endlessly shopping.

Besides which, she missed the beauty therapy clinic—the clients, the friendly staff, the contact with people.

Leanne caught sight of a parking space and slid into it. Minutes later she entered a fashion boutique and browsed idly before emerging on to the pavement.

There was a beauty clinic in the immediate vicinity, and on impulse she walked inside and requested an appointment from a receptionist who held the phone in one hand and a pencil in the other.

'Aromatherapy? I'm sorry,' the receptionist intoned with regret.

'Tomorrow?' Leanne persisted. It hardly mattered which day.

'Our aromatherapist was rushed to hospital last night for emergency surgery.' Another phone rang, and she cast it a look of flustered exasperation. 'I'm trying to locate a replacement to take our existing appointments.'

'I'm a trained aromatherapist.' The words were out before Leanne could give them much thought. 'I could fill in for you. I have my own clinic on the Gold Coast,' she added, unsure until that moment just how badly she wanted this opportunity to work out.

'You're not serious?' the other girl queried with a mixture of disbelief and hopeful reservation. 'Do you have any credentials you can show the manageress?'

'Not on me, but I can have them to you in an hour,' Leanne assured her.

'I'll call her. An hour?'

'I'll be back at ten-thirty.'

She was, with minutes to spare, and quarter of an hour later she not only had the job, but she was asked if it was possible to make an immediate start.

The day was pleasantly hectic, with a brief break at midday, during which she put a call through to Eleni to assure her that she'd be home in time for dinner.

It was almost six when she slid in behind the wheel of the Mercedes, and she eased the vehicle into the flow of traffic, feeling happier than she had in ages, for there was a sense of achievement, as well as satisfaction, in doing something she really enjoyed.

Twenty minutes later she drew to a halt behind Dimitri's Jaguar, and cut the engine. Once indoors, she let Eleni know she was back before moving quickly upstairs to shower and change.

Dimitri was in the process of discarding his jacket when she entered the bedroom, and she met his dark gaze with a cautious smile.

'Hi,' she greeted him, lifting a hand to remove the pins confining her hair, then when it fell free she raked fingers through its length and pushed a few locks back behind each ear.

'How was your day?' He loosened his tie and began unfastening the buttons on his shirt.

He knew. Eleni would have told him. Yet Leanne was unable to read anything from his expression.

'Quite different from what I expected,' she proffered with a slightly rueful smile, and proceeded to fill in the details of how she came to be employed. 'Do you mind?'

He pulled his shirt free from the waistband of his trousers, and she caught her breath in mes-

merised fascination at the set of his powerful
shoulders and the broad expanse of muscled chest.

'How temporary is the position?'

'I'm not sure,' Leanne offered slowly. 'A week,
possibly two.' She met his gaze, and held it.

His slight smile held a degree of cynicism. 'You
find the life of a wealthy socialite boring?'

'I was never a socialite,' she said evenly. 'And I
didn't ask to be wealthy.'

His eyes held hers for a few seemingly long seconds, then he conducted a slow appraisal of her
features before focusing on the generous curve of
her mouth. 'There are occasions when it's necessary
for me to entertain business associates. As my wife,
you're expected to be at my side.'

'Ever the gracious hostess?'

He closed the distance between them, and, lifting
a hand, he cupped her chin, tilting it slightly so
that she had to look at him. 'I have no objection
to your working for a few weeks, or even longer,
if it's important to you. But not in the evening.
Understood?'

'What about late-night shopping on Friday?'

'I won't countenance any situation where you
have to walk to your car after dark,' he said hardly.

'I could——'

'It isn't negotiable, Leanne.'

'You don't have the right,' she argued, then she
gasped out loud as he slid a hand beneath her hair
and held fast her nape.

'Acquaint the manageress,' Dimitri insisted
silkily. 'Otherwise I'll do it myself.'

Leanne twisted her head, and winced as he refused to release his hold. 'You're behaving like a

dictatorial tyrant!' she accused, and her eyes flashed with the brilliance of sapphire.

'Try someone who has no desire to see you frightened or harmed in any way,' he corrected her.

'Oh...go to hell!' she flung vehemently, and there was nothing she could do to prevent the slow descent of his head, or the punishing force of his kiss.

It seared right down to her soul, becoming almost an annihilation, and she wanted to cry out against him for attempting a total conflagration of her senses.

Balling each hand into a fist, she hit him wherever she could connect—hard little punches that proved ineffectual against the taut musculature of his ribs and shoulders.

With galling ease he caught first one hand then the other and held them effortlessly behind her back, and she gave an audible groan as he caught her close in against him.

There was no escape from the relentless pressure of his mouth, or the plundering force of a kiss so intense it was almost a violation as he sought to impress his domination.

When at last he released her, Leanne stood in silence, her eyes stormy.

'Care to join me in the shower?' he taunted softly, and when she shook her head he slanted one eyebrow in silent mockery. 'Pity.'

Without a further word he slid down the zip fastening of his trousers and discarded them, tossing them over the valet-frame before moving into the *en suite*.

Leanne waited until he closed the door, then she collected fresh underwear and a change of clothes

and made her way to the suite that had been her
own for the past ten years.

There, she quickly showered and dressed, then,
without bothering with any make-up, she moved
quickly downstairs to the dining-room to help Eleni
transfer serving dishes on to the table.

Dinner was a strained meal—at least as far as
Leanne was concerned. She toyed with her food,
forking a few morsels from the starter of vineleaf-
wrapped parcels of mince and rice, ate sparingly of
the excellent veal, and declined dessert.

'Not hungry?' Dimitri ventured as he selected a
tempting *baklava* and transferred it on to his plate.

'Not particularly,' she answered quietly. Their
conversation during the meal had been desultory
at best as she tempered each response with extreme
politeness.

'Don't sulk, Leanne,' he drawled, and she looked
at him carefully, aware of the hard strength evident
in the broad-sculptured planes of his attractively
moulded features.

'I don't care to be subjugated in any way,' she
ventured carefully, and he lifted one eyebrow in
silent query.

'Be specific.'

The silky tone of his voice sent a sliver of ice
scudding down her spine. To challenge him was the
height of folly, yet she was damned if she'd meekly
slip into a subservient role.

'I don't consider you have the right to lay down
restrictions, or inhibit my actions,' she declared,
watching as he lifted the napkin to his mouth and
laid it down on the table. Each movement seemed
deliberate, and his eyes never left hers for a second.

'Don't fight me,' he cautioned silkily. 'I won't allow you to win, and afterwards you may well query the wisdom of the exercise.'

'By exerting sheer male force?' she flung angrily.

His eyes resembled shards of dark obsidian ice, and she shivered at the latent anger buried beneath the surface of his control.

'*Force*, Leanne?' The single query held a degree of dangerous softness that sent a chill slithering through her veins.

Quite suddenly she had had enough, and with extreme care she got to her feet, then pushed in her chair.

'A tactical retreat?'

She looked at him carefully, almost hating him. 'If I stay here, I'll probably throw something at you.' Her mouth trembled with angry futility, and her eyes ached. Without a further word she turned and walked from the room.

It was too early to go to bed, and she had no desire to view television or read a book. Without any clear thought she moved to the rear of the house and entered the grounds.

Within minutes she was joined by Prince, the Alsatian guard-dog, and she let him nuzzle her hand before trailing her fingers up to fondle his ears. He lifted his head and playfully pawed the ground, then padded dutifully at her side as she moved through the gardens.

Trim borders, perfect blooms, and nary a weed in sight, she brooded pensively as she trod the pebbled pathway. Even the lawn was a lush green, courtesy of an automatic sprinkler system, its length clipped with meticulous precision by the dedicated George.

The pool looked cool and inviting, with covered deck-chairs placed at even intervals around its edge, and sun umbrellas still open above two tables. The light was fading as the sun sank slowly beyond the horizon, and the sky bore soft pink streaks at its edge denoting the promise of another fine day.

Without thought, she selected a lounger and sank down against its cushioned length, aware that Prince had chosen to rest on his haunches at her side.

A slight shiver shook her slim frame. There was a guard-dog at her feet, a home which resembled a fortress, and a husband who viewed her as a valued possession.

To be so involved with Dimitri Kostakidas was a terrible burden—emotionally and mentally. At this precise moment she didn't know if she wanted to be free of him or not.

Living with him was becoming a battle of wills. Yet the thought of existing without him almost sent her to the brink of despair.

Where did Shanna fit in? Was the glamorous model intent on causing trouble simply for the sake of it? Or had she genuinely believed that her relationship with Dimitri was more than just a casual affair?

Leanne sensed Prince's movement an instant before she heard his faint whine of pleasure, and she glanced up to see that Dimitri had emerged from the house and was moving towards the pool.

He walked with the easy litheness of the physically fit, and she watched as Prince rose to his feet and padded forward to greet him.

Man and beast, she mused idly as Dimitri ran a hand over the animal's body. Each as powerful as the other, and equally dangerous.

'Admiring the sunset? Or is this a means of escape?'

His voice was a quizzical drawl, and she raised solemn eyes towards his.

'Both,' she admitted succinctly.

He smiled, his lips curving at the edges as he surveyed her recumbent form. 'I came out to suggest a game of tennis.' He caught the spark of interest in her eyes before it was quickly veiled. 'We used to play together, remember?'

How could she forget? Dimitri had coached her in the evenings and at weekends in those early days, encouraging her in practice sessions so that her game lifted from the socially acceptable to an acquired edge of competitiveness. She'd partnered him against Paige and Yanis, always striving to produce her best and exalting in any praise he chose to bestow.

'Is this a desire to actually play tennis, or a veiled attempt to extend an olive-branch?' Leanne queried solemnly, watching as his eyes assumed a gleam of humour.

'What better way of throwing something at me than a racket-impelled tennis ball?'

'The best of three sets?' she countered, and saw one eyebrow slant quizzically.

'At that rate we won't finish until at least ten o'clock.'

'I plan to exhaust you.'

His laughter was deep and throaty, and she took the hand he held out, allowing him to pull her to her feet.

Leanne went indoors and changed into shorts and a top while he retrieved rackets, balls, and activated the floodlights.

She hadn't played in a while, and it seemed weeks since she'd followed her normal exercise routine.

Dimitri, on the other hand, was disgustingly fit, and it showed. The play was hardly even, yet he made no attempt to utilise his superior strength, and merely returned each ball with ease.

He won the first set by three games, and allowed the second set to reach six all before winning the tie-breaker.

'I need a cool drink, followed by a long, leisurely soak in the spa,' Leanne declared as she took the towel from him and patted moisture from her brow and neck.

It was after ten, and she was pleasantly tired. The prospect of a spa-bath was infinitely inviting, and in the kitchen she filled a glass with ice, added orange juice, then carried it upstairs.

Five minutes later she stripped off her clothes, then she switched on the jets, and stepped into the bath to enjoy the blissful sensation of tiny bubbles of pulsing warmth surging against her body.

She had little idea of the passage of time, and when the last of her drink was finished she closed her eyes in a bid for total relaxation.

'Do you intend staying there all night?' a deep voice drawled. Her lashes swept slowly open and she regarded him silently for several seconds.

He looked vaguely satanic with a dark towel hitched at his waist. Dangerous, indomitable, and displaying an indecent amount of steel-muscled flesh, she decided silently, inwardly cursing herself for taking so long.

'If you don't want to share,' Dimitri ventured with deceptive softness, 'I suggest you take the opportunity to vacate the bath... now.'

Her pulse-rate tripped and surged into a quickened beat at his expressed implication, and there was nothing she could do to prevent the instant flare of emotion deep within her, or the way it suffused her body.

'Could you please pass me a towel?' Was that her voice? It sounded impossibly husky, and she watched as he collected one and obligingly extended it within her reach.

'You want me to close my eyes in deference to your sense of modesty?' Dimitri taunted softly, and with concentrated effort she forced herself to meet his dark enigmatic gaze.

'Would you?'

His expression assumed a degree of musing humour. 'You have a beautiful body,' he proffered gently. 'Why should it distress you that I might like to admire it?'

A defiant sparkle lent her eyes a sapphire-like brilliance. 'How would you feel if the situation were reversed?'

'An invitation for me to drop the towel, Leanne?'

With deliberate slowness he reached for the twisted knot at his waist, and the movement galvanised her into action. In a few scant seconds she was on her feet with the towel clutched against her, uncaring that its edge dipped into the water.

'I'm not a voyeur, nor am I into the sort of titillating games in which you inevitably indulge,' she vowed, almost shaking with anger as she stepped out of the bath and wrapped the towel around her slim curves.

She made to move past him, only to come to an abrupt halt as his hands closed over her shoulders.

'Let me go,' she demanded fiercely.

He didn't, and she began to struggle as he urged her forward, his hands sliding down the smooth skin of her back, dislodging the towel seemingly without any effort at all.

'Don't——' Any further words she might have uttered in vilification were lost as his mouth closed over hers, firm and shamelessly possessive as he initiated a kiss so devastating that it was all she could do not to respond.

Then he raised his head, watching the visible play of emotions chasing across her expressive features, the soft trembling of her faintly bruised lips, and the darkness evident in her eyes.

'You'd be wise not to throw accusations you can't substantiate,' he warned silkily, and quite suddenly she had had enough.

'Your experience is vastly superior to mine,' she opined quietly, and his eyes assumed glittering amusement.

'Does it bother you?' When she didn't offer anything by way of response, he added gently, 'Or are you afraid you won't be able to catch up?'

She attempted to wrench out of his grasp, and failed miserably. 'You want to know what bothers me?' she vented with thinly veiled fury. '*You* do.' She was so angry she almost burned with it. 'Everything about you.'

His eyes swept her turbulent features, then slid down to the soft swell of her breasts before lifting to settle on her brilliant blue gaze. 'Have you ever given much thought as to *why*?'

'Damn you—*yes*,' she admitted shakily.

'But you're not willing to come to terms with your own analysis, is that it?'

'No.'

His faint smile held a strange gentleness. 'I suggest you go to bed.' He lowered his head and brushed his lips against her forehead. 'With luck, you might be asleep before I join you. Then you'll be spared my unwelcome attention.' He caught the edges of her towel and fastened them securely before placing her at arms' length.

Even now, in anger, her traitorous body craved his touch. It was as if her mind was totally divorced from the dictates of her flesh, and she shook her head in disbelief at her own contrariness as she moved past him and entered the bedroom.

Unfastening the towel, she slipped a silk night-shirt over her head, then slid in between the covers of the large bed.

How could she exult in his possession, and lose herself so totally in the sexual act? How could *he*? she agonised silently.

It was lust. A base, physical appetite devoid of any emotional involvement.

You lie, a mischievous imp inside her taunted. You love him. You always have. And your anger is a twofold entity: directed at him for successfully

employing the degree of emotional coercion
necessary to instigate this marriage, and at yourself,
for allowing it to happen.

Leanne was almost asleep when Dimitri entered
the room, and she registered the faint snap of the
bedside light, followed by the slight depression of
the mattress as he slid into bed.

It was crazy, but her whole body seemed to re-
awaken and become achingly alive. Almost as if in
silent recognition of the other half that made it
whole.

She monitored her breathing, consciously forcing
it into a deep, regular pattern while her heart
thudded into a quickened beat.

The desire to stretch out and touch him was
almost impossible to ignore, and she silently
clenched her fingers in a conscious effort at control.

What would he do, she agonised, if she were to
trail her fingers lightly down his ribcage, then trace
the whorls of dark hair covering his chest? Travel
lower, to the indentation of his navel, and explore
the soft, curling hair at the apex of his thighs.
Would his manhood swell beneath her touch and
become rigid with need?

She closed her eyes tightly against an erotic
fantasy so hauntingly vivid that her whole body
took fire and began to burn.

Perhaps she could turn slightly, as if in sleep, and
accidentally brush her foot against his leg. Or
maybe her hand might touch his arm. She re-
hearsed it in her mind, going over each individual
action with the precision of a film director before
discarding each and every manoeuvre as being too
contrived. Besides, if he was asleep, her actions

would fail to register. And she was damned if she possessed the courage actively to initiate a blatant seduction.

Slowly she willed her body to relax, persuading her mind into a state of tranquillity, and she slipped into a deep sleep where featured dreams seemed to focus on the man who occupied her conscious mind. Perhaps it was auto-suggestion, but they were lying in bed and he was gently teasing her into wakefulness. In the dream she smiled, then stretched like a playful kitten, openly inviting his touch as she murmured her approval in pleasurable anticipation of what was to follow...

Except that the veils of unconsciousness slowly began to lift, and she discovered that the dream had become reality.

For a moment she lay perfectly still, unwilling to move so much as a muscle, and the breath locked in her throat as he brushed light fingers across her breasts, circling first one, then the other, before trailing down to her waist.

When he reached her thigh she tensed, then gave a barely audible groan as his hand slipped beneath the hem of her nightshirt.

There was no thought of denial, and she turned towards him, her lips warm and generous as they met his, and their loving was long and slow and incredibly sweet.

Afterwards he gathered her close, and she rested her head against the curve of his shoulder, wanting to encapsulate this precise moment and hold it close to her heart.

# CHAPTER EIGHT

LEANNE parked the Mercedes, then she walked briskly towards the beauty clinic. It was a beautiful summer's day, with a clear blue sky and the sun's warmth tempered by the slightest breeze.

There was a sense of pleasurable anticipation for the day ahead, and she greeted the receptionist with a friendly smile as she entered the clinic.

'There's an early appointment due to commence in five minutes, Leanne. The morning is well-booked, and so is the afternoon.' The receptionist checked the pencillings. 'Georgina Fyfe-Smith. Her record card is in the treatment-room.'

Leanne hurried through and donned the short-sleeved dusty-pink coat that comprised a uniform before checking the card for her client's preferred choice of aromatic oils.

Aromatherapy was becoming popular as more people benefited from its therapeutic qualities, and the selection of oils was attuned to each individual client and his or her mood.

The morning's appointments spilled into the afternoon, with one client phoning in ahead to say she'd be delayed, reducing Leanne's scheduled lunch-break to an inadequate ten minutes, just enough time for a hastily eaten sandwich and cool drink.

However, it was compensated for somewhat when her three-thirty appointment failed to arrive on time, and at three-fifty she checked with the receptionist.

'Miss Delahunty hasn't phoned in. Maybe she's been caught up in traffic.'

*Shanna*? It was a sufficiently unusual name to cause Leanne's stomach muscles to stiffen.

Toorak was an exclusive area, and there was a possibility that Shanna was a regular client of this particular clinic. Leanne couldn't discount the likelihood of coincidence, for word travelled fast in the social set and the clinic was a favoured haunt of several leading socialites.

At precisely four o'clock, a good thirty minutes late, the tall brunette swept into Reception in a waft of exotic perfume, her red designer outfit a stunning complement to her striking good looks.

'*Leanne*!' the model exclaimed with feigned surprise. 'You're *working* here?'

'The clinic's aromatherapist was hospitalised for surgery,' she explained quietly. 'I'm merely filling in until they find someone to take her place.'

'Noble of you, darling,' Shanna drawled.

She was a cat, Leanne decided. Pure feline, with sharpened claws poised and ready to inflict pain. Professionalism was responsible for Leanne's warm smile. 'Please come through.' Leading the way, she moved towards a private room at the rear of the main salon. 'There's a towelling robe behind the door. I'll give you a few minutes to change and make yourself comfortable.'

There was no doubt the model possessed a beautiful, lissom body, with smooth, toned muscle and excellent skin. Leanne set to work, assuring herself that the only way to get through the appointment was to disregard any personalities and simply do her job.

With luck, Shanna would lie quietly and enjoy the therapeutic qualities without feeling the need to offer anything by way of conversation.

'One wonders *why* you're working,' the brunette began, however, 'when you have a nice little fortune of your very own. Dimitri can hardly approve, surely?'

'Why should he disapprove, when it's only such a temporary arrangement?' Leanne parried carefully, loath to allow personalities to intrude.

'As is your marriage?'

Careful, an inner voice cautioned silently. 'Whatever gave you that idea?'

'Let's just say I know Dimitri well enough to be aware you couldn't satisfy him for long,' Shanna mocked.

'Really?'

'Oh, yes, darling. He likes his women receptive and provocatively inventive,' she offered sweetly.

It took all Leanne's control not to inflict a minor injury as she forced herelf to continue with the massage. 'To match his lusty appetite?'

'He's an exciting lover,' Shanna offered with a throaty laugh. 'Earthily primitive, yet displaying incredible *tendresse*. An incredibly potent combination, wouldn't you agree?'

Leanne refrained from making any comment as she selected an aromatic oil and began the gentle, rhythmic movement, focusing all her concentration on completing the therapy without allowing Shanna to rattle her composure.

'It's amazing how many of the wealthy arrange suitable marriages,' the model observed with marked cynicism. 'A husband consolidates his position and financial standing by taking a wife whose assets equal his, for wealth is power, and a required entrée into the upper social echelons. In your case, Dimitri wanted to regain control of Paige's bequest.'

It made sense. Even if it was partially untrue, it still made sense. It also sickened her to think that Shanna was only one of several people who must entertain similar views on their alliance.

However, it was impossible that Shanna knew the extent of Leanne's inheritance, just as it was equally impossible to imagine Dimitri divulging any details. Which meant the glamorous model had taken a calculated guess, and deliberately sought to inflict wilful mental damage.

At last the session was over, and Leanne left the room in order for Shanna to dress, then she forced herself to summon a friendly smile when the brunette swept out to Reception.

'I imagine I'll see you tonight,' Shanna declared, and Leanne cast her a puzzled glance. 'The opera,' Shanna informed her, slanting one eyebrow in faint disbelief. 'Dimitri has tickets. Surely he told you?'

He had, over breakfast. 'Yes, of course.' She loved the opera, and *La Bohème* was a publicised triumph featuring an excellent cast. Tonight was a much vaunted social event, where some of the cream of the city's society could be guaranteed to gather.

'No doubt I'll see you there.' Shanna's smile was wide and infinitely lethal, and it took considerable effort for Leanne to retain a semblance of calm.

Not if I see you first, she assured her silently.

'A friend of yours?' the receptionist queried as Shanna passed through the plate-glass doors.

'An acquaintance,' Leanne corrected her. 'I didn't realise she was a client of yours.'

'I know who she is, of course,' the receptionist declared. 'But I've never seen her here before.'

There was little doubt that Shanna's appearance had been a calculated attempt to unsettle Leanne's composure, and the fact hardly aided her peace of mind as she drove the short distance home.

It was hot outside, the air curiously still, and she hurried indoors with the intention of swimming a few lengths of the pool before it was time to shower and change for dinner.

'Eleni. I'm home,' she called as she headed towards the kitchen. A delicious aroma teased her nostrils, and she felt it curl down into her stomach, stimulating her appetite and causing her to bestow an appreciative commendation on the woman who was more friend than employee. 'Have I time for a swim?'

Eleni's features broke into a broad smile. 'Of course. But no more than half an hour, hmm? Dimitri rang; he will be a little late. You had a good day, yes?'

Up until an hour ago, it was fine, Leanne felt like saying, but such an answer would provoke questions, and she wasn't sure she wanted to offer any response. 'Great.' She reached for a banana, peeled it, and bit into the delicious flesh with evident enjoyment.

'Ah—you eat now?' Eleni scolded. 'I made roast lamb, with plenty vegetables, and your favourite apple crumble for dessert.'

'I'm ravenous,' Leanne assured her with a cheeky grin. 'I was so busy, I didn't get to have lunch.'

'Go have your swim,' the housekeeper bade her. 'You want I should call you?'

Leanne shook her head, then ran lightly upstairs, only to emerge five minutes later attired in a patterned silk bikini with a towel slung over one shoulder.

The water was refreshingly cool as she plunged in at the deep end, and she surfaced to stroke a leisurely pace for several lengths, exulting in the physical exertion.

She could easily have stayed there much longer, except that the need to shower and wash her hair before dinner precluded any attempt to dally, and she reluctantly swam to the pool's edge and levered herself up on to the tiled edge.

Five minutes later she was in the shower, and, after completing her ablutions, she slipped quickly into fresh underwear and blow-dried her hair before emerging into the bedroom with the intention of selecting something suitable to wear, only to come to an abrupt halt at the sight of Dimitri in the process of shedding his jacket.

'Finished in the bathroom?'

His fingers moved to loosen his tie deftly before tending to the buttons on his shirt, and she offered a monosyllabic averment as she stepped towards the capacious walk-in wardrobe, removing the first thing that came to hand from its hanger.

'Eleni said that dinner will be ready in five minutes,' he drawled, and she slid the dress over her head, then smoothed it down over her hips and fastened the zip.

'I'll go and help.' It was an escape at best, and she breathed a small sigh of relief as she descended the stairs.

Leanne was so studiously polite during dinner that it drew Dimitri's attention.

'If something is bothering you, why not tell me?'

Leanne paused from the pleasurable task of spooning a segment from Eleni's excellent apple crumble and looked at him carefully.

'Why should you think that?'

A slight smile twisted the edges of his mouth, and his eyes held discernible cynicism. 'You're determined to make this a guessing game?'

She replaced the spoon and tried to dampen the edge of her simmering anger. 'I wasn't aware we were playing a game,' she ventured, hating his ability to perceive her every mood. She arched a delicate, finely shaped eyebrow, and met his dark, enigmatic gaze with solemnity. 'Besides, you'd only be amused.'

His eyes narrowed faintly, his scrutiny dark and direct. 'Why would you imagine I'd be amused by anything that affects you?'

A faint hollow feeling settled in the region of her heart. She'd never win with Dimitri. He was too astute, too innately perceptive ever to be fooled by any smokescreen she might attempt to create.

'It's nothing I can't handle,' Leanne revealed with a imperceptible shrug.

'I have little doubt you can,' he drawled musingly.

'Such faith you have,' she mocked, and a gleam of humour lit his dark eyes, deepening the lines radiating from each corner, and teasing the edges of his mouth.

'You're a beautiful young woman,' he told her softly. 'Possessed of a generous soul. If anyone were to deliberately hurt you, they'd have to answer to me.'

Somehow she had to inject some levity into the situation, for if she didn't she'd go to pieces, and that would never do. 'Does that mean I should make a list?'

'I'm perfectly serious.'

She pondered on his reaction if she were to reveal that his ex-lover was the source, then decided against it. 'If you've finished, I'll clear everything on to the trolley and take it through to the kitchen,' she indicated, and, standing, she began stacking plates and gathering cutlery.

'Leave it. There isn't time,' Dimitri instructed, and she gave a helpless shrug as Eleni came bustling into the room.

Upstairs Leanne tended to her make-up, swept her hair into an elegant knot atop her head, then changed into a classically designed red evening suit that highlighted the texture of her skin and the slenderness of her delicate curves. Slipping her feet into matching shoes, she gathered up an evening bag and turned towards Dimitri.

The sight of him attired in a formal black evening suit, white silk shirt and black bow-tie made her catch her breath.

He was a ruggedly handsome man whose broad, sculpted features were a visual attestation to an enviable mix of inherited genes. Yet there was so much more apparent than mere physical good looks, for he emanated an aura of power and inherent strength together with a heightened degree of latent sexuality. A quality that was instantly recognisable to women, most of whom deliberately sought to arouse his attention ... if only to assert their own femininity.

Dangerous, she decided, unable to still the thrill of pleasure that stole through her body as she preceded him from the house and took her seat in the car.

Yanis had possessed remarkably similar qualities, Leanne mused as Dimitri fired the powerful engine and sent the vehicle purring down the driveway. Yet her stepfather had had eyes only for Paige.

To want that kind of love for herself was akin to wishing for the moon.

Damn, she cursed shakily. Such introspection was not only detrimental, it was downright disruptive. Far better to concentrate on the passing scenery, and ponder on the pleasure of experiencing a performance of *La Bohème*.

The State Theatre comprised three levels in a hall reminiscent in design and décor of the elegant European eighteenth-century opera houses, and Leanne sat enthralled through the love duet between Rodolfo and Mimi at the end of Act One.

'Enjoying the performance?' Dimitri queried as the lights came on, and she directed a stunning smile at him.

'The cast is superb, and the music...' Her eyes were a dazzling blue, radiating intense pleasure. 'I love it,' she concluded without reserve, and her eyes widened in surprise as he took hold of her hand and lifted it to his lips to caress each finger in turn.

There was something infinitely sensual in the gesture, and her mouth trembled slightly as she met his dark, gleaming gaze and caught a glimpse of latent passion in their depths.

'Would you like a drink?'

There hadn't been time for coffee after dinner, and she was thirsty. 'Please.'

It seemed that several patrons entertained the same idea, and the foyer was impossibly crowded, so that managing a clear passage to the bar became a test of endurance.

'Dimitri! How *wonderful* to see you,' a voice shrieked—feminine, of course, Leanne registered as the owner carved a path towards them.

Krissie Van Hahme, hostess extraordinaire, and unequalled in the society stakes. She was also a tireless worker for charity, and a friend of Paige.

'Leanne, darling,' she greeted her, leaning forward to bestow a kiss on each cheek as Dimitri excused himself in a quest to fetch liquid refreshments. 'So sad about your dearest mother. She was an asset, such a marvellous asset. An inspiration to us all.' She caught hold of Leanne's hand. 'I heard the news of your marriage, and I'm delighted. Truly delighted.'

Effusive, gregarious, but utterly sincere, the widow had more money than she knew what to do with, and regarded its excess as slightly obscene, choosing to compensate for her late husband's avaricious acquisition of it by donating large amounts to worthwhile charities, and compounding such compensation by tirelessly serving on several committees.

'Thanks, Krissie,' Leanne returned. 'How are you?'

'Busy, darling. But that's the way I prefer to be. And you're looking so well—stunning,' she qualified. 'Love is a wonderful aphrodisiac, and I just know it won't be long before you'll fill that beautiful home with children. Paige would have adored grandchildren.' She brightened, and cast Leanne a beautiful smile. 'There are a few functions prior to Christmas. I'll send Dimitri the usual invitations. Now, if you'll excuse me?'

Leanne managed a suitable response as her mind reeled with the implications of Krissie's words.

*Children.* She hadn't thought that far ahead. *Why* hadn't she? she agonised, shocked into the realisation that if she bore Dimitri a child he'd never let her go, much less the child. Then she'd be trapped in a loveless marriage where her inimical husband held all the cards. Was she only a pawn in a manipulative game controlled by a man who wanted to continue a dynasty? Had that been part of his motive in contriving first the engagement, then the marriage?

'Your drink.'

Leanne heard Dimitri's familiar drawl, and turned slightly to take the cool glass from his hand. 'Thanks.'

'We have only a few minutes before commencement of the second act,' he indicated, turning slightly as someone greeted him by name.

Leanne was glad of the distraction, for it enabled her to sip the mineral water without his scrutiny, and it was a relief when the electronic warning sounded, alerting patrons that the intermission was about to conclude.

Instead of giving the main players her undivided attention, she focused on the stormy love-affair between the secondary characters, identifying with the portrayal of passion and anger, for in some measure it resembled the tumult within her own heart.

The foyer appeared less crowded during the intermission between Acts Two and Three, and it was a pleasure to catch sight of one of her friend's parents and hear news of their daughter's sojourn in Europe.

Not so pleasant was Shanna's appearance at Dimitri's side, and Leanne felt she should be commended for her acting ability as she offered the model a polite greeting.

There were several words equally suitable with which to describe the beautiful brunette, but Leanne could only think of one. Gorgeous. From the top of her head to the tips of her toes, she was a visual attestation to stunning beauty. Everything was superbly co-ordinated; her designer-label gown and handmade matching shoes; jewellery; make-up.

Poised at Dimitri's side, Shanna looked his perfect complement, for her height in slender high heels brought the top of her head level with his eyes.

She doesn't possess an insecure bone in her body, Leanne thought silently. She has fame, fortune, and every endowment nature could bestow.

Yet she didn't have Dimitri. Or did she? Was she content to wait on the sidelines, willing to accept whatever attention he could offer whenever circumstances permitted, until a decent length of time elapsed and Dimitri sought a divorce? Maybe Shanna didn't consider marriage that important ...

No, Leanne decided bleakly. Shanna would want it all. She was merely a temporary hindrance in the glamorous model's scheme of things.

'No, I don't think so,' Leanne heard Dimitri's deep, drawling tones as she brought her attention back to the present. 'We both have an early start tomorrow.'

His hand rested lightly at the base of Leanne's spine, and she felt its soothing movement as he trailed his fingers to her waist.

Shanna's eyes narrowed slightly, and she made a faint *moue*. 'That rarely stopped you visiting a nightclub after a show in the past.'

'I prefer to spend the time making love to my wife.'

There was no visible sign of Shanna's anger as she allowed a soft, tinkling laugh to emerge from her lips. 'All cats are alike in the dark.'

'You think so?' Dimitri parried lightly. 'Would you care to parallel that axiom to each of your lovers?'

Shanna lifted a hand and laid a perfectly lacquered red nail on the lapel of Dimitri's jacket. 'You want me to declare you the best, darling?' she asked softly. 'In the presence of your wife?'

Without missing a beat, Dimitri removed Shanna's hand and released it, his expression a polite façade that fooled no one, least of all Leanne, who felt positively sickened by the exchange.

'A graceful retreat is called for, don't you think?' he ventured with dangerous silkiness, the *double entendre* unmistakable, and, with a brilliant smile, the model murmured her excuses and melted through the milling crowd.

Leanne gave a slight start as the signal alerting the end of the intermission sounded, and she forced herself to walk at Dimitri's side as he led her back into the theatre.

Within minutes of being seated the curtain rose, and Leanne stared sightlessly at the stage, the movement, the music washing over her in seemingly discordant array, for, despite the visual parade before her eyes, all she could see was the scene between Shanna and Dimitri.

She sat perfectly still, wishing with all her heart that she could get to her feet and make a dignified exit. Damn him, damn them both, she raged inwardly.

Such was the extent of her anger that she curled the fingers of one hand into the palm of her hand, then winced as the tips of her nails bit into the soft flesh.

Without warning Dimitri reached out and covered her hand with his own, and she immediately attempted to wrench it free. But his grasp assumed the strength of tensile steel, forbidding escape, and short of making a scene she had no choice but to sit in strained silence.

Her heart thudded loudly in her chest, deepening with every beat until she felt as if her entire body was a pulsing drum, and she gave a visible start as his fingers began tracing a soothing pattern over the throbbing veins at her wrist.

Leanne turned towards him, her eyes brilliant with unshed tears, then she focused her attention on the players immediately ahead.

It was a relief when Act Three concluded, and she rose to her feet at once, only to have him unbend his lengthy frame, giving every indication of accompanying her into the lobby.

As soon as they gained the aisle she attempted to tug her hand free, barely resisting the temptation to stamp on his toes in sheer frustration when he refused to permit her freedom.

'Do you mind?' she vented quietly between clenched teeth. 'Where I'm going, no man is allowed.'

He shot her a dark, assessing glance, then released her, and she moved quickly towards the powder-room. Afterwards she crossed to the mirror and freshened her lipstick, then, taking a deep, calming breath, she emerged into the lobby.

It was late by the time they reached the car, and Leanne sat in silence as Dimitri eased the vehicle from the car park and entered the flow of traffic vacating the city.

They hardly spoke during the short drive home, and once indoors she moved towards the stairs, only to come to an abrupt halt as hard fingers caught hold of her arm and swung her round to face him.

She didn't say a word, just threw him an icy look before drawing deliberate attention to the grasp he maintained on her arm.

His eyes bored into hers, his expression ruthlessly hard. 'My relationship with Shanna was over long ago.'

She felt cold, almost chilled, despite the warmth of the summer evening. 'It's of no interest to me whatsoever,' she managed coolly, holding his gaze, her eyes silently at war with his own.

'Isn't it?' Dimitri pursued with deadly softness.

Her nerves were a quivering mess in the face of his pitiless implacability, and she was conscious of the quickened pulse at the base of her throat. A visible giveaway that defied any attempt at control.

'You want to conduct a post-mortem of your exchange with Shanna?' she demanded, aware of the watchfulness apparent beneath his inscrutable façade. 'For what purpose, Dimitri? It won't change a thing.'

'It wasn't my intention for you to be hurt.'

'In order to be hurt, you have to care,' she offered seriously, attempting to lighten the words with a slight smile and failing miserably.

'And you don't?'

His faint cynicism stung, and a tinge of pink stained her cheeks as she experienced a renewed sense of helpless anger.

'Whatever you did and with whom prior to our marriage is none of my business.'

'Expertly fielded,' Dimitri mocked as he watched the agitated pulse-beat at the base of her throat.

She was unaware of the depth of her eyes and their dilation, and the soft trembling of her mouth. She only knew the futility of pain, and the power of this one man to wield it.

If she didn't escape now, she'd resort to unenviable rage or break into ignominious tears, and there was no dignity in puffy red eyes and uncontrollable emotion. Rage would inevitably bring retribution, and she knew she'd never be able to deal with its aftermath.

'It's late, and I'd like to go to bed,' she managed evenly, and there was a mesmeric silence, intensifying until she became conscious of every breath she took.

His eyes darkened measurably for a few long seconds, then his fingers loosened their hold, and she turned away from him, ascending the stairs with deliberate economy of movement.

Inside their suite she quickly discarded her clothes, unpinned her hair, then cleansed her face of make-up before pulling on a nightshirt and slipping between the sheets.

Dimitri entered the room as she was on the edge of sleep, and she heard the rustle of fabric, followed minutes later by the soft depression of the mattress as he slid in beside her.

If he reached for her, she'd turn on him like an angry cat, and her whole body tensed as she waited for him to make a move. When he didn't she became mildly resentful, conversely willing him to begin something that would give her the opportunity to exhaust some of her hidden anger.

Soon she heard the soft, steady sound of his breathing, and it rankled unbearably to think that he'd calmly summoned sleep without any effort at all.

Consequently it was ages before she relaxed sufficiently to follow his example, and when she woke it was after seven and she was alone.

## CHAPTER NINE

LEANNE wasn't sure precisely what prompted her to be contrary. Maybe it wasn't any *one* thing, but a combination of several.

It began over breakfast when Eleni passed on a message from Dimitri to the effect that he expected her to join him in entertaining an associate over dinner that evening.

'I don't think I can make it,' Leanne prevaricated, damned if she would fall in graciously with his every whim.

'No?' Eleni queried, managing to inject surprise and disbelief into one word. 'You are working late?'

'I've already made tentative arrangements to meet a friend for dinner.' Until this minute, such a thought hadn't entered her head.

'Maybe you can change it for another night,' Eleni suggested, and Leanne pretended to consider, then she shook her head slightly in an expressive gesture of doubt.

'Perhaps.' She summoned a sweet smile that was meant to convey innocence. 'Would you mind phoning Dimitri? I have a busy day ahead of me, and I probably won't be able to make the call.'

She was a fool, she chastised herself an hour later as she showed the first client of the day into the treatment-room.

By mid-morning she was convinced of it, and expected every ring of the phone at Reception to herald a call from Dimitri demanding that she cancel any prior arrangement.

At noon, when the receptionist alerted her to a private call, it was almost an anticlimax.

'Take the name and number,' Leanne said quietly. 'I'll call back when I've finished with my client.'

By the time she put the call through she was a nervous wreck, and her fingers tightened round the receiver as Dimitri picked up the extension.

'Eleni says you've made plans to dine out tonight,' he said without preamble, and Leanne immediately summoned his forceful features to mind. His leashed strength seemed to emanate from him down the line, and she was unable to suppress a shiver of apprehension.

'Yes,' she responded with extreme politeness.

'With a friend, I understand.'

'I do have friends, Dimitri,' she said drily. 'Is it so surprising that I might like to share a meal and a few hours with one of them?'

'Not at all,' he drawled. 'Invite her to join us for dinner another evening.'

She couldn't resist the faint taunt. 'Why so sure my friend is female?'

'Bravado, Leanne?' he queried with dangerous softness, and she gripped the receiver more tightly in an effort to dampen her anger. 'I'm sure your friend will understand when you explain.'

'Are you implying that *my* plans are unimportant?' She was mad, stark, raving mad to parry words with him, but she couldn't restrain herself.

'Don't play games,' he chided silkily, and she retaliated swiftly,

'Why don't you entertain him alone, Dimitri? I fail to see why you need me...unless it's a deliberate ploy to disarm him with my charm. Is the deal dependent on providing female distraction?' She paused imperceptibly, then honed in for the kill. 'Is that the role Shanna used to play?'

She sensed rather than heard his husky imprecation, and his voice was velvet-encased steel.

'I would appreciate it if you'd postpone your arrangements.'

It was as well they weren't in the same room, otherwise she knew he would exact retribution of a kind that would emphasise her foolishness in choosing to oppose him. The distance lent her the courage to proffer, 'I'll think about it.'

'Perhaps you could be sufficiently considerate to let me know your decision?'

He was angry. Furious, she amended. And she was in the grip of some crazy form of temporary insanity.

'I have a client waiting,' she informed him, and it was true. She had bookings back to back throughout the entire day. 'And it's difficult to make personal calls.' Very gently she replaced the receiver, experiencing a mixture of apprehension and exhilaration that lasted all afternoon.

At five she rang Eleni and left a message that she would be home in an hour, and it was just after six when the Mercedes drew to a halt in the garage.

The exhilaration had completely dissipated, and in its place was a knot of fearful apprehension as she entered the house and made her way upstairs.

Dear God, what had she been thinking of? To have challenged him was some form of divine madness, she railed at herself silently.

The bedroom was empty, and she released the breath she'd unconsciously been holding, only to catch it again as she heard the shower running in the adjoining bathroom.

There was no time for hesitation, and she crossed the room to the walk-in wardrobe. With shaking fingers she removed her clothes and pulled on a silk robe, then she gathered fresh underwear, tights, and flung them on to the bed.

She was about to return to the wardrobe to select something suitable to wear when Dimitri emerged from the bathroom with a towel hitched carelessly at his waist.

Her eyes flew straight to his, and her stomach completed a series of somersaults at the hard implacability evident in those dark depths.

'I leave in thirty minutes. With or without you.' His voice held a hateful drawling quality as he crossed the room and extracted underwear and socks from appropriate drawers.

Leanne hastily averted her gaze as he loosened the towel and let it drop to the floor, and she carried the mental image of his powerfully muscled frame as she fled into the bathroom.

She was ready in time, but only just, dressed in a peacock-green silk brocade gown, matching shoes, a small emerald pendant at her neck. Her hair was left loose, simply because it was easier to brush it than fasten it in a knot atop her head. As it was she was fixing her earrings in place as she descended the stairs at his side.

In the car she sat in silence, hating the icy chasm that seemed to widen between them with every passing kilometre.

'Shall we effect a truce?' Dimitri queried with deadly softness endless minutes later, and she turned towards him, seeing the hard planes of his rough-hewn profile, the splendid assemblage of tautened muscle and bone.

'You shouldn't have played the heavy husband,' she asserted quietly.

He spared her a swift, analytical glance as the traffic slowed, then directed his attention back to the road.

Minutes later he drove into the entrance of a city hotel, arranged valet parking, then crossed to her side as they entered the restaurant.

'Your guest is already here,' the *maître d'* informed them as he led the way to their table.

A tall, extremely attractive man rose to his feet and Dimitri made the introductions before seeing Leanne into her seat.

Leon Andre murmured something in French, then laughed softly as he caught her faint blush.

'I see you understand.' He smiled without a hint of remorse for the daring compliment, and his eyes held twinkling humour as they roved with expressive pleasure over her petite frame. 'If you were my wife, I wouldn't leave you languishing at home alone.'

He was nice, and almost Dimitri's equal. It was clear they were friends of long standing, and one could understand why. Both men possessed the same degree of inherent power, as well as laying claim to more than their fair share of dynamic masculinity.

'You aren't married?' Leanne queried politely, and caught his wry smile.

'I was, once. Several years ago, when I was young enough to believe I could conquer everything in sight. Unfortunately, in order to do so, I badly neglected the one person who was more important to me than all the successful deals in the world. I was too blind to see what was happening, and she left me.'

'I'm sorry,' she said with sincerity.

'I believe you are,' Leon drawled, shifting his gaze to Dimitri. 'Be careful, my friend,' he warned him with deliberate ambiguity.

'I value what I have,' Dimitri declared with silky emphasis, and the other man gave a husky laugh.

'Yes, I think you do.' He cast Leanne a musing smile. 'I'll defer to your choice of wine.'

'Oh, no,' she declined with a faint smile. 'I won't allow you to hang that one on me. You might not approve.'

'Surprise me.'

She spared Dimitri a glance and was unable to determine anything from his bland expression. 'A Pinot chardonnay?' she offered, and her eyes widened fractionally as Leon ordered an expensive import.

'So, tell me,' he began with indolent charm. 'How long have you known this adversary of mine?'

'Ten years,' she revealed with hesitation.

'Ah.' Leon sighed. 'You were too young to be swept off your feet, so he went away and allowed you to grow up.'

Leanne's mobile mouth moved to form an infectious smile. 'Right characters, wrong script. I went away and grew up.'

'He didn't pursue you?'

The wine waiter appeared, proffered the bottle, and at an indicative nod from Leon he tended to the uncorking, soliciting Leon's approval before completing his task.

'Not until recently.' Leanne lifted her glass and took an appreciative sip.

'Shall we order?' Dimitri queried with imperturbable calm.

The food was delectable, each course a superb masterpiece in taste and decorative flair. Leanne couldn't remember enjoying herself as much in ages. Perhaps it was the wine, or the light, bantering exchange Leon deliberately sought to maintain, but she found herself caught up in a mild flirtation which saw her eyes sparkle with delicious humour and her mouth curve with laughter.

'I thought this was meant to be a business dinner,' she said when the waiter served coffee.

'The business was conducted this afternoon,' Leon enlightened her with a lazy smile. 'Tonight is wholly social. Dimitri and I have known each other since our days in university. I wanted to meet the woman who'd managed to bring him to his knees.' His features softened measurably and there was no cynicism apparent in his smile. 'His choice is estimable. You're enchanting.'

She smiled faintly, and Leon chuckled, a deep, husky sound that was synonymous with the man himself.

Draining the last of his coffee, Leon spared his watch a glance, then signalled for the bill. 'Shall we take in the nightclub on the top floor?'

'Leanne?' Dimitri's voice was a soft drawl, and she found it impossible to determine anything from his expression.

It was only ten, and she didn't feel in the least tired. 'Perhaps for an hour?'

'Why not midnight?' Leon parried. 'Then you can escape before Dimitri's Jaguar turns into a pumpkin.'

The nightclub was well-patronised, the band excellent, and it seemed an age since she'd felt so alive.

'Would you like to dance?'

They had been seated for more than ten minutes, and the beat of the music was intoxicating. 'With you?'

Leon laughed softly. 'Of course with me.'

'Dimitri?' She had to ask, and his drawled consent held a tinge of humour.

Leon was amazingly light on his feet for such a tall man, and his movements were uncontrived.

'I'm not terribly good at this,' Leanne apologised, and he grinned down at her.

'You don't normally frequent nightclubs?'

'Hardly ever,' she owned. 'My preference lies with the cinema, the theatre and the ballet.'

'And in between you stay home and watch television or read a good book?'

She laughed. 'How did you guess?'

'Dimitri is a lucky man,' he remarked softly.

There wasn't a thing she could say, and in desperation she murmured, 'Perhaps we should go back.'

The band took a small break, and when they resumed Dimitri caught hold of her hand and led her on to the floor.

Dancing with Leon had been fun, but with Dimitri she was aware of the seductive pull of sexual chemistry, and she made no demure when he pulled her close. It was all too easy to lift her arms and melt in against him as they drifted to the music.

This was where she wanted to be, and she felt strangely bereft when he disentangled her arms and led her back to the table.

Leon was engrossed in conversation with an attractive redhead, and he made an introduction, then showed no surprise when Dimitri declared an intention to leave.

'*Au revoir*, Leanne,' Leon bade her gently. 'I'll see you next time I'm in town.'

'You must come to dinner.' The invitation slid easily from her lips, and he smiled.

'Thank you.' He turned towards Dimitri. 'Take good care of her.'

'Don't doubt that I shall.'

Once in the car she sat in silence, and leaned back against the head-rest as the powerful vehicle purred towards Toorak.

'A nightcap?' Dimitri queried when they were indoors, and Leanne shook her head.

She wanted to say how much she'd enjoyed the evening, but she couldn't quite bring herself to evince pleasure in another man's company. Besides, there was a dark watchfulness apparent in Dimitri's eyes that she was unable to fathom.

'I trust your friend wasn't too disappointed when you had to change your arrangements?'

His voice was a silky drawl that seemed to reach right down into the pit of her stomach, and she lifted her head slightly and met his gaze with fearless resolve.

'I hadn't made any prior arrangements for tonight,' she informed him with studied calm. 'I resented your high-handedness, and wasn't prepared to act the part of a submissive appendage who fell in with your every command.'

His eyes hardened fractionally, and his mouth curved to form a mocking smile. 'An act of defiance?'

She looked at him carefully, and refused to be intimidated by his inherent strength of will. 'Yes.'

He moved forward until he was within touching distance, and she restrained the urge to turn and run upstairs.

'It didn't bother you that such behaviour might incur my anger?' he queried with dangerous softness, and her chin lifted fractionally.

'Not at the time, no.'

Dimitri's lips curved slightly as he lifted a hand to her hair and tucked a few tendrils back behind her ear. 'And now?'

She gave a small, helpless shrug, and was unable to prevent the traitorous pull of her body towards his. It was almost as if some celestial power had predestined them as two halves of a whole, and an exigent magnetism was intent on drawing them together. 'What good will it do to fight you?'

He took in the faint wariness in the set of her mouth, the determination apparent in those beautiful blue eyes, and stated gently, 'Yet you'd like to.'

'You do tend to have that effect on me.'

He smiled, and she almost died at the degree of lazy humour evident in that dark gaze. 'Have you ever attempted to analyse *why*?'

Innate honesty provided the courage for her to offer a trifle sadly, 'I did that four years ago.' She forced herself to hold his gaze, although she was unable to prevent her lips from trembling slightly, and her eyes widened as he lifted a hand and traced the lower edge with his thumb.

She stood motionless as he lowered his head, and she closed her eyes as his mouth touched hers.

His lips were firm and warm, caressing with a sensual expertise that made the blood sing in her veins, and she became lost, an easy prey to her own treacherous emotions as he deepened the kiss, drawing her in close against him so that she couldn't help but be aware of his arousal.

Minutes later he dragged his mouth away, then with one easy movement he swept an arm beneath her knees and carried her upstairs.

I don't care, Leanne assured herself hazily. Right now, all I want is his possession, and the sharing of something so special, so magical, it transcends rational thought.

In the bedroom their clothes were an impossible encumbrance they hastily shed, and there was a hunger in his passion, an urgency that forbade a long, leisurely entrapment of the senses. There was only immediate need, and she exulted in his erotic plunder, clinging to him in rapt abandon as he took her to the edge and beyond, then held her there for the orgasmic explosion and its shuddering aftermath.

A long time later she felt the brush of his lips against the curve of her shoulder as he trailed a path to her breast to conduct a slow, sensual tasting that brought a renewed surge of emotion, and she wound her arms round his neck, holding him close as he embarked on a gentle loving that left her feeling warm and infinitely cherished.

Not cherished, an inner voice protested as she slipped slowly towards sleep. Cherish meant love, and he felt little more for her than a healthy degree of lust.

## CHAPTER TEN

LEANNE entered the beauty clinic early on Saturday morning with a vague feeling of regret. Today was the last day of her temporary employment, for the manageress had been successful in engaging a satisfactory replacement who was due to start on Monday.

In a way she felt vaguely regretful, for she'd genuinely enjoyed working in the clinic, the contact with clients and the pleasure derived from their voiced appreciation. It made her aware of how much she missed her own clinic on the Gold Coast. Although Melbourne would always be home.

'You're fully booked,' the receptionist informed her with a rueful smile as Leanne paused to check the day's appointments.

The pencillings were distinct, and Leanne's heart sank as she saw that Shanna had arranged another aromatherapy session in the latter half of the morning.

It was unlikely that the glamorous model valued Leanne's services to the extent of making another appointment within the space of a few days. Which meant that Shanna had to have an ulterior motive. And there could be no doubt that the motive was centred on Dimitri.

Another gibe? Leanne pondered wryly as she checked the time a few hours later. Shanna was already ten minutes late. Was it a deliberate ploy to unsettle her?

Dammit, she scolded herself silently. She was becoming positively paranoid where Shanna was concerned.

'Leanne. Miss Delahunty is here.'

She thanked the receptionist and stepped briskly through to the foyer.

'Shanna. How are you?' she greeted her politely.

The model's smile was a practised facsimile as she swept through to the treatment-room.

With dedicated care Leanne set to work, grateful that Shanna seemed disinclined to offer much in the way of conversation.

But her gratitude was short-lived because on conclusion of the session, Shanna placed a detaining hand on her arm.

'I wonder if you might do me a favour?'

Sheer good manners forced Leanne to proffer a polite response. 'If I can,' she said cautiously, and glimpsed the gleam of satisfaction in the model's dark eyes.

'It's a rather delicate matter,' Shanna intimated, effecting a slight *moue*. One eyebrow arched, and her expression became faintly pitying. 'I considered despatching a special messenger,' she declared, 'then decided against it, unsure that Dimitri's secretary wouldn't open the package.'

Get to the point, Leanne wanted to scream, feeling very much like a cornered mouse confronted by a predatory cat who was bent on prolonging the agony of an imminent attack.

'After much deliberation, I feel it's best if I hand it to you.'

The brunette made no move to extract anything from her bag, and Leanne stood perfectly still, her eyes level, a polite smile firmly pinned in place. The effort almost killed her, but she was damned if she'd let Shanna gain so much as a glimpse of her distress.

'I was with Dimitri yesterday,' Shanna continued, moving in for the figurative kill. 'And...' she paused for deliberate effect '...one thing led to another. You know how it is?' she said archly with a negligent shrug.

Ice seemed to invade Leanne's veins, and she shivered, aware from the satisfied gleam in Shanna's eyes that she'd glimpsed the faint *frisson* of discomfort.

With almost theatrical precision the model reached into her bag and extracted two keys. 'Dimitri will want these back.'

Leanne took them from Shanna's extended hand and thrust them quickly into her pocket. She even managed a smile as she concluded the appointment.

'Management have found a replacement aromatherapist,' she informed her politely. 'Suzanne will start Monday.' Without waiting for Shanna's comment, she turned and left the treatment-room.

A short while later Shanna swept out, and Leanne checked the appointment book before taking an early lunch-break, during which she merely picked at the delectable chicken salad sandwich, and opted for a second cappuccino, holding the cup in both hands as if finding solace in the transmitted heat from the milky coffee.

The magazine she'd bought didn't hold her interest, and she merely flicked through the pages, seeing only Dimitri's classic features and those of

Shanna, intermingled in numerous poses, all of which aroused damnable jealousy.

Somehow she managed to get through the afternoon, and she was quite touched when the manageress presented her with a gift at the end of the day.

The thought of dining out tonight was the last thing she needed, she decided as she fired the engine and eased the Mercedes on to the road.

The evening's function was to be held in the glittering ballroom of a modern city hotel. Everyone who was *anyone* would attend, dressed in their finest, and it would be strictly smile-time as she mixed and mingled at Dimitri's side.

How would he react if she said she was tired and had a headache? she brooded as she drove the short distance home.

Leanne turned into their street seconds ahead of Dimitri's Jaguar, and after passing through the electronic gates she had the craziest urge to accelerate up the driveway and come to a screeching halt. Childish, she dismissed. Utterly childish.

So she eased the Mercedes forward with her customary care, and drove into the garage.

Dimitri was waiting for her as she gained the front entrance, and she registered the short-sleeved white knit shirt and tennis shorts. He possessed a superb physique, all honed muscle and deeply tanned flesh. An arresting force, she admitted silently. It was little wonder Shanna was loath to let him go.

'How was your day?'

His low-pitched drawl was accompanied by a smile, and she returned it, summoning all her acting ability to the fore as she responded, 'Interesting. And yours?'

His eyes narrowed fractionally as he detected the slight edge of cynicism, and he subjected her to an assessing appraisal. 'Physical,' he enlightened her drily. 'A few rounds of golf prior to lunch, followed by three sets of tennis this afternoon.'

They entered the main foyer together, and Leanne moved towards the staircase.

'What time do you want to leave?' Her hand went automatically to the banister as she mounted the first step, only to come to an abrupt halt as Dimitri's fingers closed over her wrist.

'What happened today?' he demanded in a voice that was deceptively soft, and she turned to look at him—a mistake, for he looked far too close for comfort.

'Why should you imagine anything happened?' she parried lightly, and suffered his scrutiny.

'You forget,' he drawled softly. 'I can read you like an open book.'

'How devastating,' Leanne responded with dry mockery. 'I have no secrets at all.'

'Meaning that I have?'

She held his gaze unflinchingly for several long seconds, then she lifted both shoulders in an ineffectual shrug. 'You give nothing away, Dimitri, other than what you choose.'

His eyes narrowed fractionally. 'Elucidate, Leanne.'

'Let me go,' she commanded quietly, hating him for being so acutely astute. She'd never been very good at masking her feelings, and she coveted his ability to present an impenetrable façade. Anger

bubbled at the surface, and she closed her eyes
against the force of it, only to open them again as
she attempted to tug her hand free.

'When you tell me what's bothering you.'

Her eyes flashed blue fire, and there were twin
flags of colour staining her cheeks as she regarded
him with angry defiance.

'You're not my keeper.'

'Indisputably your husband,' Dimitri drawled,
and she reined in her temper with difficulty.

'Perhaps you'd be advised to keep that in mind,'
she said stiffly, and saw his eyes harden.

'I'm inclined to demand an explanation.'

Tangling with him was akin to banging her head
against a brick wall; not only fruitless, but painful.
'Word gets around,' she began after a measurable
silence. 'Shanna made an appointment for aromatherapy early this week, and repeated it again
this morning.'

His gaze didn't falter. 'Is that an unusual
occurrence?'

Leanne closed her eyes, then slowly opened them
again. 'The receptionist revealed that she isn't a
regular client.'

He stood waiting, his eyes dark and unfathomable. 'Don't stop there, Leanne.'

'Shanna requested that I return something to
you.' It was amazing that her voice sounded so
calm, when inside she was consumed with anger.

'Then whatever it is I suggest you give it to me,'
he said silkily.

Without another word she reached into her
shoulder-bag and withdrew the set of keys, then
solemnly handed them to him.

'She said she forgot to give them to you yesterday,' she ventured drily.

'Naturally, Shanna didn't enlighten you as to their purpose.'

It wasn't a question, merely a statement, and her stomach curled at the pitiless quality in his voice.

'Tell me,' Dimitri bade her with dangerous quietness. 'What do you imagine these keys unlock?'

She didn't answer, and his eyes assumed a ruthless intensity that was almost frightening.

'My apartment?' he asked.

There was a painful lump in her throat that precluded speech, and her lips parted, only to close again as she effected a helpless shrug. Then she gasped out loud as his fingers tightened painfully on her wrist.

'What the hell are you doing?' Leanne cried as he exerted sufficient pressure to force her out to the car.

'Get in,' he directed brusquely. 'Or I'll physically place you in the seat and fasten the belt.'

'Dimitri——'

Hard hands shifted to her shoulder as he opened the passenger door.

'All right,' she capitulated with exasperation, and her fingers shook as she tended to the seatbelt while he closed the door.

Seconds later he slid in behind the wheel and fired the engine, sending the car towards the gates with a muted roar.

It took five minutes to reach his apartment block, and a further five to park the car and ride the lift to his penthouse suite on the uppermost floor.

'Here are the keys,' Dimitri said with deceptive quietness, extending them in one hand. 'Open the door.'

Leanne looked at him, saw his deadly strength of purpose, and took the keys.

The first one didn't fit. Nor did the second. Instead the security alarm went off, loud and clearly distinguishable. And it didn't stop until he inserted a coded plastic disk and punched in a series of numbers.

Her heart set up a crazy beat as it hammered against her ribs, and she almost cried out as he impelled her inside.

The door closed with a refined clunk, and she watched as he crossed to an in-house phone, lifted the handset and punched in a few digits. Quietly, distinctly, he identified himself and assured the security man that there hadn't been an attempted break-in.

Then he turned and surveyed her with cold amusement. 'Look through the apartment, Leanne.'

'No,' she refused, hating him, hating herself. But most of all hating Shanna for initiating just this scene.

'Then I'll do it with you.'

Suiting words to action, he led her into first one bedroom, then the other, pulling open drawers, flinging wide one capacious wardrobe after another, insisting on her inspection.

There was nothing remotely resembling feminine apparel anywhere. Only a variety of masculine clothing that was obviously his.

Her eyes began to ache, and she blinked to ease the emotional strain.

'Whenever I've chosen to take a woman to bed, it hasn't been here,' Dimitri informed her with uncompromising inflexibility. 'Shanna handed you keys to a leased apartment and underground car park.' He paused imperceptibly. 'One of many such apartments in a block owned by a Kostakidas subsidiary company.' His eyes raked hers, hard and implacable. 'Shall I call my secretary and have her confirm that?'

Her eyes seemed locked with his, and she couldn't tear her gaze away. Slowly she shook her head. 'No,' she managed shakily.

She had little idea of the passage of time, and it could have been mere seconds, or several minutes, before she offered quietly, 'I arrived at the wrong conclusion.'

He moved close, and, placing a thumb and forefinger beneath her chin, he tilted it so that she had no option but to look at him. 'I have little doubt Shanna intended that you should.'

She felt nervous and unsure of his mood, and, unbidden, the tip of her tongue traced the curve of her lower lip.

'You were both an item,' she managed at last, and saw the faint glitter in his eyes.

' "Were" is the operative word.'

'Shanna doesn't appear to think so.'

'You believe I would maintain a mistress after marriage?'

'In normal circumstances...no,' Leanne said honestly, and glimpsed his faint smile.

'Our relationship isn't normal?'

The sad part was that she had no knowledge as to whether he shared the overwhelming ecstasy she experienced in his arms.

'You find it difficult to condone the terms of our marriage?'

How did she answer that? With extreme caution, an inner voice prompted. Or, better, not at all. 'If we don't leave soon, we'll be late,' she reminded him, and his smile deepened, assuming a definite tinge of mockery.

'Evading the issue, Leanne?'

With a careless shrug she forced a faint smile. 'Perhaps,' she admitted, knowing that she didn't want to deal with it now. Maybe not ever. Although that was a fallacy, for eventually she would have no choice.

She looked at him carefully, seeing the strength in the depth of those dark, gleaming eyes, the sensuality apparent there, and wondered how she could possibly exist without him.

He lifted a hand to brush light fingers down the edge of her cheek, and her lips trembled as his head lowered to hers.

His mouth sought a possession that was flagrantly seductive, and any protest she might have made died beneath the mastery of his touch as he deepened the kiss. Of their own volition her hands lifted to link at his nape, her body arching towards his in silent invitation as she met and matched the depth of his passion.

His hands slid down her back to curve beneath her bottom, and she gave a soundless gasp as he lifted her up against him.

It seemed an age before he released her slowly down on to the floor, and his mouth gentled and became vaguely teasing as he tasted the lower fullness of her lip, then took it lightly into his mouth for a few heart-stopping seconds before trailing his lips up to brush against her temple.

'I suppose we *have* to attend the ballet?' Dimitri queried huskily, and she drew a deep, shaky breath.

'Krissie Van Hahme will be disappointed if we don't.'

'I could compensate for her disappointment with a sizeable donation.' He ventured, and smiled faintly as she shook her head. 'No?'

'The ballet was very close to Paige's heart. I think she attended every gala performance,' Leanne said wistfully.

'And you'd like to go.'

It was a statement she didn't deny, and without a word he caught hold of her hand and led her from the apartment down to the car, then he drove the short distance home.

Two hours later they were seated in the darkened auditorium viewing the opening scene of *The Nutcracker*. The music lilted beautifully, faultlessly crisp and clear due to superb acoustics, and Leanne was entranced by the excellent choreography, the beauty, colour and design of the scenery.

It was a magical evening, all the more special because of the way Leanne knew it would end. There was a sense of joyful anticipation as Dimitri threaded his fingers through her own and held fast her hand. Every now and again his thumb traced a soothing pattern back and forth over the softly pulsing veins at her wrist, and his smile was so incredibly warm it reached right down into the depths of her soul.

By tacit agreement they chose not to linger, refusing with polite regret Krissie's invitation to join a few select friends for coffee.

'Another time,' Dimitri promised, and the society doyenne gave Leanne a generous smile.

'I wouldn't want to waste a moment either, if I had this gorgeous man to go home with.'

He laughed, a deep, throaty sound that brought forth a wicked gleam in Krissie's eyes as she reached forward and placed an affectionate kiss on Leanne's cheek.

'Escape, darling. We'll catch up eventually.'

There was no need for words as the Jaguar negotiated the late evening traffic, and it seemed only a short space of time before the sleek vehicle slid to a halt outside the main entrance of the Toorak mansion.

Indoors they ascended the stairs, and on reaching their suite Leanne unpinned her hair, pushing her fingers through its length as she slid out of her shoes.

Dimitri was in the process of shedding his shirt, and she took a long look at him, glorying in the expanse of muscular flesh and the sheer animal grace that was his alone.

He lifted his head, almost as if he sensed her appraisal, and his eyes speared hers, dark and impossibly slumberous.

She stood transfixed as he moved towards her, and she trembled slightly as he drew her into his arms.

'It was a wonderful evening,' she said with sincerity, and his lips curved into a warm smile.

'It isn't over yet,' he promised gently as he lowered his head, and she almost cried at the depth of emotion apparent in him as his mouth closed over hers in a kiss that left her weak-kneed and totally malleable.

Her dress fell in a silken whisper to the carpet, followed by wispy underwear, then he drew her down on to the bed.

Their loving was long and incredibly gentle, becoming almost a sublimation of all the pleasurable senses as they sought to gift each other the ultimate in erotic satiation.

Afterwards they slept, tangled close together, and in the early dawn hours they made love again, then rose and showered before driving to Geelong for a picnic lunch.

It was late afternoon by the time they arrived home, and Leanne slid out from the car and turned towards him.

'Do you know what I feel like doing?'

'Should I ask?' Dimitri drawled musingly.

'What say we eat out tonight?'

One eyebrow slanted in mocking surprise. 'That's it?'

'Aren't you going to ask where?'

He moved round the front of the car and caught hold of her hand. 'OK. *Where*?'

She cast him an impish grin. 'A place I know,' she declared as they started walking towards the house. 'The chef's speciality is barbecued steak, a Greek salad, fresh bread, with fresh fruit and cheese to follow.'

'Should we ring ahead and book?' he queried, playing the game.

'They don't take reservations,' Leanne declared blithely as they gained the main entrance and entered the foyer.

'Let me guess,' he drawled indolently. 'You're planning a barbecue here on the terrace. Who gets to be chef?'

'You do. I organise the salad, the bread and the cheese.'

'Done,' he agreed, and his lips curved into a musing smile. 'Go and raid the kitchen while I check for any messages.'

Leanne inspected the large refrigerator and took out steaks, then extracted ingredients for the salad. She was in the throes of retrieving a bread-stick from the freezer when he entered the kitchen.

'Eloise called from the Gold Coast,' Dimitri revealed. 'She says it's urgent.'

Leanne closed the freezer door, then turned towards him, her forehead creased in a frown. 'Eloise works in the clinic. Why on earth would she contact me on a Sunday?'

'Perhaps you'd better ring and find out.'

Her eyes darkened, and her expression became faintly pensive. 'I'll have to check her home number in my address book.'

'I'll get things started here while you make the call,' Dimitri said, and with a murmured 'thanks' she moved quickly up to their suite.

Fifteen minutes later she returned to the kitchen to relay that the senior staff member she'd assigned to manage the clinic had been involved in a car accident and was in hospital. Another employee had been with her, and she too was injured.

'I have to go back,' Leanne declared, and caught his dark, probing glance.

'You can't delegate?'

She shook her head with regret. 'The clinic is without two operatives, one of whom manages the place for me. I'll need to screen suitable applicants, and choose someone as a replacement manageress.' She looked at him, pleading with him to understand. 'It's a good business, and I can't let it fall apart. I owe it to the staff, to the clientele.'

Something flared in his eyes, an infinitesimal flame that was quickly masked. 'How long do you envisage being away?'

'A week, at least. Maybe longer,' she offered with a slight shrug.

'You want me to arrange your flight?'

'Please,' Leanne said gratefully, chewing her lip as one thought after the other crowded her brain. 'My apartment is leased out, so I'll need accommodation.'

'Let's go into the study and take care of the details now. Then we'll eat.'

Leanne took the early morning flight to Coolangatta, caught a taxi to the hotel, organised for her car to be removed from storage, then took a taxi to the clinic.

The Gold Coast was a tropical paradise, famed for its beaches, coastal waterways, and the numerous luxury canal-front homes.

The air was fresh and clean, pollution-free, and she breathed deeply, aware of a sense of having

missed the casual lifestyle and the slower pace compared to high-geared city living.

Monday was spent making phone calls, alerting
employment agencies, and attempting to keep the
clients happy. As promised, she put a call through
to Dimitri on her return to the hotel, and after
dinner she made contact with a few close friends.
Then she showered and fell into bed to sleep until
morning.

Tuesday was very much a repeat of the day
before, except that it brought a dozen prospective
employees, each of whom needed to be interviewed
and assessed as to their qualifications, ability and
appearance.

It should have been easy, but Leanne was aware
how important it was for the staff already in her
employ to get on with any new members. If anyone
had a personality problem with a fellow employee
it created tension that was often detected by the
clientele.

To be scrupulously fair, she gave each suitable
applicant a trial period and held meetings with the
existing staff at the end of each day.

By the week's end she'd hired two operatives—
one with an immediate start, the other due to commence on Thursday, and she was still undecided
who to appoint as manageress. Colette would be
ideal, although the only problem was that she
wanted a managerial salary plus a small share of
the profits.

'What do you think?' Leanne asked when she
put a call through to Dimitri.'

'Why hesitate?' he countered. 'You say she's
good. A share of the profits provides an incentive

to keep the business running smoothly. Promote her, Leanne,' he drawled quietly. 'And come home.'

*Home*. It sounded *right*. It was certainly where she wanted to be, for although it was great to catch up with a few friends she didn't like returning to an empty hotel room at the end of the day, and she hated the long, lonely nights.

So she made the necessary call to Colette, had a contract drawn up, and took bookings for Friday and Saturday with some of her own personal clients.

On Sunday she rose early and walked down to the beach for a swim, then she ate breakfast in one of the many cafés lining the esplanade, returning to the hotel to shower and change before collecting her car and driving out to Sanctuary Cove to explore the many boutiques lining the harbour front.

It became a carefree day, and it was almost five when she reached the hotel and rode the lift to her appointed floor.

Feeling impossibly restless, she checked the room-service menu, picked up the phone and placed an order to be delivered at six, then she undressed and stepped beneath the shower, luxuriating in it far longer than was necessary as she shampooed and conditioned her hair.

There was no point in getting dressed, and she slipped into a towelling robe before switching on the television.

She had just finished her meal when there was a sharp, staccato knock at the door, and she dampened a slight feeling of apprehension as she crossed the room to open it.

# CHAPTER ELEVEN

'DIMITRI!' Leanne's surprise was genuine, for he was the last person she expected to see.

Her eyes encompassed his rugged frame with a degree of hunger, then her lashes swept down to form a protective veil. More than anything she wanted to fly into his arms, to feel their warm strength enfold her close and give herself up to the magic he evoked the instant his mouth touched hers.

Yet she felt vaguely hesitant, afraid that if she allowed her feelings free rein she would be giving away too much.

'No welcoming kiss?' he prompted with indolent amusement, and she smiled, her eyes wide and guileless as she stepped forward.

'Of course. How are you?'

His eyes gleamed with latent mockery as his hands closed over her shoulders. 'Polite civility, Leanne?'

She wanted to cry out against his faintly taunting drawl, yet the words never left her throat, and she became filled with a familiar feeling of helplessness as he drew her into his arms.

Instinctively her face lifted towards his, her mouth soft and generous as he kissed her with such primitive hunger that it almost tore her fragile emotions to shreds.

Yet there was a sense of exultation in his tenuous control, and she flirted with the challenging thrust of his tongue, accepting his ravaging exploration before conducting one of her own.

It seemed an age before his mouth gentled, and she felt a slight shudder run through his powerful body as his hands slid down her back to rest possessively on the curve of her bottom.

His lips brushed hers, sensuous and stroking as he felt their quivering softness, and she heard his faint, husky groan as his mouth trailed down the sensitive curve of her neck to savour the madly beating pulse there before travelling lower, and he traced an evocative pattern down the deep V of her towelling wrap.

Her breasts burgeoned in expectation of his touch, and she made no protest as his fingers sought the tie at her waist, dispensed with it, then gently slid the wrap from her shoulders.

His eyes were dark and slumberous as he surveyed her delicate curves, and she swayed slightly when he lifted a hand and lightly traced the tender fullness of one breast before crossing to render a similar exploration to its twin.

'You're beautiful,' he said gently, letting his hand trail down to her waist, the indentation of her navel, before brushing low over her belly. 'So sweet and warm and giving,' he added huskily. 'I've missed you.'

The feeling was mutual, yet she couldn't bring herself to say the words. Instead, her hands shifted to his jacket and eased it from his shoulders, then she removed his tie. Her fingers slid to his shirt and she slipped the buttons free before tugging it off to join his jacket. Then she reached for his belt-buckle and unnotched it before freeing the zip fastening of his trousers.

He stood silent and still, and when she hesitated his hands covered hers, holding them fast.

'Don't stop.'

She looked at him carefully, her eyes wide and faintly luminous, unsure if she possessed quite the degree of courage to continue. A slight lump rose in her throat, and she swallowed it. 'Help me,' she begged quietly, unable to tear her eyes away from his.

A shivery sensation slithered the length of her spine as he lifted a hand and shaped her cheek, caressing it gently with his thumb.

'You've gone this far; why not continue?'

Of its own volition, the tip of her tongue edged out and ran a nervous path over her lower lip. His eyes flared at the movement, and she caught her breath, unable to release it for several long seconds as she became entrapped in the darkness of his gaze.

Slowly she sank to her knees on the carpet, and with extreme care she undid the laces of his hand-crafted shoes, and eased off one then the other before removing his socks.

Then she tugged free his trousers, and reached for the thin scrap of black silk shielding his manhood, her fingers slipping beneath the elasticised hem as she pulled the briefs slowly down over muscular thighs which flexed and tensed at her slightest touch.

There was a tremendous beauty in his arousal, a potent, virile force that was awesome when swollen to its fullest extent, and the desire to explore the delicate ridges was difficult to ignore.

Her touch was as soft and tentative as the brush of a butterfly's wing as she slowly traced the pad of her finger along a fold of skin, then trailed to the dark, springy hair nesting low at the junction of his powerful thighs.

With a sense of fascination she traced the outline of hair where it arrowed up the flat tautness of his stomach, then she lifted her other hand and gently completed the exploration before leaning forward to brush the lightest, briefest kiss to his shaft.

The desire to taste him, as he had frequently tasted her, gradually overrode her inhibitions, and he growled in husky approval as she followed her instincts, employing such incredible gentleness that he soon groaned out loud and reached for her, lifting her high so that she straddled his waist as he buried his head between her breasts.

Then it was her turn to cry out as he took one hardened peak into his mouth and rendered an erotic tasting until she begged him to stop.

'Put your arms round my neck,' he bade her as he shifted slightly, and she obeyed him, her eyes widening in startled surprise as he entered her with one sure thrust, his hands holding her hips steady as he began a slow, rotating movement that made her gasp at the degree of sensation he was able to evoke.

He kissed her, gently at first, then with such passionate demand that she was unaware of anything except the deep, sensual vortex into which she was being drawn.

At some stage she began to surface, and when she did it was to discover that she was lying on the bed, sated and drowsy in the aftermath of a loving that was unequalled by anything they'd previously shared.

It was all too easy to close her eyes and allow her attention to drift...to memories of Paige and Yanis, and the reason for her now unusual marriage.

Her love for the man who lay relaxed and sleeping by her side was both primeval and shameless. But did his emotional involvement go beyond the convenience of a willing partner in his bed? Worse, would he eventually tire of her?

Sleep had never been more elusive, and she eventually gave up counting each digital change of numbers on the bedside clock in the hope that it would aid escape from consciousness.

Moving quietly, she slid from the bed and padded barefoot to a distant window where the drapes gaped slightly and a slim stream of moonlight provided a soft, eerie light.

Carefully easing aside one long fall of heavy material, she cast her gaze out over the dark ocean whose smooth surface assumed a silvery gleam beneath the moon's glow.

The view was impressive, taking in the wide sweep of pale sand, the soft, curling waves with their gently foaming crests that looked so harmless tonight yet could swell into high-rolling waves that crashed dangerously into shore.

In a way it paralleled her feelings for Dimitri. Gentleness and sweet savagery. Possession that bordered on obsession.

There were lights lining the foreshore, a fairy tracery that curved seemingly out to sea as they followed the coastline all the way down to the northern tip of New South Wales.

Within the immediate periphery were bright splashes of neon, some constant, others flickering as they vied for the tourist dollar, and there was a steady river of headlights as traffic cruised the main arterial highways.

It was a scene she was familiar with, one she'd shared often from her apartment a mere kilometre distant.

She'd frequently assured Paige that she loved the Coast, enjoyed her independence, and valued her solitude. She'd lied, for her heart had been in Melbourne—with Dimitri. As it always would be.

Leanne heard a faint movement behind her, and she tensed slightly as hands curved round her waist and pulled her gently back against a warm, muscular frame.

'Unable to sleep?' Dimitri queried softly, and she felt his breath tease the length of her hair as he bent low to bury his mouth against the softly beating pulse at the edge of her neck.

She didn't trust herself to speak as a spiral of sensation unfurled deep within her and began to radiate through her body, activating every nerve-end, every cell until she was achingly alive.

'Dimitri——'

'Come back to bed,' he bade her gently, and she arched away from him as he nibbled the soft hollows at the base of her neck.

She groaned in silent despair, hating the way her body reacted to his dangerous foreplay. He had only to touch her, and she went up in flames.

His hands shifted to her shoulders as he turned her to face him, and she was powerless to evade his searching gaze as he tilted her chin.

His eyes were dark and languorous in the moonlight, his mouth a sensuous curve that descended slowly to capture her own. She opened her mouth to protest further, except that no words emerged as he conducted a light, teasing tasting that was so incredibly erotic it was all she could do not to respond.

Her hands sought leverage against his chest as she tore her mouth away, and she was powerless to still the faint gasp as his hands urged her close in against the force of his arousal.

'Don't——' Leanne begged. 'Please.' He stilled, and she shivered slightly as one hand slid up to her nape. 'We have to talk.'

It was hard to judge his mood, and she ploughed on regardless, knowing that if she didn't continue now she might never find the courage again.

'Our marriage,' she managed at last, each word more painful than the last, 'was an arrangement we were both thrust into, and I'm sure you wanted it less than I did.'

He was so quiet that if his hands hadn't been holding her captive she might almost have thought he was some devilish figment of an over-active imagination.

'I distinctly remember that marriage was my suggestion,' he said in a deceptively soft voice. 'If you remember, I was particularly insistent.'

'It's common knowledge why you did——' she continued, but he intercepted silkily,

'Common knowledge to whom?'

Leanne was silent, recalling each and every one of those damaging barbs and the pain they had caused.

'You haven't answered my question,' he prompted quietly, and she effected a slight shrug.

'Naming names won't achieve anything.'

'Then tell me what was said,' he commanded softly, and she swallowed the sudden lump that had risen in her throat.

'You're a very astute man, Dimitri,' she allowed simply. 'I'm sure you can guess.'

He was silent for several seconds, his eyes dark and vaguely analytical as he viewed the visible signs of her distress. 'It would be advantageous to keep a considerable slice of Yanis's fortune "in the family"?' he queried with deceptive calm.

She replied with a trace of sadness, 'I've had it on good authority from several so-called friends that that was your main objective.'

His eyes hardened fractionally. 'Social acquaintances who obviously have nothing better to do than manufacture gossip and convey it by innuendo.'

'Perhaps.' She took a deep breath and expelled it slowly. 'Even so, there's some basis of fact in what they say, for if it hadn't been for Paige's illness you would never have considered marrying me.'

He looked at her carefully. 'You're certain of that?' he queried mildly, and she met his gaze unflinchingly.

'You could have any woman you want.'

'You find it inconceivable,' he ventured with deadly softness, 'that I might want *you*?'

She took another deep breath. 'I think we both have a right to happiness,' she said shakily.

'Are you unhappy?' he demanded softly—far too softly, for she saw evidence of his veiled anger in his eyes, and she shivered with the knowledge that she'd gone too far to retreat.

He reached out and switched on a wall-lamp in order to see her expression, and her eyes dilated at the invasion of light.

She closed her eyes against the sight of him, hating herself at that moment almost as much as she hated him. 'It's more than that.'

He was silent for a few long seconds, then he ventured silkily, 'Elaborate, Leanne.'

Dear God, this was far worse than her worst nightmare, for she wouldn't wake in the morning and know it was the magnification of a wicked subconscious.

'I don't think I can live with you any more,' she revealed quietly. There was nothing she could do to stop the slow ache of tears, or to prevent the well of moisture as they trickled slowly down each cheek.

'Because you love me?' Dimitri demanded gently.

She didn't possess the courage to utter so much as a single word. She wanted to dash away the tears, but she stood still, unable to move even if her life depended on it.

'Anything you feel for me is bound up in affectionate responsibility and a sense of loyalty to your father, to Paige,' she said shakily.

His hands moved to capture her face, and his eyes darkened measurably as he saw her tear-drenched cheeks and the sense of desolation evident in her expression.

'Does it feel like "affectionate responsibility" every time I make love to you?' He moved his thumbs and gently wiped away the moisture. 'Does it?' he demanded quietly.

It felt like heaven, and he had to bend low to catch her whispered negation.

'You and Paige,' he revealed quietly, 'brought so much warmth and love into my father's life, as well as to my own. I wanted to catch you close and never let you go.'

Her lips trembled. 'Yet you did.' It hurt so much to say it. 'I adored you.'

'You made me your hero,' Dimitri corrected her gently. 'Except heroes belong in fairy-tales, and you were a beautiful young girl who deserved to forge her own career and taste life before committing herself to one man. I intended to allow you a year, maybe two, of independence.' He smiled faintly, then brushed her temple with his lips. 'Except you froze me out, and became very clever at evading me, even going so far as to time your visits to Melbourne for when I was out of town. On the few occasions I managed to surprise you, you treated me with such polite civility it was all I could do not to shake some sense into you,' he concluded with dangerous softness, and she shivered slightly.

'Shanna,' Leanne ventured slowly, aware of the hidden pain deep within, 'seemed to consider——'

'I've never given her cause to believe she was anything other than——'

'A willing bedmate?'

'A pleasant companion,' he amended, and she pondered on the wisdom of pursuing the subject.

She looked at him carefully. 'I see.'

His hands shifted to her shoulders and he shook her gently. 'Do you?'

'I think so.'

'The day we married I pledged you my love and fidelity,' he reminded her quietly as he curved one arm down her back and brought her close.

'They were only words,' she declared shakily, hopelessly torn by a desire to believe him.

His head lowered and he fastened his mouth on hers in a kiss that was incredibly gentle at first, then became increasingly passionate until the mere melding of mouths was no longer enough.

Leanne gave a faint moan of assent as he slid an arm beneath her knees and carried her back to bed, where she gave herself up to the sheer delight of his lovemaking.

There was a piercing sweetness apparent, a joy that transcended the mere physical, and she clung to him unashamedly as he led her to the heights and beyond.

Afterwards she lay in his arms, content and at peace, her whispered words so low, they were little more than a soft caress. 'I love you.'

He trailed gentle fingers over her shoulder, the sensitive curve of her neck—a light tracing pattern that made her want to press her lips against his warm, vibrant skin. She heard the beat of his heart beneath her cheek, felt its strength as it powered lifeblood through his body. A beat that had pounded dramatically only a short while ago as he'd led her to a shattering climax mere seconds ahead of his own.

'You're my life,' he offered quietly. 'My dearest love. Never doubt it.'

The words whispered inside her head as she drifted into a dreamless sleep, from which she woke at the touch of a hand and the sensual brush of warm lips against her cheek.

'Mmm,' Leanne murmured, turning into his arms without any hesitation at all. 'Is it morning already?'

She heard his soft, husky laugh as he pulled her close. His mouth settled over hers in a long, drugging kiss that made her ache for more, and she gave a deep, pleasurable sigh as his lips trailed the pulsing cord at her neck and sought the valley between her breasts.

The sensual awakening was exquisite as her body surrendered to the mastery of his touch. Every nerve cell blossomed into renewed life, warm and beautifully responsive as he rendered tiny love-bites to the soft, swelling flesh beneath each breast.

The sensation drew from her a husky groan as he teased each pleasure spot to fever pitch, her body akin to a finely tuned instrument awaiting the maestro's stroke.

Her need for fulfilment was so intense that she began to plead with him, then beg as she raked her fingers down the length of his back, sinking her nails into taut, muscled buttocks as she urged him close.

Seconds later she gave a cry of relief as his fingers sought the moist crevice between her thighs, caressing the highly sensitised nub until its pulsing core drove her wild with a desire he didn't hesitate to appease.

A long time afterwards they rose and showered, then donned towelling robes when Room Service delivered their breakfast.

Leanne reached for the orange juice, then sank into a chair and began emptying packeted cereal into both plates.

'We have an hour before we leave for the airport,' Dimitri informed her musingly as he took the chair opposite.

Her hand paused in its action, and she cast him a stricken glance as a host of chaotic thoughts raced through her mind, the foremost of which was a series of appointments for the day ahead, plus a luncheon date with a few close friends.

'I can't,' she began, lifting a hand to tuck a stray tendril of hair back behind her ear. 'At least, not today,' she qualified, and saw his eyes narrow slightly. 'I promised Colette another day before she takes charge,' she hurried to explain. 'Besides, I owe it to the staff, the regular clientele. I can't just walk away before everything is satisfactorily organised.'

'I have a meeting scheduled in Melbourne for eleven,' Dimitri declared as he quartered an apple, then peeled and stoned a peach. 'One I can't postpone.'

'Dimitri——'

'Ring and let me know which flight you'll be on,' he said gently. With an economy of movement he reached for the steaming silver pot. 'Coffee?'

'Please,' Leanne murmured gratefully, taking the cup and saucer from his hand mere seconds later. 'Thanks.'

'For flying a few thousand kilometres to spend the night with you?' His eyes gleamed with humour, and she blinked at the degree of warmth evident in his gaze.

'The coffee,' she said with an impish smile.

'Hmm,' he mused as he reached out and stroked his fingers down her cheek. 'I should make you pay for that...' He trailed off suggestively, and a wicked grin curved her lips.

'You have a plane to catch, remember?'

With one fluid movement he got to his feet and moved indolently round to her side. 'Unfortunately.' He cupped her chin, then bent low and kissed her with such passionate intensity that she lost the ability to coalesce so much as a rational thought. Then he straightened, and directed a shattering smile at her. 'Don't be too long following me, hmm?'

She didn't trust herself to speak, and simply shook her head in silent acquiescence, watching as he turned and walked from the suite. Then she slid from the bed and made for the shower.

The day passed swiftly, and there was a spring to her step, a hidden depth to her smile that didn't go unnoticed by the two friends she shared lunch with in one of the newer hotels along the tourist strip.

'When are you going back to Melbourne?'

'Tomorrow,' Leanne informed them, and was greeted with two genuine and extremely voluble protests.

'We planned dinner at the Casino tonight, and Renée has tickets for a show tomorrow night. You *have* to stay. That gorgeous stepbrother of yours will never allow you to escape alone again. Oh, come on, Leanne,' Tricia pleaded. 'What's one more night?'

'I'll think about it,' she temporised. Which she did, qualifying her decision by rationalising that it wouldn't do Dimitri any harm to wait one more day. She'd waited *years*, and there was a certain degree of innate pride that forbade her from running back, no matter how much she needed to be with him.

So she attended dinner and the show, returning to her suite to sleep fitfully until she was woken by Room Service with her breakfast. Then she rang the airline, booked a late afternoon flight, and rang Eleni with the time of arrival.

The plane touched down and cruised along the runway before gliding to a halt in its allotted bay, and after disembarking she moved easily through to the arrival lounge.

'Leanne.'

Dimitri's achingly familiar drawl filled her with a treacherous weakness as she turned to face him.

There was a sense of *déjà vu*—same airline terminal, except that it was a different flight. However, this time there was no reserve or sense of uncertainty in her greeting. Only love, and a need to feel the warmth of his embrace.

Without hesitation she went into his arms and lifted her face as his mouth descended to take possession of hers in a kiss that almost blew her away.

'What took you so long?' he demanded huskily several minutes later.

She arched her head back and looked at him with such a degree of adoration that it made him catch his breath.

'I wanted to punish you a little,' she owned without hesitation, following the admission with a wickedly impish smile.

He laughed. A warm, deep, throaty chuckle that brought an answering gleam to her beautiful blue eyes. 'Indeed?'

She tilted her head a little to one side. 'I intend to make it up to you,' she promised solemnly, and he slanted her a long, musing look that sent her heart pounding against her ribs.

'Sounds interesting.'

'Oh, it will be,' she assured him. 'I had an hour on the plane to come up with several inventive possibilities.'

'I had planned to take you out to dinner,' he mocked gently.

Leanne reached up and kissed his chin, then she drew back and tucked her hand into the curve of his arm as they made their way towards the luggage carousel. 'Are you hungry?' she asked.

He reached forward and plucked her bag from the revolving belt, then led the way out to the car.

'For food? Or you?'

She slid into the passenger seat and fastened the seatbelt, waiting until he slipped in behind the wheel before venturing with teasing sweetness, 'A restaurant would be nice.'

He chose a small, intimate taverna specialising in Greek cuisine, and Leanne ordered her favoured dish of moussaka, while Dimitri settled for vine-leaf-wrapped meatballs and rice with a delicately flavoured sauce, and fresh, crusty bread. They drank fine wine, and savoured the meal, taking their time over coffee, then they walked arm in arm to the car and drove home.

Indoors they ascended the stairs to their suite, and once inside Dimitri extracted a long, slim envelope from the inside pocket of his jacket and silently handed it to her.

'For me?' Her puzzlement was genuine, and he smiled.

'Open it and see.'

Slowly she slit the seal, and removed two airline tickets... to Athens, departing the day after tomorrow.

'Dimitri——' Pleasure robbed her of words.

'A delayed honeymoon,' he relayed quietly, his arms closing round her slim frame as she reached for him. 'On a remote island in the Mediterranean. Far away from everyone.'

'Did I tell you how much I love you?' she whispered as his head lowered to hers.

'I'm hoping to hear you say it every day for the rest of my life.'

She smiled—a wonderful, achingly sweet smile that radiated from deep within her, lighting her eyes so that they resembled pure crystalline sapphire. 'I think I could manage that.' A faint laugh emerged from her throat as she tilted her head slightly. 'Of course, it's reciprocal, you understand?'

'Without question,' Dimitri answered solemnly an instant before he took possession of her mouth, and his erotic plunder made any further use of words totally superfluous.

**Michelle Reid** grew up on the southern edges of Manchester, the youngest in a family of five lively children. But now she lives in the beautiful county of Cheshire with her busy executive husband and two grown-up daughters.

She loves reading, the ballet, and playing tennis when she gets the chance. She hates cooking, cleaning, and despises ironing! Sleep she can do without and produces some of her best written work during the early hours of the morning. Michelle had her first book published by Mills & Boon® in 1988 and has since written more than 15 romances.

# *NO WAY TO BEGIN*
## by
## MICHELLE REID

# CHAPTER ONE

IT WAS a dark, dank, filthy night. One of those nights when nothing stirred, nothing but the relentless fall of fine drizzly rain from a low bank of cloud which hung oppressively overhead.

Nina Lovell stood just inside a pair of wrought-iron gates, staring across the shadowed lawns at a white-rendered mansion house. There was some kind of party going on up there. The driveway was packed with cars, and there was light spilling from almost every ground-floor window. The muted sound of music drifted towards her on the damp mizzly air.

She shivered, huddling deeper into her thin summer coat, cold hands clenched inside her coat pockets. Somewhere inside that house, the man she had come here to see was enjoying himself, while several miles away, in a house not dissimilar to this one, lay the victim of his latest *coup*, dying from the horror of it all.

'He can't do it to me, he can't——!' Jonas Lovell had cried out just before a heart attack sent him crumpling to the study floor.

But apparently he could do it, and was about to if he couldn't be stopped. Which was why she had come here tonight. She had come to beg, plead, bargain if necessary. Do whatever it took to relieve her father's stress. Did *he* know about Jonas Lovell's heart attack? And if he did know, didn't he care that in order to swell his own already massive property empire he had crushed another man into the ground?

She despised men like him, and a deep shiver shook her slender frame. Her father did not deserve what was happening to him. His whole life revolved around

Lovell's. Take it away from him and he had nothing left to live for.

'He's fretting,' the doctor had told her worriedly. 'Something has to be done to ease his mind, or I'm afraid he may suffer another attack.'

With the misty rain clinging like fine gossamer to the long loose fall of her red-gold hair, Nina started forwards, moving with a strange, ghostly grace along the line of sleek, expensive cars, the spill of light from the house catching at the stark white pallor of her skin as she went. It was gone ten o'clock, and she had hardly moved from her father's bedside for three long days and nights; fatigue was dragging at her limbs, her mind, her aching heart. Only concern for her father and a deep-seated malevolence for the man she had come here to see kept her going, forcing her to place one tired foot in front of the other, pausing only when she reached the deep circular porch supported by two white pillars.

What now? she wondered blankly.

The man she had come to see was throwing a party. Did she simply bang on his front door and demand to see him anyway?

No, she shuddered at the very idea of it. It was bad enough having to come here to beg from him without risking having an audience to watch her do it.

God, she was tired...

A pale hand slipped out of her pocket to rub across the heavy press of her brow. The worry that had become her constant companion for the last three terrible days was sapping her ability to think clearly. She wasn't even that certain she was actually standing here—or existing in some kind of misty nightmare which included her father's illness as well as this unwelcome journey.

She wished it could be a dream, she thought heavily as she lowered her hand to stare at the white-painted front door to the house. She would give anything to just wake up and find her father fit and well, and the need to place herself anywhere near the man who owned this house non-existent.

He frightened her. He had from the first moment she had set eyes on him. No one should be allowed to be as powerful as this man was—nor so disturbingly attractive.

Something inside her coiled into a tight ball in the pit of her stomach, then sprang out in a jarring wave of agitation that had her feet scuffling on the black bitumen driveway and her eyes flickering huntedly around her before she found the strength to quell the fear, and return her gaze to the white-painted front door.

It was only then that she noticed how it was standing slightly ajar, and the agitation altered to a tingling glow of excitement as an idea slid unbidden into her head.

Dared she just walk into his house without permission?

The door seemed to have been left open in invitation to any latecomers to his party. Well, she thought cynically, she was late, though not invited.

She had come here to see Anton Lakitos, and see him she would before the night was out. Even if that meant sneaking into his house and hiding away somewhere until she was sure she could get him alone.

Her chin went up, soft mouth setting in a thin line of determination, and she moved slowly forwards, stepping carefully through the narrow gap in the door.

And found herself standing in a deep inner vestibule, the floor beneath her feet ornately tiled in black and white inlaid with gold. Dark red velvet hung across the inner archway, pulled back into two deep drapes by gold tasselled cords. Beyond them was a large square hallway softly lit by oyster-silk-shaded wall-lights that glowed warmly against the oak-panelled walls and richly polished floor. A wide central stairway swept elegantly upwards to a shadowed landing, its shallow treads covered in a thick dark red carpet.

The hall was surprisingly free of people, the several doors leading from it all closed, keeping the sounds of enjoyment to a low level. And, ignoring the way the heavy pump of her heart was telling her that what she was doing was nothing short of criminal, she went forwards, slipping around the curtains to take a fleeting glance to her left and right before making a dash for the stairs, her footsteps light on the polished wood floor, some hazy sense of reason telling her that if she could only make it to the floor above then maybe she could find somewhere up there to wait undetected until the party was over.

With the sense of her own culpability running like pure adrenalin in her veins, she ran up the stairs, only just making it to the top when a door below was opened, and she dropped quickly down behind the polished balustrades just in time to see two men come out of one of the rooms, closing the door behind them.

Anton Lakitos, she saw immediately, confirmation coming with the sudden hectic clamour of her pulses. They, like she, would recognise him anywhere.

Tall, wide-shouldered and powerfully built, Anton Lakitos was the most intimidatingly attractive man she had ever encountered. Everything about him disturbed her deeply, from the way the jet-black sheen of his hair swept smoothly away from the hard-angled shape of his face, to the rigid squareness of his jaw with its inbred tilt of arrogance. His mouth was wide and firm and shockingly sensual. His nose was long and straight, an essential line to his lean-boned face. The face of a man who knew what he was and where he was going in life. A man who had been consistently undermining her composure from the first time—months ago—when their eyes had met in an electrifying clash of the senses. Dark—dark brown eyes, burning into her own with a power that was both terrifying and dangerously hypnotic.

And even while she had mentally backed off from what that look said to her, even as she had given a stunned shake of her head in outright rejection of both him and his messages, she had recognised the rich natural tan of the Mediterranean man. The eyes, the hair, the sheer muscled beauty of his body all screamed 'Italian' at her. Like the elegant cut of his hand-made suit, his shirt, his shoes, his whole manner. She had therefore been surprised to learn later that he was Greek. For he had seemed to suit her idea of a high-born Italian better than the darker, more ruggedly hewn Greek man.

Not a week had passed since that first collision when he hadn't somehow manoeuvred them into the same company. And every time they met he caused that same explosion of feeling inside her, forcing her to back right away from him in sheer self-defence of what it all meant. She didn't trust him—couldn't trust that kind of hot sexual pull. To her, he was a sophisticated man of the world, while she was nothing but a shy and nervous student of music, attending the same lavish functions he attended because her tycoon father demanded it of her.

He'd tried every ploy available to him to get closer to her, coming to stand or sit by her side at any opportunity he got, forcing her to be aware of his presence, of the white-hot static that flashed constantly between them, smiling a little sardonically when she continued to hold herself aloof from him, refusing to leave her father's side or even talk to him if she could get away with it without appearing unforgivably rude. She had rejected every approach he made towards her until, eventually, he'd backed right off and continued his unsettling of her senses from afar, dark eyes burning with a look she could only describe as a 'want'. A hot and hungry, unhidden kind of want, that had kept the colour riding high in her cheeks and her breath locked up tight in her chest for as long as they occupied the same room.

He'd begun to haunt her dreams, and she had begun making excuses not to accompany her father to the places where he might be. 'Don't be stupid, Nina,' old Jonas had snapped out irritably. 'I need you with me, and that's all there is to say about it. Anyway,' he'd gone on testily, 'it's high time you realised that there is more to life than your piano and that damned Jason Hunter!' Poor Jason

had never earned favour in her father's eyes, no matter
how hard he tried. 'And stop being so frosty towards
Anton Lakitos!' he'd added impatiently. 'I've got some
delicate business brewing with him, and I don't want
your cold manner rocking the boat.'

Well, she thought now bitterly, something had certainly rocked the boat, because Anton Lakitos was
threatening to take over her father's company, and poor
Jonas was lying sick to the heart with the horror if it.

'Are you sure, John?'

The sound of that low-pitched and grim-sounding
voice brought her attention clattering back to the two
men standing in the hallway below her.

'Yes, sir,' the other man replied. 'He's waiting to speak
to you on the telephone, right now.'

'Damn,' the Greek muttered, then, 'Damn,' again.
Then, 'OK, John, I'll speak to him in my study.' And
Nina crouched further into the shadows as both men
moved across the hall, parting at a pair of doors which
Anton Lakitos flung open and strode through while the
man called John disappeared towards the back of the
house.

A moment later, Nina heard the muffled tones of a
one-sided conversation. His voice was pitched too low
for her to catch any of the words, but she could hear
enough to know he was receiving bad news. Good, she
thought. I hope one of his rotten deals has fallen through.
I hope he's lost every penny he has!

This might well be her best chance to get him on his
own! she realised on a sudden rush of agitation that had
her jerking upright, only to gasp out painfully when her
cramped leg muscles protested at the sudden movement
after being held in a crouched position for so long.

Wincing, teeth biting down into her bottom lip, her
face so white it looked ashen against the quickly drying
tumble of red-gold hair, she took a step towards the
stairs—only to go completely still again as another door
opened below her.

The sound of music lifted, filling her ears, grating along every nerve-end, making her small teeth clench, gold-tipped lashes flickering as she glanced downwards to see a dark-haired woman leave the room Anton Lakitos had just come from.

Aware that the voice in the study had stopped speaking, Nina watched the woman walk gracefully across the hall. She was beautiful, exquisitely so. Tall, dark and perfectly shaped, she was wearing a sleek bronze silk gown that shimmered in the soft light, moving with the sensual grace of her body.

'Anton?' Her voice was sensual too, like thick cream on honey as she called out softly, 'Where have you got to, darling?'

The enquiry brought her to the threshold of the study, and Nina crouched down low again so she could see further into the room. Anton Lakitos came back into view, a glass of what looked like whisky in his hand.

'Aah...' Nina heard the woman drawl. 'So, you drink alone! You perhaps find your guests tedious company tonight?' Her arms went smoothly around his neck, and Nina felt a surprise shaft of resentment shoot through her. They were lovers, it was obvious!

'A business call, no more,' her host assured her, smiling slightly as he bent to place a light kiss on the woman's lips. 'I was on my way back to you all, Louisa.' He scolded lightly, 'You had no need to come in search of me.'

'But I missed you, darling!' the thick-as-cream voice exclaimed, and she moved closer to him, curving her body into the hard-packed line of his. 'Shall we get rid of them, Anton?' she suggested huskily. 'Send them all away so you and I can——'

'Not tonight, Louisa,' he declined, softening the blow by placing another kiss on her pouting mouth. 'Tonight I have some important business to attend to once everyone has gone.'

'More important to you than me?' she miaowed, batting her long black lashes at him.

Anton Lakitos took a sip from the glass he was holding and firmly detached himself from the clinging woman. 'Go back to the other guests, Louisa. I'll join you all in a moment,' he said, so ruthless about the dismissal that even Nina stiffened.

So did the lovely Louisa, her big eyes widening as he turned his back on her, taking another deep sip at his drink. Then she was giving a haughty toss of her head, the flash of anger in her eyes quite startlingly venomous before she was pinning a sweet smile on her face and stepping close to him again.

'Oh, darling...' she murmured coaxingly, 'don't be cross with Louisa.' Red-tipped fingers did a pretty dance along his shoulder until they reached the tense lines of his jaw where they began stroking caressingly. 'She's sorry if she spoiled your private drinking party.'

Anton shook his head, laughing softly as if in spite of himself at her childishly teasing tone. Some of the tension seemed to seep out of him and his smile was wryly mocking as he turned back to face Louisa. 'You've never been sorry for anything in your whole life, you little minx,' he scolded, hooking an arm around her slender waist to pull her against him. 'If I ask you nicely to go back to my guests, will you go?' he ruefully begged.

The sulky pout became a sensual smile. 'Kiss me properly,' she demanded, 'and I shall promise to do anything you ask of me, anything at all...'

The invitation was blatantly clear. 'Minx,' he murmured again, just before his mouth lowered to cover hers.

Disgusted with what she was seeing, Nina got up, ignoring the nagging protest in her limbs this time as she turned and escaped quickly into the shadows of the upper landing. A strange sickening feeling was erupting in her stomach, a further rejection of everything Anton Lakitos was. The man had no scruples, no morals. He might have spent the last few months lusting after Nina Lovell, but it didn't stop him taking his pleasure wherever else it was offered!

The tiredness she had been struggling with for days now came slamming down on her head again, and, without really thinking what she was doing, she opened the door nearest to her and slipped quietly through it, closing it and leaning wearily back against it with her eyes closed, heart pumping sluggishly in her breast.

What in heaven's name am I doing here? she found herself wondering for the first time since she had started out on this crazy mission.

It only took the sunken grey image of her father lying so gravely ill to remind her. She was here because of him. And on that grim reminder she sucked in a deep steadying breath of air—then went perfectly still as her senses picked up on the subtle masculine scent lingering in the air around her, and her heart gave a violent trip.

This was his room!

She had smelled that scent only minutes ago as he crossed the hallway, the musky fragrance drifting up towards her on the warm air. She had been inhaling the same heady scent every time he came close to her over the last months, been instantly drawn to it, and never quite been able to rid her senses of it since.

Slowly, reluctantly, she opened her eyes.

The room was as dark as the grave, and she shivered, her arms going up to fold across her body in an age-old act of self-protection.

Her coat was wet, she noted absently, the sleeves clinging uncomfortably to her bare arms beneath, and she shrugged it off, holding it clasped tightly in front of her while she gave her eyes time to adjust to the gloom.

Slowly, things began to take shape, dark bulks looming out of the walls: wardrobes, chests, and the squat shape of a couple of easy chairs, one of which was standing beside a rather imposing bed. She managed to make out a window, covered with heavy curtains which were blocking out all hint of light.

Taking a few hesitant steps forwards, she came to another halt halfway across the thick carpet, the silence in the room almost as oppressive as the darkness it embraced. It was like standing in some dense black void; her every sense was screaming out against it.

Her shoulders slumped wearily, the sticky dampness of her clothes and the stifling warmth of the room all helping to fill her with a hazy sense of unreality.

If she weren't feeling so tired, if she weren't so heartsick and worried about her father, if she didn't hate and despise Anton Lakitos as much as she did, then perhaps she would be able to see the humour in getting herself into this crazy situation.

But as it was she could barely think at all.

She would wait here, she decided on a stubborn firming of her quivering jaw. She would wait here until Anton Lakitos came to bed—if he came to bed—and then if he came alone.

If he didn't, then she didn't know what she would do...

God, she was tired...

The carpet beneath her feet muffling any hint of sound, she moved forwards again until her foot made contact with the base of the chair near the bed, and she sank down into it. It was a soft-cushioned velvet easy chair, big and welcoming to her weary body. A yawn caught her by surprise, and she smiled wryly at it as her aching body wilted further into the chair's yielding softness, tired fingers letting go of her damp coat so it fell in a rustling heap to the floor beside the chair, her weary brain filling with a muzzy confusion. She had not slept for three nights. Had hardly moved from the chair beside her father's bed. And his restless voice had droned on and on, mumbling senseless phrases about Lovell's and money and Anton Lakitos until she had been able to stand it no more, and she had leaned over him to ask anxiously, 'What can I do for you, Daddy? What can I do to make you more comfortable?'

'He wants everything,' he had mumbled fretfully. 'You, Lovell's, my self-respect, everything.'

'Who does?' she had cried. 'Tell me, and I'll——'

'Why couldn't you have been a son, Nina?' The age-old complaint had left his lips without his being aware of how much it hurt her. 'This wouldn't have happened if you'd been a son! God——' he choked, becoming agitated again. 'He has to be stopped——' He'd tried to get out of bed, and it had taken all Nina's strength to make him lie back down again. 'He won't be happy until he's stripped me of everything—everything...' he had gasped out as he fell weakly back against the pillows.

'Who won't?' she'd pleaded, frightened, really frightened, hating to see him like this. He was usually such a strong and forceful man, so full of life and sharp shrewd cunning, that she had found it difficult to believe that anyone could hurt him this much.

'Get rid of him, Nina, before he ruins you too,' he'd whispered fiercely. 'The greedy, no good... Get Anton... Stop him!' he had groaned, and at last had told her, without her having to ask again, just who it was who was responsible for doing this to him.

So, here she was, come to stop him. By whatever means she had available to her. Prepared to fight, claw, beg or bleed to do it. But not before she'd told Anton Lakitos what she thought of him face to face. Not until...

No, that wasn't right. Nina rubbed her aching head. You don't attack a man then beg for his mercy. You would get nowhere with those kind of tactics...

Her eyes felt hot and heavy, the pitch darkness filling her with a sense of utter emptiness, so that she couldn't think clearly, as if she weren't really here at all.

Slipping off her shoes, she curled her legs up beneath her and began rubbing at her damp cold toes, surprised to find out that she had come here without even putting on any stockings. She had just left her father's bedside, walked out of the room and down the stairs, then—then what?

She couldn't remember. It hurt to even try. She was here. How, she had no idea, but here she was, she was sure of it.

That last thought brought the wry smile back to her tired mouth. You're losing touch with your mind, Nina, she mocked herself. If you don't watch out, they'll be coming to take you away!

All she had to do now, she told herself firmly, was keep her eyes fixed on the dark shape of the door directly in front of her, and wait—wait . . .

Outside, the rain continued to fall with a silent monotony. Inside the dark room, all was quiet, peaceful. Her head began to droop, her eyelids along with it. Once or twice she managed to jerk herself awake, but eventually, inevitably, she lost the battle with sleep, curling deeper into the softly padded armchair as the minutes ticked away without her actually being aware of them . . .

Downstairs, the party began to break up. Car doors slamming, people calling out, engines revving, laughter, chatter, then nothing as a quietness settled over the whole house, and still Anton Lakitos did not come to bed.

Hours later, deep into the miserable night, the bedroom door came open and closed again. The muttered curses of a man who wasn't quite in control of his actions sounded in the darkened warmth of the room as he stripped off his clothes and left them to fall in an untidy heap on the floor. He was tired, fed-up, and too full of malt whisky to think further than his waiting bed. The phone call earlier had just about finished off a frustrating few months for him, and all he wanted to do now was sleep, sleep off the whisky and forget all his problems for a while . . .

Nina came awake with a start, eyes opening wide and bewildered, staring into the pitch blackness with a total disorientation with her surroundings. Something had woken her. What, she couldn't say, but she cried out softly as she jerked into a sitting position, a sense of an unknown fear sending icy shivers down her spine.

'What the——?'

The voice, sounding muffled and slurred, had her coming out of the chair to stand swaying dizzily, her confused mind comparing her surroundings, the muffled curse, and the chair she had been sleeping in, with her father's bedroom where she had spent the best part of the last three days.

'Daddy?' she whispered shakily, groping anxiously for the bed. Knowing she had got something wrong, but unable to work out what.

Without warning, a bulky shape launched itself at her, catching hold of her and dragging her across the bed before she had a chance to react. A moment later and the hard weight of a man's body fell heavily across her own, and in the short space of time it took her to realise just what was happening, she found herself trapped beneath the very naked body of Anton Lakitos.

'Well, well, well, what do we have here?' he murmured huskily, two hands pinning her shoulders to the bed, his warm breath fanning her face, smelling strongly of whisky as he peered at her through the inky blackness. 'Witch or angel?' he idly mused, seeming not in the least bit concerned about finding a strange woman in his bedroom! 'Or maybe a sprightly nymph sent by the gods to soothe this weary mortal's soul!'

'No!' she cried, appalled to hear her own voice leave her with hardly any volume at all. His husky intimation was so obvious that she thrust her hands against his shoulders, gasping as the sleek, smooth heat of his skin confirmed his naked state. 'No!' she choked again, 'Get your hands off me, you——'

'Tut, tut, tut,' he scolded, a long, incredibly sensitive finger coming out to tap her scorching cheek. 'This is my dream,' he announced. 'And I like my nymphs willing, not naughty. Well, maybe a little naughty,' he then amended on a husky little laugh.

He was drunk, she realised with horror. Slewed out of his tiny mind! He thought he was dreaming, when the stupid man had her...

'Let me go!' she spat, pained to find the volume lost in the tight pressure of her throat again. She hit out at him with her fists, cursing thickly to herself when he only laughed and caught her flailing hands, holding them fast in one of his own, pressing them firmly to the mattress above her head.

'Naughty nymph,' he scolded. 'I shall have to silence that pretty mouth with kisses.'

And he did. To Nina's horror, to her utter consternation, his mouth came warm and possessive on top of her own. She stared up at him through the terrible blackness, breath suspended, pulses hammering out of control as she experienced the shock sensation of heated pleasure rushing through her. Then she began to struggle in real earnest, wriggling and twisting beneath him in a frantic attempt to escape the shocking sensuality of his imprisoning mouth.

His, 'Mmm,' of pleasure had her going instantly still beneath him, shock sending blushes to every corner of her tingling flesh when she realised just what her struggles were doing to him.

God, what am I going to do now? she wondered desperately. The man was lost in a drunken stupor! If she woke him up, he could well turn nasty. If she let him go on believing he was dreaming, the consequences could be far more damning.

'Please...' she whispered pleadingly.

'Oh, yes...' he sighed, and the mouth on hers increased its pressure, tasting her, filling her with a peculiar sense of weakness that completely overrode everything else as her own lips began to part—she felt them go with a sense of bewildered horror, yet was unable to stop herself responding. His tongue touched her teeth, then the inner receptiveness of her lips, gently urging her to open further to him. A groan wavered in her throat, a desperate plea for sanity in this insane situation, then he got his own way without her being able to stop him, as her teeth parted of their own volition, and explosions went off in her head.

A hot and naked desire flicked like fire right through her. Shock, the buffeting darkness, her real hatred of this man, all culminated to fling her into a vortex of violent feeling. She wanted to scratch, kick, scream, bite! Yet her body was arching invitingly beneath his, her mouth moving sensually with his own, luring him on, even while she wanted to reject the whole sordid scene.

She was suffocating in her own responses, the breath coming from her body in short tight gasps of arousal. The fight going on inside her head was in no way strong enough to combat the feelings he was so easily awakening in her. He was big and strong, his slick smooth skin an added complication as he moved intimately against her, the heat of him awakening senses inside her she hadn't even known she possessed! The weight of him, the sheer maleness of him, touch, taste, smell, everything backing up to work against her. And the darkness, that terrible disorientating darkness, filling her with a sense of unreality that allowed her to give in to her own desperate bodily yearnings.

'My God, you're sweet.' He was trembling as he moved away a little, his breath a shivering rasp of desire that helped keep her lost in her strange passive limbo. Her hands were released, fingers fluttering as his own ran feather-light over the wild fall of her hair, brushing against her hot cheeks, finding the quivering corners of her mouth to retrace the kiss-swollen contours as though he were a blind man trying to build a picture.

Was he still asleep? She couldn't tell. She couldn't tell anything any more. He began kissing her face, light, warm, tantalising kisses that lifted the fine sensitive hairs on her skin as he brushed her temples, her fluttering lashes, her cheeks, her nose, and finally the soft quivering corner of her mouth where his fingers had just caressed. His hands slipped beneath her, lifting her mouth to the hungry heat of the kiss. Dizzy with confusion, pleasure, fear, and a hundred and one other sensations she didn't dare label, Nina felt his fingers move to the tiny buttons on her blouse, and, as her traitorous breasts began to swell in aching anticipation of his touch, at last she came alive on a horrified explosion of everything.

With a violent thrust, she pushed him off her, taking him by surprise enough to send him rolling back against the pillows. There was a startled moment when neither moved, then she was scrambling up and off the bed, gasping, choking on a build-up of strangled sobs, her only thought to get away from here before he issued the final insult to the Lovell family by taking her without even being aware he had done it!

'Who are you?' he rasped out thickly from the darkness.

Nina went perfectly still, her heart hammering beneath the hectic heave of her breasts, teeth biting down hard on her trembing bottom lip, eyes wide and stinging with wretched tears, her voice locked inside her throat, unable to answer—not wanting to answer.

There was another short pause when no one moved, the silence filling with a terrible foreboding on both sides, then Nina heard the sound of movement, as though he was stretching across the bed to drag something towards him, and she exploded into action again, bending down to search the floor for her shoes, her hair tumbling all over her face to get in her way, irritating her, sending her temperature gauge shooting high as panic completely engulfed her.

She found one shoe, her fingers trembling as they closed around the soft leather sole at the same time as a hand came gently on to her shoulder—and all hell broke loose inside her. She rose up, turning on the balls of her bare feet, and lashed out blindly at the dark bulk looming so terrifyingly close!

## CHAPTER TWO

NINA stood stricken into stillness as the dark bulk on the bed gave a pained grunt and jerked violently in reaction.

Then an awful silence settled over the room when nothing moved, nothing but the slow lowering of her hand where the shoe with its lethal-tipped heel still hung between limp, lifeless fingers. And that weird sense of unreality swept over her once again, trapping her in the centre of her own crazy nightmare.

'*You stupid bitch!*' The violent hiss of words was preceded only fractionally by the full weight of his body landing against her own, sending them both tumbling to the floor with enough force to push the air right out of her lungs. He was breathing like a marathon runner, heaving in deep, noisy gasps of air as he struggled not to completely crush her beneath his own weight.

'You stupid, crazy bitch!' he choked again, wrenching the guilty shoe from her hand and hurling it across the room.

Keeping a painful grip on her shoulders, he dragged himself to his feet, yanking her up with him until they both stood swaying in the nullifying fall-out from their mutual violence.

'You damned stupid fool! What the hell were you trying to do to me?'

Her head came up, drawn by the hoarse thickness of his voice, by the tremors she could feel shaking him. Her hair was all over her face, increasing the sense of nightmare. She couldn't speak, was too shocked by her own violence to think, so she just stood there, staring at him through the thick curtain of hair, her mind a total blank.

22

He gave her another shake, his fingers biting into the tender flesh of her upper arms as he sent her unruly hair flying out around them so it clung to the clammy surface of his contorted face. A muttered curse had him dragging the fine long strands away, tugging the thick pelt back from her face with a cruel fist so he could thrust his own darkly furious one up to hers.

'Answer me, you crazy bitch!' he snarled when she still just stood there, silent and numb. 'Why the hell are you here in my house? In my room? Trying to put my brains in with a damned stiletto?' Another shake brought her blisteringly alive at last.

'Take your hands off me!' she snarled right back. 'Don't you dare hurt me!'

'Hurt you?' he choked in utter incredulity. 'I ought to beat the life out of you, you stupid, crazy bitch!'

He seemed stuck on what else to call her. His fingers were still biting harshly into her, his teeth, pure white and sharply etched in the consuming darkness, were displaying a fury so palpable she could almost taste it.

Nina threw back her head, defiance in every line of her trembling frame. Blue eyes blazed at thunderous black. 'I hate you, Anton Lakitos!' she spat at him. 'I despise the very sight of you!'

He growled something deep inside his throat, the last threads of his control giving way as he dragged her roughly across the room and slammed her back against the door, ignoring her startled cry as he pressed a muscled arm across her throat, forcing her head back. Her chin was pushed high, and his hand curved tightly over one of her trembling shoulders. She could feel his harsh breath against her face, warm and tormentingly flavoured with whisky, stimulating senses that had been rudely woken only moments ago in the pitch-black frenzy on his bed.

Then he reached out to touch a switch, and Nina squeezed her eyes tight shut against the sudden searing crash of light to her retina. And with her heart thundering against her ribs, she stood, tensed and ready for what had to come next.

It came. 'My God...' The breath left his body on a stunned rush of air. 'Nina Lovell!' he gasped.

Her eyes flicked open, bitter blue arrowing directly on to astonished black. 'Yes!' she confirmed on a contemptuous hiss. 'And you're the heartless swine who is trying to steal my father's company away from him!'

'I'm——?' The black eyes widened, expression revealing utter bewilderment for a moment, before he closed it out on a tight mask of withdrawal. No guilt, no remorse evident anywhere on his hard-boned face as he continued to hold her bitter gaze steady. Then his arm dropped away from her throat. 'I was right,' he muttered grimly. 'You are crazy.'

Nina wilted against the door, the tremors attacking her body making it impossible for her to stand without its support. She could still feel his touch burning on her skin, still taste his kisses on her hot, dry lips, and she dropped her eyes from his, then swallowed thickly when she found herself staring at the pulse point pounding in his throat where beads of sweat glimmered like jewels against his taut brown skin. Crisp hair curled in thick profusion around the rolled-back collar of his dark brown robe—a robe he must have been pulling on when the panic hit her. His powerful chest was heaving in line with the deep gulps of air he was having to drag into his lungs to maintain some control over his temper.

An insidious heat began curling its way through her, its origins so shamefully obvious that she shuddered, a trembling hand coming up to cover her mouth as a wholly appalling desire to place her lips against that gleaming throat shook her to the very core.

In the relative safety of a room full of people, this man had frightened her, but here, with the heated intimacy of what they had so recently shared still raging in her blood, she was experiencing something beyond fear, more a raw dread of her own deeply disturbing desire for this man.

A strained smile touched her mouth. Perhaps he was right, and she was crazy. Only a mindless lunatic would stand here, literally shaking with a need to be possessed by her worst enemy!

He saw the smile and didn't like it. On a sound that came very close to a constrained choke, he grabbed her chin and pushed it up so he could glare at her, eyes so black they seemed bottomless. Black holes for any crazy bitch to fall into.

'You find all of this amusing, do you?' he bit out furiously. 'The fact that I could be lying on that bed right now, bleeding to death, doesn't touch your conscience at all?'

Her gaze flicked over the tense brown skin gleaming healthily back at her. She couldn't see any mark that said she'd actually wounded him. 'I'm—sorry,' she mumbled inadequately.

'Sorry?' he choked. 'You break into my home. Lie in wait for me in my own bedroom. Try to seduce me— then go at me with a damned stiletto!'

'I did not try to seduce you!' she hotly denied, trying to pull away from his biting grip on her chin, but he wouldn't let her, the violence they were both generating almost splitting atoms in the air around them. 'You were drunk!' she accused. 'Too drunk to even know if you were dreaming or not!'

'And what's your excuse?' he derided cynically, bringing the whole shameful episode tumbling down around her, 'No, my dear sweet *nymph*,' he taunted witheringly, 'I wasn't so drunk that I didn't know what a receptive little thing I had clinging like a limpet beneath me!'

'God, you make me sick!' she choked.

'And you, Miss Lovell, make me very—very angry. 'Now...' he made an attempt to get a rein on all the emotions clamouring between them. 'I want to know what the hell you are doing here, and I want to know now, so start talking!'

Nina sucked in a shaky breath, her senses shattered into a million fragments. It was a nightmare, she decided dazedly, just an awful crazy nightmare...

'Talk!' he barked.

No nightmare, not unless you class the last three days as one long waking nightmare, she thought on a shuddering wince as her mind went winging off to that awful moment it had all begun when she had heard her father shouting at this man down the telephone. 'And you can keep your greedy hands off my daughter as well as my company!' had been the final explosion. 'Neither are for the likes of you!'

That, she knew now, had been the moment her father had signed his own death-warrant. You just didn't insult a man like Anton Lakitos and expect to get away with it. Whatever the Greek had answered in return, she didn't know, but when she had rushed into the room after hearing the receiver being replaced with a resounding crash, she had known it must have been catastrophic, because his face had been wiped clean of every vestige of colour. 'He can't do it to me!' he had choked out breathlessly. 'He can't——!' Then the pain had creased his face, and she had had to stand there, watching in horror as he crumpled, clutching at his chest, to the floor.

'The day you had that bitter row with my father, he had a heart attack,' she whispered thickly, anger diminished on a sudden wave of despair.

His black brows drew together in a puzzled frown, and Nina sighed impatiently, further disgusted by this man who couldn't even recall the moment he had caused another man to break apart in horror. 'Three days ago!' she snapped out bitterly, as if talking to an imbecile. 'My father had a heart attack three days ago!'

The frown remained in place, the puzzlement. 'So I found out this evening,' he informed her grimly.

'You didn't know before?' Her head came up, disbelief in the haunted turbulence of her blue eyes.

He shook his head, holding that look. 'I've been away,' he explained. 'I only got back this evening—though what the hell that has to do with any of this, I have no idea...'

He was darker skinned than she'd thought him to be. Taller too, close up, and broader, more—more everything. She dropped her eyes from his again, staring at the way her fingers fumbled with the buttons of her pale blue blouse. A blouse she had put on this morning without any thought to what it looked like, her only concern to shower, change her clothes and get back to her father.

'Since then, I've had to listen to him going on and on about you!' she continued wretchedly. 'Listen to his restless mumblings, w-watch him fade slowly further away f-from me with each new curse he sends you!' She sucked in a deep breath, bitter derision in every line of her tired young face. 'I wanted you to know that, Mr Lakitos. I wanted you to know the results your greed has on your victims. And that is why I'm here tonight,' she finished thickly. 'To tell you that no matter how other people may believe your Midas touch deserves respect, I abhor you! You and your kind make me sick!'

'Thank you.' His dark head dipped in a parody of acknowledgement for every insult she had thrown at him. 'And it was worth leaving your father's sick-bed to impart all of this.' Not a question, but a grim observation of fact. Then he cleverly brought the whole shameful episode into perspective by adding drily, 'Including risking your innocence, it seems.'

'My innocence—or lack of it,' she instantly flared, 'has nothing to do with this!'

'It hasn't?' The dark head tilted to one side, narrowed eyes touching hypersensitive nerve-ends as they ran glitteringly over her. 'I would say it has everything to do with it.' A smile touched his hard mouth, but it was a bleak, uncomfortable thing which stood miles away from humour. 'Anything else you would like to...' he flung out a mocking hand '...get off your chest before we put an end to this—highly informative evening?'

The sarcasm made her cringe, but her chin came up bravely. 'Yes,' she admitted. 'I came here tonight to ask...' It stuck in her throat, and she had to swallow before she could go on. 'To—ask you not to do it to him!'

'Oh?' He didn't sound very receptive, in fact he sounded downright unreceptive, his expression unmoved, eyes grimly implacable.

Nina shifted uneasily. 'Stop trying to make this harder for me than it already is!' she muttered irritably, all too aware that she had made a terrible mess of the whole thing. 'You must surely know what you are without my opinion having shocked you much. OK, so you're angry because I sneaked into your house and tried to hit you, but——'

'Tried?' The black fury was suddenly firing sparks at her all over again. 'A fraction of an inch, Miss Lovell,' he rasped, tugging at the roll-neck collar of his robe and thrusting his left shoulder up to her face. 'That's all, and the steel tip of your shoe would have sunk neatly into the main artery! Are you sorry it did not?'

For the first time he sounded Greek, harshly guttural and shiveringly Greek. Nina swallowed, the pink tip of her tongue tracing the heart-shaped outline of her mouth as she forced herself to look at the ugly red mark slicing across the beautiful dark skin where corded neck met muscled shoulder. It was already beginning to swell around the bruised tear where her shoe heel had cut into the skin. 'I...' Words died in her throat, and she had to drag in a shaky breath to make herself speak. 'I'm sorry,' she mumbled. 'I...' Guilt darkened the blue of her eyes, and, without her actually knowing she was doing it, her hand fluttered up to touch the angry mark with the trembling pad of one finger.

He jerked in response, his own hand coming up to capture hers, fingers tangling, his strong and dark, hers so fine-boned and pale that they looked like delicate porcelain against his. Then the brown of his eyes deepened into a hot dense blackness, and Nina went perfectly still. He was going to kiss her again, she knew it.

Her trembling lips parted. His chest expanded on a harsh intake of air, and her precarious world went topsy-turvy again as their mouths moved to meet in a hungry collision that sent everything else flying.

'God!' It was he who broke the burning contact, dragging himself away from her in angry disgust. 'What are you?' he bit out hoarsely. 'Some kind of sex-starved siren?' Nina bowed her head, shaking the long red curtain of hair. The blood was pounding in her veins with a need so strong she was shaken by it, utterly shamed. 'Damn and blast it, you stupid fool!' he exploded forcefully. 'Have you any idea just what you're inviting here?'

'Mr Lakitos, please listen to me.' She came away from the door to stand trembling in anxious appeal. 'I didn't mean any of this to happen! I—I came here tonight simply to talk to you! About my father—about his illness and—and his distress! I wanted to beg you to help me!' she cried, when he spun the rigid length of his back on her.

'By sneaking into my house?' he growled. 'By throwing insults at me? By trying to put me in my grave before your father was there?' Broad shoulders lifted and fell on an angry breath, his hands thrusting into the deep brown pockets of his robe.

'I—I'm sorry,' she said again. 'I'd fallen asleep in the chair and—and you frightened me...' Small teeth pressing into her trembling bottom lip, she walked forwards, laying a tentative hand on his arm. 'I lashed out instinctively, I...' It was her turn to suck in a deep breath, the pressure in her lungs so great she felt they might explode soon. 'I w-was at my wit's end when I came here tonight. My father has been lying there for days, restless, mumbling incoherently about his company, money—you,' she told him wretchedly. 'In the end, I couldn't stand it any more!' she cried. 'The doctors are worried that he'll have another attack, and I wanted to ease his restless mind! I—I asked him what was worrying him, w-what I could do to help.' An anguished sob broke from her, and he turned around to view the effects her terrible vigil had wreaked on her pale young face. 'He needs Lovell's, Mr Lakitos,' she finished thickly. 'He has nothing to live for without Lovell's.'

'He has you,' Anton Lakitos said gruffly, glinting eyes hooded by thick black lashes. 'Surely, you are enough to make any man want to live.'

Her smile was pure self-derision. 'I am not a son,' she cynically pointed out. 'You, being Greek, should know exactly what I mean by that.'

'Then you must be crazier than I imagined you to be, if you don't know how much your father cares for you.'

Nina lifted her eyes to stare at him, surprised by the depth of rough-voiced sincerity he'd put into that last statement. And, instantly it was back again, that stinging, stifling, drumming pulse of attraction, glowing in his blackened gaze, throbbing in the space between them, driving the breath from her body and bringing her hand up to cover her lips in horrified recognition of what was charging between them.

Then everything was shifting again, the conflict of emotions swerving from that violent flow of passion to an eruption of anger so unexpected that Nina cried out as he grabbed her wrist in a biting grip.

'What's this?' he bit out harshly, dragging her hand away from her face to dangle her fingers in front of her anxious face. 'What in God's name is this?'

The fingers shook, the bright sparkle of a single diamond glinting accusingly at her.

Nina quaked. 'It—it's a ring,' she breathed.

'I can see it is a damned ring!' he snapped. 'What I want to know is who put it there?'

'My—my fiancé,' she whispered, going pale as a picture of Jason's handsome face leapt up to haunt her. She hadn't given Jason a single thought until that moment! The ring had only been placed on her finger the night before, urged on her by an anxious Jason who wanted her to feel secure in the event of the worst happening to her father.

'Your fiancé,' he repeated, drawing the word out in soft and crushing sarcasm. 'And the name of this—very lucky young man?' he demanded tightly.

'I—Jason,' she stammered thickly, as aware as the man standing in front of her that she had betrayed Jason tonight. 'Jason Hunter.'

'God in heaven.' He threw her hand aside, and Nina caught hold of it with her other one as once again he spun away from her. 'No wonder old Jonas is going——' He stopped himself in mid-sentence, spinning back to face her, eyes narrowed and sharply assessing. 'Jonas does know about this, I presume?' he asked grimly.

'I...' Nina bit down hard on her bottom lip, then shook her head in answer, a new kind of guilt deepening the blue in her eyes. No, she hadn't told her father.

'You know how upset he'll get,' Jason had said, and his smile had been all self-mockery. He knew as well as she did that old Jonas would never accept him as his son-in-law. 'But, at this moment, my concern is for you, not your father's crazy aversion to me. You need the comfort of knowing someone cares about you if—if the worst happens.' And, weakly, she'd given in, too tired to think clearly, and too in need of that comfort he offered to think of refusing it as she should have done.

'Get out of here, Miss Lovell.' The hard, flat tone in his voice made her wince. Anton Lakitos was looking at her through hard, contemptuous eyes. 'Go on, get the hell out of here before I call the police and have you arrested for breaking into my home.'

'Do it!' she instantly flared, angered by his dismissive tone—or maybe because she knew she deserved his contempt. Whatever, she came back spitting, 'Call the police, and I'll tell them how you tried to rape me!'

His eyes flashed coldly. 'Don't make the silly mistake of challenging me,' he grimly warned. 'Or you may find that you have bitten off more than you can chew! Rape, Miss Lovell,' he continued witheringly, 'does not leave the victim panting for more of the same!'

He cynically watched all the colour drain from her face, the ruthless truth of his taunt holding her locked in the horror of her own making.

'Go home,' he repeated grimly. 'Get out of my room, out of my house, and out, Miss Lovell, of my damned life!' Hard eyes sliced her in two where she stood. 'Get back to where you belong, at your father's bedside, in your fiancé's waiting arms, and seek your sexual solace there! But do it now, before I change my mind and take you back to that bed over there to enjoy what you were so recently eager to give me!'

'I wish I hadn't missed with my shoe!' she choked out woundedly.

'*Get out!*' he shouted. And all at once his control snapped, the harsh mask slipping from his dark face to reveal the rawly angry man.

Without waiting for her to move, he grabbed her arm and swung her back towards the door, flinging it open so it banged back against the wall behind it. Then he was dragging her along the half-lit landing, down the stairs and across the hall to the velvet-draped vestibule.

The cold air hit her flushed face as he opened the front door. Without a single word, he shoved her outside, and she had barely steadied from her inelegant exit before the door had closed firmly behind her.

It was still raining, the steady drizzle falling from the sky to cover everything in a fine veil of silver mist. Nina stared out across the darkened spread of lawn to where a line of tall trees stood quiet and still, tinged purple by the slowly lightening sky. There was a sense of unreality about everything, including herself as she hovered there.

A cold shiver sent her arms wrapping around her body, icy fingers curling around the bare flesh of her arms where the short-sleeved style of her blouse left her flesh vulnerable to the dank, cold chill. Feeling thankfully numb, she stepped out of the porch, the fine rain sheathing her as she walked, her bare feet sinking in the soft spongy grass as she crossed the lawn and then went out through the wrought-iron gates, pausing then to look to her left and her right, wondering vaguely how she had got here.

Taxi, she recalled. She hadn't felt fit enough to drive herself and had come here by taxi. A pale hand lifted to her throbbing brow.

How tired she was. So tired she could sink down here on the cold, wet pavement and sleep, sleep forever. A tremor shook her, deep and cruelly felt, and she turned to the left, bare feet making no sound on the damp, cold pavement as she went.

Within minutes she was drenched to the bone, her slender frame racked with intermittent shudders, the chill seeming to strike from inside out rather than the other way around.

What kind of madness had driven her to come here tonight? she wondered despairingly, covering her eyes with a hand where the tears she had been holding back for a long time were threatening to fall at last.

All she'd seemed to see when she had left her father had been the dark, handsome face of Anton Lakitos smiling at her as he had done so often, offering her a promise of such raw and burning passion that she'd had to stand aloof from it or go up in flames with him. She'd wanted to wipe that smile off his face! Wanted to hurt him as much as he was hurting her! And, she admitted to herself, see if the desire glowing in those devil-black eyes gave her any power over him at all—enough, maybe, to extract some mercy from the man?

It hadn't. She had made an absolute mess of everything, done nothing to help her father, betrayed Jason, and, in the end, she concluded wearily, betrayed herself.

'Oh, God,' she choked, ashamed, bitterly regretting the whole mad night.

It was then that she became aware of a car, crawling slowly up behind her, and she stiffened, a new dread trickling icily down her spine. This was all she needed, a kerb-crawler believing she was a...

Her head twisted sharply as a silver Mercedes drew up close beside her, fumes belching out of the exhaust pipe to mingle with the mizzly mist, and her heart stopped dead in her chest.

The driver's door came open, and Anton Lakitos stepped on to the road, leaving the door swinging wide as he stepped around the car bonnet to open the passenger door.

'Get in,' he said.

Nina stood there, so totally used up inside that she just stared blankly at him. He was dressed, looking completely different in a thick navy sweater and stone-coloured casual trousers. His face wore a mask of grim calm, eyes telling her nothing.

'Get in, Nina,' he repeated quietly. 'I'll take you home.'

Something...the slight softening of his tone, or the brief glimpse of pity she saw in his eyes, or maybe it was just the simple fact that, even after everything, he could not live with himself by allowing her to walk away in the state she was in...whatever, it was enough to crack wide open the control she had been exerting on herself, and her pale face crumpled, chin lowering to her chest as the deep sobs came, and there, in the colourless quiet of the early morning, she experienced the ultimate humiliation, her own emotional collapse in front of this man.

His arm came gently around her shoulders, and, without a word, he guided her over to the car and saw her seated inside, squatting down beside her to personally deal with the seatbelt and flick a car rug over her cold, wet legs. The car door closed with a quiet click, and a moment later he was seated beside her, setting the car into smooth, quiet motion.

They drove in a silence broken only by the sounds of her soft crying, the car's efficient heater trying its best to penetrate the chill of her body. After a while, he leaned across her to twitch open the door to the glove compartment, eyes kept firmly on the road ahead while he rummaged around until he came out with a handkerchief which he dropped into her lap before straightening up again.

'Nina...' he began huskily, once she seemed to have gathered some control over herself. 'We have to——'

Whatever he'd been about to say was cut off as he swerved the car to avoid hitting a big black cat that ran right in front of them. Nina was thrown against his shoulder, and he put out a hand to steady her. His touch burned right into her skin, shocking her into stillness, the brief, wry smile he turned on her telling her that he had experienced the same thing.

'Good luck or bad luck in England?' he quizzed, bringing her eyes flicking warily up to clash with his. He was smiling. 'A black cat crossing one's path means different things in different parts of the world,' he explained the question. 'In Greece, it is a sign of good fortune, but then...' he gave a rueful shrug '...the Greeks are renowned for the love of lucky omens, even if it means altering the fable to suit their needs.'

'You don't sound very Greek,' she observed huskily, shaking with a different emotion now.

Another shrug brought her gaze back to study him. He sat long and lean and lithe in the seat beside her. There wasn't a spare ounce of flesh on him anywhere, yet he exuded a daunting power, the muscled firmness

of his body too obvious to be masked. He was a man
of disturbing masculinity and her stomach coiled so
tightly in response that she had to look quickly away.

'I've lived most of my life in different parts of the
world,' he informed her, driving the car with the smooth
precision of one who was at ease with power. 'My late
father was a member of the diplomatic service, and
throughout my formative years I learned to speak all of
the most necessary languages quite fluently. English
comes the easiest because I was educated here.'

'Black cats are good luck,' Nina stated suddenly and,
even as she said it, knew she was taking a leaf out of a
Greek book, and turning the superstition to suit herself.

'Then perhaps we will be saved,' he smiled. She could
sense his gaze on her. 'Or perhaps not,' he then added
drily, and that shocking pulse of awareness came back
again, the remnants of what they had shared in the pitch
darkness earlier, weaving itself into the air around them,
confirming all those feelings she had refused to accept
before tonight, forcing her now to recognise her own
uncontrollable attraction to this man. He knew it too,
Nina could tell by the quick, assessing glances he was
giving her. He wanted her, had wanted her from the first
moment he had ever set eyes on her, and all she had
achieved tonight was letting him see that she was vulnerable to him. He wouldn't let an opportunity like this
pass. He wasn't the kind of man who backed off when
he saw victory within his grasp.

She shivered, turning her face away from him so he
couldn't see the apprehension in her gaze.

'Cold?' he asked. 'I have your coat and shoes in the
back of the car, but they are so damp I don't think they
would be of much use to you.'

'I'm—all right,' she assured him thickly, and they finished the rest of the journey in silence.

It was the sway of the car as it turned into the driveway
that brought her gaze jerking forwards, and the breath

left her lungs on a shaky sigh when she recognised her own home.

Tell-tale lights glinted from cracks in the curtains, telling her that no one had gone to bed. She must have left without telling anyone she was going. She couldn't remember. An amnesia born of physical and mental exhaustion had left great gaps in her memory.

She wished she could blank out the events that had taken place since, but she couldn't; they lived sharp and clear in the forefront of her mind, reminding her of what a fool she had been—the stupid, crazy fool, Anton Lakitos had called her.

The silver Mercedes drew to a stop behind another car, and Nina's heart sank. 'The doctor is here,' she said flatly. 'My father must be worse.'

The man beside her turned, shifting in his seat until he was facing her, the movement disturbing the warm air inside the car, and Nina inhaled that clean, musky-scented smell of him, her foolish senses lurching out to grab at it.

'Will you be all right?' he asked quietly.

She didn't answer. What would be the use? She could say yes, she'd be fine, but it wouldn't be the truth. She was suffering from a real dread of finding out what had happened in her absence, of facing the curious looks, the questions, and, inevitably, the truth about her actions tonight.

'God,' she whispered, burying her face in her hands. 'I don't want to go in there.'

'I am coming in with you,' he said firmly.

'No.' She pulled her hands down and fumbled for the door handle, stunned by the way her heart leapt at the offer.

'Yes,' he insisted. 'You can't face them alone. Not in the state you are in. You asked me for my help, and the only way I can give it is by coming inside with you.'

'But...' Now she had it, Nina was no longer sure she wanted his help. Her eyes clouded on her own confusion, and he laid a gentle hand on her shoulder.

'No buts,' he said. 'It's too late now, anyway, the door to your home has just opened and a rather handsome though very aggressive young man has appeared in the doorway.'

'Jason,' Nina noted dully.

'Ah,' drawled the man beside her, and something hard entered his eyes. 'The—affianced. Wait there,' she was told, then he was climbing out of the car and striding around the smooth silver bonnet and opening the passenger door.

# CHAPTER THREE

ANTON'S grip on Nina's arm was firm as he helped her out of the car, and she needed it. She was shaking so badly she didn't think she could support herself alone.

'Nina!' Jason stood in the open doorway, looking as though he'd spent the night tearing his hair out worrying about her, and her heart twisted guiltily. 'Where the hell have you been? Have you any idea of the trouble you've put us all to?'

'Hello, Jason,' she answered quietly, her eyes not quite managing to meet the angry concern in his, wondering how the hell she was going to explain tonight's escapade away, and not sure she wanted to even try.

She gave a tug at her arm, but Anton refused to let go of her, guiding her up the steps towards Jason as though he were delivering a rather recalcitrant child back home. Nina felt like a child. A silly, stupid, burdensome child who deserved a good slapping for what she had done tonight.

'You've been gone all night!' Jason's angry voice jarred on her frayed nerves. 'Sadie's been going out of her mind! So have I for that matter! God,' he gasped, 'just look at the state of you!'

Her free hand lifted shakily to her untidy hair. Eyes fixed on her feet where her bare toes were curling in on themselves in shame.

'What the hell got into you—just taking off like that?'

'Nina has been with me,' a deep voice put in smoothly.

'And who the hell are you?' Jason's tone bordered on the downright rude.

'Th-this is Mr Lakitos, Jason,' Nina put in quickly, not liking the way both men were sizing each other up. 'I h-had to see him about——'

39

'You are Anton Lakitos?' Silver eyes sharpened, flicking narrowly from one face to the other, and Nina cringed inwardly, knowing exactly what he was thinking. She had told him all about the arrogant Greek who had been pursuing her. 'What the hell is going on?' he demanded.

'I . . .' Where did she start? she wondered wretchedly. And worse, where did she finish? Her tongue did a nervous flick around her dry lips, and for the life of her, she couldn't look Jason directly in the face. 'I h-had to see Mr Lakitos about something important,' she mumbled in the end.

'And it took you all night?'

She nodded, lifting her hand to her brow. Her head was thumping, the cold morning air was making her shiver, her feet were numb, and she felt utterly used up inside. 'I had to wait until Mr Lakitos was free to——'

'You spent the night with him?'

'No!' she denied, feeling her cheeks go hot, and silently cursing them for it.

'Do you think this is the kind of discussion we should be having on the doorstep of a sick man's home?' Anton Lakitos put in grimly.

'My father!' Nina gasped, horrified that she had forgotten all about him.

With a tug, she released herself from Anton Lakitos's grip, and blindly pushed by Jason to dash into the house. Sadie was standing by the bottom of the stairs, her old face drawn in deep lines of concern, and, swallowing on a bank of fear, she ran quickly up the stairs.

She couldn't go inside. Every single instinct she possessed was rebelling against the idea of entering her father's bedroom, she was so terribly afraid of what she might find.

'Easy does it,' a quiet voice murmured just behind her. She was trembling so badly that her teeth were chattering in her head, the slender body beneath the limp blouse and skirt shaking violently.

'Is he . . . ?' She couldn't ask it, the words clogging in her fear-thickened throat.

'No,' Anton Lakitos gently assured her, catching her to him when she sagged in relief. 'Apparently, he's had another attack—a minor one,' he added quickly when she turned to bury her face in his shirt, too needful of his presence to thrust him away as she should be doing. 'The doctor is with him now, and he is comfortable.'

'Thank God,' she breathed. 'I would never have forgiven myself if he'd . . .' Swallowing again, she straightened up. 'W-where is Jason?' Her gaze flicked searchingly along the softly lit landing.

'He seemed—reluctant to come near your father's room,' he remarked drily.

'Of course,' she accepted. Her father would have another attack just suspecting Jason was in the house!

God, she thought heavily, what a mess it all was. If only her father didn't resent Jason so much, he could have been a great source of comfort to him while he lay so ill. As a qualified accountant, Jason could have lifted the burden of Lovell's right from her father's shoulders—had offered to—despite the older man's aversion to him. But she hadn't even dared put the suggestion forward. It was sad that the two most important people in her life should be at such loggerheads.

'Now, if you feel ready, we will go and see your father together, and see if we cannot find a way to give him peace of mind,' Anton Lakitos said firmly. 'That is what you want, is it not?' he added when she glanced uncertainly at him.

'I—yes,' she frowned, not sure of anything any more. Perhaps, if her father could have accepted Jason, she wouldn't be standing here having to accept the help of his enemy.

'Good.' The tone was quietly satisfied. 'So pull yourself together. Pray to God your father is too exhausted to notice your atrocious state, and let us go in.'

Atrocious, he called her. Nina looked down at her cold, dirty feet, and placed a hand to the limp, wet tangle of her hair. Atrocious just about said it.

Dr Martin was just packing his bag away when they entered the room. He glanced up expectantly, showing relief when he saw her. 'Ah, Nina,' he said. 'Thank goodness. Your father has been fretting for you.'

She nodded, eyes going worriedly to the frail figure lying so still on the bed. 'H-how is he?'

'There's no fool like an old fool, so the saying goes,' he drily observed. Dr Martin was an old friend of her father's, their family practitioner for as far back as Nina could remember. 'I've got him taped this time, though.' A rueful glance at his patient said it hadn't been easy. 'He won't be trying any more silly tricks for a while.'

'What did he do?' She moved towards the bed. There was a single low-watt bulb burning beside it, illuminating the awful grey cast of her father's face.

'Got out of bed,' Dr Martin announced. 'Actually got himself as far as the phone in his study before he collapsed. Getting someone to sort some other poor bloke out, so he said—couldn't catch who, the name was too foreign for my English ears.'

'Me, probably.' Anton stepped over to offer his hand to the doctor. 'Anton Lakitos,' he introduced himself, his gaze sliding over to where Nina was now kneeling by the bed, her father's limp hand held between both of hers. 'Is he going to be all right?'

The doctor shrugged non-committally. 'I've been warning him for months to slow down. He brought these attacks on himself. Wouldn't listen to the experts, wouldn't do anything he was told to do. But then, old Jonas isn't known for his listening powers,' he concluded drily.

Anton Lakitos nodded grimly, as though in complete agreement, his gaze still fixed on Nina where she knelt talking softly to her father. Jonas Lovell's eyes were closed, and there was no sign that he was aware she was even there.

'I wanted to shift him to hospital when the big one hit last week, but he wouldn't hear of it,' the doctor was saying. 'Said if he was going to die, then he would do it in his own bed—stubborn old mule damned near achieved it with this last escapade. If Nina had been here, he wouldn't have got beyond putting a foot out of the bed, but then, she's taken enough these last few days. He's a bloody awful patient, and I'm worried about her too.'

'There is no need to be,' Anton Lakitos murmured, eyes still locked on Nina's washed-out profile. 'I will be here to share the burden with her now.'

'Nina...?' The rusty croak brought everyone's attention to the man in the bed.

'I'm here, Daddy,' she thickly assured him.

'Where've you been?' Eyes which had once been the same vibrant blue as his daughter's looked grey and dim as they opened slowly to look at her. Tears split Nina's vision, an anguished sob trapping inside her throat.

'With me, Jonas,' Anton Lakitos inserted levelly. He had moved to stand behind Nina the moment the sick man spoke, leaving the doctor to see himself out of the room.

'My God,' Jonas huffed. 'You're quick off the damned mark.' He sounded relieved rather than angry, which completely confused his listening daughter.

'True.' A faint smile touched the younger man's face. 'But not by either your or my own persuasion, Jonas. Your daughter came to me to plead on your behalf.'

'She did?' Surprise showed on the sick man's face. 'She's a good girl,' he whispered weakly.

'And you are a foolish old man.' Anton scolded with an odd kind of gentleness that made Nina glance at him in surprise. 'Things had no need to get this bad.'

'I am about to lose everything,' was the tired reply.

'You should have trusted me sooner, Jonas. Now things have gone too far, and you will have to let me deal with it all in my own way.'

'I had to try it my way first. It was my duty to try.'

'And I admire your dedication to the task,' Anton acknowledged, while Nina became more bewildered as the conversation progressed. 'But at the cost of your own health?'

'At the cost of anything!' Jonas gasped out fiercely.

'Even at the cost of your company, old man?'

It was an unfair dig, and Nina's head spun around to glare at the man standing behind her, but her father spoke first, seeming to understand and accept where she was just horribly confused.

'Yes...' he hissed out wearily. 'Even at the cost of that.' His weary old eyes drifted downwards, the desire to give in to the drug-induced sleep beginning to win against his resolve to stay awake. 'But it's up to you now,' Jonas conceded. 'Do your worst if you must.' The resentment towards Anton Lakitos seemed to have left him completely. 'I suppose you'll want everything now.'

'I want only one thing, and you know it.' The hand coming warm on Nina's shoulder seemed to be trying to offer comfort, but she gave an impatient shrug, annoyed at them both for talking about Lovell's as though it were a living breathing person! The hand tightened, fingers curving delicately into the rounded bone, and the sudden hectic leap of her senses brought the colour rushing to her cheeks, and she subsided, cowed by the man who seemed to be in control of all their lives now.

'Now what?' Jonas wanted to know, struggling desperately against the drugs Dr Martin had given him.

'Rest,' Anton advised. 'Leave everything to me. Then, when you are feeling stronger, we will talk.'

'About my company?' the old man asked hopefully.

'About a whole lot of things,' Anton threatened. 'Not least about the trouble you've put me to tonight. Your daughter seems to think me a black-hearted devil, Jonas,' he added drily.

'She does...?' A slow smile stretched the bloodless contours of his mouth, and a hint of the old wicked humour eased some of the strain from his face. 'She must be confusing you with someone else,' he said, then actually laughed as if something really funny had been said. 'That's my girl, Nina.' Weakly, he patted her hand where it lay beneath his own. 'Trust no man. They're all black-hearted, man and boy alike.'

'Thanks for that vote of confidence,' Anton drawled sardonically.

'Think nothing of it,' Jonas said, still smiling that strange smile as he fell into instant sleep with a single blink of a twinkling eye.

'I wish I understood a single word of all that,' Nina sighed as she came slowly to her feet.

A hand beneath her elbow helped her rise. 'In several ways, so do I.'

Nina glanced at him, frowning at the mockingly cryptic reply, then shook her head. 'Whatever,' she dismissed it all for now, too tired to struggle with it. 'Thank you for this.' She looked back at her father, resting peacefully for the first time since he took ill.

Then reaction set in, sending her into a paroxysm of shivers that had him drawing her into his arms as he murmured roughly, 'Don't thank me yet, Nina Lovell. You have no idea what my terms for helping you are going to be.'

With that, he led her out of the room, his closeness disturbing her senses all over again. 'Th-that sounded very much like a threat to me,' she whispered shakily as the bedroom door closed quietly behind them.

Anton Lakitos turned her in his arms, forcing her with the superior power of his will to look at him. His eyes were dark and hooded, but glowing with that terrible look she had always seen written there. 'It was much more than a threat, my beautiful nymph,' he murmured huskily, his arms folding her hard against him. 'It was a vow...'

He kissed her then, taking her lips with a hunger that was too easily matched by her own. His mouth was warm and knowing, moving so sensually over her own that he urged a response from her without having to try very hard. And they clung together, relighting flames which had never really been doused since the incident on his bed, hours ago.

It was as his tongue tangled with hers that the horror of what she was allowing had her groaning and she dragged her mouth away from his. 'No!' she whimpered. 'Please, I can't take any more!'

'No,' he sighed. 'I don't suppose you can.' Black eyes glinted hotly down at her, and Nina trembled as she fought not to meld her mouth on to his again. 'But this isn't going to be the end of it, Nina Lovell,' he warned raspingly. 'And the quicker you come to terms with that, the better it will be for all of us!'

They stared at each other for a moment, the awful truth in what he was saying holding her trapped in sheer horror of it. Then he growled, the sound coming from deep inside his cavernous chest, and his mouth caught hers again with a swift but lethal kiss which left her emotions naked.

'Which is your room?' His gaze flicked impatiently along the landing.

Nina just pointed, too weak to do much more. But when he bent to swing her into his arms she came alive in a way that sent the dizziness flying. 'No, Anton!' she cried out hoarsely. 'You can't——!'

'I can,' he growled. 'And if I wished to I would!' The door opened inwards with a jerk, and he swung them both inside. 'But now is not the time, nor the place for what you have in mind, and I am, though you probably don't believe it, not so insensitive as to make love to you here, with your father lying ill not far away, and your fiancé waiting downstairs!'

Jason! she thought with a shiver of guilt. Once again, she had forgotten all about Jason!

He dropped her feet to the floor, keeping hold of her only long enough to be sure she was steady before he let go and moved right away from her, taking only a small amount of the violent static emanating between them with him. 'Now,' he went on grimly, 'you will shower yourself into some semblance of sanity, and change your bedraggled clothes, then we will talk, you and I. Talk,' he repeated for a second ominous-sounding time. 'Before we go and deal with that angry fiancé of yours!'

'We?' She was still trembling from that kiss he had just branded her with, literally pulsing with a need to throw herself at him. Appalled at herself, at him, at everything, she turned angrily on him. 'What do you mean—*we*? There is no *we* about it! Any explanations which need to be made to Jason will be done in private!'

'How long have you been involved with him?'

'What has that got to do with you?' she cried.

His eyes grew hard. 'Don't, Nina, make the mistake of trying to challenge me,' he grimly warned. 'How long?'

'F-five, maybe six months,' she answered in a subdued voice, niggled at how easily she backed down.

The grimness increased. 'And your father, how has he responded to the association?'

She shifted uncomfortably where she stood. 'I...he— he's prejudiced against Jason,' she reluctantly admitted. 'My father and Jason's were partners years ago. They had a row, and he's never forgotten it.'

'But you just never bothered trying to find out why?'

Yes, she had tried. But it had been a hard, black period in her father's life, and she had been very young, and she didn't blame her father for not wanting to remember it. In a few short months he had lost his wife in a terrible car accident, and then his best friend and business partner through a row that had been so bitter that it had persisted through all the years that followed it.

Grief-stricken and disillusioned, he had buried himself in his work, cutting everything else out—herself out to a certain extent. Lovell's had become his great passion. Then along had come this man, determined to take even that away from him!

'Hell,' Anton muttered suddenly. 'It's no wonder Jonas is going out of his mind!'

'And whose fault is that?' she cried, stung by his condemning tone. 'You've been lying and cheating your way into my father's life since the first day you met him. It's down to you that he's lying where he is now, worrying himself to death about some awful deal you're obviously forcing on him, and no one, not even my father, can blame Jason for that!'

His gaze slewed back to clash with hers, and something dark and nasty passed between them, something which had Nina physically backing away though he didn't move a single muscle towards her.

'Go and get that shower,' he advised, 'before I change my mind about my own sensitivity and throw you on to that bed to make love to you until you can't remember your own name, never mind that of your damned fiancé!'

She went; a single second longer holding on to that suddenly threatening gaze had her stumbling across the room to lock herself behind the relative sanctuary of her connecting bathroom door.

When she came back, he was relaxing in her window seat. It was fully light outside now, though the overcast sky could do little to lift the heavy mood from the pretty blue and peach room.

'I need to fetch some clean clothes,' she mumbled, defiantly aware of the inadequacy of the short towelling robe she was wearing.

Her hair lay in a thick wet pelt down her back, the warmth of the shower had put some colour back into her cheeks, and she was angry, angry at the lingering sensations she was having to deal with because of this man, angry at the way he had so casually staked claim over her life.

Anton lifted his head, eyes hooding lazily as they ran over her, taking in everything from the warm moist V of creamy skin at her throat to the long length of slender leg left exposed by the skimpy cut of the robe. By the time he lifted his black eyes to hers, she was blushing fiercely, and hating both of them for it.

A nerve twitched a bit of wry humour into the edges of his mouth. 'Perhaps I should call your fiancé in here right now...' he mused cruelly. 'Then there would be no need for explanations of any kind.'

'God, you're despicable,' she breathed, moving stiffly across the room to throw open her wardrobe doors. 'You think you can take control of people the way you can your petty companies. Well...' she turned to glare at him '...I am not for sale, Mr Lakitos. Just remember that when Jason is around, because if it were a choice between you and him I would choose Jason any day!

'So, you are not for sale, heh?' He didn't sound angry, just curious.

Nina sent him a disdainful look before she turned her attention back to the contents of her wardrobe. 'No,' she said, and snatched a pair of cream linen trousers from their hanger. 'I love Jason!' she announced forcefully. And she did, she told herself desperately. She did! 'And, as soon as my father is well enough to hear the news, I will be marrying him!'

'You will not,' Anton Lakitos smoothly drawled, 'because, Miss Lovell, you will be marrying me.'

Nina went still, the pale green silk shirt she had been about to pull from its hanger sliding uselessly through her fingers as she stood, trying to convince herself that she had misheard that last incredible statement.

'What did you say?' she demanded breathlessly, once she could get her throat muscles to unlock.

'You heard,' he said, eyeing her coolly. 'You've known how badly I want you from the moment I set eyes on you, so why are you looking so shocked?'

Because want and marriage were two completely separate issues. Something clamoured inside her, then settled to a quiver low down in her stomach. She reached up and pulled the shirt from its hanger. Trying to appear calm, she laid the clean clothes on the bed, then moved to the tall chest of drawers to slide open the top drawer. 'And you heard me,' she said as carelessly as she could in the circumstances. 'Thank you, but no, thank you. Jason is the man I love, and he is the man I will marry.'

'Sit down, Nina, you're trembling,' was all he said, and she turned on him like a virago.

'Will you just get out of here and leave me alone?'

'No.' The dark head shook, black eyes intent on her.

'What is it you want from me?' she cried, suddenly so agitated she didn't even know she was clutching a pair of fine white lacy briefs in her hands, tugging and stretching at the delicate fabric in a way which brought a rueful twist to her tormentor's attractive mouth. 'An apology?' she asked shrilly. 'Is that it? You want an apology for the way I broke into your house and hit out at you and insulted you?'

'Don't forget the way you tried to seduce me,' he reminded her lazily.

'I did not try to seduce you!' Almost stamping a childish foot in frustration, Nina saw the humour in his gaze too late to realise how beautifully she had risen to his bait. 'Stop being so flippant,' she muttered, at last seeing the mangled briefs and stuffing them quickly back in the drawer, her cheeks on fire.

'Then stop trying to convince me that you love that young fool downstairs,' Anton threw derisively back. 'My God,' he sighed, all hint of humour leaving him as he got up while she stood dry-mouthed watching the lithe movement of his long body. 'He can't be more than a year older than you.'

'Three,' she corrected.

'He looks younger,' he growled, shoving his hands into his trouser pockets.

'And how old are you?' Nina decided to get in a few taunts of her own. 'Thirty-one—thirty-two?'

'Thirty-four actually.' His grimace acknowledged the fourteen-year gap between himself and Nina.

But she rubbed it in anyway. 'And you think that makes you more acceptable to me than Jason? I don't know whether that makes you a cradle-snatcher, or just an ageing old——'

'Watch it,' he warned, and her tongue cleaved itself to the roof of her mouth, as she became aware that once again she had almost gone too far with this frighteningly aggravating man. 'I'll tell you this much, Nina Lovell,' he went on grimly. 'I may seem old to you, but just try turning those kisses you branded on me on to your precious Jason and see what he does! He's not man enough for a hot-natured little siren like you. Marry him, and you'll burn him out in a night—or, worse, hide your own desires behind a scenario of invented gasps and contrived shudders while you burn with frustration inside rather than frighten your poor darling Jason!'

'God, you're so crude!' she choked, turning her back on him so she could hide the look of mortified truth written on her face. She had never allowed Jason to kiss her like this man had. Nor had she ever felt the desire to kiss Jason as she had kissed Anton Lakitos!

'It is crude,' he derided, 'to sentence you both to that kind of pathetic relationship. You think you will be happy with it? Do you think he will be?'

He won't know, Nina thought, then shocked herself rigid with what she was actually admitting to herself. 'Oh, hell,' she groaned, slumping her slender shoulders. 'I hate you.'

'Well, that is a whole lot healthier an emotion than the kind of brotherly love you feel for him,' he snapped irritably. 'And I will promise you this much, Nina

Lovell——' He reached out to take her by the shoulders, bringing her to stand in front of him, the fire and the passion alight in his eyes as he glared dwon at her, put there by the anger throbbing between them '—marry me, and I'll match those wonderful passions of yours, fire by fire, ache by ecstatic ache!'

'Stop it!' she whispered, beginning to tremble. Her hand snaked up to clutch at the gaping folds of her robe, her heart accelerating out of control as she stared darkly up at him. She was falling into the fathomless blackness of his eyes again, drawn by the fire, the need to feel its heat, to feel his body weighing heavily on her own again!

'You'll marry me,' he pushed on relentlessly, the words rasping from his throat, grating along her every sense, tripping live wires of feeling as they went. 'For your own sake! But if you can't bring yourself to accept the truth in that then you will marry me for your father's sake, because it is the only way he will keep his company!'

'No!' she breathed, trying to pull away from him..

'Yes,' he hissed, long fingers winding around the thick wet pelt of hair so he could tilt her head back until the creamy length of her throat was exposed to his passionate gaze. 'Feel this?' he murmured huskily, placing the moist tip of his tongue against the pulse-point pounding in her throat so that it leapt, throbbing all the faster. 'That is what I can do to you with just a simple caress! Marry me, Nina,' he urged, 'and I will promise you that neither you nor your father will suffer by my hand.' He buried his face in her throat, the taunting tongue trailing fire as it slid across her sensitive skin.

His body throbbed against her own, hard-packed and shockingly aroused. Nina gasped, struggling to fight against the thick clouds of sensual need he was wrapping around her. 'Please . . . !' she whimpered. 'Don't do this to me!'

'Marry me,' he pushed on passionately, 'And I will even forgo all the money your father owes me, every last——'

'He owes you money?' If anything had the power to tumble her back to hard reality, then that piece of information did.

'You didn't know?' Anton let loose a soft curse, sounding angry with himself. He allowed her to put a few desperately needed inches between them. 'Of course he owes me money,' he muttered. 'He owes me a damn sight more than his company is worth,' he informed her grimly. 'More than you could even begin to appreciate.'

'Oh, God.' She sagged all over again, this new shock sending her reeling into a whole new nightmare.

Strong hands moulded the rounded bones in her shoulders. 'He borrowed a large amount of money from me several months ago to pay off some—large debts he had acquired, and put up Lovell's as security against the loan. He was supposed to pay me back within three months, but he hadn't a cat in hell's chance of doing that while——'

'Then why did you lend it him, if you knew he couldn't pay you back?'

He didn't answer, his hard mouth snapping shut as if he'd said too much already.

Nina's eyes narrowed on his closed face. 'Unless you did it for that reason,' she therefore concluded, pulling right away from him. 'Because you knew he couldn't pay you back, and the company would be yours anyway.'

His hands dropped wearily to his sides. 'I thought I had just explained to you that he owes me more than Lovell's is worth.'

'Then what other reason could you have had to throw good money after bad?'

'You already know the answer to that, Nina.' His eyes held hers for a long and killing moment before he added huskily, 'You.'

'Don't...' Icy shivers went slinking down her spine, and she turned her back on him, arms going up to wrap tightly around herself. 'You're frightening me.'

'I frighten myself, believe me. I have never in my entire life wanted a woman as badly as I want you!' He came to stand right behind her, his fingers running in unhidden agitation along her towelling-covered arms. 'And if you think I like it any more than you do, then think again! But at least admit it is the same for you,' he ground out huskily. 'Even if you cannot say it out loud to me!'

He turned her then, catching the horror of truth in her eyes and growling at it just before his mouth hit hers with enough force to knock any attempt at denial right back down her throat.

His hard body pressed against the fragile softness of her own. Hot, dark and excitingly alien. He burned for her, and it was knowing that which lit an answering fire inside herself. Her arms went up, sliding along the soft wool knit of his jumper, fingers spreading out to trace the ripple of muscle beneath, muscles she had been yearning to touch again ever since her hands had made contact with them in the pitch-black battle on his bed.

He shuddered, groaning against her straining mouth, and she shuddered too, her spine arching upwards as his hand slipped inside her robe to search out her waiting breasts. His fingers trembled as they caressed her, and she bloomed for him, aware only of the man and the kiss and what his touch was doing to her.

The kiss deepened, and the robe slid smoothly from her shoulders, his arms trapping her to him as he made her feel the force of his desire for her. There was something incredibly erotic in having her naked breasts crushed against the rough texture of pure wool. She felt frail and helpless in his arms, so very feminine, that she moved enticingly against him.

The knock at the door was a mere hearsay before it flew open, the solid wood banging back against the opposite wall, allowing Jason to walk angrily in on them.

# CHAPTER FOUR

'DO YOU usually barge into someone's bedroom without invitation?' Anton gained his composure a whole lot quicker than Nina could, speaking calmly into the drumming silence while she just stood there shaking, feeling Jason's pained abhorrence as if it were her own.

'How long has this been going on?' he bit out harshly.

'Long enough,' Anton replied, smoothly shifting his body until he was effectively hiding Nina from view by the superior height and width of him. Then, with a slow deliberation, he began straightening her robe, sliding it back over her shoulders and tucking it gently beneath her lowered chin, her mortification obvious by the dark red flush colouring her cheeks. She felt his mouth move lightly over the top of her head, and trembled on a remnant of desire, her fingers clutching at him for support. His hand came to lift her chin, black eyes searching her pained and guilty face, going grim at the sight of shamed tears glinting in her blue eyes. 'Ssh,' he murmured, and kissed her softly on her trembling mouth.

'God, will you leave her alone?' Jason grated in thickened disgust. 'She's wearing my ring, for God's sake!'

'An opportune move on your part, I think,' Anton said quietly.

'What's that supposed to mean?' Jason demanded.

'Oh, I think you know.' Anton twisted his dark head to level Jason with a look. 'It would be advisable to close the door if you don't wish to be overheard.'

The door slammed shut, and Nina winced, struggling to pull herself together, placing the palms of her hands against the rock-hard wall of the chest she was trapped against, and Anton let her go, watching grimly as she drew herself up and took a deep breath before stepping around him to face her fiancé.

Tall and reed-slender, he looked demolished, and her heart wept. His face was as pale as his light blond hair, grey eyes silver with shock. He was staring at Anton Lakitos as though he'd just thrust a knife into his chest.

The silver eyes slid sideways to accuse her. 'You're lovers, aren't you?'

Nina swallowed, tears backing up in her tight throat. 'I...'

'Yes, we are lovers,' the man beside her answered for her.

'I wasn't speaking to you!' Jason sliced at him, eyes flashing a hatred Nina could well understand. 'Nina...?' he appealed hoarsely.

She stared mutely at him. What could she say? Her heart was bleeding for him, for herself and the terrible mess she had placed them all in with her madness to-night. But the awful truth of it was, she and Anton had become lovers tonight. Oh, maybe not in the way Jason was thinking, but as near as mattered. She lowered her head, and said nothing.

'I should have guessed!' he rasped, shock turning to bitter contempt. 'When you first mentioned the damned Greek's name to me, I should have guessed your father was up to something!—I should have remembered how history has a habit of repeating itself! You Lovells have always meant the kiss of death to my family!'

'Oh, no, please, Jason!' Nina pleaded painfully. 'You have it all wrong, my father didn't have anything to do with——'

'Of course it's his doing!' he derided, eyes lashing her with scorn. 'He hates me enough to do anything to stop you marrying me! The conniving devil has set you up— and you're so damned stupid, you don't even know it!'

He had good excuse to feel maligned by the Lovells, Nina acknowledged as a fresh wave of guilt washed over her. History was repeating itself in a way. Ten years ago, when their two fathers had had their blistering row, Jason's father had been the one to lose out to the much shrewder Jonas who had quite ruthlessly forced Michael Hunter out of Lovell Hunter, even going as far as to have the Hunter name taken from the company. Michael Hunter had never succeeded in business again after that. According to Jason, he had died a year ago a bitterly disillusioned man.

'I'm sorry that my father refuses to accept you, Jason,' she whispered huskily, ashamed as always at the way her father had stubbornly refused to let the past die. Even though Jason had been quite prepared to let it go—for her sake, she acknowledged painfully. He had been prepared to put his own resentments aside for her sake.

She lifted pained and guilty eyes to his. 'But this has nothing to do with my father,' she insisted. 'This,' she sighed, 'is all my fault.'

'You're damned right it's all your fault!' He was literally throbbing with anger and wounded pride, the hard look in his eyes withering her where she stood. 'If you hadn't been such a gullible fool, we could have had everything. Everything!'

'And now you will leave here with nothing,' a grim voice put in, its total lack of compassion so cruel that Nina gasped at it.

'For goodness' sake!' She turned on him, a trembling hand going up to touch her brow in despair. 'Why are you doing this?'

'Yes, Mr Lakitos...' Jason sneeringly provoked. 'Why are you doing it?'

It was a challenge, and one so deadly serious that the whole room seemed to go still. Anton stood to one side of her, his poise so finely balanced that Nina could feel the tension emanating from him, and held her breath, sensing that something utterly destructive was being tempted out into the open, although what it was she had no idea, only that the threat was definitely there.

Then Anton moved, his hands coming warm and possessive around her waist, ruthlessly staking claim. 'Nina came to me,' he stated the unpalatable truth of it, 'and to me she has given herself. Unlike old Jonas, I share nothing—nothing. Do you understand?'

'And you expect me to just accept that and walk meekly away?' A finely etched eyebrow rose in calculated challenge. The anger seemed to have gone from Jason, leaving a hard, cold shell behind it, and she found herself staring at a stranger. A tall, fair, bitterly cynical stranger. And it was as if she weren't the issue here any longer, dismissed by something far more important. 'She's wearing my ring, remember?' he added smoothly. 'Surely that must count for something?'

'Ah, yes,' Anton drawled, 'The ring.' One of his hands left her waist to grasp her left hand, lifting it out in front of them, then slowly, carefully, while the tears washed her eyes all over again, he slid the small solitaire from her finger, twisting it thoughtfully between finger and thumb. 'And what price do you put on your—broken heart, Hunter?' he enquired curiously, and, while Nina choked in horror at his filthy suggestion, he named a figure that had her going rigid with shock.

'Double that may be nearer the mark.'

'Oh, Jason,' she choked, feeling the nausea begin churning inside.

'Done,' Anton said, and threw the ring to Jason, who caught it deftly. The smile he turned on Nina was hard and contemptuous. 'What does it feel like to be sold down the river for the price of a Rolls-Royce?' he taunted her.

She shuddered, the sickness almost overwhelming her. He had done it to get his revenge on her, accepted Anton's offer because he'd known it would hurt her more than anything else he could have said or done.

'Here...' She looked up in time to see the diamond ring floating through the air towards her, and caught it instinctively. 'Keep it as a memento,' he invited as he opened the door. 'I certainly don't want it—any more than I want you.' He turned to slice them both with an insolent glance. 'Second-hand goods were never to my taste. Don't forget the money, Lakitos. I am not by nature a very patient man.'

Then he was gone, striding out of the room and out of Nina's life, leaving the atmosphere thick and tainted behind him.

Nina sank down heavily on the edge of the bed. 'I'll never forgive you for this,' she whispered thickly. She knew Jason, and all that careless insolence had just been a front he'd erected to hide his real pain behind. It was the same careless insolence he had used to hide her father's hostile rejection of him. The same careless insolence he had shown when he told her about the straitened circumstances of his upbringing after his father and hers broke apart. And now he had used it to hide his feelings of hurt and betrayal. 'Isn't it enough that you want to ruin my father—did you have to ruin my happiness too?'

Anton spun his back to her. 'I don't remember promising you happiness, Nina,' he murmured flatly.

'I wasn't talking about any hope of happiness with you!' she cried scathingly.

'You honestly believe you would have been happy with that mercenary devil?' If she had thought her own tone scornful, then his eclipsed it.

'He needed to leave with his pride,' she explained, staring at the small diamond lying in the palm of her hand. Betrayer, it seemed to be accusing her. Betrayer—and she shuddered. 'The only way he could do that was by making me appear insignificant next to your blood money. You men and your damned pride,' she sighed, thinking of her father who had been prepared to die for his precious pride. 'You live and die by it, but what about my pride, my self-respect?' she demanded thickly. 'I don't think I shall ever feel clean again!'

'And you blame me for this also? You came to me for help, Nina,' he reminded her. 'Not the other way around.'

'I should have gone straight to Jason,' she whispered, still gazing tearfully at the ring.

'Perhaps you should,' he agreed, sounding infinitely weary of the whole affair, 'but you didn't. And now you must pay the price for your mistake!'

Without her expecting it, he reached down and pulled her to her feet. His eyes glinted black fire at her as he wrenched the ring from her and slid it arrogantly into his pocket.

'Forget Hunter and his damned ring,' he bit out roughly. 'You belong to me now!' Before she could do more than gasp out a protest, she was in his arms, and the kiss was hard and punishing, but staking claim all over again. By the time he let go of her, she was trembling badly, and the tears of sensual defeat were hot in her eyes.

'An—interesting price, is it not, *agapi mou*?' he taunted cruelly, sounding more huskily Greek than he had ever done. His gaze narrowed meaningfully on the parted fullness of her kiss-swollen lips. 'One, I think, you are more than willing to pay.'

He put her from him, contempt at her easy submission twisting his hard features as he moved right away from her, and Nina sank back on to the bed, head lowering in weary defeat.

'I want your solemn promise that you will tell me if Hunter tries to make contact with you,' Anton said suddenly, bringing her head shooting right up again.

'But why?' she asked bewilderedly. 'He isn't likely to do that. Not after what I've just done to him! He would cut me dead rather than speak to me again.'

His eyes hooded over. 'Nevertheless,' he insisted, 'I want that promise.'

Nina stared at his grim face for a moment, then shrugged. 'All right,' she said. 'You have it—for what good it will do you. But I won't be hearing from Jason again.'

'I hope sincerely that you are right,' he murmured grimly. 'I *prefer* to hope you are right, for your sake, Nina, as well as his . . .'

The first letter arrived only three days later, proving her wrong and Anton Lakitos right. Jason wrote with all the pain and passion he was feeling right now, and his words confirmed her belief in him.

> I ripped up the cheque from Lakitos. I only accepted his bribe because I knew it would hurt you, but all the money in the world couldn't make up for the loss I'm suffering now. I loved you— still love you, and, no matter how the evidence of my own eyes wants to tell me otherwise, I can't believe you would willingly wish to hurt me like this. It has to be an elaborate scheme to break us up. Your father has always hated me, enough to make sure I never become a member of your family. Can you bring yourself to meet with me, darling? So we can talk? Call me, I need to see you. I need to understand . . .

With tears of misery in her eyes, Nina sat in her father's study with the letter clutched in her hands, desperately torn between a desire to do as Jason begged, and go and see him, at least try to explain, and the heavy knowledge that explanations would not change anything.

She was trapped, and she knew it. Trapped by her own reckless stupidity and concern for her father. And she forced herself to admit the full and chilling truth about her own weak character. From the moment Anton Lakitos had kissed her, her feelings for Jason had faded into the shadows of her life.

Getting up, she stood over the waste-paper basket, and let the letter fall into it, tears blinding her eyes as it slithered hollowly to the bottom. Discarded, she made the comparison as she walked away; discarded, just like Jason.

It was a week before Jonas Lovell was deemed fit enough for that talk that had been promised by Anton. And it was a week when Nina learned the full torment of her own wretched anxieties, aided and abetted by the steady flow of correspondence she received daily from Jason. In one letter he posed a telling question.

> Have you asked yourself why Lakitos is so willing to help in the conspiracy against us? Lovell's owns some very lucrative property in the centre of London. Property which any speculator would give his eye teeth to obtain. Ask your father if you don't believe me. Lovell's is suffering from a worrying cash-flow problem at the moment, but nothing that could not be put right once your father is well again. But who aims to gain if the worst should happen and your father does not recover? I am concerned, Nina, dreadfully concerned that Lakitos is manipulating you into his clutches to get his hands on Lovell's. We have to meet again, if only to discuss my suspicions...

Could Anton have lied when he had said Lovell's was worth less than her father already owed him?

The letter went the same way as all the others, while her emotions flittered through a whole new set of uncertainties. And, as if to confirm all Jason's suspicions, Anton himself had become so cool and remote that she shivered when he came into the room. A man who professed an uncontrollable desire for her, he had barely glanced at her since declaring it!

He called around every day, asked about her father, asked about herself with all the polite interest of a stranger, then retired to her father's study to go diligently through the sick man's mail before he left again, leaving her wondering if the madness they had shared had already burned itself out!

By the time a week was over, every single resentful feeling she'd ever felt towards Anton Lakitos had re-asserted itself, and the only softening of this frame of mind that she would allow herself was a small gratitude for the change he had helped bring about in her father. Jonas was working hard at getting well now instead of waiting to die. The spark of life was back in his eyes, and, where before he had been restless and awkward to deal with, now he was content to rest and willing to please, which, in that contrary way things had of playing with your feelings, Nina resented because he had not wanted to get better for her sake, but the mere glimmer of hope where his company was concerned had worked wonders!

'The doctor thinks it will be OK for me to speak to your father today,' Anton coolly informed her when he arrived one morning, looking so much the powerful businessman in his dark, sophisticated suit and snowy white linen shirt that Nina went dry-mouthed just looking at him.

'Change your mind,' she pleaded impulsively.

They were standing in the hall, he towering over her and looking every one of his daunting thirty-four years with that austere expression he was wearing on his face, and she feeling so painfully young and ill-equipped to deal with this man who had so thoroughly taken over her life.

'In what way exactly?' he drawled unapproachably.

His cool gaze was fixed on her face, and each indi-vidual pore was tingling as if he'd reached out and ca-ressed her. She shivered delicately, her slender hands clutching together across the simple pale lemon cotton knit dress she was wearing.

'A-about marrying me,' she stammered. 'I—you—we don't even like each other!' she cried out desperately, seeing no hint of softening in his hard face.

'We don't have to like each other to feel what we do for each other,' he oh, so cynically pointed out.

'It was a silly—crazy night, when everything got out of hand! Can't you just—just give my father more time to pay back the money he owes you, then leave it at that?' she suggested hopefully.

'But you forget,' he said, seeming fascinated by her agitation, 'it isn't Lovell's I want.' His narrowed gaze dared her to challenge him. 'It is you I want,' he stated silkily when she said nothing but only looked more hunted. 'And it is for you that I am going against all my better instincts and allowing him to heap all his problems on to me!'

'I'll hate you until the day I die if you make me go through with it!' she vowed hectically.

'Then hate me!' he snapped, suddenly losing all that ice-cold reserve and reaching out to pull her to him. 'But marry me you will! Or I'll take you without the respectability of the ring, and your father will get nothing— not one concession from me!'

She was trembling. The moment he touched her the heat began burning its sensual trail through her body. He glared down at her, the light of desire thoroughly lit in his eyes, eating her, consuming her in the deep dark blackness so that she cried out, a choked, husky little sound that drew an answering groan from him just before his mouth took hers in a kiss that sent her flying back across the fraught days to a night when this man had changed the whole course of her desires.

'Deny that, if you dare,' he challenged as he drew away. She was breathing heavily, hardly able to lift her drugged lids from her eyes. 'You want me, Nina,' he claimed raspingly. 'It sings as powerfully in your blood as it does in mine!'

'I'm afraid of you,' she whispered wretchedly.

'I know.' He loosened his grip on her, moving his hands along her spine to gently cup her nape beneath the fine silk fall of her hair. 'But I think you are even more afraid of yourself.'

His thumbs drew lazy caressing circles on the soft skin at her jawline, his expression brooding as he looked down at her pale, anxious face. Then he let her go, sighing softly as he did so.

'Why not make this easy on yourself, and pretend you are in love with me?' His voice was loaded with a sardonic whimsy that made her shiver. 'You never know,' he went on drily, 'if you work hard enough at it, you may even manage to convince me! There is a lot of power in a woman's love for her man, Nina. It can buy her everything she could ever desire.'

'Except the man she really loves.'

'Don't start that again.' He turned away from her, sounding wearied to death as he moved towards the stairs. 'Just remember when you see your father next to make him believe we are besotted with each other.'

'Anton?' she called out hesitantly as his foot took the first stair. He stopped, turning slowly back to face her. Nina stared at him, her lovely eyes despising him, even as they drank him up. 'I w-want to know how long this—sentence you're inflicting on me has to last.'

His eyes narrowed, and he suddenly looked very much the arrogant Greek. 'Explain,' he clipped, nothing else; the hard-hearted businessman was back on show, and he used a harsh economy of words, most of them cuttingly intimidating.

Nina swallowed tensely. 'If I agree to m-marry you——'

'You already have agreed,' he pointed out, reinforcing that remark by glancing at her kiss-swollen mouth.

She flushed, her lips quivering a little as she pushed herself to say what she had been working up to say to him all week. 'You must know that the doctors have warned me not to expect my father to...' She couldn't say it, the word just got stuck in her throat. 'The day he—goes...' she went for the closest substitute, 'is the day any commitment I make to you ends also.'

He didn't say anything for a while, and the tension in the hallway inched itself up a few more notches while those narrowed eyes continued to study her pale young face with its small determined chin and anxiously staring eyes. She was aware that she had no bargaining power here. She had given all that up the night she had begged him for his help. Anton Lakitos wanted her. And, God help her, she wanted him. She had no weapons to fight him with. She only had to look at him to have her newly awakened senses screaming.

His nod of agreement was curt and grim. 'All right,' he said at last. 'If—when the time comes, and you still wish to dissolve our marriage, then I won't stop you.'

'Thank you,' she whispered, aware that he had allowed her that one concession where none was due.

'Oh, don't thank me, Nina,' he drawled, the sardonic man well and truly back in place. 'After all,' he pointed out, 'the condition will automatically apply to me as well as to you. I may well be glad to see the back of you by then.'

Those hard black eyes held hers for a moment longer, and she felt their impact with an ice-cold shiver that struck deeply into her, washing the colour right out of her face. A slow smile stretched the hard contours of his mouth. He had won that round, just as he won every battle they waged with each other. He wanted her, and had made no secret of the fact. But it wasn't love, and sexual desire could wither and die as quickly as it had risen to life. She had only demanded of him what he himself wanted. A loophole, to free himself when this awful gnawing ache had left him.

He turned away from her and began climbing the stairs while she watched him go, numbed into silence as something terrible shuddered through her.

No! she denied its terrible warning, and spun away from the tall, lean sight of him, shivering violently at the suspicion that she was halfway to loving him already.

She hadn't been able to get him out of her mind since the first time he had levelled those hungry eyes on her. She'd held him at arm's length then, not understanding why, but certain that she didn't dare let him come close to her. Now she had to wonder if her instincts had always known he could be a real threat to her very existence.

Anton Lakitos was a man of deep-running passions. She had seen him with at least four different women on different occasions, each of them clinging seductively to his side, as familiar as only lovers could be. She had known then that she could never compete on that sophisticated level. And there had been Jason, dear, caring Jason, who posed no threat to her emotions at all.

Pain streaked through her at that final confession, the ever-present guilt withering her insides as she began to acknowledge, truly acknowledge how carelessly she had confused her friendship with Jason for love.

Jason had a right to hate and despise her. And she couldn't understand why he didn't. She hated and despised herself—and Anton Lakitos because he had forced her to recognise her own sleeping devils within.

It was an hour before she found the courage to go into her father's bedroom, her troubled thoughts putting the bruises back around her eyes.

Jonas was resting against a mountain of pillows, talking genially to Anton who was relaxing in the chair in which Nina had spent her long hours of vigil when her father had been so gravely ill.

'So.' Her father smiled when he saw her. 'You've come to your senses about Hunter at last.' He sounded relieved, which only helped to chafe at her conscience. 'You two were never meant for each other,' he huffed out pompously.

Meant for each other or not, she and Jason could have been very happy together. They shared the same likes and dislikes. Their accidental meeting had come about when Jason had joined the same music group she belonged to. It had been such a wonderful surprise then,

to find out he was the same Jason Hunter she hadn't
seen since they had both been small children. They had
got on well together from the very beginning, and even
the bitterness that had remained firm between their two
fathers throughout the years hadn't been enough to stop
them wanting to be together.

It had taken Anton Lakitos to do that, and she glared
her loathing at him across the room. What interest did
they share, except this animal desire for each other's
body?

He caught the look and fielded it with a quizzical tilt
of one dark brow, then lifted his hand in arrogant
command that she go to him. Gritting her teeth, she went
obediently, flushing with embarrassed annoyance that
he didn't just stop at taking her hand, but drew her down
on to his lap.

'Your father gives us his blessing, *matia mou*,' he
murmured warmly, his fingers snaking around her trim
waist to issue a sharp dig of warning that she put a convincing smile on her face.

The smile arrived, pinned there by sheer strength of
will. A look passed between the two men, one which had
her puzzling over its meaning. Could Jason be right? she
wondered suspiciously. Had her father been plotting for
this result the whole time? She recalled how cross he had
used to get every time she rebuffed Anton's approaches
towards her. Then she dismissed the idea as unworthy.
Even her father, for all his faults, couldn't produce a
heart attack just to make his daughter toe the line.

'You make a magnificent couple.' Jonas was smiling
appreciatively at them. 'Can't wait to see the grandchildren you'll give me! Be an interesting mixture, if my
guess is right!'

Something stirred deep inside her, what, she couldn't
explain, but Anton felt it too, because he shifted tensely
beneath her, and a shower of electric sparks brought
goose-bumps out on her skin.

'I think, if you can be patient for a while, Jonas,' Anton murmured, the warmth of his body suddenly too intimate for Nina to draw breath easily, 'we will wait for a while for the children. Nina has years ahead of her to play mother. Let her become used to being a wife first, then——'

'Rubbish!' Jonas dismissed. 'The younger the better is my motto! Why, Nina's mother was only a year or so older than Nina is now when she gave birth to her!'

And she's dead, Nina thought heavily. After spending a life trying her best to please a man who made no secret that his real love was his company, and the excitement it alone gave him.

She got up, her feelings in utter turmoil yet again. Was she destined for a similar fate to her mother's? Tied to a loveless marriage with a man who offered nothing more than the physical satiation of his body? What could children do, but trap her irrevocably into that kind of hell? In the end, her mother had not been able to take her unhappiness any more, and she had left, packed her bags and left both her husband and her child. 'I'm sorry,' her note had said. That was all. Not even a word of love for Nina. She had died, ironically, not by her own hand, but by that of a drunken driver who had thought he could drive faster than the wet roads would allow.

Yet something had stirred inside her at the idea of having Anton's child. A natural maternal stirring, maybe, or something much—much more frightening.

Folding her arms across her breasts and moving right away from both men, she could feel their eyes on her, her father's in mild surprise, and Anton's with a deep burning intensity.

'As I said,' he placed quietly into the silence, 'we have plenty of time to make those kinds of decisions.'

'But, Anton, you and I were just——'

'It's time I left, Jonas,' Anton cut in brusquely, leaving the older man gaping as he got up from the chair, his eyes, hooded by thick frowning brows, fixed on Nina. 'Nina?' he summoned quietly.

She was standing across the room, staring at the portrait which hung over the fireplace, studying the beautiful smiling face of her mother, painted at a time when she had been happy with them. I will never desert a child of mine! she thought fiercely. Never!

'Nina...' The deeply compelling voice had her turning slowly to face him. His hand was held out in invitation, and she found herself staring unblinkingly at it, feeling oddly shut off from the world. The hand remained outstretched and waiting, palm up, long fingers curved invitingly at the ends, as though urging her to go to him.

As if in a dream she went, pulled by a force far stronger than her own will. When she reached him, she unclipped her fingers from where they were biting into the opposite arm. She was so tense she couldn't seem to breathe properly, a dark sense of her own entity holding her in a strange void somewhere between the now and the never.

His fingers closed around her own and she watched them curl, drawn, fascinated by them, by their warmth, and the pulse of life they seemed to be transferring to her. She sucked in a deep breath then let it out again shakily, and Anton's frown darkened into concern.

With only a muttered farewell to her father, he drew her out of the room and along the landing, his grip firm but gentle as he took her down the stairs and out of the front door.

The sunlight blinded for a moment and she winced. His car stood by the front steps, its long sleek lines unnervingly familiar to her. He saw her inside then moved around to get in beside her, driving away without a single enquiry as to whether she wanted to go with him or not.

# CHAPTER FIVE

'WHEN was the last time you stepped out of that house?' Anton turned to glance frowningly at Nina then away again, long hands resting lightly on the steering-wheel.

'I can't remember,' she answered vaguely, looking out of the side window at the blur of passing scenery. She still felt strange, so utterly depressed that she could barely summon up the energy to speak.

'Have you been out since I took you home last week?'

She thought about it, then shook her head. No, she hadn't been out. She had been too busy grappling with the conundrum her life had become to do anything else but brood. Not least through the fault of Jason's letters. She had written him a long letter in an attempt to explain, but had never posted it. It hadn't seemed to do anything but offer him encouragement to hope when none was there. Whatever strange paths her life took from now on, they would not be leading her back to Jason. The man sitting beside her had seen to that, with the ruthless power of his sensuality and the control he held over her father's destiny. Jason was now a part of her past, and a guilty part too. She didn't think she would ever learn to forgive herself for the way she had hurt him.

'Where are you taking me?' she enquired listlessly.

'Somewhere where you can unwind a little.' She received another searching glance from those frowning black eyes. 'You are very near a complete mental collapse, you do know that, don't you?'

Am I? she wondered. Then, yes, perhaps I am. Again, the fault of the man sitting beside her. It was the stress of confusion that did it. She just couldn't understand how, in the space of a few short hours, Anton Lakitos

71

could have gone from being her father's sworn enemy
to his most trusted friend! But every time she'd tried to
broach the subject her father had shied right away from
answering it, mumbling something about better the devil
you know than the one you don't, and then become so
anxious that she had had to drop the subject. None of
it seemed to add up, least of all, why, knowing all she
did know, she still only had to glance at the man sitting
beside her to feel that hot sting of awareness strike into
her. She couldn't, no matter how she tried, justify it in
her own mind. She should hate him, and perhaps she
did in a way, but did she have to want him so badly?
She didn't like herself much for feeling as she did. In
fact, she found her own desires harder to accept than
Anton's desire for her. He was a man, after all, and, as
all women knew, their sexual needs followed more ani-
malistic paths than a woman's did. So what did that
make her? An animal, like him? She shuddered, liking
herself even less. She had the awful feeling that was
exactly what she was, a sexually woken animal.

The car slowed, and she blinked, snapping forcefully
out of her heavy mood when she recognised the driveway
they were just turning into. 'Why are you bringing me
here?' she demanded sharply.

'So you can do what I said you need to do, and unwind
a little away from the constant worry of your father's
illness.'

'Here?' God in heaven, she thought, as she stared at
the white-rendered mansion house. This is the last place
on earth I could wind down in!

'Don't put your imagination on overdrive,' he drawled
as he stopped the car. 'I have not brought you here with
the exclusive intention of ravishing you.'

The cynical mockery brought an uncomfortable flush
to her cheeks, and he smiled tightly at it as he climbed
out, striding around the bonnet to open her door, his
hand determined as it closed over her elbow to help her
alight.

'You know, Nina,' he went on grimly, 'if you could bring yourself to trust me a little, maybe you would find I am not the complete sex maniac you seem to believe me to be.'

She shook her head, and said nothing. How was she supposed to trust him when she couldn't even trust herself? That terrible flow of attraction was already humming between them. And he only held her lightly by the arm!

She heaved in an unsteady breath and let him lead her into the same house which, only a week ago, he had so angrily ejected her from.

'John!' he called out the moment they stepped beyond the curtained vestibule and into the polished warmth of the inner hallway.

The man she remembered seeing him with that same night a week ago appeared in the study doorway, his curious gaze flicking from his employer to Nina then back again.

'Find Mrs Lukas and ask her to prepare a light lunch to eat by the pool,' he ordered briskly. 'Then take the rest of the day off; we won't be doing any work today.' He was pulling Nina along behind him as he spoke, so they had gone past the man called John when Anton added as a mere afterthought, 'Oh, and by the way——' stopping so abruptly that Nina cannoned into him. He caught her gently by the shoulders and turned her around to face the other man. 'This is Nina Lovell, and we will be getting married in three weeks, so I will want you to get on to all the arrangements as soon as you can.' He turned again, either not seeing or arrogantly ignoring two completely stunned expressions. His arm was firm around her shoulders now, clasping her to his side. 'But not today, John!' he called over his shoulder. 'Today I want some peace and quiet to be alone with my fiancée!'

The poor John's muffled, 'Yes, sir' fell on indifferent ears. Anton was already opening a door and guiding Nina

through it into a glass-canopied room that made her
completely forget the shock announcement he had just
made to his assistant.

'Oh!' she gasped, gazing around the luxurious pine
room where the sun glinted down through the glass-
domed roof on to a large swimming pool. White plastic
tables and chairs were dotted in a kind of organised ran-
domness around the pool edge, their seats thickly padded
with pale peach, lemon and green-striped cushions. The
heavy drizzle of a week ago had been blown away on
the fresh breeze now cleaning the summer air outside,
making it cool enough to strike a chill into the body,
but in here the air was warm and humid, the steam gently
rising from the expanse of clean, calm water telling her
that it was invitingly heated.

'What better place to unwind than spending a lazy
hour here?' Anton claimed. He was already dragging his
tie from his throat and shrugging out of his expensive
jacket.

His movements drew her eyes to him, and her senses
began to stir when she saw how the fine fabric of his
shirt had pulled taut across his broad chest, revealing
the dark shadowy evidence of what lay beneath, as-
serting disturbing memories of crisp black chest hair
rasping against her searching fingers.

Dry-mouthed, she looked quickly away from him, 'I—
I can't swim here,' she said a little breathlessly. 'I haven't
brought anything to wear.'

'No problem.' He waved a casual hand to a door across
the pool. 'You should find something suitable in there...'
He was already moving off towards a matching door on
the other side of the pool. 'You have ten minutes to
change and join me,' he added smoothly before he
disappeared.

She stayed where she was for a moment, wanting to
refuse, but not quite finding the courage to do so. It
didn't need any special powers to know that he was not
prepared to take no for an answer. If she didn't change

and join him in the allotted time, he would take steps to make sure she did.

'Damned man,' she muttered to herself as she moved to obey him.

Ten minutes later to the second, she slid shyly out of the changing-room wearing a bright blue one-piece which was the only thing in a veritable store of female swimming gear that she'd considered half decent enough to wear, and even that was too cut away at the thighs for decency, its fine silk lycra fabric clinging to every single curve of her body so she felt almost as naked with it on as she'd felt without it.

Anton was already in the pool, pounding up and down with the brisk smooth strokes of the born swimmer, his brief white trunks doing little to soothe her fevered imagination. His skin was bronze and slick, muscles rippling as he cut a clean line through the water. Chewing uncertainly on her bottom lip, she lowered herself carefully down the steps and into the pleasantly warm water, relieved to get under out of sight before he realised she was there.

He powered up the pool towards her, dark head lifting on every other stroke so he could draw breath. She watched him in breathless awe, envious of his style, of his air of easy elegance, even in such a casual situation. His hand touched the end of the pool and up came his head, water cascading down his face as his eyes arrowed right on her, and she went still, waiting for she knew not what, then he grinned, did a neat rolling turn and powered away again leaving her wilting with relief.

It took time, but eventually she began to relax, mainly because he took no more notice of her after that one quick grin, and she swam more leisurely around the pool, feeling the slow erosion of her tension, and even managing to smile at it in the end. Anton had promised no seduction, and he obviously meant it.

She was floating lazily on her back when he eventually came up beside her. The sun was glinting down through the overhead glass dome, and she had her eyes closed, but at the light touch of his hand on her cheek her lids flicked open to glance warily at him.

'You are feeling a little more relaxed?' he enquired.

She nodded, feeling foolish for her strange mood earlier, and she told him so shyly.

His eyes were thoughtful, giving little away of himself. 'You have been under a great strain,' he made excuse for her.

Nina just smiled. She was still under a great strain, but instead of her father being the cause of it this man was, this dark and frighteningly attractive man who could raise goose-bumps on her skin just by looking at her.

'We all have to find time to relax and play, Nina,' he said after a moment. Then he grinned, perfectly square white teeth flashing in a suddenly satirically mocking face. 'Even I—wicked devil that I am in your eyes—like to take time off to play!'

She couldn't help it—she laughed too, the light sound pealing delicately in the high-domed room.

'That's better,' he murmured in wry satisfaction. 'I was beginning to wonder if you knew how to smile.'

'The same could be said of you,' she said, blushing a little.

'Yes,' he sombrely agreed. 'Ours has been a grim association until now.' Then, just as the mood threatened to grow heavy on them, he was smiling again, and reaching out to capture one of her hands, laying its palm flat on top of his own. 'See how pearly white your skin looks next to mine,' he mockingly observed, 'It looks almost as though your poor skin has never been exposed to the sun.'

Her stomach did a somersault and she dropped her legs, pulling her hand away as she trod water beside him, eyes making an involuntary sweep of his beautifully tanned body. 'Only because you Greeks are a race of thankless sun worshippers,' she answered scornfully, happy to continue the playful mood. 'While I have far more absorbing things to do with my time!'

With a resounding splash, she hit the water just by his face, then dived off, laughing as he spluttered beneath the surface in surprise.

She was just pushing herself out of the pool when he caught her, dragging her back by the waist and twisting her around to face him, his strong arms wrapping right around her in an effort to hold on to her slippery figure.

'Don't you dare kiss me!' she shrieked, seeing the intention in his gaze when he turned her around to face him, and rueing her own recklessness in daring to tease this man of all men.

'Why not?' His voice was full of lazy amusement. 'This is my pool, my water, and you are my own personal water nymph. I caught you, so I can kiss you whenever I want to!'

His feet were planted firmly on the pool bottom, but Nina's didn't reach, making her reliant on his grip on her to keep her head above water, and her hands went to clutch at his shoulders, fingers splaying out across the cool wet silk of his skin. Her gaze was drawn to the sleek cord of muscle where his shoulder met his neck, and her mouth went dry when she saw the darkened line which was all that was left of the wound she had inflicted on him over a week ago.

The sudden urge to place her lips against the mark had her heart clamouring wildly in her breast. 'Please let me go, Anton,' she pleaded breathlessly, panicked by her own feelings.

'No.' He shook his head, still amused, this lighter-hearted and playful man just as dangerous as the sexually hungry one she was used to seeing. 'Kiss or forfeit for splashing me,' he offered generously. 'You choose.'

'I...' The pink tip of her tongue threaded nervously around her lips. It was a kiss or a ducking, she realised that, and she had to choose the forfeit of course; even he was expecting her to. But the kiss was suddenly a real temptation. His mouth was very close to her own, so close she only had to move a fraction to... 'Forfeit!' she cried out in outright denial of her own traitorous desires.

'Too late,' he murmured, and did what she had been aching to do, and closed the gap between their hungry mouths.

It was fascinating, this feeling of weightlessness on the outside with the water lapping around her shoulders, and the weightlessness on the inside with the deep drugging sensuality of the kiss. Anton drew her closer, her long legs automatically tangling with his beneath the clear surface of the water. She could feel the texture of his hair-roughened limbs chafing pleasantly against her own, and her toes curled, the soft padded soles of her feet sliding delicately along his legs.

His arms tightened around her. 'Open your mouth,' he commanded huskily.

'No,' she refused, then melted anyway, bringing a warm laugh bubbling up from his chest as he acknowledged her easy surrender.

Then there was no laughter, no playfulness in the game whatsoever as the mood flipped over from the passive to the passionate, and the kiss was deepened by a mutual desire that sent them both straining desperately against each other.

'Well, well, well,' a thick-as-cream voice drawled from somewhere above them. 'This is—nice.'

If anything had the power to bring them both clattering back to a sense of the present, then that voice did. Nina froze in his arms, feeling at the same time Anton stiffen just before he slowly withdrew his mouth from hers.

'Fate seems determined to spoil our more—pleasurable moments, *matia mou*,' he murmured drily, sighing his dissatisfaction as Nina hid her hot face in his throat.

'Hello, Louisa,' he said. He didn't look up, keeping Nina against him, his mouth sliding lazily across her heated cheek, playing sensuously with her as if the other woman's unexpected appearance altered nothing. 'This is a—surprise.'

He wasn't being nice, and both women knew it. Nina pushed at his shoulders, her embarrassment total when he pressed a final clinging kiss to her lips before giving in to the pressure of her hands. But only in so far as to transfer his own hands to the tiled edge of the pool, effectively trapping her against the pool wall and the rigid planes of his richly tanned body.

'Let me go,' she whispered uncomfortably. She couldn't look up; she was just too aware of the other woman standing directly above them, appalled at what she must have witnessed—appalled at her own wanton behaviour. They had been so engrossed in each other that they hadn't even heard Louisa enter the pool-room!

'No,' he refused, turning his attention on their intruder. 'I did think I had given orders not to be disturbed, but...' a long sigh left him, lifting the black shadowed expanse of his bronzed chest then letting it fall again in a way that held Nina's breath locked tightly in her throat '... I must have been mistaken.'

'Oh, you know Mrs Lukas, darling,' Louisa dismissed lightly. 'She knows you never mean me.'

'Is that so?' It was rather like a dangerous cat playing with its equal. 'How stupid of me not to make my meaning clearer.'

'Very.' Louisa agreed. 'Are you going to stay in there much longer, Anton?' she enquired. 'Because, if so, I may as well undress and join you.'

'Not if you value your health, Louisa,' Anton said, and at last slid sideways from Nina so he could lever himself out of the pool, the water cascading down his beautiful body as he went.

'My, but we are being modest today, aren't we?' Nina heard Louisa taunt, dark eyes mocking the brief white swimming trunks he was wearing. 'I haven't seen you wear those in years, Anton, not in years!'

'Do you want slapping, minx?' he threatened, the indulgent use of that pet name stinging Nina's memory.
These two were so intimate with each other that it
screamed 'lovers'—just as it had done that night she had
watched them go into each other's arms!

Anton turned to offer her his hand as an aid to help
her out of the water. She didn't want to take it, she would
much rather have turned tail and dived beneath the
surface out of view of the lovely mocking eyes of Louisa.
Yet, and oddly, it was that exact same look which asserted her composure, bringing her chin up, blue eyes
hinting at defiance as she accepted Anton's hand and let
him haul her easily from the pool.

'Thank you,' she murmured as she landed neatly
beside him.

'My pleasure,' he mocked her trite remark. 'Let me
introduce you to an—old friend of mine.' For 'old friend'
replace 'mistress', Nina thought as a fierce shaft of pure
jealousy streaked right through her. 'Nina,' he went on
softly, pulling her closer to his side while his bland gaze
fixed itself on Louisa's mocking face, 'I would like you
to meet a very old friend of the Lakitos family, Louisa
Mandraki. Nina Lovell, Louisa,' he continued in that
same soft careful tone. 'My future wife.'

There was a stunned silence. Louisa's composure
slipped, her magnificent Yves St Laurent frame going as
rigid as a pillar of ice as she stared at him.

'You can't mean this, Anton?' she managed to gasp
in horrified disbelief.

'A real surprise, is it not?' He deliberately ignored
Louisa's horror. 'You are stunned,' he kindly allowed.
'And rightly so. I am rather stunned myself!'

'B-but what about...?' she faltered, lush mouth
quivering slightly, and Nina began to wish herself a
million miles away. 'Does your mother know about this?'

Mother—what mother? Nina hadn't known he had a
mother!

'Of course,' he calmly assured her. 'I informed her personally via the telephone only yesterday, or I would not be telling you now, Louisa,' he oh, so silkily pointed out. 'You know what a stickler for convention my mother is.'

'Yes...' Louisa's gaze narrowed as it slid over to Nina's stiff, uncomfortable face. Her composure was quickly restored. 'May I offer you my congratulations, Miss Lovell?' She lifted a long limp hand towards her, the length of its red-tipped nails so potentially lethal that Nina shuddered.

My God, she thought as she let her own hand slide briefly across Louisa's. She wants to kill me. 'Thank you,' she answered as coolly as she could.

'And you, darling, of course...' The smile she turned on Anton was warm and seductive, lovely face lifting up to him for his kiss.

He let go of Nina so he could oblige, leaving her standing there in seething silence while the two dark heads closed on each other with easy intimacy, the only thing stopping them from folding each other in a real clinch being the fear that the droplets of water still clinging to his hard, bronzed body would spoil Louisa's exquisite designer suit!

By the time he drew away, Louisa's eyes were smiling cat-like into his gleaming black ones. 'I think this calls for champagne, don't you, Anton?' she suggested huskily. 'Why don't you go and see if you have a bottle on ice somewhere while your—fiancée tells me all about your—romance?'

'What a good idea!' He turned back to Nina, laying one of his white-toothed smiles on her as he bent to place a kiss on her unresponsive lips.

Don't you dare leave me alone with her, her eyes warned him. The grin just widened. He was enjoying this, she realised angrily. He thought it all just a huge joke to have his future wife faced with his mistress! 'I'll only be a moment!' he assured her, touching her scorching cheek with a teasing finger, then sauntered off, whistling softly beneath his breath, leaving Nina with the nagging suspicion that he had left the two of them alone like this on purpose, just to see who would still be alive when he got back!

Well, she for one, refused to take the test. 'If you'll excuse me,' she murmured politely, 'I'll go and get changed while...'

'Running away, darling?' the thick-as-cream voice taunted. 'I really can't blame you. It was very naughty of Anton not to tell you about me.'

Nina's chin went up, her wet hair flying across her shoulder as she let her cool blue gaze fix with Louisa's hard black one. 'Oh, I already know all about you, Miss Mandraki,' she said sweetly. 'You are Anton's—old friend.'

'My dear girl.' Louisa's smile was full of humiliating mockery. 'There is a lot more between us than just a mere friendship.'

'That's—very nice,' Nina remarked insipidly, refusing to bite the bait, even while she was a seething mass of antagonism inside.

'His mother will not accept you, you know,' she was told. 'Ianthe has strict ideals where her only son is concerned. She does not believe in mixing the races. A Greek wife is the only kind of woman she will welcome into her family, and Anton knows it, which...' she paused to look curiously at Nina '...which only makes this— announcement of his all the more intriguing...'

If she wanted to make Nina feel even more uncomfortable with this marriage idea, then she was succeeding. The daunting prospect of having to face a hostile mother-in-law did not appeal at all. 'I won't be marrying his mother,' she said, keeping her expression cool with effort.

'You won't be marrying her son, either, if Ianthe has anything to do with it,' Louisa stated with calm certainty. 'Lovell...' she then murmured thoughtfully, sending her narrowed gaze on a crucifying scan of Nina's scantily clad figure. 'Lovell... now why does that name ring a shrill bell inside my head...?' The black eyes studied Nina's proudly defiant face for a moment, then a sly smile ruined the lush contours of her mouth. 'Ah, yes. It is Jonas Lovell's company which owns several properties in central London, is it not?' she mused silkily. 'The ones Anton has been trying to get his hands on for several months now, unless I am mistaken...'

No, you're not mistaken, Nina thought heavily as the silky observation hung in the air between them, making Nina look away and Louisa's smile widen as she noted her reaction.

'I wonder if knowing that will make you more acceptable to Ianthe?' Louisa went on curiously. 'We Greeks are all for marriages of expediency. And you never know, several million pounds' worth of good development land may just swing things in your favour—but what does it feel like, Miss Lovell,' she then taunted softly, 'to know yourself bought and sold like that?'

'Now wait a minute...' Stung by the damning truth in the words, Nina's chin came up. 'You have no right to——'

'I have every right!' Louisa cut in, and suddenly the silk gloves were off, revealing the furiously angry woman beneath. 'Anton is mine, do you hear?' She took a threatening step towards Nina, her stilettoed shoes screeching on the tiled pool-room floor. 'He has always been mine! We have been lovers for years!'

'Which makes you—what exactly?' Nina found it in her to taunt right back.

Louisa went pale. 'If you believe he will stop coming to me just because he marries himself to you, then you are a fool!' Her lush mouth turned down in a sneer. 'You, with your cold English passion, what do you have that will stop a man like Anton Lakitos straying back to more—satisfying favours?'

Blue eyes flashed their contempt for Louisa and all she stood for. 'Virginity, Miss Mandraki,' she heard herself reply, and was almost as shocked as Louisa at hearing it. 'Isn't that as precious to a Greek as the property you say I shall bring with me into our marriage?' Louisa couldn't know it, but the words were hurting Nina to say as much as they were hurting the Greek woman to hear. 'Surely,' she pressed her point scathingly home, 'even his high-principled mother will see the asset in having a daughter-in-law who hasn't *been around*, as we cold English like to call it!'

A direct hit, Nina noted as the beautiful Grecian face contorted, dark eyes flashing a single warning at her just before rage transformed itself into action, and Nina shied jerkily away as a beautifully manicured hand came winging out towards her face.

She landed in the pool with more urgency than grace, her heart pounding in frantic response to the distasteful scene she had just endured, followed by the eruption of violence. Her own quick reactions were the only things which had saved her from the vicious swipe from Louisa's red-tipped nails, and she swam away beneath the water, staying submerged for as long as she could, listening to the angry click of Louisa's feet echoing in the water, and praying that the terrible woman was leaving and not intending jumping in after her.

'My God,' she gasped when eventually her bursting lungs insisted she come up for air.

'Greek women are renowned for their shocking tempers,' a smooth voice drawled.

Nina spun around in the water. Anton was leaning against the pool-room door, an ice bucket containing a bottle of champagne tucked into the crook of his arm.

Her eyes spat angry fire at him. 'How much of that did you hear?' she demanded.

'Not much, I am sorry to say.' He looked disappointed. 'But by the look on Louisa's face as she pushed by me just now I would say you must have come out on top. Well done,' he dipped his dark head in sardonic applause, then spoiled it by adding balefully, 'Though I think it will now take some careful pampering on my behalf to bring her back into good humour.'

'Well.' She turned away from him in disgust. 'I'm getting out of here,' she told him angrily. 'Before any more of your—women arrive to stake their claim!' Swimming to the side of the pool, she pulled herself out of the water, her wet hair lying in a thick pelt down her back as she walked angrily towards the door he was so arrogantly propped up against.

'This annoying habit you have of leaving my home only half dressed will have to be curbed, Nina, my love,' he drawled lazily, the infuriating humour in his voice bringing her to a skidding halt so that she could glare at him—only to wish she hadn't when she caught the way his appreciative gaze was running freely over her. 'Only, I can't have my wife flaunting her...' the eyes did another run of her body '...charms for all and sundry to see.'

'I am not your wife yet!' she snapped, cheeks running hot with colour as she swung away again, making this time for the changing-room where she had left her clothes, furiously aware how well she deserved the taunt because that had been exactly what she had been intending to do: to walk out of here wearing only a skimpy blue bathing suit!

'Need any help?' he offered maddeningly.

'Go to hell!' she snarled and slammed the changing-room door shut.

# CHAPTER SIX

WHEN Nina came out again, Anton was sitting by the poolside waiting for her. He was dressed again, and looking just the same as he had when he'd arrived at her home that morning. Only the sleek dampness of his hair said that he had been doing anything other than sitting at his desk working all day. Nina's mouth went dry as she looked at him, and she damned the dryness just as she damned the way her heart fluttered at the mere sight of him.

'You are lovers,' she accused, keeping the full width of the pool between them.

'Louisa and I are a lot of things to each other,' he answered smoothly.

'As I've said before, you're despicable.'

Dark brows rose at her. 'How does it feel,' he enquired, 'to desire such a despicable fellow as me?'

The taunt hit home, heating her cheeks and closing her throat in despair. He was right. She did desire him, even while she hated the very sight of him. 'I would like to go home now, please,' she informed him primly.

'I am sure you would,' he agreed. 'But not yet. Not until you've sat down here and eaten something.' He waved a hand towards a loaded tray his housekeeper must have brought in while Nina was changing. 'We need to talk, you and I, and you are too thin. I would go as far as to say that you have lost almost a stone in weight since the first time I saw you.'

He could actually remember back that far back with so many women passing through his life? Nina was derisively surprised. She stayed where she was, eyeing him uncertainly, wondering if she dared defy him and just walk right out of here. She'd had enough of Anton Lakitos for one day!

'If I have to come and fetch you, you won't like it.'

He reads minds too, she grumbled to herself as lack of courage sent her around the pool to sit down opposite him, selecting a sandwich with a churlishness that only made him smile at her as though she were a silly child which, in turn, sent the resentment deeper.

The sandwich was surprisingly good though, she allowed, sinking her teeth into fresh salmon and finely chopped celery, keeping her eyes firmly averted from him while he seemed content to sip at his black coffee, prepared to stretch the tension between them out to breaking point before he began his threatened 'talk'.

She took another sandwich.

'Have you heard anything from Hunter since last week?'

Nina went still, the sandwich hovering halfway to her mouth. Obviously, he wasn't going to stretch it out. 'No,' she answered, her heart slowing to a heavy thump at the outright lie. He couldn't know about Jason's letters—could he? she told herself. She had thrown them all away. 'Did you "pay him off" as you promised to do?' she felt confident enough to throw right back.

He ignored the taunt. 'I am sure you have considered the consequences if I ever find out that you are lying to me,' he warned her levelly.

Nina lifted curious blue eyes to his. 'And will you inform me of any contact you have with the lovely Louisa from now on?' she asked, and her small white teeth closed over the sandwich.

He smiled at that. 'Are you sure you want to know?' he drawled. 'I saw the green devils glinting in your eyes earlier. Jealousy has a way of clouding the truth, and the truth of the matter is, I can't promise no contact with Louisa because we do—business together from time to time.'

'Don't forget the family connection,' she reminded him, not believing him for a minute. He had no intention of staying away from the lovely Louisa. She was enough to knock any man's eyes out.

'As you say,' he seemed happy to agree. 'She is also the daughter of my mother's best friend. Whereas your Jason has no excuse whatsoever to get in touch with you.'

'Except our music,' Nina put in, taking another sandwich and biting eagerly into it. The swim had made her hungry, or maybe it was the kisses—no, she dismissed that thought with an angry toss of her head. 'Jason and I belong to the same music group,' she explained, glad to have something to annoy him with. 'So we are bound to meet once—' she gave a careless shrug '—maybe twice a week.'

'Which brings me nicely on to another—rather delicate subject,' he said quietly, and Nina felt her nerves tingle to the surface of her skin. She wasn't going to like what was coming next, she was sure of it. 'Your college education.'

Nina put aside the sandwich, her suspicions confirmed. 'What about it?' she said warily. 'I begin a new term in October, that shouldn't be any——' She fell into a choking silence. He was already shaking his head, his meaning so horribly clear that her heart dropped to her stomach. 'No!' She refused to believe what her suspicions were saying to her, stretching out a hand as if to ward him off. 'You can't mean it. You can't really mean to take my music away from me.'

He caught the hand, holding it tightly in his own. 'You have to understand,' he urged her. 'It will be impossible for you to continue once we are married.' He was sorry; there was genuine sorrow in his voice as he said it. 'I travel a lot, I will expect you to travel with me. We will be man and wife in every facet of the union, Nina. I want you beside me in whatever bed it is I have to sleep in!'

'No.' She rose shakily to her feet, her hand still caught in his, the fingers cold and trembling. 'I won't give up my studies for you. I'll live here in your home with y-you. Be w-whatever it is,' she swallowed thickly, 'it is you want me to be to you, here, while in this house! But I won't throw away years of study because you are Greek enough to believe your wife's only place in life is to be stuck to your side!'

'I entertain a lot,' he persisted. 'You will naturally be my hostess—whatever country I happen to be in. I want and expect you to take up that role.' Dark eyes took on a hard immovable cast. 'There will be no time for your college studies, Nina. I am sorry, but there it is.'

'No.' The quickly drying tumble of glorious red hair trembled as she shook her head. 'No, I refuse to agree to it.'

He stared grimly at her for a moment, studying the set contours of her mouth, the angry heat in her cheeks, and the determined tilt of her small chin. Then something flickered across his face, the merest hint of pain, or was it irritation? Whatever, he sat back suddenly, releasing her hand as though it repulsed him, and the new look on his face was pure irony which seemed, oddly, to be aimed entirely at himself.

Then he said, quite flatly, 'I am not really giving you any choice, you know,' and watched, without any feeling whatsoever, all the colour drain from her face.

He had to be bluffing, she was thinking hectically. He wasn't that rotten, surely? He was just trying to put the fear of God into her for some reason, that was all, force her to acknowledge who had control over their——

'Of course,' he continued when she hadn't managed to utter a single word in response, 'if your music is worth more to you than trying to build a successful marriage with me, then by all means forget the marriage and go chase your rainbows. What right have I to deny you? But,' he added silkily, 'are those rainbows worth more to you than your father's health and happiness?'

'I'll give up my studies!' she choked, sitting down with a bump, beaten, as always, beaten by his more ruthless will.

He should have been triumphant, when all he looked was bitterly cynical. 'So, you will fight me to the death if I beg you to accept something on my behalf alone,' he jeered. 'But as soon as your father and his precious company is mentioned, you surrender without a second thought!'

'That is what this is all about, isn't it?' she choked, hating him with the pained blue of her eyes. 'My father and his company—or I wouldn't be sitting here with you at all!'

'That is certainly the truth,' he muttered. Then, without any warning, he leapt forwards in his chair, his hand snaking out to slam down on top of hers where it lay trembling on the plastic table-top, making her jump in surprise and the tray of fine crockery rattle dangerously, and Nina found herself looking at the frighteningly angry man she had always known lurked just beneath the surface of that urbane mask he liked to wear.

'So, now we will have the full truth,' he demanded gruffly. 'And you will tell me all about those secret love-letters you have been receiving from your darling Jason!'

Her eyes went wide in horror. 'You know about the letters?' she breathed.

'I know about the damned letters,' he scathingly confirmed. 'You will not be given the chance to cheat on me with Hunter,' he bit out grimly. 'No woman makes a fool out of me—especially one who is such a consummate liar as you have just proved yourself to be! Or one I know already has a penchant for sneaking into other men's bedrooms when the mood takes her!'

'That's not fair!' she jumped to her own defence. 'When I came to your room that night, it wasn't to...'

'Seduce me?' he offered when her own throat clammed up on the word. 'But how do I know that?' The black eyes were cynically mocking. 'You may have been planning all along to—place me in a compromising situation so you could blackmail me into leaving Lovell's alone. Or you would ruin my reputation by telling the world how I was capable of seducing a sick man's daughter at the same time as I stole his company from under him!'

It hit her then, just what was going on here, and she sighed, sitting back in her seat in much the same way he had done earlier. 'You actually read my letters from Jason,' she flatly accused, trying to recall just how Jason had worded it.

> We could threaten to tell the world how he blackmailed you into letting him seduce you. Think how much he would be prepared to pay to squash that kind of slur on his character. In the speculator business, a man relies on his social contacts to keep him in the know. He would become a social pariah if it ever got out that he was capable of seducing a sick man's daughter at the same time as he stole his company away from him. With a bit of clever planning, we could make him pay enough to put Lovell's back on an even keel again, then your father could do nothing else but accept me, and be grateful that we'd plucked him out of Lakitos's greedy clutches.

'How did you get hold of them?' she asked now, turning dulled blue eyes on him.

His shrug was pure indifference. 'I fished them out of the waste-paper basket.'

Of course, she thought. How stupid of her. He had used her father's study every morning—after she had used it to read Jason's letters before discarding them. How utterly stupid of her not to guess that he would be arrogant enough to retrieve and read them.

'Jason wrote a lot of lies in those letters, Anton,' she murmured huskily. 'He was talking wildly, and I didn't want you misinterpreting his meaning.' It was his own pain and confusion that had made Jason write what he had. He just could not come to terms with the fact that it was over between them.

'And which, in your opinion, were the lies, and which the truth?' he enquired cynically. 'Perhaps all his insinuations about me were the truth—or were they lies? Or maybe the intensity of his love for you was the truth—or was that a lie also?' Nina wriggled uncomfortably where she sat, and he leaned forwards suddenly, grasping her chin between a hard finger and thumb, forcing her to look at him. 'And what about all those—emotive pleas to meet with you, Nina?' he demanded roughly. 'Were they just wishful thinking on his part, or have you actually been meeting with him behind my back?'

The finger and thumb pinched painfully, and Nina set her mouth tightly shut in outright refusal to answer him. Sparking blue eyes warred with burning black, and the air around them began to buzz, with anger, with disdain, and with that forever present sexual turmoil that always complicated any issue they took up with each other.

'Have you been meeting with him?' The hard black eyes demanded an answer.

'Why, are you by any chance jealous?' she threw back tartly, then sat watching in wide-eyed fascination as two streaks of revealing colour whipped across his high cheekbones. He *was* jealous, she realised, as her senses clamoured in hectic triumph at the discovery.

'Bitch!' he breathed out hoarsely, hating her for surprising that piece of truth out of him. 'You damned beautiful bitch!' Her triumph was very short-lived as he yanked her mouth on to his, using the cruelty of his finger and thumb to do it, and punishing her mouth with a fury that pulsed frighteningly between them.

By the time they broke apart, they were both struggling for breath, gasping on the excitement of a hot and hated sensuality.

'Now you will tell me what I want to know,' he insisted huskily.

'Why should I tell you ánything?' she muttered, lifting trembling fingers to the tender flesh of her bruised mouth. 'You want to take everything away from me, yet give nothing back in return!' She wouldn't cry, she would not! 'As long as you deprive me of my college studies, I won't tell you anything I don't want to!'

The anger left him, replaced with a grim resolve which showed no hint of softness anywhere, 'You can play your piano in our home until my ears ring with the sound of it, Nina. But you will not be returning to college after the summer recess.'

'But Jason doesn't even attend the college!' she burst out wretchedly. 'Only the music group. I'll give that up!' she promised eagerly. 'I'll——' the uncompromising set of his jaw slewed her to a thudding stop. 'Oh, God,' she choked, and buried her face in her hands, wondering painfully if there was anything left for him to do to her.

'Come on,' he sighed, sounding as beaten as she felt. 'I'll take you home.'

The journey was not a happy one. Neither of them spoke; it all seemed to have been well and truly said. When he drew the car to a halt outside her home, Nina was relieved that he didn't switch off the car engine. It meant he wasn't coming in.

'I have to go away for a few days,' he informed her. 'John Calver, my assistant, will be in contact with you about the wedding arrangements. Leave everything to him.' An order, not negotiable. 'All you have to do before we marry is buy yourself a gown which will do honour to us both.'

'Black,' she mumbled bitterly. 'Mourning black to match my——'

'Listen to me, you aggravating fool!' he snarled, making her blink as he pushed his angry face close up to hers. 'Remember just who all this is being done for! And if that doesn't help seal your vicious tongue, then try remembering this!' His hand snaked out to grip her nape. 'I only have to touch you like this——' his mouth landed on top of her own, driving the breath from her body and the will to fight him from her soul as he kissed her with such agonising thoroughness that she was whimpering by the time he dragged his lips away '—to have you aching for more of the same!' he finished as if the long passionate gap in the middle hadn't been there.

'I wish I had never set eyes on you!' she choked, shamefully aware of how her throbbing lips burned for his to plunder them once again.

'The feeling is entirely mutual,' he gratingly agreed. 'I cannot think of anything less palatable than marrying myself to a crazy, mixed-up child who does not know when to curb her impulsive tongue!'

'Then why are you?' she cried in bitter challenge.

Black eyes flashed across her strained face. 'You know why,' he growled. 'Because I can hardly keep my hands off that responsive little body of yours.'

'You don't have to marry me to do that,' she pointed out wearily. 'You are in the position of calling all the shots—are still calling them!' She turned her face away from the grim hard cast of his. 'Haven't I already proved to you that I'll do anything to make my father happy?'

'Then be glad I am prepared to marry you to get what I want,' he snapped, then sighed heavily. 'Go inside, Nina,' he advised. 'Before this really degenerates into the slanging match you seem intent on. And Nina,' he added as she went to scramble quickly from the car, 're- member with whom your loyalty now lies.' He grimly warned, 'Hunter is in your past, and in the past is where I intend to keep him. No more lies. I want to know if he so much as sends you a postcard, got that?'

'Yes.' She'd got it. She now belonged to Anton Lakitos. Bought, body and aching soul.

He was away almost a week, and it was a week when she didn't know what was worse: having him around to constantly remind her why she was letting herself be coerced like this, or not having him around so her mind could work overtime conjuring up all kinds of horrors that could befall her under his uncaring hands.

In the end, she went to her piano to search of escape, and found it in the complicated absorption of teaching herself a new Mozart piece.

'That was nice to hear,' her father said when she entered his room later that day. He had been improving steadily, and was now allowed to sit in the chair beside his bed, though he spent most of his time there dozing. 'I hadn't realised how much I'd missed hearing you play until today.'

'I haven't felt much like playing while you've been so ill,' she explained her neglect of the piano, then smiled a little wanly. 'Anton doesn't want me to continue my studies after we're married,' she confessed sadly.

Her father glanced sharply at her. 'I guessed he might feel that way,' he said gruffly. 'He loves you,' he smiled as if that said it all, and Nina wanted to weep. 'And these Greek fellows can be damned possessive of their women. Give him a few children,' he advised. 'That'll soothe his ego a little. Then, if you still want to, maybe you can convince him to let you return to your studies.'

She sent him a jaundiced look. 'Do you male chauvinists always stick together?'

'There can be as much self-fulfilment in being a wife and mother as there can be in academic achievement, Nina,' he said carefully. 'Don't let the feminists' view brainwash you into believing yourself only half a woman because you've chosen love and marriage to a good man over your career.'

Love, she thought heavily. What was love? Perhaps, if love were there between herself and Anton, she could accept any sacrifice she would be forced to make.

'And think how it would gladden your old papa's heart to bounce his grandson on his knee,' Jonas added, blue eyes glinting with their old foxiness again after weeks of being so dull and lifeless that Nina didn't have the heart to douse the light with the cutting reply that naturally jumped to her lips.

But she wasn't above putting in her own little dig. 'So you don't mind the father of your grandson being the man you once hated enough to murder?'

'That was all a—misunderstanding,' he huffed out dismissively, his face closing up on her as it always did when she tried to discuss his relationship with Anton. 'I—I owed him money, you know,' he added suddenly.

'Yes.' Nina nodded. 'Anton told me.'

'He did?' Jonas looked surprised, then added defensively, 'I could have paid him back if the old ticker hadn't gone on the blink!'

'I'm sure you could,' Nina allowed, not sure of it at all.

'But, as it is,' he murmured tiredly, leaning back in his seat and closing his eyes, 'I can rest easier knowing he's taking care of Lovell's. There are a lot of sharks out there, Nina, waiting to pounce on a sick old man like me; Anton was only one of them. At least, now you're marrying him, I'll always know that everything I've worked for through the years will stay in the family. It's a good feeling, that.' He sighed with satisfaction, then peered slyly at her through the narrowed slits of his lowered lids. 'Just do your part, and make sure of that grandson I need to inherit. Then this old man can die contented.'

Could you see it? Nina leaned closer to her dressing mirror to peer at her own reflection. No, her smile was lopsided and faintly cynical. You couldn't actually see the rope being slowly tightened around her neck, pulled steadily by her father on one end and Anton on the other. It didn't show; it was an invisible noose.

It was Saturday evening, and Anton was due to come and collect her in a few minutes. She had received the royal summons, as she mocked John Calver's telephone call of yesterday. Anton was apparently arriving from

Greece today, and would be bringing his mother to meet her.

She was invited for dinner.

What a treat, she grimly mocked. I am to be looked over to see if I come up to the high standards his mother apparently has for her son's bride. Well, there was one thing for certain, she knew as she applied a final touch of blusher to her too-pale cheeks: not even the daunting Ianthe could fault her appearance tonight; she had spent too many long painstaking hours making sure of it.

Nevertheless, there was a definite lump of nervous tension in her throat as she stood up to view the finished effects in the long mirror. Her gown was a long, sleek, knitted silk thing that covered her from throat to wrist to ankle except for the upside-down heart-shape cut out of the bodice just above the rounded slopes of her breasts. She had bought it to wear to one of her father's formal receptions because its elegantly classical lines had the courage-lifting effect of adding years to her paltry twenty, putting her more on a par with the kind of highly sophisticated women who usually attended those affairs. The shimmering turquoise colour of the silk echoed the blue of her eyes and reacted beautifully with the rich red colour of her hair, caught up tonight in a smooth coroneted pleat. And the whole effect held a certain dignity about it which went a little way to soothing her hectic nerves.

It was also the dress she had been wearing the first time Anton had seen her, she reminded herself as she turned away to collect her wrap and purse. But that didn't mean anything—she dismissed the sudden tingling low in her stomach. She hadn't chosen to wear it for that reason, but because it was the dress she felt most confident in.

With a firm lifting of her chin, she walked out of her room and across the landing to say goodnight to her father.

Anton arrived on time, looking so terribly handsome in full black tuxedo that her breath caught in her throat.

His hooded gaze glinted over her, giving nothing away.

'You wear no jewellery,' was his only personal comment, and Nina felt instantly deflated.

'No,' she answered defensively. 'I don't particularly like wearing it.'

A black brow rose in faint mockery. 'Then I hope you learn to like wearing this...' He stepped forward, and instantly her senses were reacting to his sudden closeness. His hand slid into his jacket pocket and came out with a high-domed box which he flicked open with his thumb, and Nina couldn't hold back the gasp of surprise as a huge blue sapphire circled with tiny diamonds winked richly up at her. 'Give me your hand,' he commanded gruffly.

'I...' She touched her dry lips with the moist tip of her tongue. 'Are you sure it is necessary to——?'

'Very sure.' He reached down to capture her left hand when she made no move to offer it to him. 'This ring belonged to my grandmother,' he informed her as he slid the beautiful thing over her slender knuckle. 'My mother will expect to see it on your finger. It was left to me for just such a purpose.'

'I... Thank you,' she whispered, feeling oddly like weeping.

He smiled a little grimly, then did a strange thing, bending his dark head over her hand and pressing his lips against the ring. When he straightened, he didn't look at her, but Nina caught a brief glimpse of something intensely moving on his face before he quashed it, and wondered at it as he led her out to the waiting car.

They were to be chauffeur-driven tonight, she saw as Anton helped her into the back of a long black limousine where the driver sat hidden behind a sheet of obscure glass. 'I am probably a trifle jet lagged,' he explained his reason for the chauffeured car. 'And not really fit to drive myself.'

'I—I thought you had been with your mother in Greece,' she remarked shyly, feeling a little overpowered by the man and the ring glowing deep, deep blue on her finger. 'People don't usually suffer jet lag on such a short plane journey.

'I was in Greece this morning,' he agreed. 'But before that I was in the States, and only stopped off in Athens long enough to collect my mother to escort her to London. I have been continent-hopping,' he informed her sardonically, watching her. She could feel the heat of his gaze on her, though she refused to look back at him. 'Trying to fit two months' work into just a few days.'

'And how...?' Her fingers twisted together as a sign of tension. 'How is your mother taking the news about me?'

Her anxiety had shown in the husky quality of her voice, and Anton was silent for a moment as he studied her. 'She isn't an ogre, you know,' he murmured drily at last.

'No?' She sent him a thin smile that barely touched the edges of her tense mouth. 'Her son is. He must have inherited it from somewhere.'

He laughed softly, shaking his head in rueful appreciation of the little thrust. 'Subdued but not dead, I see,' he drawled. 'Poor unfortunate darling...' he taunted softly. 'You look like Joan of Arc, going bravely to her fate.'

Nina shifted restlessly where she sat, disturbed that he should make such an assessment of her plight.

'I wonder,' he then added musingly, 'if, with hindsight, Mademoiselle d'Arc thought the cause worthy of the sacrifice?'

'How is my father's company doing since you took over its affairs?' she got in her own little dig. Anton might have drawn back from actually taking over the company, but he dealt personally with all Lovell's business affairs now.

'A lot better than it had been doing,' he answered quite seriously. 'No company worth its salt could afford to fritter away its assets as Lovell's had been doing. Heard from Hunter while I've been away?' It was his turn to change the subject, and make her stiffen at the same time.

'No,' she answered stiffly, and it was the truth this time; Jason's letters had stopped abruptly. She levelled him with a suspicious look. 'I suppose you threatened him or something,' she accused.

'I—advised him it would be better if he let sleeping dogs lie from now on,' he amended carefully.

'Same thing,' she said, turning a stony profile on him. 'Whatever, you won't have been nice about it. You don't know how to be.'

'Oh, come here!' he sighed impatiently, taking her completely by surprise when his hand snaked across the gap separating them and pulled her ungently towards him. 'Enough is enough, Nina,' he muttered as he settled her into the warm crook of his arm: 'Your fighting spirit is to be admired, and, God knows, I enjoy sparring with you. It puts such an enchanting light in your beautiful blue eyes. But I am tired,' he sighed, dark eyes roaming her pale and anxious face, 'and in no mood for any of it tonight.'

'Then let me go, and I'll be as quiet as a mouse,' she promised, already having to quell her clamouring pulses.

'What you need is kissing into a better humour,' he stated huskily. 'And I need this, quite desperately in fact,' he groaned as his mouth came slowly down to hers.

The colour was running high in her cheeks by the time he released her, the glow in her eyes easily outshining the bright glitter of precious stone she wore on her finger. With her lips still parted and trembling invitingly, Anton took his time taking it all in, holding the tension like fierce static around them while Nina waited, praying he wouldn't kiss her again—and hoping achingly that he would.

'Just hold that look, *agapi mou*,' he murmured after a while. 'We are almost at my home, and this is exactly how I wish my mother to see you.'

'You did it on purpose!' she cried, sitting bolt upright and hating him all over again.

'Not entirely,' he denied, settling himself comfortably into the corner of the car so he could continue his unnerving study of her at his leisure. 'Five days without you, Nina, is long enough for any normal man to endure, but for one whose desires run as deeply as mine, those five days have been utter purgatory!'

'My God,' she choked, 'You are——'

'Despicable, I know,' he sighed. 'You have told me so often that I am now bored with hearing it. But just remember this, my scratchy little kitten.' His hand found her chin and turned it around to face him. 'My mother is about as innocent as anyone in all of this, so keep your claws sheathed in her company, or I may have to take drastic steps to make sure you do.'

'Threats again, Anton?' she taunted recklessly.

'You had better believe it, Nina,' he confirmed. 'You play the besotted bride, or else. Got that?'

'Yes,' she whispered, the defiance dying as quickly as it had risen. 'I had no intention of doing anything else.'

'Good,' he said, letting go of her. 'We are here.'

# CHAPTER SEVEN

'GOOD evening, Miss Lovell.' John Calver was waiting for them as they entered the house, and, after his polite greeting for Nina, he turned an apologetic look on his employer. 'I'm sorry to waylay you just as you've arrived, Anton, but that call from New York you've been expecting has just come through.'

'Damn their lousy timing,' Anton cursed, his eyes warming as they turned on Nina, taking in the lovely picture she made in her deep turquoise gown against a backcloth of richly polished wood. 'I have to speak to them,' he told her huskily.

Nina nodded, unable to manage more than that over the nervous tension she was suffering.

'Where is my mother?' Anton asked John Calver.

'In the drawing-room,' he was informed.

'Then tell New York I will be a few minutes.' He reached out to take the fine silk matching wrap from Nina's shoulders and handed it to his assistant, his dark gaze concentrated on her in a way that had her heart beating shallowly in her breast. How could it be, she wondered achingly, that she could hate this man so furiously, yet want him so badly?

'All right?' he enquired as he drew her towards the door she had once watched people coming and going from one dark and fateful night not so very long ago.

She swallowed. 'Yes,' she said, and lifted her chin.

His soft laughter said he'd noted the mental arming. 'Don't worry,' he soothed as he opened the door. 'My mother is going to love you. How could she not when you look so enchantingly beautiful tonight?'

The compliment flushed the colour back into her cheeks, and Anton smiled his satisfaction as he took them both over the threshold into his mother's presence.

It was a lovely room, was Nina's first hazy thought, the furnishings classically European in shades of pale ivory and gold. She managed to gain an impression of contained luxury and quiet elegance before Anton was demanding her full attention, and drawing her towards the woman just rising from a long ivory sofa.

And immediately Nina's heart sank. She was a woman of formidable presence, tall and strong-boned with the expected jet-black hair swept away from her beautifully preserved olive-skinned face—a face which bore no welcome in its cold black eyes whatsoever.

'Mother,' Anton greeted her warmly, his hand transferring itself to Nina's slender waist as he bent to accept his mother's kiss. 'The New York call I have been expecting has just come through. So I am going to have to make rushed introductions then leave you both to get to know each other. Nina?' He drew her forwards. 'Darling,' he murmured, 'this is my mother. Mother, this is the beautiful creature who has delighted me by promising to be my wife!'

Triumph or challenge? Nina wondered at the emphasised tone in his voice, 'Good evening, Mrs Lakitos,' she greeted her nervously, holding out a decidedly shaky hand, then shivered at the pair of frigid black eyes that turned on her.

'Miss Lovell,' Ianthe Lakitos said formally, ignoring the outstretched hand, but stepping forwards instead to brush her lightly perfumed cheek against Nina's. 'It is a—pleasure to meet you at last,' she murmured as she moved away, but her eyes said otherwise, and Nina's heart sank a little further. So, Louisa had been right, and she was not to be accepted by Anton's mother with any warmth.

'I have to go,' Anton cut into the tension filtering between the two women. 'Look after her for me, Mother,' he requested smoothly. 'Nina was just a little nervous of meeting you. Do your best to make her feel at home.'

Again, Nina picked up the hint of challenge in his voice, and knew for certain then that Anton had not had an easy time convincing his mother that Nina Lovell was the woman he wanted for his wife. Nina could understand it; she wasn't in the least bit convinced herself!

Nevertheless, she attempted to keep things on a polite footing. 'It—it was very good of you to come all this way to meet me, Mrs Lakitos,' she broke the stiff silence Anton left behind him.

'My son insisted on it.' Nina was bluntly informed. 'But I have to tell you, Miss Lovell, that Anton has grieved me bitterly with this shock decision.'

'I—I'm sorry.' The apology was genuine. She was sorry his mother was disappointed in her.

'You are not even Greek!'

Nina's smile was dry. 'No,' she confirmed. 'I am afraid I can't claim any Greek blood whatsoever.' But her chin came up in that brave way Ianthe's son would have recognised with wry dread. 'But my blood runs red, Mrs Lakitos,' she said, then added spiritedly, 'Just as I must assume yours does.'

'As red as your awful hair, no doubt.' The black eyes flicked contemptuously to Nina's silken halo of red-gold hair.

'I will not apologise for the colour of my hair.' Her hands were beginning to tremble, and she hid them into the folds of her gown. Anton had warned her not to spar with his mother, but it seemed he hadn't bothered warning his mother about the ground rules, because she was more than determined to provoke Nina!

'You are nothing but a child, and too slender for my taste!' The stiffly held mouth turned down in dislike. 'Will you apologise to me when that frail body of yours cannot produce the sons my son requires?'

'I am not marrying Anton for the exclusive function of giving him sons, Mrs Lakitos,' Nina answered stiffly, rising fully to the indignity of the inquisition.

'And why are you marrying him?' the Greek woman questioned coldly. 'For his money, is that it? Your own father's wealth is drying up, so you thought you would find yourself a nice rich husband?'

Nina laughed at that; she couldn't help it, it was so ridiculous. 'Why?' she threw back sweetly. 'Can't you believe your son capable of making a woman love him for himself alone?'

Ianthe stiffened with haughty affront. 'Anton can have any woman he likes!'

Nina nodded. 'Because his money draws them.' Too angry to care, she pressed home only what the woman herself had just implied. What was it with these Greeks that made them so condescendingly superior to everyone else?

'That is not what I meant at all!' his mother said irritably. 'You have to understand the ways of a Greek to understand what my son's announcement has done.' She went on coldly, 'Anton was expected to marry well. A Greek girl, one whose wealth and fortune would complement his own.'

Like the lovely Louisa for instance? Nina thought. She was well aware of the kind of money the Mandraki shipping family had behind them. 'My own father is not exacty penniless, you know,' she said defensively.

'We are talking pounds, not pennies, Miss Lovell,' Mrs Lakitos scorned. 'And we are talking blood. Good Greek blood which would reinforce the strength of our own pure Greek bloodline, not that weak stuff you were referring to a moment ago. You have to know what you are allowing him to throw away by agreeing to marry him.'

Nina was beginning to feel a bit like a Victorian maid, condemned for thinking she could marry a prince! 'So, what are you trying to suggest, Mrs Lakitos?' she enquired. 'That I jilt your son for his own good?'

'Ah.' Ianthe Lakitos smiled at last. 'I see you are beginning to understand.'

'That your son's happiness is up for sale like any commodity sold in the market-place?' she said. 'You're right, Mrs Lakitos, I am only just beginning to understand!'

'That is not what I meant!' Ianthe protested impatiently, actually looking uncomfortable at last. And Nina was angry enough to enjoy seeing it.

'You are still standing?' a deep voice remarked in surprise, and both women stiffened, glancing sharply around to find Anton just closing the drawing-room door. 'And no drinks!' he declared, seeming completely oblivious to the hostility permeating the air.

He strode forwards, smiling easily at both of them. 'I apologise for taking so long. It was a silly matter, but those are always the ones which seem to take up more of your time than they actually deserve. A sherry, Mother...?'

It was an awful evening, and Nina had never been so glad to be helped into the back of the car as she was when Anton eventually brought the traumatic evening to an end.

'She hates me,' she said dully.

'Not hate,' he denied. 'Just—resentment of anyone who gets in the way of something she wanted very much.'

'The rich little Greek girl with the pedigree blood?' Nina jeered.

He had settled himself into the corner of the car as soon as they moved away, a mixture of jet lag and strain hollowing out the richly tanned lines of his face. 'Is that what she said?' His eyebrows rose in wry appreciation, mouth showing a humour which only served to make Nina more angry. 'She will come around eventually,' he assured her, closing his eyes. 'Just give her time.'

'If that is supposed to make me feel better, then let me disappoint you,' Nina snapped, 'I don't want her

approval.' A full evening of having to endure his
mother's only slightly less acid barbs while her son was
present made her more than ready to pour all her frustrated anger over his thankless head. 'Or anyone else's
for that matter.' Her angry eyes glinted at the darkness
rushing by them outside the car. 'I am marrying you
because we made a bargain, not with the ambition of
becoming the light of your mother's life!'

'Or mine, for that matter.' The eyes remained closed,
the voice flat.

'You want me, and you're going to get me,' she muttered. 'Don't expect more than that.'

'Oh, I shall expect a whole lot more than that, my
spitting little kitten!' And with an economy of movement
that set the nerves stinging across the surface of her skin
he pulled her to him, sealing her mouth with kisses,
turning her anger to passion without having to try very
hard to do it. And at the same time forcing her to accept
what any amount of words had failed to do: that even
if she could escape the net being so ruthlessly thrown
around her, she wouldn't want to.

She wanted this too much. Wanted him.

The private jet tilted as it hit an air pocket, and Nina
stirred from the light doze she had fallen into. It had
been a long and tiring journey, finishing off a long and
tiring day.

They had been married that morning at a small church
not far away from her home. She had worn traditional
white satin and lace, and covered the strained pallor of
her face with a full tulle veil. Her father had had tears
in his eyes as he watched her come down the stairs. He
was leaning heavily on the two sticks he was determined
to discard once they reached the church. He still wasn't
well, and Dr Martin had been concerned enough to insist
he go straight back to bed once the traditional wedding
toast had been drunk.

'Goodness, girl,' he muttered rustily, 'you look just like your mother.' And there were tears in his eyes as he bent to place a kiss on her cheek through the enveloping folds of tulle.

Anton's mother attended the ceremony, and her manner had not softened one iota since their first meeting. Louisa was there too, invited by Ianthe, who, Nina was sure, had done it solely to discomfit her, and she could feel the septic sting of Louisa's eyes on her back as she walked down the aisle to take Anton's waiting hand.

He looked devastating, dressed in a conventional dark suit and plain white shirt; nothing could take away the man's special charisma. His gaze narrowed on her face obscured by the veil, and she was glad of the cover, feeling the tiny muscles around her heart squeeze as she looked up at him.

His hand was warm and firm on her freezing cold one, long fingers closing around hers in a way which stated ownership.

Behind her followed a single bridesmaid, the only one from the music group who hadn't condemned her for jilting Jason. 'No contest,' Tina had announced after meeting Anton at the small dinner party her father had insisted on holding a few nights before the wedding. 'Want Jason after meeting him?' Her big eyes had rolled upwards expressively. 'It's like tasting caviare when you're only used to tuna fish. There is no comparison. You lucky devil, Nina.'

But Nina didn't feel lucky. She felt unbearably sad, and just a little afraid of what came after this very respectable ceremony. During the weeks leading up to the wedding, Anton had turned back into the remote stranger she had known while her father had lain seriously ill. He had visited her, been very polite, even quite gentle with her, but he hadn't kissed her once since that last passionate exchange in the rear of his chauffeur-driven car when he had pulled away from her, muttering, 'God, this has to stop, or you will be coming to me on our wedding night a very experienced woman!'

'What makes you think I'm not already experienced?' she'd flared, annoyed at his confidence in her innocence.

Black eyes had flashed darkly at her. 'You had better not be, Nina,' he'd warned, 'or you will find out just how Greek I am!'

'Is that why you wouldn't marry Louisa?' she had hit back tartly, certain as anything that it was Louisa whom his mother had picked out for his bride. 'Because you know she's no virgin?'

A dry smile had touched his mouth. 'You would have to go a long way back into Louisa's past to trace her virginity. No,' he'd then denied more seriously. 'I am not so primitive as to expect virginity from my wife on her wedding night—so long as it was I who took it from her in the first place.' He had cupped her cheek with a hand, holding her gaze with the black density in his. 'My Greek breeding demands total commitment from my wife, Nina. Remember that,' he'd advised. 'It will hold you in good stead if you ever consider cheating on me.'

'But I am not to demand the same of you, I suppose?'

'Before we met? No,' he'd said. 'The double standard raising its ugly head,' he had admitted drily. 'But since we met?' He'd pressed a final kiss to her lips before moving away from her. 'I give you leave to beat me to within an inch of my life if you ever catch me with another woman.'

'Catch being the operative word.'

He had just laughed, and settled himself back into his corner of the car to study her lazily while they finished their journey. Since then he had kept his distance, and the man she had become so reluctantly drawn towards had once again become the stranger she instinctively wanted to cower away from.

But his eyes were burning when he lifted the veil from her face. *Mine,* the look said, and she trembled when he bent to kiss her cold, stiff lips, as every fear she'd ever felt of him leapt starkly back to the surface.

'You will never keep him,' Louisa said confidently when she managed to corner Nina at the wedding breakfast. 'You just are not woman enough.'

'I shall learn to be,' she replied, refusing to let Louisa see how her words had struck home.

'I believe my son to have made the biggest mistake of his life today,' her new mother-in-law told her coldly. 'And I hold you entirely responsible for it all.'

Which probably held more truth than Ianthe actually realised, Nina acknowledged heavily to herself.

'Look after my girl,' her father gruffly commanded when at last he gave in to the doctor's urges to get him back to bed. 'And remember those grandsons you promised me!'

Her expression was troubled as she watched Dr Martin lead him away. 'Leave a sick old man his dreams,' Anton murmured quietly beside her, understanding the reason for her frown. 'Is it not the foremost hope of every parent when their offspring marry? Even my own mother has that broody glint in her eye,' he drawled, making Nina glance across the room to where Ianthe stood frowning at them. She wasn't brooding, Nina thought acidly. She was busy casting evil spells! 'What she loses on the swings, she hopes to gain on the roundabouts,' Anton mocked lightly.

'Which is why she continues to treat me like a leper.'

'Wait until the children come along,' he soothed, 'Then see how she responds to you.'

'What children?' she threw back tartly, aware of the odd clutching of her body at the thought of conceiving his child.

'The ones we will forge in a storm of fire and passion,' he promised, and she trembled at the deep growling promise in his voice. 'Frightened, Nina?' he taunted softly.

She went to deny it, then found she couldn't, lowering her eyes instead. 'I have to change,' she mumbled, desperate to get away from him, if only for a short while. And, thankfully, he let her go, but his soft laughter taunted her as she went...

'We are almost there,' a quiet voice said beside her, and Nina sat up straight, smothering a yawn as she turned to look out of the aeroplane window. 'The island is small, but large enough to accommodate a landing strip.'

'Does it have a name?' she asked, watching the baked brown oval shape of an island rise out of the Aegean sea. It was getting late, gone seven o'clock in the evening, and the August sun was polishing everything below them a rich copper colour.

'It is Lakitos Island, of course,' he said, sounding amused and not a little arrogant. 'It has been in the family for generations. The island is home to me—the only real home I ever really knew as a child because I used to spend all my holidays from school here.'

The wandering life of a diplomat's son, she recalled, feeling an odd sympathy for the boy who must have found his gypsy existence lonely sometimes.

'There is one small village—there...' he leaned across her to point down to where a cluster of flat-roofed white-washed buildings stood blushing in the evening sun. His arm pressed against her own, making it tingle, the musky male scent of him teasing her nostrils. 'It is a small island, dependent mainly on itself for its needs, and the boat that calls here once a fortnight during its round trip supplying all the smaller islands.'

'No tourists?' He was so close that she was hardly breathing, and desperately tried to keep her voice level.

He smiled—she sensed the movement of his mouth almost touching her cheek. 'We discourage tourism on this island. The tourists have more than enough of our homeland to assuage their hunger for sun-soaked mythology, and we have nothimg to offer them either in the way of history or accommodation. We are a simple people at heart, Nina,' he informed her drily. 'Give a Greek a modest home, a good wife, and a place he can congregate with his neighbours in the evening to drink *ouzo* and put the world to rights across a simple wooden table, and he will be content.'

At that moment, the plane banked sharply, throwing Anton hard against her, and he instinctively threw a hand across the front of her to hold her steady in her seat, brushing across the sensitive tips of her breasts as he did so. She sucked in a sharp breath, and he glanced at her, his eyes darkening as her soft mouth began to quiver.

'And th-the big house I can see on the hill-top?' she enquired breathlessly, knowing he wanted to kiss her, and praying to God that he wouldn't. She had a feeling she might shatter if he did, she felt so brittle.

He grimaced, easing the sexual pressure between them by sinking back into his own seat, arching a brow at her audible sigh of relief. 'Our villa,' he announced, then smiled ruefully. 'And not so modest, I suppose I had better add before you do.'

Nina stared down at the lovely sun-kissed villa with its two-storeyed verandas and whitewashed walls. She could see the rich blue rectangle of a swimming pool laid out in the middle of a mosaic patio, and the surprising lushness of lawn which swept down to a rock-rimmed beach.

'Water is not a problem on the island,' Anton said as though he only had to look at her to read her thoughts. 'It has its own natural spring which gives us more than enough not to have to worry about wasting it on keeping at least some of the land alive and fertile during the long hot summer.'

The plane lurched and landed on the ground with a bump, making Nina start in mild alarm. One moment they had been circling low over the island, the next landing without any warning whatsoever.

'Primitive but effective,' Anton drawled as the drag on the plane's brakes forced them back into their seats, pulling them to a stop almost as soon as they had all wheels on the ground.

He got up, smiling at her as he held out a hand to offer her assistance. She took it, dry-mouthed and tongue-tied. He was still wearing the same clothes he had worn to their wedding—minus the jacket and silk tie, and looking ten times more attractive without them. The white cotton shirt clung to the rigid walls of his chest, forming shadows where the thick mat of body hair curled in a dark disturbing triangle beneath. His hips were slim and spare, his stomach flat-planed so the dark trousers fitted snugly before following the powerful length of his legs.

He manoeuvred her in front of him, his hands possessive on her waist as he guided her down the aisle to where the steward was already unlocking the door. At the top of the steps, she paused, momentarily stunned by the bank of heat which hit her full in the face.

'All right?' Anton enquired from just behind her.

'Yes,' she whispered, her voice sounding rusty even to her own ears. 'I just didn't expect the heat to be so intense so late in the day, that's all.'

'Hmm.' His hands tightened a little on her waist. 'We must watch that delicate skin of yours does not burn, *agapi mou*. I couldn't bear to see its perfection marred by the ruthless heat of my Greek sun.'

'I shall be careful,' she promised, moving down the steps so that she could break free of him. He let her go, but only for as long as it took him to join her on the makeshift runway, then he was reaching for her shoulders and turning her around to face him.

'Welcome,' he said simply, and bent to capture her lips.

It wasn't a passionate kiss, or even a kiss that expected a response, but her breathing was unsteady when he drew away, and her cheeks had grown warmer, a bout of painful shyness completely overwhelming her.

'Let's go.' She heard the husky rumble of his voice and shivered delicately. Did she have any choice? she wondered sadly as she let him take her to where an open-topped Mercedes stood waiting for them not ten yards away, parked beneath the shade of a huge old olive tree. Any choices she might have had, she had let slip through her fingers weeks ago, she reminded herself heavily. Forfeited on the night she had set out on her crazy mission of doom.

'Don't tremble so much,' he scolded as he walked beside her, his hand like a loose manacle around her own. 'I am not going to jump on you the moment we are alone.'

'I d-didn't think you were!' she denied, daring to send him an indignant glare.

'Liar,' was all he said, and she had to look quickly away from the lazy mockery in his deep brown eyes.

He saw her seated in the Mercedes before returning to the plane where the steward and the pilot were already taking off their luggage. The three men chatted genially for a few minutes, then shook hands, and Anton was picking up the two large suitcases and striding back to the car. He threw them on to the back seat, then climbed in beside her, his attention on acquiring his own comfort as he rolled back his shirt sleeves to the elbows and loosened several buttons on his shirt before reaching over to fire the car engine.

Nina had watched it all in a kind of hypnotic fascination, but now she turned away from him as the suddenly heady temptation to reach out and touch the newly exposed skin at his throat had her stomach knotting in appalled acknowledgement of her own hectic emotions. It was humiliating, the way her senses responded so violently to him.

The dark sapphire on her finger glinted blue fire at her in the steadily dying sunlight, the addition of a heavily engraved wedding ring still feeling strange to her. She twisted the rings around absently, remembering how neat Jason's single diamond had looked on her slender hand, and a new sadness filled her heart.

Poor Jason, she had treated him so badly that she didn't think she would ever manage to justify it to her conscience. Yet, she admitted dully, even if she could have found a way to avoid committing herself so totally to the man beside her, she knew she wouldn't have used it. Anton had spoiled her chances of ever being content with any other man but him. He fired her senses in a way that exalted her even as it appalled. One kiss was all it took, one small, insignificant kiss like the one he had laid on her lips as they left the plane just now, and he could turn her into a shaking mass of emotion.

She heard the revving of the plane engines as Anton turned the car on to a dusty track and began accelerating away. The speed pushed the warm air through her loose hair, and she lifted her face to it, staring up at the rich expanse of deep blue sky above.

So, this is it, she told herself bleakly. This was what she had committed herself to. A husband she knew she would never be sure of, and the unnerving prospect of a wedding night she knew was going to alter the whole substance of her life.

'There will be a small reception committee when we arrive, I'm afraid.' Anton's rueful tone broke into her bleak thoughts. 'People from the village,' he explained. 'It is customary for them to welcome you as my wife.'

She turned to look at him. His black hair was blowing in the breeze, his beautifully honed face looking more arrogant, more handsome than she had ever seen it, with the warm caress of his own Greek sun highlighting the richness of his skin.

He caught her staring at him, and a rakish grin cut a dashing line across his features. 'Do you think you will be able to handle it?' he challenged lazily.

'I don't know.' She looked away from him. 'Do you think I will?'

'Oh, I think so,' he drawled. They were driving up a gently winding incline, the view blocked off on either side by tall stately fir trees. 'You will probably send them that shy little smile of yours which holds a certain charm along with the reserve, and they will be bewitched, just as I was when I first encountered it. And if that does not work...' he continued while she gasped, stopping the car with a jerk then turning fully to face her, his gaze running over the tumble of fiery hair '...then that lovely hair will. They will think I've brought my own personal goddess to the island, and, before you know it, they will be erecting shrines to you!'

'Shrines are for saints!' she snapped, disturbed by his light-hearted flippancy, for it held a hint of pride which moved her oddly. 'And God knows,' she sighed, 'I am no saint.' Saints didn't seethe with lust every time they look at a man.

There was a small silence, when Nina found she couldn't look at him and Anton sat beside her studying her pale tense profile for so long that she thought she would have to start screaming just to ease the tension around them.

'W-why have we stopped?' she asked instead, glancing around and seeing nothing that even vaguely resembled the lovely white house she had seen from the air.

'Come on.' He got out of the car, obviously expecting her to do the same, which she did, and they met at the car bonnet. Anton took her hand in his and began drawing her between two fir trees, then stopped, bringing her to stand in front of him.

'Look,' he said. 'I thought it might give you pleasure to see this. We could not have picked a better moment to be driving by this particular spot.'

'Oh——!' she gasped in pleasant surprise, focusing on the beautiful spread of Aegean sea basking in the glory of a red fire sunset. Everything around them seemed to be blushing, from the semicircular curve of sun-bleached rock that formed the sides of a tiny bay, to the soft golden circle of sand on the beach below. Deep purple shadows stood out as if etched in by an artist's pen, and out at sea the large ball of fire seemed to be performing a careful balancing trick on the very edge of the horizon.

'Apollo,' Anton chanted softly, his arm closing around her waist to gently urge her back against him, 'the sun god, joins Zeus in the heavens with Poseidon in the sea. It is an awesome meeting, is it not?'

She nodded, her body unconsciously leaning into his as they continued to watch as the sun slowly sunk into the sea, the scene in front of them changing fascinatingly as it did so.

Then it wasn't the heavenly view in front of her which held her attention, but the man standing so close behind, as his hand began tracing a light caress along the smooth flesh of her uncovered arm until it reached the feathery ends of her hair, and began absently fondling the silken strands, making her scalp tingle pleasurably and her heart beat faster.

'Beautiful,' he murmured huskily.

'Yes,' she whispered, turning her head so she could smile at him. 'It's...' She got no further, the words dying in her throat when she saw the darkened heat of his gaze. He was looking at her, not at the sunset, his tanned face burnished by the quickly fading sun.

'You are beautiful, Nina,' he murmured again, and lowered his mouth on to hers.

She thought of protesting, even stiffened a little in his arms with the beginnings of rejection, but something in the magic of the moment had her mouth parting beneath his, and she allowed him to turn her fully in his arms, her body arching sensuously into the kiss.

'Nina...' he sighed against her lips. Then the world seemed to stand still, life beginning and ending with this poignant moment. And her mouth blossomed for him, their tongues touching on an electrifying meeting of the senses.

It was the most intimate kiss they had ever exchanged, overshadowing anything that had gone before it, and she found herself held by it, her hands drifting along the rigid muscles of his arms until they wound around his neck, her body stretching and bending with such innate sensuality that he shuddered as he held her.

By the time they broke apart, the darkness had fallen all around them. Nina swayed dizzily, disorientated by the kiss, by the inspiring sunset, and by the man who held her so possessively to him.

'Let's go home,' he said, and Nina trembled, knowing with a fresh surge of trepidation just what that meant.

## CHAPTER EIGHT

NEITHER Anton nor Nina spoke as they drove the few hundred extra yards to the villa; neither seemed capable. Nina could sense the dark tension in him as he drove, felt the exact same thing in herself, and sat very still beside him, not knowing what to do to ease the terrible pressure and afraid of what would happen once he decided to.

They turned a bend in the road, the car headlights swinging in a wide arc across the night sky, filling her with an alarming awareness of their isolation. Then the villa was there, the white walls illuminated by the car's lights, mingling with the added warmth of light spilling golden and welcoming from the villa windows.

At least half a dozen people were waiting at the top of the veranda steps. Nina felt the tug of apprehension for this next ordeal in a long line of ordeals, and made a firm effort to get a control on her nerves before anyone noticed.

He brought the car to a stop at the bottom of the steps, ignoring all the expectant faces as he murmured, 'Stay there,' to her and got out of the car, coming around to her side to open the door himself then bending to take her arm.

She hadn't done a good job at calming her nerves, she realised when he bent his head to urge softly, 'Be brave—this will only take a moment, then we will be left alone.'

Was that supposed to make her feel better? She wasn't sure which alarmed her more—the prospect of meeting all those dark, beaming faces he was guiding her towards, or all that aloneness he had so casually referred to!

He began speaking in Greek, his smile rueful, the arm
he had around her possessive as he led her up the steps
and to an over-large lady dressed all in black, her round
face smiling warmly.

'Agnes,' he informed Nina. 'Our housekeeper and the
woman who tanned my backside more times than I care
to remember when I was a child on this island.'

Nina sent Agnes a shy smile, then found herself en-
veloped in a smothering bear-hug of an embrace, the
flourish of Greek spoken to her sailing right over the
top of her self-conscious head.

Then Leon, Giorgio, Athene... her mind began to
boggle as she was passed from one person to another,
all smiling a warm welcome, all holding some important
post on the small island, though the significance of them
was way beyond her powers of comprehension. Anton
was smiled at, teased, slapped on the back by the men
and embraced by the women. Her shy blushes were ignored as she was remarked over, dissected in detail then
put back together again, and, in general, made to feel
more welcome by these strangers than she had ever been
made to feel in her life.

Then Anton was sending out some rueful command
that had everyone laughing as they made their mass
exodus from the veranda—except for Agnes who had
obviously decided to take charge of Nina, her plump
hand firm on her arm, her tongue clicking in a Greek
version of motherly attention in between rapping out
stern commands to Anton who, to Nina's surprise,
obeyed without a single protest.

She was led into the coolness of a hallway, the cream-
painted walls and honey-coloured tiled floor all seeming
to endorse the warmth of her welcome here.

'See—see...' Agnes kept saying eagerly, taking Nina
up the stairs and along a spacious landing to a raw-
grained light wood door which she threw open then stood
back to allow Nina to precede her inside. 'See...!' she
exclaimed again, using the only English word she seemed

to know, and waddled past Nina to go over to the bed, pressing energetically down on the mattress, white teeth shining as merrily as her eyes. 'See...'

'What she is trying to say...' drawled a lazily amused voice that made Nina spin around to find Anton standing there with their suitcases '... is that this is our bedroom. She is not...' he then added drily as he swung into the room '...trying to order us straight into the marriage bed!'

Had her terrified expression told him that much? She blushed, looking away from both dark faces which were grinning like alien monsters to her agitated mind.

The room was, she found when her eyes managed to focus on her surroundings, quite nice, the simplistic taste of the wealthy Greek having an underplayed luxury about it that pleased the eye. The walls were cream-painted again, on bare plaster, the furniture, like the doors, a pale wood, hand-carved and tailor built to fit the room. Island made, she guessed, with love and pride worked into every detail. The most beautiful handmade lace curtains hung across the open window, billowing gently in the evening breeze, and the same snowy lace covered the bed—a huge bed—a bed she absolutely refused to look at while those two pairs of eyes were watching her so intently.

The sound of cases being dropped on the floor made her start nervously. 'The bathroom is through that door.' Anton pointed, ignoring her nervous reaction. He ignored the second one too when his hands came warmly on her shoulders. 'Say "thank you" nicely to Agnes.' The mockery in his voice made her blushes darken. 'Then we will leave you alone to—get your bearings.'

She turned shyly to face the waiting housekeeper whose round face was looking expectantly at her. 'How do I say it in Greek?' she asked the man standing close behind her.

For some reason, the enquiry affected him, because he didn't answer right away, his thumbs tracing gentle circles on the tensed muscles at her nape. 'You are a thoughtful child, Nina Lakitos,' he murmured eventually, and the simple sound of her new name on his lips made her quiver a little desperately inside. 'Say "*efkharisto*, Agnes," and she will be your slave for life.'

Sending Agnes a nervous little smile, she repeated what Anton had instructed her to say. Sure enough, the housekeeper's face became wreathed in smiles, a bewildering flow of Greek coming right back at her which made her blink and Anton grin. 'She wants me to tell you that she thinks I am the luckiest man on earth to find such a lovely wife.'

Nina began to wonder if her cheeks would ever be allowed to cool down as once again she felt the betraying blush creep along them. 'Th-thank you.' she said shyly. '*Efkharisto*, Agnes,' she repeated, receiving yet another stream of bewildering Greek in return.

Anton laughed, and made some amused reply. 'Agnes says she will spare your blushes and see us both in the morning,' he translated as Agnes nodded, beamed, and bowed herself out of the room.

Which left only him.

She was so uptight that her nerve-ends felt stretched to breaking point. She couldn't look at him, and a tense silence inched its way around them. After a moment, he sighed softly and moved away, walking back to the door while she bit down hard on her bottom lip, waiting for him to leave her alone as he had promised to do.

So when he didn't leave, but closed the door instead, she almost wept. 'No, Anton, please...' She was already backing away from him although he hadn't moved from the door.

'"No, Anton, please"—what?' he taunted huskily.

His eyes were filled with lazy heat. He looked like a man with a brand new possession, excited, eager to learn all about it, and she swallowed tensely.

'D-don't tease me,' she whispered, lowering her hot face from his gaze. 'Y-you said you would give me time alone to—to get my...'

'Bearings,' he finished for her. 'Yes, I did say that, didn't I?' He sounded as though he was regretting that moment of charity now. 'A kiss.' He decided. 'One small kiss, then I will leave you alone, Nina, and that is a promise.'

The husky quality in his voice alone made her tremble, the hungry gleam in his eyes drying her mouth until she had to moisten her lips with the nervous flick of her tongue. She shook her head, the long flow of red-gold hair like a halo of fire around the creamy perfection of her face.

'Come here,' he commanded gruffly.

Her stomach turned over and she shook her head again, 'Please...' she pleaded unsteadily, her blue eyes much too big in her pale young face.

'Now.'

Not daring to take him on in this mood, she moved forwards on shaky legs to come to a nervous standstill in front of him.

'So shy.' His hand came out to curve the side of her jaw. 'So utterly sweet and innocent. It almost seems a shame to take it all from you.' His wide chest lifted and fell on a despairing sigh. 'But take it I will,' he vowed. 'With fire and passion and a devastating sensuality. I'll change the child into woman, then worry myself to grey hair at the Pandora's box I will have opened!'

'I'm not like that,' she denied, inhaling sharply as his hand came up to boldly cup her breast in an outright gesture of ownership. The firm young peak beneath his palm stung as it swelled in response.

'No?' he mocked her denial. 'You are too inexperienced to know what kind of woman you are going to be. A child, Nina,' he muttered thickly, all signs of gentle indulgence gone as he suddenly pulled her against him.

'You are a child, who has no idea of the power her womanhood will have over mere mortal men!'

'No——!' Frightened by the words, by the hot passion he threaded into each one of them, she tried to pull away.

'And mine!' he growled, refusing to let her go. 'Mine, to have and possess—and know as no other man will ever know!'

Ever since the kiss in the sunset, he had been vibrating with a need she feared was bordering on the uncontrolled, and now that fear was confirmed as his hand tightened on her breast, crushing the breath from her lungs as a thousand needles of hot, sharp pleasure scattered through her. He muttered something beneath his breath, then his mouth came on to hers with an ardour that bordered on the angry, and she melted, hating herself for it, but unable to stop the degeneration of everything sensible inside her. He was like a drug in her system; she hated everything about it, but couldn't get enough of it, and the more she got, the more she wanted.

She was a trembling mass of emotion by the time he dragged his mouth from hers. She kept her lashes lowered so he couldn't see the agony of confusion rioting inside her. Her kiss-swollen lips were hot and quivering, and she wanted desperately to lift her fingers to them, feel the changes he had effected on them, knowing that, like her breast, her mouth had blossomed for him, and hating that weakness also.

'Be at ease,' he muttered, thrusting her away with hands which weren't quite steady, his dark face flushed as he turned abruptly away. 'I am not so savage that I would rip your virginity from you on the first moment we have been left alone.' Then he left the room with a controlled violence that displayed the battle going on inside him.

Nina sank down weakly on the bed. He wanted her so badly that there seemed little chance of him managing to be gentle with her. He had to know that as well as she did, which was, perhaps, why he had uttered that final supposedly comforting statement.

And suddenly the full magnitude of what she had let herself in for by marrying him almost had her jumping up and running, screaming from the room.

But there was no escape. Not from him or his island. She was committed, trapped in every way a woman could be. Married to a man whose desires terrified her even as her own leapt up to greet them. Married to a man who didn't love her, though, again, she had an awful feeling that she could just have been foolish enough to fall in love with him. And married to a man who could, at any moment, tire of her, walk away and leave her, and in so doing shatter everything she had left within.

Getting up, she wandered over to the lace-curtained window and lifted the fine fabric aside to step out on to the veranda. The air was cooler now, though still warm to her unaccustomed skin. She sighed softly, moving to lean against the white-painted balustrade, looking up at the velvet-dark sky above, with its celebration of twinkling lights. It was a beautiful night, the silence broken only by the intermittent call of the cicadas hidden in the sweet-smelling shrubbery below. Her fingers picked lightly at her folded arms, the action unconsciously comforting.

She was here, the wife of a man whose blood ran as hot and free as the sun that drenched his island with its scorching heat each day. Up there, beyond the curtain of glittering stars, played his gods, the mythical conquerors of life itself.

Were they watching her now, she wondered fancifully, waiting curiously to see how the little English girl coped with one of their blessed descendants?

She smiled, a half-wry, half-bitter smile, and turned back to the bedroom. She knew how she would cope. Anton would consume her, devour her with his passion, and she wanted him to.

That just about said it all, she accepted heavily as she went in search of the bathroom.

She found Anton in a pleasantly old-fashioned kitchen when she went looking for him, seated at a scrubbed kitchen table with a cup of strong Greek coffee at his elbow and a Greek newspaper spread out in front of him. He glanced up and smiled as she entered, but other than that showed no hint of that barely leashed hunger she had witnessed earlier.

'There is coffee if you want it,' he murmured casually, returning his attention to his paper.

'I—anything cold?' she asked, shifting nervously from one foot to the other.

Lowered eyes observed her hoodedly, but didn't look up. 'Of course. In the fridge.' A hand made a lazy wave across the kitchen. 'Help yourself,' he invited.

She found a jug of freshly squeezed orange juice, the smooth glass chill to the touch. Her mouth watered as she took it out of the fridge and went in search of a glass, pouring herself a generous amount and gulping at it thirstily.

He flipped over a sheet of newspaper, and she found her gaze drawn to the contrast between the white paper and his long brown fingers. Something moved inside her, an awakening of the senses again, and she held her breath for a long high-pressured moment to contain the feeling, then exhaled slowly, and made a concerted effort to behave like an adult rather than a fool, moving with the jug and glass to sit down opposite him.

'Everything looks very—prepared,' she observed.

Black eyes flicked towards her then away again. 'Agnes would be appalled if you had said otherwise.'

She lifted the jug and poured herself another glass of orange. 'Would she normally live in here if we weren't— we weren't . . . ?' God, this was awful! She couldn't even speak without . . .

'Agnes has her own house just a ten-minute walk away,' he put in smoothly, taking a sip at his coffee, reading his paper.

Nina ran her fingertips down the ice-cool glass where the condensation had already hidden the contents from view. He really was the most attractive man she had ever seen. She couldn't seem to keep her eyes off him, was fascinated by every nuance of the man. Like his hair, so black and sleek, expensively styled and cut to suit his well-shaped head. His lashes were long and thick, lying in two perfect arcs against his high cheekbones. His dark brown eyes so...

'But she cares for this place as if it were her own...'

... Brown eyes so warm and seductive, except when he was angry, then they turned into black voids, hard and chilling. His nose was long and slender, not quite Roman, not quite Greek. His mouth was wide and naturally sensual, his chin square, a rock, like the man, a rock a woman could maroon herself on if she had the courage.

Another sheet of paper flicked over, and she started, blinking as she caught his sudden glance in her direction from beneath those beautiful dark lashes, and she quickly dropped her gaze. The tension inside her inched up a few more notches. She wasn't going to be able to carry this thing through, she thought desperately. He looked so different here, in his natural surroundings, dark and...

'Agnes prides herself on always being prepared for my arrival with or without prior warning...'

... And alien. That worldly sophistication transforming itself into something far more...

'Though I usually like to give her fair warning. It is only courteous...'

... Intimidating. She lifted her eyes to him again, finding them drawn to the deep triangle of warm skin exposed at his chest where the white shirt had been tugged open to low down on the taut planes of his stomach. The dark hair was thick and crisp, a curling mass of masculinity, the breastplate beneath firmly muscled, the brown skin sheened like stretched silk over...

'Nina...'

She jumped violently, almost spilling the glass as her eyes jerked upwards to clash with his.

He looked grim, the paper lowered to the table, long fingers clenched tightly on the flimsy sheets.

'If you don't stop it,' he warned her quietly, 'you will find yourself in a whole lot of trouble...'

His mouth had a fascinating shape to it when he spoke, it seemed to form words with a...

A hot flush mounted her skin, beginning at the agitated rise and fall of her breasts and running along her throat and across her cheeks. 'I...' She licked her dry lips. He looked tense, angry almost. 'I was miles away,' she lied. 'W-what did you say?'

'I said,' he murmured silkily, holding her still with the fixed darkness of his gaze, 'I said, be careful or you may find yourself...'

She got up, the chair scraping across the tiled floor and making her cringe inside. 'Is it all right if I go for a walk outside?' she asked jerkily, sounding like a child asking permission from an adult, and she groaned inside at the mess she was making of all this. He had been speaking to her in a studiedly calm and easy flow, as if he knew what was going on inside her and was trying to gentle her out of her fears. But even his voice sounded different here, the depth more liquid, the accent more seductive. She could barely breathe through the sexual tension she was experiencing, and what made it all worse was that she knew just who was generating it, and it wasn't the man sitting watching her!

'You can do whatever you want to do here, Nina,' he said softly. 'So long as you don't try running away.'

It was that obvious? 'I—I'm sorry,' she stammered again. 'It—it's just that I...'

'That you are so uptight about what happens next that you can hardly think of anything else!' he bit out angrily. 'For God's sake!' he sighed. 'calm down! I have already assured you that I am not going to jump on you. I'm not that desperate.'

But he was! She was! Oh, God, what was happening to her? She moved warily backwards, her wide blue gaze never shifting from his darkly frowning face.

Anton muttered a soft curse beneath his breath. 'Come on, then,' he said impatiently, getting to his feet. 'We'll go for a walk outside. Maybe that will help you to relax a little. Then I will——'

'No—please!' The very thought of his coming anywhere near her turned her limbs to jelly. There was a terrible battle of wills going on inside her. She only had to look at him to want him shamefully, yet the very thought of him touching her made her quake with fear.

He was standing tall and grim now, watching her through the brooding curve of his lashes, and she lifted pleading eyes to his, not knowing what she was begging for except maybe her sanity, for she had a feeling she was losing it rapidly.

He continued to study her for a few moments longer, taking in the way she trembled, the whiteness of her strained face, the shocking battle going on behind the turbulent blue of her eyes, then he sighed heavily.

'What's the use?' she heard him mutter, shaking his dark head as he began walking towards her, and Nina whimpered at what she saw written in his eyes, horrified by her own behaviour, frightened by his. 'We may as well get it over with,' he said grimly. 'Then maybe you will stop jumping like a terrified kitten every time I so much as glance at you!'

'No, Anton, I...' Her hand went out in trembling appeal in front of her, she backing off as he came relentlessly forward. He caught the hand and pulled her determinedly against him.

'God, just look at you,' he growled, the impatience tinged with a pity that made her want to weep. 'Why does the idea of becoming one with me seem such a terrible thing?'

'I'm tired, Anton,' she pleaded in her own defence, the wild flurry of awareness already attacking her with just the simple act of his touch. Her frantic gaze caught his again, and her mouth began to tremble uncontrollably. 'Please,' she appealed. 'Let me go—just for tonight, let me sleep alone so I can——'

'No.' It was an intractable refusal. 'Putting off the inevitable will not make the horror any easier to face tomorrow—or the next day, or even the next if you were thinking you could hold me off that long.' A wry smile twisted his fascinating mouth. 'You are my wife now, Nina,' he reminded her. 'And tonight you are going to be treated as such.' And with a determined tug he pulled her against him. 'You've showered,' he murmured as he bent his face to her clean-scented throat, his fingers burrowing into her hair so he could tilt her head back for his seeking mouth. 'You smell of roses and maidenly innocence.'

'Please...' she cried, straining away from his searching mouth.

'Too late, my poor confused darling,' he whispered, 'You should not have admired me with your eyes just now. I am man enough to be aroused by such blatant invitation.'

His mouth came warmly on her own, easily parting her lips to accept the moist caress of his tongue and, scooping her into his arms, he began walking, moulding her to him as he strode out of the kitchen and up the stairs, the kiss holding her captive as he walked into the bedroom and over to where the huge bed waited expectantly for them.

Lowering her feet to the floor, he lifted his mouth only long enough to study the effect of his kiss in her dark, slumberous eyes, then he was kissing her again, no rush, no urgency any more, but with a slow deepen-

ing of sensuality which held her still and compliant in
his arms.

He undressed her slowly, the slight tremor in his fingers
making her breath leave her lungs in soft, agitated gasps.
Discarded pieces of clothing were replaced by the tantalising caress of his lips. Nina squeezed her eyes shut
and prayed she would get through this without dying.
She felt as though she were dying; every sense in her was
fluttering in desperate need to escape from the rigid
control she was holding over them.

She flinched when his hand came to cover her breast,
the stinging contact forcing her eyes wide to clash with
the dark intensity of his. She was standing naked in front
of him, the gentle breeze drifting in through the window
disturbing the fine threads of her hair as he stepped back
a little to look at her, black eyes hot and dense.

'The lights, Anton,' she pleaded huskily. 'Put out the
lights.'

'No,' he refused. 'The last time you came to my bed,
it was in darkness. This time we will finish what began
there in the full glory of fire and light!'

He scooped her up again, lying her on the bed and
bending over her to press a hard kiss to her lips before
straightening away to remove his own clothes. Nina
closed her eyes, and heard his soft, mocking laugh taunt
her shyness.

He was already breathing disjointedly when he joined
her on the bed, his arms reaching for her with an eagerness which fired the need in her own blood and had her
moving to him without protest, curling into the shocking
beauty of his body with such unconscious sensuality that
he shuddered.

'My God, Nina,' he whispered hoarsely. 'You want
this as much as I do!'

She didn't deny it, couldn't. He was right, and she
did want him, with a fire that easily matched his own.

And every prediction he had made about their coming
together came to fruition that long, hot, turbulent night,

as he opened up the Pandora's box of her desires and let them fly wild and free.

It was awful, it was shocking, it was shamefully exhilarating. And the sheer intensity of it sent her soaring to incredible heights. She opened her eyes to see the shock mingling with the rapture on his passion-locked face, and knew it had stunned him too.

Her arms snaked up around his neck, pulling him down on to her, some terrible she-devil inside her exulting in the power she had discovered over this man.

He shuddered, his mouth opening on her breast, 'Nina...' he whispered thickly. 'God, Nina...'

In the grim grey cast of the early dawn, when at last he had fallen into an exhausted sleep, she lay looking at the shocked pallor of his face, and tears filled her tired eyes, tears of shame and horror and a certain hopelessness.

Months ago, when those black eyes had first looked at her and announced their desire, she had instinctively backed away. Weeks ago, in the confusing aggression of her own folly, she had been forced to recognise why. Now, in the grey half-light of a brand new day, she knew it all, and the tears brimmed and fell, tracing lazy channels down her pale cheeks. She loved this man, loved him with every fibre of her being, and there wasn't a single thing she could do about it.

The tears dried as she lay there, and slowly her own eyes grew heavy, closing out the sight and sounds echoing in her mind, the aching replay of her own total capitulation, and her only saving grace in it all had been that small cry she had made as he entered her.

'I hate you, Anton,' she'd whispered threadily as the fire threatened to consume her forever.

'No, you don't,' he'd muttered, his voice nothing but an ebbing wave rasping over her desire. 'You only wish you did.'

He was right, as he had been so right about everything from the very beginning. She didn't hate, she loved. And as sleep dragged her slowly into its darkened pits, her hand slipped lightly across his chest to curve into the warm moist nape of his neck, and she sighed, with no idea that the black eyes flicked open at the first whispering touch of her hand, and that the man beside her took over the sleepless vigil for a while, watching her as she slept, his thoughts as bleak and brooding as her own had been.

They slept on into the fierce heat of the morning, waking with their bodies curved together and the rattling sounds of cups on a tray to tell them they were no longer alone. Nina pushed her blushing face into his shoulder as Agnes chatted out a stream of Greek to the wry-faced man holding his new wife so closely to him.

'She's gone,' he said teasingly when at last the silence came back to the sunny room.

Nina couldn't look at him, the drama of the night before holding her trapped in an all-consuming shyness. His hand touched her cheek, drawing a soft caress down to the point where her small chin curved delicately into her throat, and, with a gentle pressure, he urged her face up to his.

'All right?' he questioned gravely.

His eyes were dark and sombre, the genuine concern in them warming her. 'Yes,' she breathed, unable to manage more than that before her lashes were letting her hide again.

'I didn't—hurt you?'

She shook her head. No, there had been no pain, or none she could remember. Only the wild, white-hot need to feel him inside her, and the short, sharp stab of that union, welcomed by her overwrought senses.

'But I shocked you,' he said, not a question but a statement of grim fact.

She had shocked herself. The depth of his passions had always been clear. Her own had shocked both of them.

'I'm sorry,' he was saying, his hand drawing an absent caress down the side of her body where it curved intimately into his own. 'I lost control. The waiting had been such utter hell...'

Yes, she could accept that, understanding as she now did. The terrible build-up of sexual tension over the weeks had brought about the violent explosion, on both sides.

She trembled as his hand found her breast and cupped it gently, and she lifted disturbed eyes to his, the need inside her flaring in a way that held her trapped, and caught at his breath as he observed it.

'Hell, Nina...' He moved to lean over her, eyes dark and troubled even as his own need leapt to meet with hers. 'You terrify me,' he groaned, and covered her waiting mouth with his own.

## CHAPTER NINE

IT SET the pattern for their whole stay. Nina and Anton were supposed to spend a fortnight on the island, but stayed a month, and during that time found a certain kind of peace with each other that Nina instinctively knew would not survive the return to reality.

Perhaps he knew it too, which was why he decided to stay on, though he was forced to spend some time in his study, dealing with business via the telephone and the complicated-looking computer system he had installed in there.

But by tacit agreement neither of them mentioned subjects liable to bring a return of the resentments they had managed to set aside. The woven threads of this new relationship were just too thin to take any pressure from outside sources, and the hostility which had brought them together in the first place was still there, lurking in the background, biding its time, holding a part of her back from him that she knew annoyed him.

But to commit her whole self totally to this man would be foolish, although she almost succumbed to the need to do just that the morning after their night of frenzied loving, when he led her into the sunny sitting-room at the villa and said huskily, 'I was going to buy you diamonds, but I remembered you voicing a dislike for jewellery and thought maybe you would get more pleasure out of this.'

*This* was a beautiful creamy white grand piano, standing in a shaded corner of the room. And Nina felt her heart fill with emotion.

'Oh, Anton...' she quavered, too moved to say anything more.

'I have had one installed in every home we have,' he informed her, that possessive 'we' sending warm tingles up and down her spine. 'I may have taken away your studies, Nina, but I had no wish to take away your music.'

'Thank you.' Her eyes were shining with happy tears when she turned to throw her arms around his neck in her very first unreserved move towards him.

And that precious moment was the closest she ever came to telling him how deeply she loved him, especially when his arms came tightly around her, and he murmured fiercely, 'I want you to be happy with me, *agapi mou*,' as though it meant more to him than anything else in the world.

But then, as she lifted her face to offer those fateful words which would commit her to him forever, she saw that the dark gleam was back in his eyes, and, on a lusty growl, he picked her up and took her back to bed. And any thought of using words of love to him died at that moment. His own feelings were all too clear.

Physical, nothing more, nothing less.

He wanted her, all the time, any time, and the desire didn't show any signs of abating as the days went by, more the opposite, his Greek nature making him jealously possessive of every smile, every moment of her time, until she began teasing him about it.

Then the day came when everything came to a head, as, she supposed later, it had to do when a man like Anton Lakitos found himself stuck with a woman who had suddenly realised the power of her own sexuality, and was taunting him ruthlessly with it, heady, almost drunk on the little victories she could win over him with just a look, or a certain provoking word. It was a sop to her own aching heart, she knew that; but couldn't stop herself from behaving like a siren when it provoked such exciting results.

He caught her talking to the fishermen down by the village one morning. She had left him at the villa working in his study, her usual routine of spending her time alone sitting at the piano, broken by a sudden urge to walk barefooted along the water's edge until she found herself by the village where several small fishing boats were just putting in after a long night out at sea.

It must have been the lack of piano music drifting around him as he worked which alerted him to this change in her routine, and Anton came looking for her, his face like thunder when he found her, wearing nothing more modest than one of his own white linen shirts over a skimpy white bikini, her wild hair in a glorious tumble down her back as she stood there laughing delightedly at the silly hand signals she was having to use to make herself understood, the fishermen grinning white-toothed with amusement as they struggled with their own pidgin English replies.

'You are not safe to be let near any man!' Anton growled as he dragged her away with the fishermen's teasing laughter ringing in their ears.

'Why not?' she challenged, thrilling inside at his jealous rage. 'Do you think I'm going to tear off their clothes if you let me escape long enough?'

'I will never give you the chance to try!'

'Then God help you when we get back to civilisation,' she drawled, pulling provokingly against the hard clasp of his hand as he launched them both back up the incline from the village to the villa. 'Unless, of course, you're planning to shut me away in a darkened room, and only let me out for your own pleasure.'

'I may never let you leave this island!' he threatened, stopping so he could glare down the long length of his nose at her in what she had come to recognise as his haughty look—he only did it when he wanted to intimidate.

'But that would mean leaving me alone with all those hot-blooded fishermen,' she reminded him silkily, and watched fascinated as dark colour streaked across his cheek bones.

'I'll kill you if you so much as look at another man! Got that?'

'Yes, sir!' she snapped to a mocking attention, looking so utterly wild and wanton with her hair flowing all around her taunting face that he yanked her to him, his mouth covering hers with a kiss meant to punish rather than please.

In equal aggression, she kissed him back, absorbing the punishing thrust of his tongue with the sensual flick of her own. Battles, they battled on every level. Where she got it from, Nina had no idea, but there was an inner devil inside her that made her want to match him whatever he did to her, though she had an awful feeling it was born out of fear, the fear that if she didn't keep his interest alive, then his passion would die along with it, and then she would have nothing left to hold him with.

His arms gripped her shoulders to push her at arm's length from him, black eyes boring into defiant blue. 'I'll get the better of you yet, you provocative little witch!' he scowled, and dragged her back to the villa to make love to her until she begged for mercy.

And when she lay, nothing but a boneless mass of aching compliance in his arms, he got up and left her, walking out of the room to leave her cold and trembling, shaking with frustration, and appalled at how easily he had been able to turn his own desire aside, his point well and truly made.

He locked himself in his study and she didn't see him for the rest of the day. And she punished him by going nowhere near the piano and let the silence filling the villa speak for itself, though neither did she venture outside. By the time they sat down to dinner, the tension between them was about as bad as it had ever been. Nina was riding her high horse of indignity, and he had withdrawn behind a cold shell of arrogance she knew she couldn't penetrate, even if she wanted to, which she didn't, she told herself mulishly as she dragged herself off to bed that night.

For the first time in a month, she had the bed to herself.

The next morning the telephone call came, ruining with a single shattering blow any hope of their resolving this first real dissension between them.

She was sitting drinking Agnes's freshly squeezed orange juice on the sunny patio when he came looking for her. And she was alerted the moment he sat down beside her and took her hands in his.

'Nina...' he began quietly.

'What's happened?' she gasped, eyes already wide with fear as they leapt up to meet the dark gravity in his.

'It's your father,' he said very gently. 'He's had another heart attack.'

They travelled back by private jet, Anton quietly supportive, wisely allowing her to sink into herself to wait out the long journey home.

Jonas wasn't dead, but very ill.

They arrived at the house in the cool dusk of an early September evening, Nina shivering a little at the drastic change in the temperature from Greece to England. She left Anton's side the moment they entered the house, going straight upstairs and into her father's bedroom to almost faint at the sight of his grey, sunken face.

Anton followed at a slower pace, to find her kneeling by her father's bed in much the same way he had seen her once before, his limp hand clutched tightly between hers. After a while, he moved away, drawing up the big easy chair and silently urging her into it. She didn't acknowledge him, and he left her, coming back hours later with the nurse the doctor had employed when Jonas took ill; stubbornly removing Nina from the room and down the stairs, he forced her to eat something

'I can't leave him,' she said flatly.

'Did I say I expected you to?' Dark brows lifted in faint affront at her inference. 'Of course your place is here while Jonas is so ill.'

Relief took some of the strain from her face, a face which had lost most of the lovely golden bloom it had acquired on the island.

'I shall stay here with you, of course,' he went on decidedly. 'It will prove no hardship to move my business operations into your father's study and——'

'No!' Her slender body stiffened out of the chair, the lingering shock and the awful worry bruising the soft skin around her eyes. 'I—you—I can't sleep with you here!' she cried, covering her face with a trembling hand at his look of pained surprise at her unexpected outburst. 'You have to understand,' she pleaded thickly, shuddering at the very idea of lying boneless in his arms while her father lay so ill. 'I can't be that person I was on the island. I j-just can't...'

His arms, coming warmly around her, cut off her broken attempt to explain. 'It's all right,' he said quietly. 'I do understand.'

'I'm so sorry,' she whispered, allowing herself the luxury of leaning against the solid support of his body. 'I know this w-wasn't part of our bargain, but——'

'What are you talking about?' he cut in gruffly, thrusting her away from him and frowning down at her with those dark eyes suddenly harsh with anger. 'You are my wife! Not some inanimate object bought and paid for, for my own exclusive pleasure!'

'I...' She thought that was exactly what she was, and her face told him that.

'Sometimes, Nina,' he sighed as he let go of her, 'I can actually bring myself to despise you.' He turned away from her, the long body, beneath the conventional suit he was wearing, tight.

Nina shuddered, accepting that she had hurt him, and said nothing. What could she say? She still believed herself to be bought.

'I will, of course, accede to your wishes,' he continued stiffly, sounding so grim and remote that it brought fresh tears to her eyes. 'But I will not allow you to stay here alone. I will send for my mother and——'

'But I don't want your mother here!' She stared at him as if he had gone mad. Was he totally blind to his mother's dislike of her? 'I don't need her.'

'To listen to you, you don't need anyone!' he ground out, spinning back to lance her with a bitter look. 'Nevertheless,' he insisted, 'you will accede to *my* wish in this!'

His voice brooked no argument and Nina sank heavily on to a seat. 'But, w-what will she think, if y-you aren't...?'

'She will think we have a very strange relationship,' Anton mocked tightly. 'But I will attempt to console her worries by explaining that it is I who needs to be on hand at my home due to business, and not your aversion to having me anywhere near you!'

'But that isn't what I——'

'You know where I am if you find by some off chance that you need me,' he cut in brusquely, and Nina watched him miserably as, grimly, tensely, he moved to the door. 'If not,' he added as he reached it, turning to glance coldly at her forlorn figure slumped in the chair, 'I will come tomorrow, with my mother.'

His mother arrived, cold, stiff, and so obviously under protest that Nina smiled bleakly to herself and showed her to the guest-room.

It was Sadie who brought her the letter much later that same day. 'I forgot all about it in the panic over your father,' she apologised as she handed it to her. 'It came while you were away.'

Nina gazed down at the familiar black scratchy handwriting, hesitating uncertainly before, with reluctant fingers, she broke the seal, and within seconds was trembling with loathing.

It was a hard, hurting, soul-destroying letter. A letter in which all Jason's pain and contempt spilled out in a hot lava flow of bitter hatred gone so deep that Nina could only stand in the middle of her bedroom, locked in the horror of his terrible lies. He had brutally dissected her with his bitterness, her father, and worst of all, her mother. He had written such vile lies about her mother, lies that made her feel sick to her stomach, and ripped away every last ounce of feeling she had left for him.

> She and my father were lovers. Had been for years before your father found out. He knew I knew, and was so terrified that I might tell you what a faithless bitch you had for a mother that he made it easy for me to make him pay for my silence. And you made it easier for me to keep on the pressure by being so sweetly gullible to every lie I handed you. He hated seeing me with you, having to watch as another of his women was taken from him by a Hunter. It really stuck in his throat, and I enjoyed watching him choke on it.
> Your mother was leaving you to come to us the night she died. Jonas never forgave my father for that. He ruined my father to get his precious revenge on him. And I wanted to ruin him in return. I would have succeeded, too, if that damned Greek hadn't messed it all up. He wanted Lovell's for himself, but I stood in his way. Until he came along, you were mine for the taking. Just as your mother was my father's for the taking. She was nothing without my father. And my father was nothing without Jonas Lovell. He died a miserable failure, and I wanted to see your father go the same way. He had it coming to him. I was going to take it all: Lovell's, his money, his pride and his precious daughter.

I wanted you to know all this, before I leave
this damned country for good. Your Greek paid
me well enough to make that possible, but not
well enough to buy my silence. So, consider this
my parting gift to you, my dear Nina. The truth,
written down in black and white.

The paper crackled as her fingers screwed tightly
around it. The sheer ignominy of it all quivered sick-
eningly through her. There was more, much more, but
she couldn't read on, didn't need to to know how the
letter became more objectionable, more abusive. She was
able to forgive Jason almost anything after the cruel way
she had treated him, but not this, not these awful ma-
lignant lies that were already beginning to eat away at
her even as she utterly rejected them, and, on a muffled
choke, she got up, the awful letter rending in two as she
ran, trembling, to her bathroom so she could be sick.

For the next few days, she devoted all of her time to
her father, avoiding Ianthe as much as she could, though
she had to be grateful for the cool, efficient way her
mother-in-law kept the house running smoothly around
them, answering all telephone calls, all enquires about
Jonas Lovell's health, and, in general, easing Nina of
any burden that did not involve her father's well-being.

And Jason's letter was not as difficult to put out of
her mind as she thought it would be, when another entirely new problem began to worry her. One which might
have begun with Jason's letter, but had not abated since.
She was having to be sick each morning, and her body
warned her to fear the worst. She could be pregnant with
Anton's baby, and she didn't know how she was going
to tell him.

Now that the first flush of passion was over, the man
she had come to love so completely had become a
stranger again. He seemed averse to even coming close
to her.

How did you tell a man like that that you might be
going to have his child?

So, once again, their ever-changing relationship took on a new pattern. She would hear his silver Mercedes draw up with a crunch of tyres on gravel each evening, and her heart would give a pathetic leap of pleasure, but she didn't move from her father's side, which was where Anton would find her, coming to stand silent and grim while he studied Jonas Lovell's wasted face before taking a firm grip on her arm to take her firmly from the room. Then he and his mother could preside over her like a pair of disapproving judges while she ate a decent meal, then he would get up and leave them, going into her father's study to deal with anything there was which might require attention, before leaving the house altogether.

No kisses, not even a soothing embrace. Ianthe's onerous presence dissuaded her from making any attempt to heal the breach growing wider and wider between them with each passing day. Feeling empty inside, she would return to her father, to stay there until the nurse came to take over from her so she could get some sleep. And another day would slip by without her sharing her secret with Anton, almost hugging it to herself as if the knowledge of the baby was her only comfort in her black little world.

A week later and Jonas was showing signs of improvement. He was still very weak, but could answer slurredly any questions put to him, and was no longer lying so frighteningly still as he had been doing.

Anton began spending a short time with him while Nina showered and changed for dinner, and she would come back to find them conversing in quiet, comfortable tones. It still niggled her, the way her father had so easily accepted a man who, mere months before, had been set to ruin him. It niggled her how easily she had accepted him too. Nothing fitted, nothing ever had, and she would remain quiet and withdrawn within herself, constantly struggling with it all, and still getting no real answers.

A week after that, she was smoothing a nice clean pillow behind her father's head when he suddenly reached out to grip her wrist with more strength than she had thought him capable of. 'You love him, don't you?' he demanded hoarsely. 'You do love him?'

She didn't even try to evade the question. 'Yes,' she said, smiling in such a way that Jonas could not be anything but convinced.

'Good.' His old eyes closed tiredly as he relaxed back into his pillows. 'I worried for a time that you'd married him for my sake.'

Nina took his hand in hers, feeling the ever-present lump in her throat thicken. She was going to lose him, she knew she was, he just didn't have it in him to fight his way back from this one.

Silvered lashes flicked upwards again. 'Just like your mother.' He smiled at her. 'Hair like hers, and her lovely face and pretty figure.' His eyes roamed her face for a while. 'My eyes, though,' he claimed proudly. 'You got those blue eyes from me.'

'Yes.' She managed a husky laugh. 'And your stubbornness,' she added teasingly. 'And your temper.'

'Oh, I don't know about the temper,' he argued. 'Both I and your mother had one of those. I remember when she...' His voice trailed away, eyes clouding over as his thoughts went inwards. 'She was a good woman, Nina,' he said suddenly. 'Always remember that. I loved her very much, though I may not have shown it much.'

'I know,' Nina soothed, holding back the tears.

'Perhaps if I'd actually said it to her more, she wouldn't have——'

'I think she knew,' Nina put in quickly, seeing with a slight twinge of alarm that he had begun to get agitated. 'She was just—unhappy with herself, that was all.'

'Unhappy, yes...' he sighed. 'But not always,' he claimed with an oddly bleak smile. 'A lively little thing once, your mother. Get up to all kinds of tricks. Impulsive?' He let out a soft laugh. 'The devil himself would get into her sometimes, and I used to wonder what she would do next just to torment me. We got on well then . . .'

Nina's smile was misty as she recalled that bright, glittering, almost hectic side of her mother's nature. It had used to frighten her a little, she remembered, her child's mind likening the brilliance to a brightly flaming torch in real danger of burning itself out—which it had in the end, she remembered sadly, snuffed out in the most tragic way possible.

'Until he took a fancy to her.'

Nina frowned. 'Who did?' she asked, wondering what she'd missed hearing him say.

'Wrecked our lives . . .' he mumbled restlessly. 'Wrecked his own in the end. Couldn't let him get away with it, not and live with myself. Pride.' He grimaced, and it was only then that Nina realised he was not really aware of her any more, his mind had taken off on some tangent of its own. Back into his past.

And suddenly she went very still, a fine silken thread beginning to weave several separate things together in her mind in a way which had her blood congealing in her veins.

'Damned Hunters,' he muttered, and Nina stood up abruptly, staring across the room to where her mother's portrait hung in pride of place above the fireplace in her father's bedroom, the full and true horror of what he was actually saying hitting her full in the face. 'Damned blasted Hunters wanted to take both my women away from me! Where are you going?' he demanded suddenly.

Her blue eyes flickered as she dragged them back to him. 'Nowhere,' she whispered, her heart thundering in her breast. She forced a smile on to her face.

'Sweet girl,' her father sighed. 'My sweet, sweet girl. Can't touch you now. I've seen to that.' His mouth stretched into a weak contented smile, and he slipped into sleep as he often did, with a single blink of an eye.

Nina stared across the room at the portrait of her mother, waiting while every illusory veil she had worn throughout the years was peeled painfully away.

Jason had been telling the truth in that final letter.

Her mother had been involved in a passionate affair with his father.

She had been leaving them to go to Michael Hunter the night she died.

On an anguished groan, she fled from the room, so blinded by the horrors taking form in her mind that she didn't see Ianthe and cannoned right into her.

'Nina!' she said sharply. 'Is your father all right?'

She couldn't even manage a yes, instead she just pushed past her and ran into her own room, only just making it to the bathroom before she was horribly sick.

'Take this.' A hand appeared in front of her blurred vision, holding a glass of water.

She took it in a trembling hand, feeling Ianthe's curious gaze on her as she sipped carefully at the water. 'I'll be all right now,' she said after a while, her eyes carefully guarded as she turned them on Ianthe. 'Sometimes it just gets too much,' she explained, 'w-watching him fade away like that.'

'Yes.' Her mother-in-law's tone was studiously flat, convincingly neutral. 'Do you love my son?' she asked, so unexpectedly that Nina's head shot up, eyes wide and startled for a moment.

Then she smiled wanly at the question. It seemed as if everyone wanted to know her feelings for Anton today. 'Yes,' she answered rather flatly. 'Yes, I love him.'

'Well, that has to mean something, I suppose,' Ianthe muttered, and turned and left her to her privacy.

Nina gripped the sides of the wash-basin, listening to Ianthe's quiet exit, her eyes squeezed tight shut against the pounding going on inside her head.

Poor Daddy, she thought wretchedly. Betrayed by his wife and his best friend and business partner. God, how they must have hurt him! It was no wonder he had refused to even speak about it.

And it was no wonder he had wanted her to have nothing to do with Jason, she added painfully. He was the man who had driven him to his first heart attack.

'And you can keep your greedy hands off my daughter as well as my company!' he'd cried out the morning all of this began. 'Neither are for the likes of you!'

Hot tears split her vision.

She had thought it was Anton who had been threatening him, but it had been Jason all along!

Every tender word, every loving gesture Jason had made towards her had just been a part of his plan to make her father pay for what he believed he'd done to his own father. He had never cared for her—only for what he could get out of the Lovells by way of revenge.

'He wants everything!' That terrible, plaintive cry of her father's reverberated around her throbbing head. 'You, Lovell's, my self-respect, everything!'

Something shuddered inside her. But it had nothing to do with Jason's duplicity, nor was it even the shock of her mother's errant behaviour which caused such a violent reaction inside her. It was the hard realisation that she had gone to plead with the wrong man on that awful rainy night months ago!

Slowly, she lifted her pained gaze to the mirror above the wash-stand, seeing clearly for herself the ravages taking place on her face as every carefully structured image she had had of Jason and Anton went through a complete metamorphosis right in front of her.

Anton had been completely innocent of every crime she'd thrown at him.

Or was he? a small, anguished voice questioned inside her head.

Her stomach revolted, and she swallowed wretchedly. Anton, like Jason, had wanted something from the Lovells and had been prepared to go to any lengths to get it.

Was there much to choose between them?

She thought not. She had still been used. Bought by one man, sold by another. And all for the sake of a silly old man's pride, and his desire to keep his wife's memory spotless for his daughter's eyes.

'My mother tells me you were—ill today.'

Nina looked irritably at the two grim faces frowning at her from across the dinner table, then looked away again. She didn't want to talk, or even pretend everything was all right, when it had to be obvious from her face that everything certainly was not. It had taken all the courage she had to come down here tonight, and worse, walk back into her father's bedroom later that afternoon as if nothing out of the ordinary had taken place. He had helped, by seeming to have forgotten their earlier conversation.

'If you are feeling unwell,' Anton persisted carefully, 'then you should speak to the doctor. There may be something——'

'I'm fine,' she put in flatly, wishing he would shut up, just ignore her as he usually did, leave her alone with the confusion of thoughts going around and around inside her head. She didn't need...

'Nina...' His hand came out to cover hers. 'This isn't doing——'

'I'm all right, I tell you!' she snapped, standing up with a jerk, fingers as cold as ice and trembling as she dragged them out from beneath his.

Face white, the strain of the last few weeks doubled in just a few short excruciating hours, she stared at the two dark faces studying her, and wondered just how much of all this they actually knew.

Anton's face told her nothing, cold, grim, as it always was these days. She felt the beginnings of a hot flush of distress creep beneath her skin, and turned away, stumbling a little in her eagerness to get out of the room before she broke down in front of them.

He caught up with her in the hall. Taking a firm grip on her arm, he marched her into her father's study and closed the door firmly behind them.

'Now,' he said, letting go of her so she whirled away to stand, hugging herself, by her father's big old desk. 'Perhaps, with the histrionics out of the way, you will explain that rude outburst just now?'

No answer. She didn't have one, and just stood there trembling instead, her glorious hair quivering against her slender back.

Anton studied her angrily for a while, then let out a long sigh. 'Nina...' he appealed more gently, keeping his distance from her, as if he could sense how brittle her control was, and didn't want to shatter it completely. 'What's wrong? Can't you tell me?'

He actually sounded as though he needed her to, and her heart lurched in helpless yearning to do just that and pour the whole sorry mess out to him. But she had made that silly mistake before, and look where it had got her: married to a man who might never feel more for her than desire.

'Is it all getting too much for you?' he persisted when she said nothing. 'Would it be easier if I employed another nurse to help you with——'

'I don't want it making any easier,' she interrupted thickly, 'I just want leaving alone.'

Another silence stretched between them. 'Has your father said something to upset you?' he then asked carefully. 'My mother said you came rushing out of his room as though something or someone had upset you deeply.'

She turned at that, the terrible bleakness in her gaze drawing in the tense corners of her mouth. 'He's dying, you know.'

'Yes.' Anton didn't even try to pretend otherwise. 'I know.'

He looked beautiful. And her love for him spilled into the anguished blue of her eyes. Even here, in the dim fusty atmosphere of her father's old-fashioned study, she felt her lonely senses reach out towards him. This man who had given her so much, yet never offered her more than the unhidden heat of his passion in return.

But even that was missing from his dark brown eyes now.

She looked down and away, knowing what she had always known, that when the hot sting of desire left him there would be nothing else left to hold him to her.

Except a baby, maybe. The tiniest flutter of hope made a desperate attempt to draw life inside her. Would their child hold him to her? Would he love her then? Could he love her then?

Or would a child only tie him more indelibly to a woman he'd been forced to marry by the insatiable clutch of his own loins and the desperate straits of a sick old man.

She drew herself up, forcing her eyes to level with his. She had to know if he felt anything for her other than the lust he had never denied. 'Y-you made a promise to me once,' she began huskily. 'You s-said our commitment to one another would end the day my father dies.'

'Ah.' It was his turn to lower his gaze, a strange smile that told her nothing touching the grim contours of his mouth. 'And you are now calling in that promise.' Not a question, but a grim statement of fact.

'I n-need to know if that agreement still stands,' she explained.

'So you can make plans?' The eyes flicked back to her. 'So you can, perhaps, go back to your music-loving Jason?'

'No!' She shuddered at the very thought. 'I—I never want to lay eyes on him again. He——'

'Good.' Anton said, cutting her off before she could even begin to explain why she'd had such a complete change of heart about Jason Hunter. 'Because he is the one man I would never let you leave me for.'

'But you will let me go to anyone else?' She smiled ruefully at the idea, and so did he, the same bitter twist of a thing that held no humour.

'That all depends,' he drawled, pausing to study the wretched anxiety in her guarded blue eyes, 'on whether you are pregnant or not.'

# CHAPTER TEN

NINA'S slender frame jerked in an uncontrolled response. 'W-what do you m-mean?' she stammered, lashes flickering as she forced herself to meet his black, probing gaze.

'I didn't bother taking any precautions against such an event—did you?' said Anton.

A small shake of her head gave him his answer, eyes searching his face in an attempt to read his expression. He couldn't know, she told herself anxiously, he just couldn't...

'Why not?' he wanted to know. 'Because of your father?' he suggested cynically. 'Was that to be your final sacrifice for him, Nina? To grant his wish for a grandson before he died?'

'No!' She shook her head again, denying that absolutely. She had thought about guarding herself against getting pregnant, then, in the end, done nothing about it. But not because her father wanted it. The trouble was, she couldn't actually say what had made her disregard the need for protection, except maybe because some deep inner part of her already knew, well before she married Anton, that she loved him, and it had wanted to have at least a small part of him to hold on to when the inevitable happened, and he tired of her.

'But a child could be possible,' he persisted thoughtfully, eyes narrowing on her, faintly challenging, giving nothing of himself away. 'When was the last time we made love?' he mused, 'Ah, yes,' he said. 'I remember...'

The moment he began speaking in that soft silky voice, needle-sharp tingles of awareness started piercing the

153

thick shell of self-defence she had grown around herself to guard against both him and his addictive sensuality, and she straightened warily, knowing what he was going to say.

'Two weeks and three days ago to be exact.' He began walking across the few yards' gap between them, 'It was very early in the morning, just as my hot Greek sun was rising above the villa, and you decided it would be fun to taunt me a little with your beautiful body.' His hands came up to mould her shoulders, and she began to tremble. 'You seduced me,' he said, taunting her with the mocking smile on his lips.

Nina closed her eyes, her traitorous mind conjuring up the pictures he was cruelly calling up, of a wild moment when she had woken him up from a contented sleep to insist he walk with her up the hill at the back of the villa so they could watch the sun rise. Up there, overlooked only by the sea and the trees and the slow lifting of the sun, she had seduced him, using every sensual wile he had taught her to bring his body into full throbbing life.

'How could I ever forget that wanton creature who spun her magic spell around me that morning?' he sighed, the sensual rasp of his breath on her face sending tiny white-hot shivers chasing across the surface of her skin. 'A woman whose searching lips paid homage to my body. Whose hair became a cloak of living flame around my face as she rode me out into the heavens, defying the gods, her silken limbs urging me onwards, forever upwards——'

'Stop it,' she breathed, shaken to her very depths by the quick-fire sensual flow he was so easily creating inside her.

'Could we have seeded our child that morning, *matia mou*?' he wondered throatily, his body so close to hers that it took all her will-power not to arch invitingly to him, just as she had that magical morning. 'It would be a glorious beginning for him if we did, would it not? Forging a life beneath the stinging heat of a hot Greek sun. His mother turned fiery goddess, while I...' he paused to make her quiver at the beauty of his rueful smile '...I the lowly mortal, lost in her wild enchantment.'

'No,' she groaned, hating him for reminding her, making her vulnerable to him all over again. 'No,' she said again, dragging in a shaky breath of air. 'It—it isn't possible.'

'Not possible?' Silkily he questioned her certainty. 'But surely, anything, my fiery enchantress, was possible that day.'

'Not th-that.' she denied, and her stomach quivered, as if the child itself wanted to acknowledge his father's claim. 'It—it was the wrong time.' She knew exactly which moment it was they had conceived their child. Not the morning Anton wished it to be, but another, far more devastating moment, on the very first night he took her tumbling over into womanhood. That, she was sure, was the moment he had laid his child in her, and she lifted her eyes to tell him just that, but the cold hardness she saw enter his cleaved her tongue to the roof of her mouth.

'That's a relief,' he said, all sensual mockery suddenly wiped clean from his voice. 'Your body I am happy to use to satiate the desires that run between us. But as a vessel for my child?' He shook his black head, watching with a kind of grim detachment her hot face blanch a sickly white. 'I want no child of mine conceived by a woman who is already planning her exit from my life barely two months after she entered it!'

Caught in the trap of her own making, Nina could only stand and stare as he lifted his hands from her as though the closeness repulsed him, and knew, as every vestige of hope withered inside her, that he would never love her. Not now, not ever. No man could utter such cruel words and feel even the smallest amount of love.

She might still excite his body—she had just seen proof of that glowing in the blackness of his eyes. But she would never touch his heart.

'And as for any decisions about your future,' he continued grimly as he turned abruptly and made for the door, 'shall we set them aside until your father is actually gone?' His harshly critical tone cut right into her, and she flinched. 'It seems the more—respectful thing to do, don't you think?'

They didn't have to wait long.

Early the following afternoon, Jonas Lovell had another heart attack. It happened without warning, only a vague restlessness about him that wasn't enough to prepare Nina for what was to come. Dr Martin arrived swiftly, called for by the nurse who read the signs. He was lying very still, barely conscious or aware of what was going on around him. Nina stood at the end of the bed, arms folded tightly across herself as cold fear and dread began to creep slowly over her.

'Nina,' Jonas called out weakly.

'Yes, Daddy.' She was beside him in an instant, the doctor's grim expression telling her there was little he could do. 'I'm here,' she quavered, taking his frail hand between hers, her pale features finely drawn against the onset of what was to come.

'Anton will look after you, sweetheart,' he whispered. 'You, Lovell's, you'll be all right with him.'

'Don't talk like that,' she scolded, trembling. 'This is just a small setback. In a few days you will be growling at me all over again.' A weak smile touched his bloodless mouth, and her eyes blurred with tears. 'I love you, Daddy,' she choked, lifting his hand and holding it there against her paste-white cheek.

The fingers flexed and curved, gently stroking the smooth, pale skin beneath them. 'Just like your mother,' he whispered threadily.

Tears washed her vision. 'No,' she groaned, knowing it was the end, yet unable to accept it. 'Daddy?' she whispered thickly, pleading with her shimmering eyes that he open his own and look at her. 'Daddy, listen to me. I have something to tell you!' Nothing, not even a small twitch of his mouth to say he had heard her. 'I am going to have a baby, Daddy!' she cried out urgently, moving her cheek so she could kiss his fingertips. 'I'm going to have a baby! Your grandson! So you have to get better, don't you? You have to——'

'Nina...' The doctor's hand coming gently around her arm felt like the cold clutch of hopelessness, and she quivered at it. 'It's all over, dear,' he broke to her, gently removing her from the bed. His voice sounded rough in the terrible silence in the room. 'It's all over, I'm sorry.'

'He didn't even hear me,' she whispered tragically.

'He heard you,' Dr Martin assured her, watching, with a fierce lump in his throat, her eyes fill with tears. 'I'm sure he did.'

'Nina——?'

The sound of that deep, familiar voice had her spinning around in search of its owner. Anton was standing just inside the bedroom door, his dark face white and grim. Through her glazed vision, she saw him glance questioningly at the doctor, felt the grim negative response emanating back from him, and it came then, the hard rasping choke of grief that shook her whole body and brought Anton striding over to her, his arms folding her in a crushing embrace.

That was the first night in almost a month that she slept in her husband's arms. While the house readied itself for mourning, Anton stayed with her in her room, absorbing her pain and grief until eventually exhaustion sent her tumbling into sleep.

She didn't wake again until deep into the night, finding herself cocooned in the warmth and comfort of his arms.

'All right?' he asked when he noticed she was awake. Nina lifted her dulled blue eyes to his. He had not slept; she could see the alertness in the grim cast of his face.

'Yes,' she breathed, and lowered her gaze from his, feeling thankfully numb inside now. 'How did you know to come?'

'My mother called me,' he explained. 'I'm sorry I couldn't make it before he——'

'He believed we loved each other, did you know that?' A small sob which was supposed to be a laugh broke in her throat. 'He died believing you the big white hero, come here to save his company and his daughter in his final hour!'

The hand curving around her tensed slightly. 'But you know otherwise, I suppose,' he sighed.

'I know the truth,' she said flatly.

'And what is the truth?' the man holding her enquired grimly.

I was bought, she thought, and moved away from him, feeling the coldness of loss sweep over her once again. Anton might have helped save her father's company from Jason's greedy hands, and she would always be grateful to him for that. But she had sold herself to him to get his help.

She found no solace in any of that, none at all.

He made a movement beside her as if to draw her back into his arms, and she tensed as she waited, every aching pore in her going out towards him in miserable yearning. She loved him so much! Needed so badly for him to love her too!

The tears flooded her eyes again, and she bit down hard on her quivering bottom lip, not wanting to cry, refusing to cry, feeling so lost and alone, it hurt almost as much as her father's going.

Then the arms were gathering her in anyway, and she went. Like a weak little kitten she went, curling herself into that warm hard body and burying her face in the scented hollow of his shoulder.

Just this one last time, she told herself weakly. Just let me lie here in his arms and inhale that warm musky smell of him this one last time.

She might never allow herself the beauty of it again.

'Nina...' His voice was low and roughened, sending threatening sparks of something she refused to acknowledge skidding out across her skin.

'Don't talk,' she whispered pleadingly. 'Please, don't talk.'

Jonas Lovell was buried one still morning a week later. Ianthe stood to one side of her, her manner towards Nina softened slightly by her grief. Anton stood on the other, his arm supportive around her slender waist.

He had hardly left her alone since her father's death, his mood quietly sympathetic but grim. He had taken over one of the other guest-bedrooms, and not even Ianthe questioned why he wasn't sleeping with his wife when she, like everyone, could see how utterly exhausted Nina was now the physical caring for her father was over.

And if she lay awake deep into the dark night, shivering with loneliness and a stark yearning to feel his warm body infuse some life into her own numbed one, then at least no one else knew it.

It was too late. Her father had gone now, and taken with him her right to hold on to the man she loved.

Except for their baby, an insistent little voice in her heart kept prompting urgently. Surely their child gave her the right to hold on somewhere?

She must have trembled, because Anton's arm became more supportive around her waist. 'Let's go,' he murmured, turning her gently from the grave side, and she felt Ianthe's hand rest on her shoulder for a brief moment before it was withdrawn again.

Sympathy? she wondered blankly. And wanted to sob her heart out.

The chauffeur-driven limousine took them back to the house, leading a cavalcade of funeral cars containing people who had been friends of her father's, business colleagues, people who, though they were virtual strangers to her, helped to instil a small ball of comfort inside her because they cared enough for Jonas Lovell to break off from their busy day to attend his funeral.

She said as much to the man sitting beside her.

'Your father was a well-liked and deeply respected man,' Anton replied sombrely. 'Of course they cared enough to pay their respects to him. He will be sadly missed.'

The slight hint of censure in his voice sent her sliding back behind her cloak of withdrawal, and they finished the rest of the journey in silence. But the moment they entered the house Ianthe took one look at her pale, drawn face and sent her firmly to her room, and Nina went, glad of the excuse not to have to put on a brave face in front of all those people, leaving Anton and his mother to entertain them in her absence.

He found her still in her room hours later. Black coat, hat and shoes discarded, she was sitting in the window seat, her cheek resting on her drawn-up knees as she gazed sightlessly out of the window.

'You have not packed,' he observed as he stepped inside the room and closed the door.

Nina turned her head as he spoke, running the question through her mind several times before its meaning sank in. He was expecting her to return with him to his home today.

'I'm not coming,' she said.

He stopped mid-stride, his gaze sharpening on her, then he grimaced. 'I suspected as much. May I be allowed to enquire why?' he drawled sarcastically.

'I read my father's will,' she informed him flatly.

'Ah,' he said, as if that explained it all when, really, it was only the very tip of the iceberg encasing her.

'He had a copy in his bedside drawer. I found it while I was clearing out his personal things. He left you everything,' she concluded heavily.

'Yes,' he sighed, sitting down on the end of the bed. 'In trust,' he made it clear. 'For our first-born son. But I hope you will believe me when I say I didn't know he was going to do that.'

'It doesn't matter,' she murmured indifferently. She actually understood why her father had done it. He had believed he was protecting her from any other Jason Hunters who might think it worth preying on his daughter's naïveté. 'He owed it to you, anyway,' she shrugged, thinking, What a pathetic person I must be to make my own father go to such lengths to protect me.

'Of course it damn well matters!' Anton exploded gruffly. 'I wanted none of it!'

'You wanted Lovell's.'

'I wanted you, Nina. And I refuse to let you forget that fact.'

He wanted her... She remembered the first time he'd ever said that to her, here in this very room, what seemed an age ago now.

With her pale cheek still resting on her upturned knees, she let her eyes run over him. His posture was heavy, the stresses of the last few weeks beginning to affect him also. Something fluttered inside her, and she damped it down hard, refusing to give it space to grow.

He looked up suddenly, catching her gaze, and for once she didn't look away. It was a slate-grey September day outside. Her own curled-up figure was blocking most of the natural light from the room. She couldn't see his face clearly, but could sense his grimness. The mood in the room was grim, the air they breathed, the words they spoke.

'It is time to come home, Nina,' Anton stated quietly, refusing to accept her earlier refusal.

'No.' Home to her was a sun-kissed island a million miles away from here. It had been the only place she had found happiness recently. Straightening her stiffened limbs, she got up. 'I—I need some time to be by myself,' she insisted, hugging herself as if cold.

'What is that supposed to mean?' His body was stiff as he stood up too.

Nina turned away from the aching beauty of his tall, lean frame, an unwanted need to simply throw herself at him almost overwhelming her. 'I need time to think, plan what I am going to do with my life now.'

'You are coming home with me!' he stated arrogantly, sounding so utterly Greek that she almost smiled. 'Where you will take up your responsibilities as my wife again!'

'In your bed, I suppose you mean.'

'Yes, in my bed,' he snapped, reaching out for her to pull her around to face him. 'Wife, lover—what's the difference? It is your place. To be with me, wherever I am, not living and sleeping separately!'

'But my father is dead!'

'Yes.' He nodded curtly, fingers tightening on her upper arms. 'And I respect your grief, but from now on you will grieve in my home! I will not tolerate this foolish separation any longer! God knows,' his breath rasped her face on an angry sigh, 'I should not have let this begin in the first place! But now it is time to put an end to it. And you, Nina Lakitos, are to come home with me. Today!'

'But you promised to free me of any commitments to you on my father's death!' Just tell me that you love me, Anton, she pleaded wretchedly inside, and I'll walk over hot coals to be anywhere with you! 'We talked about it, only a few nights ago, and you promised——'

'To discuss it,' he cut in grimly. 'And discuss it we will, at home—our home!'

His angry insistence alone made her want to give in
to him. She wanted to let him take the weight of her
worries from her shoulders, let her hide behind the
strength of his autocratic will. But it wouldn't be right.
Not any more. Not with her father dead and their bargain
finished. She was pregnant with his child, and she needed
more than just his desire for her as a woman now. She
needed desperately, his love.

'Please...' she pleaded with the dark anguish in her
eyes, head back, hair tumbling in wild disarray down
her back and with no idea how tragically beautiful she
looked to the man glaring right back at her. 'Try to
understand! I can't just walk back into things as they
were before!'

'And what were they?' he challenged. 'A man and a
woman barely setting out on learning about each other!
And you want to throw it all away because—because of
what?' He actually looked confused as his black eyes
pierced angrily into hers.

'B-because it was part of our bargain.'

'Just a silly pact,' he dismissed with contempt. 'Made
to salve your guilty conscience because you wanted me
so badly that you abhorred yourself for it!'

'That isn't true!' she denied, knowing inside that it
was the exact truth.

'It isn't?' His gaze sliced darkly over her, raising the
fine sensitive hairs on the back of her neck as it went.
'Let us just test that theory, shall we?' And before she
could even think what he meant to do, he pulled her
angrily against the hard tension of his body.

His mouth came cruel and punishing on top of her
own with a kiss that burned itself into the very depth of
her being and swung her away on a hot current of ruthlessly incited sensuality which left her nothing—nothing
of herself to salvage from it.

'The truth,' he jeered as he pushed her away, breaking
the kiss so abruptly that she stood there swaying in front

of him, staring at the scathing mask of his contempt with her mind still lost in a whirling pleasure. 'What do you know about the truth, when you have such an unerring ability to tie the truth into knots just to suit your own purposes?'

He turned away from her, striding tensely for the door. 'Stay here if that is what you want to do!' he decided bitterly. 'But this is the last time I walk away from this house without you,' he warned as he reached it, turning to flay her with a last bitter look. 'You know where I am if you change your mind. Just pray to yourself that I will not have changed *my* mind by then!'

With the hard slamming of the door, he was gone, leaving her wondering dazedly just what she had been hoping for as her heart split wide open to allow all her pain to ooze out, and, on a broken sob, she threw herself down on her bed, crouching there to cry, cry as she had never done before. She cried for herself, for her father, for the child she carried so secretly inside her, and even for the man who had just walked so angrily from her life.

The sudden sharp knocking at the door brought her jerking into a sitting position, her heart giving a pathetic leap in her breast.

It is not Anton, she told herself hectically as she scrambled off the bed. He said he wouldn't come back, and he won't.

And it wasn't.

Nina had barely managed to dry the tears from her wet cheeks before the bedroom door was opening to allow Ianthe to walk in on her.

'Nina!' she cried, looking more anxious than angry. 'Why has my son just stormed out of here in a black rage?'

Nina turned away, moving back to the window again, hiding, hiding as she always seemed to do these days. 'Why don't you go and ask him, Ianthe?' she suggested dully. 'It is his feelings you are most concerned about, after all.'

In all her life, she had never felt so lost and alone, and it must have shown in the bleak quality of her voice, because, contrary to her expectations, Ianthe did not come back at her spitting her usual contempt, but sighed heavily instead, and came to stand right beside her, a gentle hand reaching out to touch her arm.

'Aye, aye, aye,' she sighed in tragic dismay. 'Have you not enough grief to contend with at the moment, Nina, without bringing more upon yourself by alienating my son?' The arm beneath Ianthe's touch trembled, and she sighed yet again. 'I thought you assured me that you loved him,' she persisted softly. 'Why is it, then, that I have had to watch the way you are slowly breaking his heart?'

His heart? Nina thought bitterly. What heart? And what about my heart? The tears came back to her blue eyes. 'Anton doesn't have a heart,' she derided thickly, 'He has a slab of rock in its place!'

'Oh?' Far from being offended by the insult, Ianthe's voice actually gentled even more! 'And have you ever bothered trying to prove that statement to yourself?'

'I know what I know,' she mumbled.

'I suppose, by that, you are referring to your father's company being the only reason my son went against his mother's wishes by marrying you?'

'I am talking about lust, Ianthe,' Nina was stung into replying, not caring what she said any more. Things had gone way beyond the need for pretence now. 'It was the only way he could get me into his bed, so he married me!'

She felt Ianthe go stiff beside her. 'Then, if you agreed to marry him knowing that, why are you not using every ploy you know to keep those lusts alive, rather than sending him away as you obviously must have done?'

'I... You just wouldn't understand,' she sighed, watching the steadily dying grey light outside fade into a miserable darkness.

'You perhaps expected more than Anton offered you?'

'No.' Nina even managed a small smile at that suggestion. 'I never expected more than he offered me.'

'But, because you love him, you automatically expect him to love you in return,' Ianthe assumed.

Feeling empty inside, Nina turned away to go and sit down heavily on the chair beside her bed. Not once had she ever expected him to love her, she thought bleakly. Wished for it maybe, but never expected it.

Ianthe remained where she was, studying her for a while as the room grew steadily darker, then she began to move briskly around, switching on lamps, forcing the light to lift the grim atmosphere from around them. 'You know, Nina,' she said as she moved about, 'love does not come with the blinding flash of wonder the romantics would like us to believe. It takes time and careful nurturing to grow. It means working hard at getting to know someone, learning their likes and dislikes, making them feel so content to be with you that they could not even consider looking elsewhere for consolation. I should know,' she murmured rather drily, coming to sit down on the bed, and reaching out to grasp Nina's cold hands in hers.

'My own marriage was not a love-match as you English like to describe the union,' she admitted, the wry twist of her lips bringing Nina's gaze jumping to meet hers in surprise. 'The Greeks do things differently from you,' she explained. 'I was just sixteen when my father first introduced me to my future husband, and I hated him on the spot.' The smile became a grimace. 'He was fifteen years older than I, and so frighteningly sophisticated that I thought him old and stuffy—told him so too!' She laughed softly at the memory. '"Then you must teach me how not to be stuffy, must you not, Ianthe?" he said to me, and cleverly laid down a challenge I was more than willing to take up.' Black eyes came up to level with vulnerable blue. 'He made me fall in love with him first, Nina, then made me work even harder at earning his love.'

'And did you?' Her voice was hoarse, and Nina had to clear the lump of pathetic hope from her throat before she could go on. 'Did you make him love you?'

The older woman's face had softened into something almost beautiful as she talked about her late husband, but her gaze remained solemn on Nina. 'A Greek man,' she began by way of a reply, 'is different from any race of men in the world. Do not, Nina, expect more from my son than you are prepared to give, or he will always disappoint you. Hide your feelings behind your pride if you must, run away from them if you have to. But if you do, then do not then live in the thankless hope that he will some day come and lay his heart at your feet, because he will never do it. You say my son only married you to satiate his lust,' she went on grimly. 'Then, is that not enough to begin the fight for more? Or is, perhaps, your own love not strong enough to support you in the fight?'

Nina looked down at her lap where her fingers lay buried beneath Ianthe's darker, much, much stronger ones. 'Why are you bothering with all of this?' she questioned huskily. 'I thought it would please you to think I was letting him go.'

Ianthe's finely sculptured brows rose in full hauteur. 'You are carrying my grandchild, are you not?' Blue eyes flicked up to clash with black in startled surprise, and Ianthe smiled in grim satisfaction, the heat which spread across Nina's cheeks giving her all the confirmation she needed. 'That, above everything,' she said, 'earns my respect.'

'But not your son's,' Nina choked, and the bleak tears brimmed all over again. 'He didn't marry me to give him his sons, Ianthe,' she whispered thickly. 'He told me that himself.'

Ianthe went stiff with shock, then scorned Nina with a look. 'Rubbish!' she denounced, getting up to move impatiently away. 'If my son said something as terrible as that to you, then you would spend your time better wondering just what you had said or done to bring such an outright lie from his lips, rather than wallowing in the hurt he inflicted on you.'

'You don't understand...' Nina sighed.

'I understand enough to know that if you do not do something positive about your relationship with Anton then it will soon reach a very hapless end.' She turned her grim face on Nina. 'Think about it, my dear,' she advised. 'There are plenty of other women out there, more than willing to help him forget all about you. Is that what you really want?'

Want? Nina wondered unhappily as Ianthe left her alone. How was she supposed to know what she wanted when she was so confused that she could barely put two coherent thoughts together?

Fight, Ianthe had advised her. But she didn't know whether she did have the strength to take such a huge battle on. And did she really want to commit herself so completely to a man who only wanted her because her body excited him?

It would not be many months before the lithe and slender figure he so loved to eat with his eyes would be blown out of all proportion, growing big with the child they had made between them. Would he even want to look at her then?

And there was another grim consideration. She loved this baby already, and would kill to keep it safe. But if she decided she could not live with Anton without his love, would he try to take the baby away from her? If it was a son, then he would be Anton's heir. His Greek nature surely would not allow his own son to live separately from him?

She could of course just quietly disappear from his life. Move away, go and live...

Live where? Go where? Her heart wrenched at the utter bleakness of it all. She knew where she wanted to be. Love or not, wanted or not. She knew exactly where she yearned to be.

# CHAPTER ELEVEN

SEPTEMBER was curling its way out of the year on dry misty frosts that put a silver haze over the orange street lamps and turned the ground black and hard.

Nina stood just inside the pair of wrought-iron gates, staring at the white-rendered mansion house. Unlike the first time she had stood here like this, the house seemed at peace, no cars filling the driveway, no sound of music drifting towards her.

She pulled the collar of her warm woollen coat closer to her throat, trembling slightly as she began moving forwards, still unsure if she was doing the right thing, but, as on the first time she made this journey, she had to see the man inside, talk to him.

'Is...your own love not strong enough to support you in the fight?' Ianthe had challenged.

Well, she had come here to find that out.

Heart beating a little too unevenly for comfort, she stepped up to the front door and rang the bell. She was afraid, she had to admit it, afraid of his welcome, or if he would welcome her at all.

'You know where I am if you change your mind!' he'd snapped at her. She could only hope and pray he meant it.

The door swung inwards, golden light spilling out from the hallway to show John Calver standing there, his expression startled before he managed to mask it.

'Hello, John,' she said, stepping past him into the inner vestibule.

'Mrs Lakitos,' he greeted her politely, hesitating slightly before closing the door, then moving around to

170

stand in front of her, almost as though he were trying
to block her progress into the house.

'Is my husband at home?' She looked at him curiously, wondering if that was the reason for his odd behaviour. Perhaps Anton hadn't even waited one day
before going out to seek that solace his mother mentioned. Perhaps...

'Yes, of course.' His eyes went flickering across the
hall towards the closed study door then came guardedly
back to Nina. 'If—if you'll just wait here a moment,
I'll——'

'No.' She stopped him with a hand as he went to stride
away, sending him a dry smile when he glanced warily
at her. 'If you don't mind, John, I would rather an-
nounce myself.' She didn't want Anton pre-warned, she
wanted to see for herself his initial reaction at finding
her here. It could tell her everything she needed to know.
Swallowing tensely, she lifted her gaze across the hall.
'Is he in his study?'

'Yes, but...' He seemed uncertain of what he should
do, then, on a shrug, offered to take her coat instead of
arguing any further.

'Thank you.' She relinquished the black wool coat to
reveal a simple black silk knit dress beneath, then walked
across the polished wood floor towards the study, aware
of John Calver's tense gaze on her all the way, but too
nervous to be curious about it.

At the door, she paused, taking a moment to quell
the hectic hammer of her heart, then, on a determined
lift of her chin, turned the handle and stepped quietly
into the room, her eyes flicking quickly around the
strange surroundings until they settled on the man who
was standing just in front of a paper scattered desk.

And everything inside her shuddered to a halt as the
icy clutch of a hand closed tightly around her heart.

He wasn't alone. Louisa was with him, her slender
body leaning intimately against his, her arms wound

possessively around his neck in much the same way as
Nina had seen them before. Anton was smiling indulgently into her eyes, his mouth curved in that sensual
smile Nina recognised only too well.

They were so engrossed in each other that they hadn't
even heard her enter. 'I can't believe it is happening at
last!' Louisa was saying excitedly.

Anton smiled down at her. 'Well, it is about time
someone made an honest woman out of you, minx,' he
teased, and lowered his mouth to Louisa's waiting one.

The hand clutching at her heart let go suddenly, allowing the pain it had been holding in such tight restraint to spring outwards in a jarring wave that had
Nina swaying dizzily. She must have made a sound of
pain, because Anton glanced up at that moment, their
eyes clashing over the top of Louisa's dark head, his
showing a total disbelief for one split second before he
was pushing Louisa from him with such force that the
action screamed guilt.

'Nina!' he breathed in stunned amazement.

Louisa's startled head shot around to stare at her, her
olive skin burning up with a guilty colour that only
helped to condemn them both, and Nina turned away,
stumbling a little in her eagerness to leave the room, get
out of here before they witnessed the total degeneration
of everything she had left inside her.

But before she could move further than the open
doorway, a strong hand closed on her elbow, 'Don't be
stupid, Nina,' Anton murmured gruffly. 'This isn't what
you——'

'You are every awful thing I ever thought of you, aren't
you?' she cried, pulling at her captured arm.

He muttered something nasty beneath his breath,
trying to keep her still in front of him while she struggled
to get free.

'Stop it!' he bit out tightly.

'Let me go!' With panic blurring any sense she might have left, she moved desperately, tugging at her arm again, and this time Anton made the mistake of letting her go, because she turned on him like a wild thing, only becoming aware of what she had done when she heard the shrill sound of a slap, and the stinging heat of her palm told her it had collided with something warm and hard!

His entire body jerked under the force of the blow, his eyes growing murderous for the moment it took him to control the urge to slap her back, then silence fell around them, broken only by the shallow gasps of her own hectic breathing while he stood there with the white-lined marks of her fingers firmly imprinted on to the side of his face.

'Your—penchant for causing me bodily harm has raised its ugly head again, I see,' he bit out tightly, pulsing with a fury she hadn't witnessed since their first explosive meeting in the all-consuming darkness of his bedroom months ago.

'Y-you deserved it!' she spat out furiously, hot tears pressing at the backs of her eyes, her heart hammering way out of control as she stood there, hating him with every wounded part of her, 'You deserve everything you get!' she choked, and spun away from him, needing to get out of here, having to get out of here before she——!'

Her wrist was caught in a steely manacle of a grip, pulling her to a mid-flight halt, sending her hair flying out wildly as he spun her back to see the black blaze of fury burning in his eyes. 'John,' he bit out from between tightly clenched teeth. He was so angry, he was throbbing with it. 'See Miss Mandraki to her car and then get the hell out of here yourself.'

'Yes, sir.' It was only then that Nina remembered the two other people present, and she began to tremble, tremble with shock, with horror, and with a real fear that Anton was not going to let her get away with humiliating him like this in front of them.

'Anton—I...' Nina stiffened violently as that thick-as-cream voice began to speak. Her eyes flashed blue hatred at him all over again.

'Get out of here, Louisa,' he ordered roughly. 'I love you very dearly, but get the hell out of here. I don't need any witnesses when I commit murder!' he added silkily for Nina's benefit.

There was a short pause, filled with a throbbing silence while everyone in the hall took that last threat in, then John Calver was moving, his actions jerking Louisa into life, and they both strode off towards the front door, leaving Nina and Anton glaring angrily at each other.

A hard silence settled over the house. Nina was still trembling, the desolation she was trying desperately to hold in check forcing her to breathe in small hurried gasps. The kind of emotions darting around them were keeping every sense they possessed on stinging red alert.

'What was she doing here?' she demanded when she could stand the drumming silence no longer.

'What right have you to think you may ask that question?' he threw back bitterly.

'A wife's right!' she snapped, glaring into the angry beauty of his dark face.

'You're no wife,' he sneered. 'You never have been.'

Throwing her wrist aside, he turned away from her, striding angrily across the room to a drinks cabinet where he poured himself a large brandy.

'W-what's that supposed to mean?' she demanded, the cheek she had slapped seeming to taunt her with the angry red lines running at an angle across it.

'A child is what you are, Nina,' he said, slicing her a contemptuous glance before looking away again. 'A silly aggravating child who is more trouble than she is damned well worth!'

'If you think that,' she choked out wretchedly, 'then why did you marry me?'

'You know why.' He took a deep gulp at his drink. 'Because I couldn't keep my lecherous hands off your body.'

His derision cut right into her. 'A problem you've managed to cure, I now see,' she threw right back, having to clasp her hands tightly together in front of her they were trembling so badly.

'Don't you believe it,' he bit out, flashing her another scathing glance. 'I could drag you upstairs right now and tumble you on to the bed if it weren't for that— pathetic ethereal look you've managed to develop over the last few weeks.'

'My father has been ill!' Hurt tears filled her eyes all over again.

Black eyes glinted malevolently at her, then he sighed heavily. 'Yes,' he said. 'I know, and that was a low thrust, I apologise for it.' He took another gulp at his drink, and Nina stared bleakly at him.

He was still furiously angry, the usual rich quality of his skin lost to a pallor she had never seen on his face before, and her heart lurched achingly in her breast; he hadn't enjoyed being caught out by her like this. It had touched his pride, his self-esteem.

'I'm sorry,' she mumbled, feeling more the culprit than he for some crazy reason. 'I should have called to warn you I was coming here tonight.'

'Should you?' He sent her a strange look, then lowered his dark head to stare grimly into his glass. 'Why have you come?'

Why had she come? An empty smile touched the tight corners of her mouth. Her reasons for coming here tonight had now been rendered null and void, seeing him with Louisa had seen to that.

It was time to hide again, she realised bleakly, At least attempt to leave here with some pride still intact.

Making a firm effort to control the anguish clamouring inside her, she lifted her small chin to send him a cold stare. 'To tell you it is all over between us,' she managed to say with credible calm.

That seemed to hit a sensitive nerve somewhere, she noted as he stiffened jerkily, then grimaced, more at himself than at her. 'I suppose I should have expected that,' he murmured cynically. 'But, oddly, I didn't.'

'I—I've decided to return to college,' she told him, wanting to see him hurt as much as he had hurt her, and knowing it was a hopeless wish. She had been right earlier when she'd told his mother Anton had no heart—he hadn't.

'Ah, the all important musical studies,' he drawled, and took another sip of his drink. 'And the all important Jason, I suppose,' he then added bitterly.

She couldn't let that remark pass without correcting it. 'I know about Jason,' she informed him. 'And I know about my mother.'

That brought him swinging around to face her fully. 'How?' he asked sharply.

'Apparently, Jason didn't think you had paid enough for his silence,' she mocked acidly, then shot him a half-questioning, half-accusing look. 'He bled my father so dry that he had to go begging to his friends just to keep his head afloat, didn't he?'

He didn't answer, the averting of his grim face an acknowledgement in itself.

'And all to keep my mother's memory clean,' she sighed, sucking in a deep breath and letting it out again as the full weight of all her disillusionments settled heavily on her once again. 'It wasn't worth it. He should have known I would far rather have had him safe and happy, and my mother's image ruined, than what I have now.' The onset of grief-stricken tears showed in her voice.

'And what do you have?' he enquired grimly.

'Nothing much,' she said, looking away from him, her face ashen against the brilliance of her red-gold hair. 'An empty marriage based on an old man's frantic attempts to salvage something from the mess he had made of his life, and your insatiable lust.' She gave a bitter smile.

'Don't forget your own lusts, Nina,' Anton prompted cynically. 'It takes two very attracted people to generate the kind of sexual charge you and I manage to produce between us.'

Shame engulfed her, then she lifted her chin to him, eyes like iced blue glass. 'Which is why I have decided to return to my studies. I refuse to be used by other people ever again. You made me want you, Anton,' she added bitterly. 'I didn't want to feel like that.'

'And you think I did?' He put the glass down with a thud, the atmosphere between them so bleak that it made her shiver.

'I suppose that was all my fault too,' she sighed. 'Turning up here that night, begging like a fool for you to help us.'

'No, you are wrong there,' Anton drawled. 'It began a long time before the night you came here looking for me, Nina.'

Her heart stopped in her breast, sensing a fresh attack on the way. 'What are you talking about?' she breathed.

Anton shrugged lazily. 'I knew all about Hunter's blackmail, his attempts to inveigle you into his plans, his desire to get Lovell's for himself. I knew everything there was to know before you came to me that night—except for the engagement ring,' he added with a small smile. 'Now that was a surprise, even to me.'

'I . . .' She didn't know what to say—strange things were beginning to happen inside her. 'Why?' she asked breathlessly. 'Why did my father confide all of that in you when he was prepared to lose everything just to keep it all a secret?'

'Because he knew what I wanted,' Anton said simply, black eyes hard on her through their narrow slits. 'Which made me the only person he could trust who would be prepared to help him out of the mess he was in.'

'Me,' Nina whispered, going paler by the second.

He nodded. 'I never tried to pretend otherwise,' he reminded her. 'The night you came here looking for my help, your father already had it. We had already struck our deal,' he informed her. 'I was to get Hunter off his back with a large pay-off, and in return I was to get control over Lovell's, and you in my bed,' he told her brutally. 'Legally, of course. Your father was not about to save his daughter from the greedy clutches of one man just to land her in the lecherous ones of another.'

Nina swayed as if he had hit her. 'I hate you for that,' she choked, turning away from the hard cruelty of his smile.

'So, what's new?' he drawled, calmly refilling his glass again. 'You have always hated me, so you say. Still,' he added coolly, sliding his eyes her way as she took a trembling step towards the hallway, 'try to leave here now, Nina, and I promise you, you will be sorry.'

'Why?' she cried, spinning around to stare at him. 'Why do you still need me here when you have Louisa! Or is one woman not enough for the likes of you?'

Her angry contempt brought a flare of answering fury from him, bringing him striding across the room towards her. Nina stood her ground, chin up, eyes defiant, even while she hurt so badly he had to see it.

'One day that vile tongue of yours will get you into real trouble!' he grated, coming to a stop barely half an inch away from her to thrust his taut face up to hers.

'Then let me get out of here, and you'll never have to listen to my vile tongue again!'

'Not on your life!' he refused, a finger and thumb coming up to grab her chin and holding her hot face up to his. 'We have unfinished business, you and I,' he in-

formed her tightly. 'The very important business of a
son to keep your father's company in my control.'

Without even knowing she was doing it, her hands
whipped around to cover her stomach. 'No,' she whispered shakily. 'You can't mean that!'

'You think not?' he drawled, eyes lost beneath cruelly
narrowed slits. 'I have been fighting to get Lovell's in
my power for too damned long to give it up now because
you have decided to renege on our deal!'

'But all that died along with my father!' she cried.

'And what about our deal?' he reminded her. 'The
one where you sold yourself to me body and soul?'

'That died too,' she whispered breathlessly, trembling
with a real fear of him now. 'You will never father a
child in me,' she thickly vowed, knowing she could never
tell this cruel and ruthless man about their baby now.
Never. 'I will never let you get that close to me to try!'

'Too late, my love...' he drawled softly '...when we
both know my child already grows inside you.'

She swayed, her eyes closing on a dizzying wave of
horror.

'You see, *matia mou*,' he persisted in a deadly voice,
'your instincts about me have been right all along. I
bought you, like a slave girl in the market place, just as
you always accused me of doing, and until I have everything I want from you—including that child you are so
lovingly nurturing—with me is where you will stay!'

'No!' The pained negative broke from her thickened
throat, while he stood watching her, his eyes black and
grim, mouth set in a thin, uncompromising line that told
her once and for all how little he really cared for her as
a real living breathing person.

'And to think,' she whispered tremulously, staggering
back from him, 'I actually believed myself to be in love
with you.'

She continued to stare bleakly at him for a moment,
seeing the way all the colour left his face on that last

pained confession, then she turned and fled, running across the hall and grappling with the front door until she was stumbling outside, wanting to get away, having to get away before he saw the complete devastation of everything in her.

'Nina!' she heard him call out hoarsely, but she was already speeding across his lawn with no real idea of where she was going and not really caring any more.

He caught up with her when she was only halfway across his garden, his hands landing on her shoulders to pull her to a jarring halt before spinning her around to face him.

'What did you just say?' he gasped out thickly.

At last she seemed to have shaken him, she noted numbly. He looked stunned, so pale it washed all the natural richness from his skin.

'Let go of me,' she choked. 'You want to take everything from me—everything!' With an angry wrench, she managed to free herself, swirling away to come to a quivering halt three yards away from him, 'And now you want to take my baby away from me!' she sobbed out brokenly.

A spasm of real pain rippled across his stark white features. 'Nina, for God's sake...' he groaned. 'I didn't mean a single word of what I said back there!'

'This baby is mine to keep,' she choked, her hands covering her womb once again in fierce protection. 'And neither you nor your deals with my father are going to take it away from me!'

'I wouldn't take your child away from you, Nina,' Anton said hoarsely, his eyes strained as he watched the way she trembled. 'I was angry back there,' he sighed. 'You were talking about leaving me for good, and I re-taliated. Hell!' he exploded, when she just stood there staring at him through those wide, wounded eyes. 'I have known about the baby since the day my mother said you had been ill! I even tried to make you tell me about it, but you wouldn't—would you?' And suddenly, it was his turn to be bitter, to scorn her with a look. 'You keep denying our own child to me, and wonder why I can find it in me to want to hurt you?' he choked out bitterly.

Her tumbled head shook, refusing to take responsibility for any hurt inflicted on him. 'You planned this with my father too, didn't you?' she accused. 'You planned it between you that I should get pregnant. It was just another part of your terrible bargain with him!'

Anton moved impatiently. 'There is no child on this earth I would condone being used in any deal!' he ground out harshly. 'What kind of man do you think I am that could do such an inhuman thing!'

'You used me,' she choked. 'I was only a child compared to you and my father.'

'Your father loved you, Nina,' Anton said wearily. 'He loved you so much that he was prepared to do anything to keep you safe from harm—whether it be from your mother's unsavoury past, or Hunter's greedy clutches—or my hungry ones! There is no way he would have made a deal which included you the way I implied back there.' He took in a deep breath and let it out again slowly, the colossal weight of their mutual pain clouding his grim black eyes. 'He gave me his blessing to try to make you care for me—if I could get rid of Hunter for him. But that was all,' he stated heavily. 'The rest was up to me, and I took up the challenge willingly! Nina...' he pleaded roughly, lifting a hand out between them. 'It's freezing cold out here, and you are shivering. Let's go inside so we can finish this, hmm?' he appealed. 'Please. We can——'

'I can never live with you again, Anton,' she told him, holding her place, her hair beginning to silver in the frosty night air.

'Why not?' His eyes darkened painfully. 'Because of your college studies?' he asked. 'All right!' The outstretched hand gave a dismissive flick. 'I give you back your studies!' he granted with a flash of his old arrogance. Then he added in a roughened voice, 'We are good together, you and I, Nina. You know we are. Don't throw it all away on a few crazy misunderstandings.' He took a step towards her only to groan in frustration when she fell back a couple of paces.

'You say you love me, but you will not let me even come close to you!' he rasped out angrily. 'What is it you want from me, for God's sake!'

I just want your love, she whispered wretchedly inside her head.

Silence fell between them, the crisp night air broken up by the smoky gasps of their hectic breathing. And it was only as his head came up sharply to reveal the look of shocked disbelief on his face that she realised, with a sense of horror, that she had said the words out loud!

And slowly, as the silence seemed to stretch into eternity, and still neither of them moved or spoke, Nina felt all grasp on reality begin to slip away from her.

He saw her begin to sway, and, on a broken curse, covered the space between them, snatching her back from the temptation to faint by wrapping her into a bear-hug of an embrace.

'You've always had it,' he muttered thickly into the sparkling softness of her hair. 'From the first moment I ever set eyes on you, I have been totally and irrevocably captured by you!'

'Because you desire me, that's all,' she choked, not daring to let herself believe him. It meant too much.

Anton growled impatiently, and pushed her at arm's length so he could glare at her. 'If you were not pregnant with our child,' he growled, 'if you didn't look so damned frail—I would shake the living daylights out of you, you blind stupid fool! God in heaven, Nina!' he sighed. 'Are you the only person on this earth who does not know that Anton Lakitos took one look at Jonas

Lovell's daughter and fell flat on his besotted face for her!'

'B-but Louisa——'

'Louisa is an old friend of the family,' he dismissed impatiently. 'She arrived here tonight to tell me the good news that she has just betrothed herself to another mutual friend of ours.'

'But I've seen the hungry way you kiss her!' Nina accused jealously, stubbornly refusing to believe a single word he said—especially while her foolish heart wanted to open wide and scoop in every claim so it could hold them there as tightly as it could.

'When?' he demanded. 'When have you ever seen me kiss Louisa the way I kiss you?'

Nina shifted restlessly beneath his black flashing gaze. 'When I was hiding in your house that first night,' she admitted guiltily, then lifted her chin to flay him with her eyes. 'She wound herself around you like a serpent, and you were enjoying it!'

Anton let out a rasping sigh. 'The only enjoyment I got from that kiss,' he snapped, 'was the prospect of seeing the back of her as soon as I could! I had just received news about your father's first heart attack, and the last thing I wanted was Louisa making a nuisance of herself with me! I was worried to death about you being alone and vulnerable to that leech Hunter!'

Something began to warm inside her, the first tentative glow of real hope. 'You were lovers,' she accused outright.

'Before I set eyes on you?' His mouth gave a cynical twist. 'There were probably a hundred and one other women before I saw you, Nina,' he said grimly. 'But I cannot remember a single one of them now.'

'You forced me into marrying you,' she charged. 'Bought me—just as you said, like a slave in the marketplace. How can you have done that then claim you love me?'

'Oh, no.' Anton shook his dark head at that one, not for a moment showing any guilt for the way they had married. 'If anyone did any buying, then you bought me, Nina. I sold myself to you—willingly, I do admit—for the price of a sick old man's company that wasn't worth the trouble I have already put into it!'

'What do you mean?' She arched away from him so that she could stare into the dark gravity of his eyes.

'I mean,' he explained, 'that the only real asset Lovell's has is a broken-down old piece of London property which has a conservation order on it that says we cannot touch a single brick or rot-ridden block of wood in it without spending a large fortune renovating it to a strict specification.'

Nina went pale. 'Then all that money you said my father owed you, he—he could never have paid back, even if he hadn't taken ill?'

Anton shook his head. 'Not in our lifetime, no.'

'How——?' She cleared her suddenly dry throat. 'How much altogether did we cost you?'

He told her, and she swayed in his arms. 'Goodness me,' she breathed, 'That certainly is a lot of money.' She was so shocked that she could barely breathe for the minute it took her to take the enormity of it in. 'All these months while I have been thinking myself bought,' she murmured wonderingly, 'when really...' she sent him a curious look '...I got rather a bargain in you, didn't I?'

Blue eyes began to gleam at him, and black went blacker, her smile became a taunt, the tilt of her chin a downright provocation that made him stiffen tensely as he watched in angry wonder the beautiful woman in his arms turn before his eyes into the wickedly wanton creature he had once set free on his island.

And on a rueful grimace he let go of her, taking a step back to eye her sardonically. 'You are never going to let me forget that confession, are you?' he murmured drily.

'Nope,' she said, eyeing him up and down as though he were up for sale all over again. 'Still want me back?' she taunted sweetly.

'God,' he growled, 'come here!' and, with an angry tug, he brought her back into his arms to bruise her mouth with a kiss she more than willingly matched for passion. 'Of course I still want you!' he muttered when he at last managed to slide his mouth away from the clinging heat of hers. 'I cannot remember a moment when I did not want you!'

'Just for my body?' Her fingers made a tantalising sweep across his sensitive nape.

She felt a shiver of pleasure ripple through him. 'For whatever crumb you are willing to throw my way!' he conceded drily. 'As I have just confessed—to my eternal folly, I should imagine—I am your slave for life to do with as you will. I will be content to sit at your feet if that is all you will allow me to do.'

'Liar,' she drawled, using the word to taunt him with the sensual hush of her voice. 'You can't keep your lecherous hands off me, and you know it!'

And while he shook his head in rueful appreciation of that mocking taunt she slipped out of his arms, turning to saunter away, back across his lawn.

'Where are you going?' he demanded bewilderedly.

She spun back to face him, every inch of her so sensually provocative that he almost groaned. 'I'm going inside,' she informed him, then issued her worst provocation yet by waving a lazy hand at him. 'Come on, slave,' she commanded. 'It's cold out here, and I want to—get warm.'

Her blue eyes gleamed a wicked promise at him, and Anton sucked in a deep breath before letting it out again harshly, then, on a husky growl that sent tiny shivers of excitement chasing up and down her spine, he came after her, scooping her up in his arms without even pausing on his way back to the house.

'I will get the better of you yet,' he warned as he carried her into the house and up the wide curving stairway. 'One day, I will win a battle with you, and see how much I taunt you then!'

Nina put her lips to his ear. 'I love you, Anton,' she whispered softly.

It brought him to a shuddering stop outside his bedroom door. 'Have you any idea what it does to me to hear you say that?' he said in a shaken voice.

'Have you any idea what it did to me *not* to hear you say it?'

He looked down into her sombre face, and sighed a little bleakly. 'It was no way to begin, was it? A marriage based on so many lies and deceptions.'

'No,' she agreed, still a little sad as she studied his beautiful, serious face. Then she reached up and placed her lips against his. 'I still loved you despite it all, though.'

His eyes darkened, the black heating with a fire she recognised with a thrill of anticipation. 'Open the door,' he commanded gruffly.

Blue eyes grew wicked all over again. 'What,' she teased, 'this door?'

'Yes, this damned door,' he growled. 'Open it, you tormenting little vixen, or, so help me, I will lay you down right here on the landing and have my lecherous way with you!'

'That sounds interesting,' she mused, the blood beginning to pulse through her veins in delicious triumph at the easy way she could arouse this man.

Then his mouth landed on hers with no warning whatsoever, and she gasped, startled for a moment until that wonderful hot sensual swell began to mushroom inside her, and she gave herself to him without reserve, her pulses racing as she felt his body tremble in response, her fingers scrambling out to find the requested doorhandle.

'Where it all began for me,' she murmured much later when she lay satiated in his arms, glancing around the room she had not entered since that dark mizzly night months ago when her senses had been blasted awake by their mutual pitch-black frenzy of desire.

Anton lifted himself on to an elbow to look at her, a gentle hand going to smooth her tangled hair from her face. 'Then we shall call this a new beginning for both of us,' he suggested tenderly.

'A new beginning.' Nina smiled up at him. 'I like the sound of that.' She reached up to arch an arm around his neck. 'A beginning with no end,' she whispered as she drew his mouth down on to hers.

'Believe it,' Anton said fiercely. 'Because I will never let you go—never!'

On a contented sigh, Nina offered herself up to his hungry demands.

# MILLS & BOON®

## *Makes any time special*

**Enjoy a romantic novel from
Mills & Boon®**

*Presents™   Enchanted™   Temptation®*

*Historical Romance™   Medical Romance™*

This month's
irresistible novels from

## DODGING CUPID'S ARROW! Kate Hoffmann

*The Men of Bachelor Creek*

Perrie Kincaid couldn't believe she was being sent to Muleshoe, Alaska—population *twenty*! But then she met sexy pilot, Joe Brennan, and those endless northern nights began to sound promising... But would warming up with Joe be a big mistake? After all, he'd sworn to stay a bachelor *forever*!

## PRIVATE FANTASIES Janelle Denison

*Blaze*

Kyle Stevens wanted Jade—in his life and in his bed. But even though the sexual energy between them was almost out of control, something was holding her back. Then he discovered her journal of private fantasies...and he decided to make every one of them come true. He just had to hope Jade didn't find out what he'd done...

## A DIAMOND IN THE ROUGH Selina Sinclair

Sara Matthews was tired of letting everyone else have all the fun. She wanted to be adventurous, daring, *wild* and Dakota Wilder was just the man to teach her how. So they struck an outrageous deal: Dakota would tutor Sara in the ways of the world, and, in return, she would let him have his way with her!

## MANHUNTING IN MEMPHIS Heather MacAllister

*Manhunting*

Justin Brooks didn't know how he'd got himself into this. One minute he was telling Hayley Parrish that the 'groom' she'd hired couldn't make it. The next minute he'd *become* her pretend fiancé. Not that he minded getting close to this gorgeous brunette...especially if their charade took them all the way to the honeymoon suite…

# JoAnn
# Ross

# a woman's
# heart

In *A Woman's Heart*, JoAnn Ross has created a
rich, lyrical love story about land, community,
family and the very special bond between a man
who doesn't believe in anything and a woman
who believes in him.

**Available from February**

# EMILIE RICHARDS

## FUGITIVE

Tate Cantrell froze, the stranger wielding a revolver was an escaped prisoner. He was also badly hurt—and in desperate need of her help. Carl longed to spend a life sentence in her arms, but he had to keep running, or he might not be the only one to pay with his life.

**MIRA®**

**Available from February**

# DIANA PALMER

## ONCE in PARIS

Brianne Martin rescued grief-stricken Pierce
Hutton from the depths of despair, but before
she knew it, Brianne had become a pawn in an
international web of deceit and corruption.
Now it was Pierce's turn to rescue Brianne.
What had they stumbled into?
They would be lucky to escape with their lives!

**MIRA®**

1-55166-470-4
Available in paperback from March, 1999

# The Drifter

# SUSAN WIGGS

*"Susan Wiggs turns an able and sensual hand to the…story of the capable, strait-laced spinster and sensual roving rogue."*
—Publishers Weekly

**MIRA®** **Available from 19th February 1999**

# PENNY JORDAN

## *The Hidden Years*

Unlock the
shattering
secrets...